I0822092

Praise For

KEYHOLDER

"KEYHOLDER is a nail-biting journey through a captivating world with villains at every turn. The expert storytelling, high stakes, and swoon-worthy romance gripped me from page one. I haven't stopped thinking about it, and I can't wait for book two!"

— **Sarah Limardo, author of *All She Ever Wanted***

"It's difficult for any author to cross genres, but to go from Dystopian to Fantasy in such a seamless and perfect manner is nothing short of astonishing. Danielle has created a world so rich in style and substance, with characters who grip your heart so tightly, that you simply cannot put the book down. KEYHOLDER has become one of my all-time favorite fantasy reads. I'll be waiting with bated breath for book two."

— **Josh Langlois, author of *The Supernatural Adventures of Ryan Bumble***

"From beginning to end, I was hooked! KEYHOLDER is unique, action-packed, and romantic, with suspense around every corner."

— **Monica Shantel, author of *Seven Deadly Sins* and *Beauty of a Crimson Soul***

"From its incredible plot and world-building, to its emotional turmoil, to its ever-increasing stakes, this story holds nothing back. You will *devour* this book and be left wanting to read it again!"

— **Kayla Ann, author of *Well of Dreams* and *Tree of Ash***

"Danielle Harrington has always written with great skill, but she hit her stride with KEYHOLDER. It's everything a fantasy book should be. There are many great indie authors out there, but Danielle is my favorite!"

— **D.E. Carlson, author of the *Empire of Ash and Song Series***

"KEYHOLDER perfectly captures the essence of a true fantasy with its incredibly unique story, high stakes, emotional moments, and fantastic world-building. You will be left wanting more after every single chapter."

— **Nicole Velazquez, author of *A Touch of Destiny***

ALSO BY

DANIELLE HARRINGTON

THE HOLLIS TIMEWIRE SERIES

(young adult dystopian)

The Diseased Ones

The Unseen Ones

The Pure Ones

The Empowered Ones

KEYHOLDER

The WELLS *of* POWER

BOOK 1

by

DANIELLE
HARRINGTON

Key illustration for chapter headers & page breaks created by Kyannah Durocher (Instagram: @piecebypiece_artworks)
Cover design by miblart (miblart.com)
Map created by Danielle Harrington using Inkarnate
Hardback case laminate book cover design by Sandpiper-Ink
Interior design and formatting by Debra Cranfield Kennedy
Illustrations by Efa (Instagram: @efa_finearts)

Printed in the United States of America

ISBN-13: 979-8-9906502-1-3 (hardcover)
ISBN-13: 979-8-9906502-0-6 (paperback)
Library of Congress Control Number: 2024908768

Content Warning

THIS STORY CONTAINS dark fantasy themes and is not recommended for readers under the age of 18. While there are no explicit sex scenes, there is sexual content. Content warnings include: violence, murder, depictions of torture, sexual assault, sexual threat, attempted rape, discussion of rape, and attempted self-sacrifice. Reader discretion is advised.

Dedication

For all those who have forgotten
that sometimes the fruit of
walking through the darkness
is better than having it removed.
I hope you know how strong you are.
For God sees you in your suffering,
in your willingness or unwillingness,
and He has not abandoned you.

GENESIS 6:5-7

Then the LORD saw that the wickedness of man was great upon the earth, and that every inclination of the thoughts of his heart was altogether evil all the time. And the LORD regretted that He had made man on the earth, and He was grieved in His heart. So the LORD said, "I will blot out man, whom I have created, from the face of the earth—every man and beast and crawling creature and bird of the air—for I am grieved that I have made them."

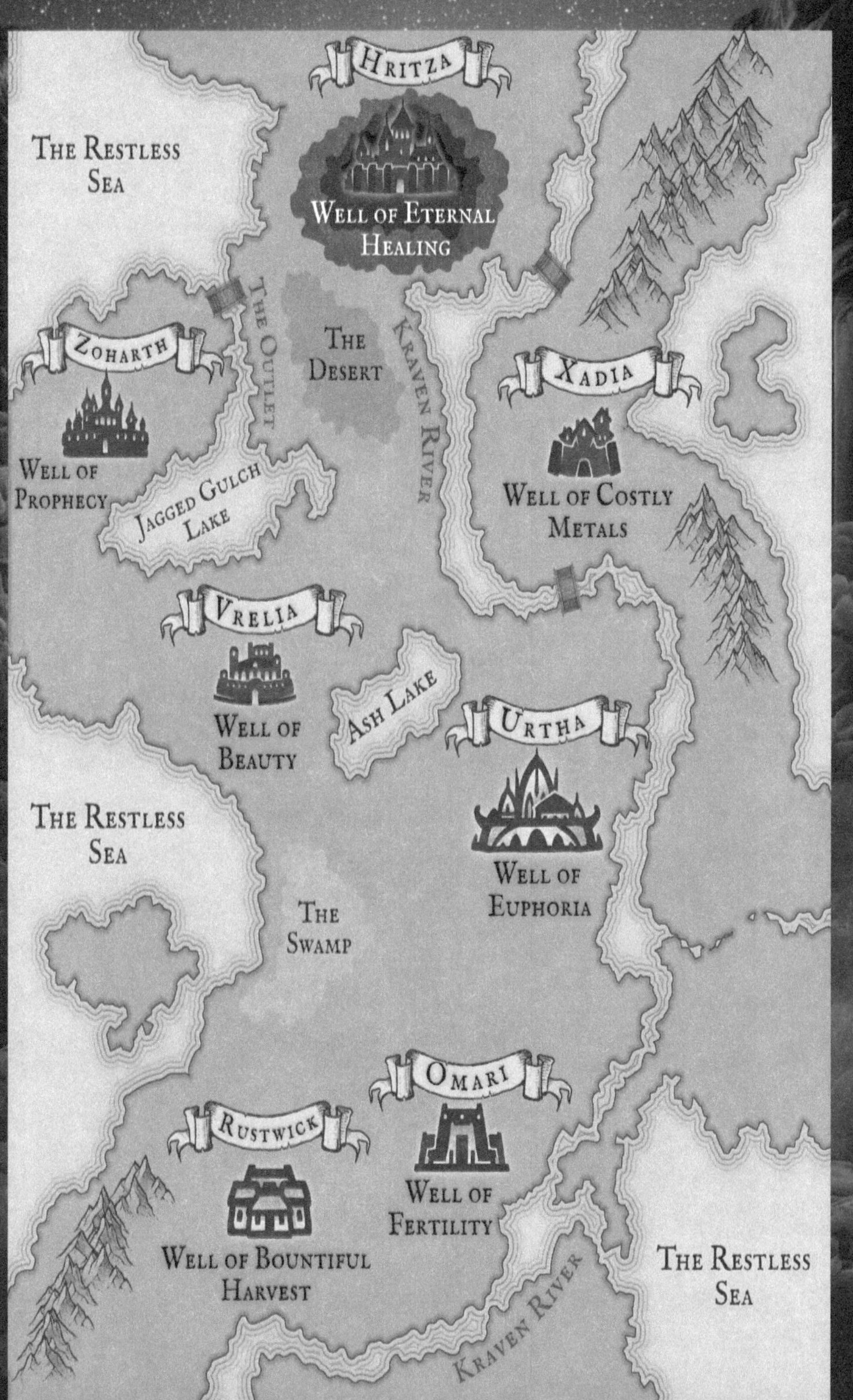
Hritza
The Restless Sea
Well of Eternal Healing
The Outlet
The Desert
Kraven River
Zoharth
Xadia
Well of Prophecy
Jagged Gulch Lake
Well of Costly Metals
Vrelia
Well of Beauty
Ash Lake
Urtha
The Restless Sea
Well of Euphoria
The Swamp
Omari
Rustwick
Well of Fertility
Well of Bountiful Harvest
Kraven River
The Restless Sea

The WELLS *of* POWER

BOOK 1

1

Insult

If Octavia Fletcher had known ahead of time that punching Mildred Creevy in the face would land her in Rustwick's jail, she *still* would have done it. It was worth losing the moral high ground of "being the better person" to finally knock the ever-living snot out of that self-righteous trout. Papa would rebuke her. She knew it. But right now, she didn't care. Mildred didn't get to talk about Mama that way and get away with it—*gods* knew she had done it for far too long—and Octavia had let her snide remarks slide one too many times.

Octavia paced the six feet of space that her wooden, straw-strewn cell provided, running her fingers through her trio of thick brunette braids. Even though her hand hurt and she was now confined to this filthy, stench-filled space, a smile curled her lips. It was quite a sight—blood spurting from Mildred's nose like a fountain . . . and the sounds of her squealing like a pig? Priceless.

Mildred deserved the broken nose, and Octavia wouldn't apologize for it.

She brushed the creases of her mud-covered tunic off, flicking bits of dried muck over the straw. It didn't help her appearance in the slightest. She was covered head to toe in grime. Rustwick's guards had wrestled her to the ground before she could get away from the scuffle, and all the while, Mildred had been shrieking about how Octavia had tried to kill her.

Liar.

If Octavia had wanted to kill Mildred Creevy, she certainly wouldn't have punched her . . .

A harsh banging caused Octavia to jump. One of the guards was slamming his fist against the wooden bars.

"Your father is here," he grumbled.

Octavia glared at him but let a small sigh slip out, swallowing hard against a dry throat. She wasn't intimidated by the imposing Rustwick guard. She was more intimidated by the conversation she was about to have with Papa.

"You're lucky your father is rich, girl," the guard huffed, his caterpillar eyebrows crawling down his forehead in a frown. "Always bailing you out of your own messes." He shook his head. "Spoiled. That's what he's made you."

Octavia had to bite her tongue to keep from retorting. She was in enough trouble already. She didn't need a few ill-advised words to extend her stay in this grungy hole. Five hours was long enough. She was starving and cold and not ready to see the disappointment on Papa's face, but she was thankful that she didn't have to spend the night here.

The cell door scraped open, and the guard grabbed Octavia's upper arm. Her immediate instinct was to pull away from his rough touch, but she quelled the feeling, allowing him to lead her from the dark and damp interior of the jail out into the brisk springtime air. The sun was maybe half an hour from setting, but it wasn't the creeping shadows of the surrounding town or the two dozen Rustwick guards standing outside the rotting jail that chilled her, it was Papa's grim stare.

He was sitting atop Bugs, their male brown and white horse, and in his hand, he held the reins of Billa, their female speckled horse.

"Here she is," the guard muttered, pushing her forward. He looked back at another guard and then pointed at Papa. "Did he pay?"

The man nodded.

Unceremoniously, the guard holding Octavia shoved her. She stumbled, almost tripping, but she was able to regain her balance quickly. She threw the guard a vile look, brushed herself off, then joined Papa's side.

"Thank you," Papa said to the man who had shoved her. "I'm sorry for the trouble she has caused."

"Keep control of your daughter, Theodin," he growled. "Next time your money won't help her."

"Of course," he replied, bowing his head. "She won't be causing any more trouble." Papa looked down at Octavia, his eyes sharp. "Get on Billa. Let's go."

Octavia obeyed him without a word, hoisting herself up onto the brown and white speckled horse. The clop of the horses' hooves against cobblestone was the only sound for nearly ten minutes as Papa and Octavia wound their way through the town, riding past shops, through evergreen trees, and then out along the Kraven River, which bordered the Kingdom of Rustwick. It was only when the sounds of the frigid water rushing by became thunderous that Papa finally spoke.

"Octavia, what were you thinking?"

His tone wasn't harsh. In fact, it was so quiet that Octavia could barely hear him.

She clenched her hands against the reins until her knuckles turned white. "Mildred called Mama a *Hritza*. She called our whole family *Hritza*."

Papa's almond-colored eyes widened in alarm, the wrinkles on his forehead becoming more prominent. Then he sighed, brushing strands of pepper gray and black hair from his eyes. "Octavia—"

"No! She went too far. I don't care if Mildred is the daughter of a Wellminder. She could be the daughter of the king! I still would've punched her. No one gets to talk about Mama that way. *No one*."

"You can't punch people who insult us. You're a grown woman, Octavia. You're twenty-two years old."

She ground her teeth. "So is Mildred."

"And *she* has the protection of Asa Draydon! *You* do not!" Octavia flinched at the sudden sharpness of his voice. Papa continued. "It may not be fair, but Wellminders have privileges the rest of us don't."

"But Papa, we're not *Hritza*!" she pressed, unnerved by his willingness to overlook the deep insult. "We are not from that *gods*-forsaken place!"

"Then you are smart enough to realize that a mere insult isn't worth losing your family over. Your mother couldn't handle that. And Bowan? He looks up to you, Octavia. You're his whole world. You're lucky the guards only held you in Rustwick's jail and didn't drag you to the palace. King Asa isn't forgiving . . . and I couldn't have helped you if that had happened. I almost couldn't help you anyway." Papa cleared his throat, giving her a grave look. "It took a lot of *convincing* to get you free."

She ran her tongue along the inside of her teeth, grimacing as Billa continued to walk along the river's edge. How much had Papa spent on her freedom? Shame replaced her anger over the insult Mildred had used as her mind shifted to how Papa must have perceived this . . .

The Fletchers oversaw Rustwick's wheat production. They were blessed by the Well of Bountiful Harvest like everyone else in the Kingdom of Rustwick, but wheat carried a currency with it that other crops did not, making Octavia's family considerably wealthy. Wealth, however, did not make them invincible. They were just as susceptible to King Asa's whims as the rest of Rustwick. Money only gave Papa a certain amount of pull, and it seemed he had to use quite a bit of it to get Octavia free.

She breathed out slowly, pursing her lips.

Things could have gone far worse for her. Mildred Creevy had always been relentlessly cruel toward Octavia, but Mildred had never gone as far as using *that* term—a term that referred to those who had angered the *gods of old* a thousand years ago and triggered the impenetrable darkness. The *Hritza* were a curse. The lowest of the low. They were the reason humanity had lost access to the Well of Eternal Healing. Using that term was nearly as unforgivable as cursing the *gods*. The fact that Mildred dared to call Mama that—to call them that—churned Octavia's stomach. Still . . . if the guards had opted to take her to King Asa instead of Rustwick's jail, she had no doubt that she would've never seen her family again.

She silently scolded herself, promising the *gods* that she would do better—for Mama's sake and for Bowan's.

"I'm sorry, Papa," Octavia said. "Please forgive me. Thank you for bailing me out. I won't . . ." She bit her lip. She would never apologize to Mildred, but she would promise Papa to control herself in the future. "I won't do that again. You have my word."

He gave her a sad smile, his tired eyes crinkling. "You are forgiven."

Their journey lasted another fifteen minutes as the two of them rode against the flow of the Kraven River until they came upon a vast clearing. There was a large brown-red barn in the distance where more horses were gathered, and to the barn's left, a two-story farmhouse stood tall against the lush green of the pines beyond. The structures were just visible in the falling light, but now that the sun had dipped below the horizon, night was swallowing everything in haste.

"You better get yourself washed up," Papa said, eyeing her with slight amusement. "You look like you rolled around in a mud pit. Did you tackle Mildred as well?"

Octavia shook her head. "No, but I didn't exactly go easily. The guards had to pin me to the ground before I would relent. Three of them actually."

Papa huffed, but even in the low light, Octavia caught the grin that quirked his mouth. Although he would never admit it because he was a peaceful man by nature, Octavia knew he was proud of her ability to put up *that* much of a fight. She supposed it was something that gave him comfort—the fact that his daughter wasn't totally helpless when it came to defending herself—but she also knew it had been the source of many conflicts over the years. Octavia Fletcher . . . always getting into trouble. Always getting into fights. Nothing as big as punching a Wellminder's daughter in the face, but enough that she had gained a reputation amongst the townspeople of Rustwick.

Octavia slid off Billa as Papa slid off Bugs. Papa grabbed the reins from Octavia and nodded to her. "I'll tend to the horses. You go inside."

"Yes, Papa."

The instant Octavia crossed the threshold into the warm glow of the farmhouse, a blur of a figure tackled her around the middle, nearly knocking her over.

"O!" A boy with dark brown hair and tanned skin squeezed her tight. Dried clods of dirt fell from her tunic as the boy embraced her, sprinkling the wooden floorboards, but he didn't seem to mind the mess or notice it at all.

"Bowan," she murmured, smiling and hugging him back. He stood a head shorter than her, but at eleven years of age, Bowan Fletcher was growing fast, and it would only be a matter of time before he outgrew her.

"Papa said you got into trouble." A mischievous look pinched Bowan's face. He checked over his shoulder, lowering his voice to a whisper. Octavia knew he was checking for Mama, but they were the only two standing in the living room. Mama must be upstairs. "He said you were in jail?"

"I was," Octavia said, matching his mischievous tone.

Bowan looked flabbergasted. "What did you do?" Then, as if the question triggered his ability to see clearly, he backed up to take in her appearance. "Why are you covered in mud?"

Octavia hashed out the events of her day, not sparing a single detail, and when she got to the part about Mildred's insult, her brother's eyes became saucers and his jaw dropped. Color flushed his cheeks, and he put up his fists.

"That ugly pig!" he hissed. "I would've punched her too. Did you make her cry?"

Octavia tousled his hair, smug delight written in her expression. "I made her bleed."

"Good," Bowan said, cracking his knuckles.

"How's Mama doing?" Octavia asked. She should probably go upstairs to see her, but she needed to clean herself up first.

"She's . . ." Bowan stalled, wringing his hands together. "She's not been lucid today. She didn't even know you were gone."

Octavia's heart pulled in two different directions. On the one hand, Mama wouldn't know about her skirmish and short stay in jail—a blessing, really, since it would only upset her, and the stress could weaken her body even further. But on the other hand, Bowan's comment meant Mama had racked up another bad day. She was still so young—a mere forty-two years of age—but her body was giving out on her, and so was her mind. They had been to every doctor in Rustwick, but no one had any answers for them. Tabitha Fletcher was dying, and there was nothing they could do but watch.

It was her Mama's sudden illness that triggered the use of *Hritza* from Mildred's lips—Octavia knew it—and it boiled her blood again just thinking about it.

According to legend, the *gods of old* didn't just curse the Kingdom of Hritza by sealing the Well of Eternal Healing and shrouding it in darkness, they also cursed the descendants of those who escaped the destruction. As punishment for their transgressions, the *Hritza* would die young. From illness or injury or accident . . . But no one could prove the theory was real since no one could prove that any descendants from the Kingdom of Hritza lived. It was simply a story, evolved over the ages by the sheer span of time.

"Okay," Octavia murmured, pulling Bowan into another hug. The two of them fell silent. They never spoke about the possibility of Mama actually dying, but every time Mama had another episode, the reality of it grew sharper.

Bowan wriggled out of his sister's embrace, scrunching his nose. "You smell."

Octavia chuckled. "I know."

She walked to the kitchen to grab the pail of clean water they kept on the floor next to their wooden dining table. She would refill the pail later. It would probably be easier for her to jump into the river with this much muck caked all over her, but it was chilly outside, and she didn't want to be out in the dark.

"Fix me a bowl of Mama's stew while I get washed up?" Octavia asked with a devilish smile.

Bowan gave her a stern look and crossed his arms, but then he sighed, resigning himself to her request with a smirk. "Fine. But only because you punched Mildred."

"You're the best!" she called, already halfway up the stairs.

When she got to her room, she peeled off her clothes, tossing them to the floor by the foot of her bed. It was a modest space, but roomy enough. The only things in here were a bed, a small dresser with three drawers, and a wooden chair Papa had made. It was simple, but perfect. Papa liked it that way, and so did she. Octavia had always admired Papa for his rustic approach to life, even with their wealth. He made things with his hands and worked hard to provide for his family. The Fletchers were not above anyone else just because they had money—and it was that sentiment that Papa had instilled into her and Bowan.

Octavia gave a longing look toward the bed. She yearned to cocoon herself into the blankets and pass out, but she was too hungry to sleep.

After dunking a rag into the pail of water so she could mop up the grime coating her skin, she pulled on clean trousers and a new tunic, cinching the fabric around her waist with a belt made of old leather. Then she shoved her feet back into her leather boots.

"Mama?" Octavia called in a soothing voice, walking down the short hall.

She poked her head into her parents' bedroom. Mama was sitting up, tucked under a large handmade patchwork quilt, and she looked exhausted. Dark bags hung under her brown eyes, and her thin black hair was woven into a disheveled braid. Her face, once so full of life, was now hollow and empty most days, and since falling ill, she had lost a lot of weight.

Octavia walked over to the bed and sat down on the edge, grabbing Mama's hand.

"How are you feeling, Mama?" she asked softly. "Do you want me to bring you a bowl of stew? Bowan is heating some up over the fire."

She stirred, looking up as if just now noticing Octavia's presence.

"You look lovely today," she murmured. "Do you think you could..." She paused, locking eyes with her daughter, and then a delighted smile lit her face. "I have to tell you something, Sissy. I simply can't keep it in anymore." She clasped Octavia's hand tightly. "But you have to promise not to tell Mother, okay? She wouldn't approve."

Octavia felt a lump building in her throat. Mama thought Octavia was her sister again . . . She fought against the desire to cry, stuffing it down as deep as it would go. Since the onset of this illness, Octavia had learned to play along with Mama's failing mind, because trying to coax her back to reality in the past had only ended with Mama dissolving into hysterics.

"I promise," Octavia said with a smile. "I won't tell."

Mama's face gained the smallest tinge of pink. "There's this man I met at the marketplace a few weeks ago. He's lovely, and I have seen him every day since. I can't stop thinking about him, Sissy. He's the kindest, most handsome, most amazing man I have ever met!"

Octavia's chest felt hollow as she gazed into Mama's excited face, but she maintained a cheerful expression. "He sounds wonderful."

A giggle passed Mama's lips. "This is going to sound crazy but . . . I want to marry him, Sissy! And he wants to marry me too. We've talked it all out. He's going to build us a farmstead and grow wheat. Wheat!" Her voice was giddy. "Oh! I can't wait for you to meet him. I know you will love him!"

"I'm sure I will."

"I'm sorry I haven't told you about him yet, but I wanted to *know* first. And people might say a few weeks isn't enough time to know, but for me, it is." She peered into Octavia's face intently. "You're not mad I didn't tell you sooner, are you?"

Octavia shook her head, squeezing Mama's hand. "I'm not mad. I promise. I'm really happy for you."

Abruptly, Mama's eyes seemed to take on a slight surprise, but then they appeared to cloud over. She sat there without saying a word.

"Mama?" Octavia whispered.

But she didn't reply. She simply stared past Octavia, her gaze fixed on the far wall of the bedroom. Octavia dug her fingernails into the flat of her palm and took several deep breaths.

Every time Mama became like this, the episode would last longer, and Mama would slip further away. It was only two weeks ago that Mama had started asking who they were when she wasn't lucid, and that was the first time Octavia felt truly afraid.

With a heavy heart, she leaned over to kiss Mama's forehead. "I'm going to bring you some stew."

She rose from the bed and walked to the door, feeling like a lead weight was pressing down on her chest. She felt so helpless . . .

"Octavia?" Mama whispered.

Octavia froze with her hand on the doorknob. Then she turned around to look Mama in the face, now noting the clarity that filled her eyes.

"Could you go into town tomorrow to get me more of that herbal tea? The one with lemongrass and chamomile? I think it also has cinnamon and hibiscus in it. That one helps me . . . it helps me feel better."

She nodded. "Of course, Mama. I'll go first thing tomorrow morning."

Mama closed her eyes, breathing deep. "Thank you, my love. I think I'm going to rest now."

As Octavia closed the door, a deep sadness clung to her, burrowing into the pit of her stomach. She couldn't imagine losing Mama, but she also understood that it was going to happen. Octavia didn't know how much time Mama had left. All she knew was that she had to cherish it.

2

Tea and Trouble

The next morning, Octavia woke up later than normal. The sun was already well above the horizon, peeking through her window slats to light up her bedroom with bright orange hues. She silently reprimanded herself for not rising earlier, even though her body must have needed the rest. Getting tea for Mama was Octavia's top priority today, and she didn't want to dawdle for fear of Mama losing her senses again. As she got dressed, she sent a quick prayer up to the *gods* that Mama would remain lucid today.

When she got downstairs, she was greeted by Bowan and Papa, who were both seated around the dining room table—and already done with their bowls of porridge.

"Hey there, sleepy head," Bowan teased.

"Good morning, Octavia," Papa said.

"Morning."

She skirted around Bowan to grab an apple from the bowl that sat at the center of the table. She took a bite, and the sweet juices ran over her tongue. Then she moved to the door. "I'm going into town," she announced. "I'll be back in a few hours."

"Hold on a moment, Octavia." Papa eyed her with a stern countenance. "Don't you think you should take a few days away from town? I don't think it's wise for you to be around any Rustwick guards right now, considering what happened yesterday. And I can't imagine Heston Creevy would be pleased to see you if you were to run into him."

"Mama wants me to get her some tea," Octavia explained. "She asked me last night. Plus, I already promised I wouldn't hit anyone again. I *will* control myself."

Papa considered her for a few seconds and then said, "Take Bowan with you."

She huffed, slightly exasperated. "Do you really not trust me? I won't get into trouble, Papa. I'll keep my head down, get the tea, and come straight back."

"I trust that Bowan's presence will keep you out of trouble more than your promise will," he replied knowingly.

Bowan flashed Papa a playful grin. "Don't worry, Papa. I'll make sure she behaves."

Octavia stuck her tongue out at her brother, who returned the gesture, and when Bowan hopped up from his seat to join Octavia at the door, she hooked her arm around his neck and dug her knuckles into the top of his head.

"Hey!" Bowan yelped, squirming. "Cut it out!"

"Alright you two," Papa chuckled. "Be civil."

Bowan wriggled free, tugging himself from Octavia's grip. "You know, I'll be bigger than you one day, O."

"Not today!" she said with a smirk.

"Straight home after grabbing the tea," Papa insisted. "You really need to lay low and let the situation with Mildred Creevy die down."

"Yes, Papa. We'll be quick."

Fifteen minutes later, after saddling up Billa and Bugs, Octavia and Bowan began their ride to town. The brisk morning and the comforting scent of the evergreens gave Octavia a boost of energy. Today was going to be a good day. She could feel it.

When they arrived at town, bustling activity filled the cobblestone streets, and a waft of smells hit Octavia's nose. Gregg's Bakery filled the air with hints of sourdough, sugar, and spice. Just past that, the Lawson's Butcher Shop storefront was open, and their selection of salted meats was tantalizing. As far as the eye could see, the town was vibrant with life. The Treeta Tavern across from the bakery was overly boisterous as usual, the sounds of laughter and chatter seeping from its depths. Octavia had never gone into Treeta to drink in the morning—her tastes were better suited to an occasional evening drink—but she could see the appeal. Rustwick's beer was one of the most sought-after beverages in all the lands due to the quality of wheat that the Well of Bountiful Harvest allowed the earth to produce.

"Where's the tea Mama wants?" Bowan asked, nudging his horse to walk alongside Octavia's.

"Quite a ways down," she answered. "Here, let's tie Billa and Bugs up in front of Treeta and walk."

She dismounted, leading Billa to a horse post just outside the noisy tavern. Three other horses were already out front, dipping their heads lazily into a trough of water that sat underneath the long horizontal wooden post.

Bowan followed suit, sliding off Bugs and leading him to stand next to Billa.

"Remember, O, we've got to be quick."

"I know . . ." She gave him a devilish look. "Need anything else while we're here?"

"Octavia."

"Kidding! Lighten up." She hooked his neck again and pulled him into a wrestle-like hug. "The tea is at Powders and Plants, right next to the Apothecary."

As the two of them took off down the long cobblestone street, they passed a myriad of storefronts, all nestled together into a cramped but cozy marketplace. There were vendors selling fresh produce, their stands full of tomatoes, corn, onions, garlic, potatoes, peppers, and squashes. Other vendors provided a selection of fruits, including apples, berries, apricots, pears, plums, grapes, and a large, deep purple fruit called yatchka, known for its tangy-sweet flesh. The brown outer rind of yatchka was sour, but inside the rind, the pods were as sweet as honey.

The bounty of the marketplace was magnificent. Every possible crop of the earth could be found in Rustwick, thanks to the Well's incredible blessings. And there was just about every kind of pickled fruit a person could imagine at Peachy Preserves—one of Octavia's favorite shops. She liked it particularly for the candied cherries.

There were also shops that had a more eclectic feel to them. Madame Trinkets sold talismans meant to help the wearer garner the favor of the *gods*. It was a popular shop in Rustwick because the materials used in the talismans were imported from the Kingdom of Xadia, which oversaw the Well of Costly Metals. There was another shop called Classically Quaint that was quite popular as well. It sold all kinds of antiques, from jewelry boxes to porcelain plate sets to hand-carved decorative furniture pieces.

Octavia and Bowan continued at a brisk pace until they came upon the frumpy and posh storefront of Powders and Plants. The doorway was a stark pink—almost offensively so—and when Octavia crossed the threshold into the small shop, an overpowering wall of perfume accosted her nostrils.

"Octavia!" a stout, curly-hair woman called cheerfully. She was standing behind a counter, rustling through a cabinet mounted against the back wall, and she was wearing a vibrant lilac apron. "Oh, hello, Bowan! Good to see you, dear."

"Hi," Bowan said with a wave.

"Back again for more tea?" the woman asked.

"Yes, ma'am," Octavia replied. "Mama loves it."

"Oh, you don't need to 'ma'am' me, dear. Makes me feel much too old."

"Of course, Mrs. Putnam," she said with a nod.

"How is Tabitha?"

Bowan and Octavia exchanged quick glances. While the townspeople knew of Mama's illness, the Fletchers had kept quiet about how bad it had gotten. Papa had decided that it was best for them to deal with their circumstances in a private manner—at least, as private as possible given their status in Rustwick—and Octavia agreed.

"Some days are better than others," Octavia offered in a measured tone. This wasn't a lie, but it was also vague enough to not give too much away.

"The poor dear," Mrs. Putnam murmured, her eyebrows creasing together. "Come to think of it, I haven't seen her out and about in a spell. I should come visit."

"I'm sure Mama would love that," Octavia said.

"Well, let's see here," Mrs. Putnam muttered, now turning back to her cabinet of glass bottles filled with herbs and powders. "I believe Tabitha enjoys the hibiscus herbal blend, yes?"

Octavia nodded. "That's the one."

Mrs. Putnam rose all the way onto her tippy toes to grab a glass bottle that was on the top shelf. She then slipped the bottle into a small fabric bag and cinched it shut, handing it to Octavia. Octavia fished in her pocket for the coins she had brought with her, but Mrs. Putnam shook her head.

"My gift to Tabitha."

"Are you sure?"

"Of course, dear. Tell her I said hi, and that I'll come visit soon. And give Theodin my regards as well."

Octavia clutched the small bag tight. "I will. Thank you."

"I look forward to trying more of Tabitha's yatchka cream pie at the harvest festival this year! That woman sure knows how to bake." Mrs. Putnam gave them both a warm smile.

"She sure does," Octavia replied. "Thanks again."

She pocketed the tea and then joined Bowan's side, steering him from the shop back onto the busy cobblestone street.

"That was nice of her," Bowan commented.

"Yeah, that was."

Now out of the stifling atmosphere of thick perfumes, Octavia took a deep breath. She couldn't wait to brew the tea leaves over a fire and tuck a hot cup into Mama's hands. Maybe they could sit together on the porch and get Mama some fresh air—if she was feeling up to it.

Bowan took off back the way they had come, and Octavia followed him, weaving through the crowded marketplace, but just as the two were coming upon Gregg's Bakery, Octavia stopped in her tracks, her heart jumping up in her throat. She grasped Bowan's shirt near the back of his neck and tugged.

"Hey! What the—"

Octavia pulled him into the cramped space between the bakery and the butcher shop.

"Octavia!" Bowan protested. "What are you doing?"

She pointed out to the cobblestone street, and Bowan's gaze followed her hand. A dozen Rustwick guards were standing outside the Treeta Tavern, and with them, adorned in rich taupe fabrics, was Heston Creevy.

"Mildred's father," she whispered.

Bowan paled and then poked his head out from behind the bakery a bit further. "How are we going to get to our horses?"

"We're not," Octavia answered. "Not right now, at least. Papa's right. I don't want to run into him."

Bowan gasped, whipping his head back from the edge of the bakery and retreating further into the crevice between the shops. "He's walking over here!"

"What? Did he see us?"

"I don't know!"

Octavia's pulse spiked, and she shuffled back a few steps, drawing closer to her brother. The two of them stood silent, the chatter from the townspeople filling their ears. Footsteps padded closer to the spot where they hid, and a nasally voice cut through the air.

"Havka, darling, did they have those little cakes Mildred likes?"

There was a scrape of rusted hinges as the wooden door to Gregg's Bakery opened. A woman's voice answered him.

"I got two dozen of them. She deserves it, my poor baby. Being attacked like that! And unprovoked too! That horrid girl!"

Octavia's anger boiled over, and she clenched her fists. Unprovoked? Mildred was a liar! Octavia's actions were *far* from unprovoked. She felt the urge to launch herself around the corner of the bakery to tell them as much—even though she knew that would be foolish—but Bowan's hand clamped over her wrist before she could take a step. He shook his head furiously, pulling her back.

"Theodin's feral brat of a daughter didn't even spend the night in the jail!" Heston growled. "I stopped by to talk to the guards earlier. It seems Theodin's money persuaded them to free her."

"How wretched!" Havka sighed, sniffling slightly. "What has this town come to? Letting someone like that go with no consequences!"

"If I could, I would stop parceling out the *waters* to that family to teach them a lesson. But the king would have my head if I did that. The Fletchers oversee too many workers and cultivate too great a crop to deny them the blessings of the Well. All of Rustwick would suffer from a decision like that," he grumbled. "Still . . . the girl won't go unpunished." Heston Creevy's voice turned sinister. "I've thought of something much better than denying the Fletchers their parcel of *waters*. It's all been taken care of."

"Oh?" Havka probed, intrigued. "And what's that?"

But before Heston could reply, there was a shuffle of footsteps and what sounded like half a dozen people exiting the bakery.

"Pardon me," a girl's voice sounded.

In the heavy foot traffic, the Creevys wandered off, moving too far for Octavia to hear the rest of their conversation . . .

She and Bowan both stared at each other for a moment, and Bowan's mouth parted.

"What did Mr. Creevy mean?" he whispered. Octavia could hear the unease in her brother's voice. "What's he going to do to you?"

Her stomach twisted into a knot. "I don't know."

"We better tell Papa."

"Yeah, I think that's a good idea."

After waiting another twenty minutes for the Rustwick guards to clear from the front of the Tavern, Octavia and Bowan mounted Billa and Bugs and took their route home in haste. During the ride, apprehension fired through Octavia's body. Mildred Creevy. That lying, manipulative shrew. How dare she! She openly used the term *Hritza* and lied about the skirmish . . . and she was getting cake out of it?

And Octavia was getting . . . ?

She didn't know what.

The short conversation she had overheard between the Creevys made her feel sick. What could Heston Creevy have done in retribution for Octavia's impulsive punch? She knew he was a Wellminder and a powerful man, but surely he couldn't hurt her . . . could he?

Upon entering the clearing, Octavia and Bowan both nudged their horses faster, reaching the barn in record time. They quickly dismounted, not even bothering to unsaddle the creatures before racing to the farmhouse.

Bowan sprinted faster than Octavia, arriving at the door a few seconds before she did. "Papa!" he called, but then he froze in the doorway, causing Octavia to nearly crash into him.

"Bowan!" she scolded, but when she looked up to see why Bowan had stopped running, she froze too.

Mama was standing in the center of the living room, clutching the front of Papa's shirt, but it was not Mama's stark, sickly appearance that frightened Octavia most, it was the three Rustwick guards standing in their home.

"Are these your children?" the tallest guard asked in a deep voice, turning around to face the doorway.

"Yes," Papa said.

The guard eyed both of them but then turned back to Papa briskly. He handed Papa a scroll that contained the wax seal of Asa Draydon. "The king requires your service. You've been conscripted to his army. You'll find all the information you need in the scroll. You are to report to the palace in three days."

Octavia felt her insides turn to ice.

"Conscripted?" Bowan protested. "What? Why? Rustwick's not at war."

"Bowan." Papa's tone was sharp, warning him to keep quiet.

The guard's cruel eyes fell on Bowan once more, scrutinizing him from head to toe. Then his gaze returned to Papa. "How old is he?"

Octavia's breath caught in her throat. Bowan definitely looked older than he was, but he was much too young to be conscripted—although the Rustwick guards could take him anyway.

"Eleven," Papa said.

The guard considered Bowan for another second before clearing his throat. "By the king's hand."

And with that, the guards pushed their way past Octavia and Bowan, leaving the Fletchers alone.

Octavia's lungs felt stuck in place. It was only when the sound of the guards' horses faded into the distance that she felt like she could breathe again. Papa pulled Mama into a tender embrace, whispering to her in low, soothing notes, but she didn't seem lucid enough to understand what had just happened.

Bowan caught Octavia's gaze, and the two of them exchanged a silent look of dread. It was overwhelming enough that Mama's condition made them feel like they had already lost her. But in the span of one day, a decree from the king had now taken Papa away from them too. Reality wound its icy fingertips around Octavia's heart. Families who headed up Rustwick's key crop productions were meant to be excused from royal decrees such as these in order to keep up the booming production across the kingdom. Papa shouldn't have been a part of this.

But Heston Creevy's words slithered back into her mind, and now Octavia knew . . .

Papa had been conscripted because of her.

3

Fish Fry

"You can't go!" Bowan protested.

Papa's defeated look made Octavia's stomach clench. "I have to."

"But Mama needs you! *We* need you! King Asa can't just break our family apart!" Bowan cried. "Why does he want you anyway? I'm sure there are a lot of other men who can go. Why does it have to be you?"

"What does the scroll say?" Octavia's voice barely surpassed a whisper.

Her heart felt like a hand was squeezing it to death. This didn't feel real. Her stupid temper. Her stupid, impulsive temper. She wanted to scream at Heston Creevy. What a vile, hateful man! He must have talked to King Asa directly with this request. She silently cursed his name to the *gods*.

Papa broke the wax seal that held the scroll shut, and in silence, his eyes scanned the page. As he read, his face grew so pale that he looked like a corpse, and this only made Octavia's unease grow.

"Papa, what does it say?" she asked again, this time more insistent.

For several seconds, Papa didn't speak. When he lowered the scroll, his voice came out hoarse. "Rustwick's army is marching to the outskirts of the Kingdom of Hritza."

Octavia's breath caught in her throat, and all thoughts of Heston Creevy momentarily fled her mind. "What?" She gaped at him, unsure of whether she had heard him correctly. "Papa, what do you mean?"

She strode over to him and pulled the scroll from his hand. She read over the looped writing of the conscription, and sure enough, it mentioned that Rustwick's army would leave in a week to march on Hritza. It also contained instructions on where Papa was to report, and it didn't specify a service term limit, which meant Papa was now a part of Rustwick's army indefinitely . . .

What on earth could have possessed King Asa to want to march on a kingdom cloaked in a darkness that could kill? Were the other kingdoms doing the same? Was there a war on the horizon? As far as Octavia knew, there were no conflicts between Rustwick and the other five kingdoms. Humanity now shared access to the Wells of Power as they should have from the beginning. The impenetrable darkness that shrouded the Kingdom of Hritza was an everlasting warning from the *gods of old*. It stood as a reminder that the Wells of Power were meant to be shared—not hoarded or fought over.

She locked eyes with Papa, and his face changed from shocked to deeply disturbed.

"Papa, what? What is it?" Octavia couldn't help the stress that had snaked its way into her voice.

Papa's lips parted, and he spoke with a paralyzing whisper. "Someone has the key . . ."

Octavia's whole body stiffened, and the hairs along the back of her neck stood on end.

"The key?" Bowan repeated. "What does that mean?" He looked between Papa and Octavia several times, and when neither of them answered his question, he asked it again. "What does that mean? What key? For what?"

"But that's just a story," Octavia murmured. Her voice gained strength. "The key isn't real! Has King Asa lost his mind?"

As Octavia continued to peruse the parchment, Papa led Mama to sit in the rocker in their living room. Something was stirring behind Mama's eyes, almost as if she were coming out of the fog that clouded her mind, but she only mumbled incoherently as Papa situated her under a knit blanket.

"Will someone talk to me?" Bowan exclaimed. "What key?"

Papa sighed and gestured for Bowan to sit on the settee next to Mama's rocker. Octavia gave Papa a resigned look. Bowan didn't know the lore that surrounded the fallen Kingdom of Hritza as well as she did. Octavia grew up on Papa's stories of death and destruction, but Mama disliked them, so when Bowan became old enough to start learning, Mama insisted Papa stop telling them. Bowan only knew pieces—but a lot of people only knew pieces. A thousand years was a long time for humanity to tell the same story.

"Bowan," Papa began. "A thousand years ago, when the Kingdom of Hritza waged war on the lands to gain sole control over all the Wells of Power, the *gods of old* punished them for their greed by destroying their kingdom and sealing off the Well of Eternal Healing with a veil of darkness so that no one could access its *waters*."

"I know that already," Bowan said, batting his hands as if he were sweeping away cobwebs. "What does that have to do with King Asa wanting to march on Hritza?"

Octavia took a seat next to her brother. She glanced at Papa, and he gave her a nod, as if passing off permission to continue the history lesson. She pursed her lips. "According to legend, the *gods* created a key that could unveil the darkness and restore humanity's access to the Well of Eternal Healing. It's said that only the Keyholder can walk through the darkness without perishing and restore the Well to its previous state. The Keyholder would be the one to redeem humanity in the eyes of the *gods* . . . or something like that."

Papa nodded. "As you can imagine, many have searched for this key, but no one has found it. The Well of Power in Hritza belongs to the darkness."

Octavia felt a sudden tug of sadness at Papa's statement. She was thinking of Mama. If Hritza's Well of Power were available, Mama wouldn't be sick. She wouldn't be dying. Its *waters* could have restored her the moment she had fallen ill. But it was foolish for Octavia to linger on thoughts such as these because the Well of Eternal Healing was never going to belong to humanity again—and the key was simply an old wives' tale spun by those who wanted to hold on to the hope that humanity could gain back the gift it had so carelessly squandered.

"So King Asa thinks he knows who has this key?" Bowan asked.

"It would seem so," Papa replied, his eyes landing on the scroll still clutched in Octavia's hands. "I can't imagine another reason for marching up to the darkness."

"But Papa, that's crazy!" Octavia insisted. "The key doesn't exist. Why does King Asa think someone has it? How would he even know?"

"I don't know," Papa admitted.

Octavia pushed herself to her feet, unable to sit still from the confusion and stress weaving through her mind. She began to pace the length of the living room. "And what? Does King Asa think he's going to fight the other kingdoms over this key? Or worse yet, fight for control over a Well no one can use? Isn't that why the *gods of old* cursed Hritza in the first place? Because of their greed?" She ran her hands through her thick braids, tugging on them with force in her frustration. "Papa, don't go!"

The way she said this reminded her so much of Bowan that it gave her pause. They were so alike, she and her brother. Octavia knew that asking Papa to stay was an impossibility. He couldn't defy a royal conscription. He would be imprisoned, and then what hope would their family have of being whole again someday?

But Octavia found herself repeating the words anyway. "Don't go . . ."

Papa walked over to Octavia and held his hand out for the scroll. Her fingers itched with the desire to tear it to pieces, but she pushed the impulse away, handing the paper back to Papa. She stared at him, a storm of emotions working its way up her throat to choke her. Papa's eyes were pooling with tears, and this made Octavia's eyes well up too.

Again, thoughts of Heston Creevy swarmed her, making her blood boil.

This was her fault. Papa was going to Hritza, and it was *her* fault. She almost opened her mouth to spill the conversation she had overheard in town, but Papa pulled her into a hug before she could. The two of them stood there without words for nearly a full minute, and when Papa spoke, she could hear the restraint it was taking him to keep his voice from breaking.

"You need to take care of your mother and Bowan now."

Octavia's throat closed as she fought to keep her own words from falling into a sob. "I will, Papa. I promise."

Bowan shook his head. "No!" He ran to Papa and wrapped his arms around his waist.

Papa embraced him. "And you, Bowan," he said as he smiled through his tears. "You're a man now."

"But I don't want to be a man! Not if it means you have to go."

Octavia backed away a few paces to give Papa and Bowan some space.

Papa was trying his best to hold himself together—Octavia could tell—but it was proving impossible. His eyes crinkled with sadness. Then, he held Bowan's shoulders gently, giving him a good look up and down. "It's often not our decision when life hands us our circumstances. I wish I could stay so that you could be free to finish growing up, but I need you to be the man of the house now. It's not fair of me to ask you so early. I know that. But I wouldn't ask if it wasn't important. Octavia and your mother need you just as much as you need them. Do you understand?"

Bowan looked like he wanted to argue, but his face also expressed what Octavia was more adept at hiding: he was heartbroken.

"Yes, Papa."

Papa gathered Bowan into a tight hug, kissing the top of his head.

The rest of the day was as somber as death. Octavia made Mama the tea, but Mama barely drank any of it. She was non-verbal today, clouded and tucked away into her own mind. Trapped. And Octavia was doing everything she could to keep herself from sobbing her eyes out.

When evening fell and Bowan and Mama went to bed, Octavia sat on the settee in the living room, numb. Her mind was feverish with the desire to tell Papa what she knew, and when he came downstairs from tucking Mama in, their eyes met.

"Papa, I have to tell you something."

Shame stirred in her until it felt like a poison lacing her veins. What would Papa say when he discovered that the reason he was leaving his family behind was because of her? Would he be angry with her? Would he ever look at her the same way again? Papa's tender instructions over the years had always been the same: "You need to control yourself, Octavia. You must keep out of trouble. You can't behave that way, Octavia. Stop and think first. Take a breath before you act, Octavia . . ."

She had finally gone too far . . .

And instead of paying for the mistake herself, Papa was bailing her out, like he always did. Only this time, it wasn't his choice.

Papa sat on the settee next to her. She grasped his hands, and tears finally spilled from her eyes. "When I went to town, I heard Heston Creevy say he was going to punish me for hitting Mildred. He said he thought about denying us the *waters*, but since King Asa wouldn't allow that, he did something else to get back at us . . ." She had to fight with herself for a moment to actually say the words. "He asked the king to conscript you, Papa. To make us pay. To make *me* pay."

A violent tug of shame yanked at her chest as the tears continued to spill down her face.

"It's my fault, Papa. The king would've never conscripted you if I hadn't hit Mildred. And now you're going to—Hritza—and—and what if you're hurt? Or even worse! What if you—" She couldn't finish her sentence. Her voice grew thick with remorse. "I'm sorry, Papa. I'm so sorry. I wish I could take it back."

Papa's eyes widened, then his mouth pursed. He looked her in the face, and anguish overcame him. Then he lowered his gaze to their hands, which were still woven together. For a long time, he didn't speak, and Octavia swore her heart was going to give out on her. It was the loudest silence she had ever heard, but she dared not break it.

When Papa finally spoke, his voice was fractured. "Oh, my beautiful Octavia." He gazed into her dark brown eyes. "I love you so much. You know that, don't you?"

She tried to say something, but she felt like rocks had been lodged in her throat, so she nodded instead.

"Listen to me." His eyes grew fierce, and his tone became more forceful, but his face still carried the softness she had come to know well. "No more fights. No more getting into trouble. They need you.

Do you understand me? Your mother and Bowan *need* you, and I can't be there to bail you out anymore. You have to promise me."

Her lower lip trembled. "I promise you, Papa."

"Swear it."

"I swear it."

He gripped her hands tighter, peering at her with intensity. "I *don't* blame you for this."

A shiver passed through Octavia's body, and it overwhelmed her. How could he mean that? Papa's severe stare continued.

"Please hear me, Octavia. I don't blame you. I'm not angry with you. I know how you can get sometimes, so caught up in your own head . . . but you can't let this get to you. You must be strong for your family."

Octavia's eyes brimmed over again, and a salty tear traced down her cheek, landing in the corner of her mouth.

"Even though you can't control what happens, you *can* control how you react," Papa affirmed. "You *can*."

Octavia let out a low cry. How was she supposed to do this without Papa? How was she supposed to continue their family's trade and be there for Mama and Bowan all by herself? It was too much to bear.

Papa pulled her into an embrace, and for a long time, they simply sat there in each other's arms.

"I love you," Papa murmured.

"I love you too," she whispered.

The time Papa had left with them passed all too quickly. Octavia tried to cherish it, but it was tainted by the thought that she might never see him again. When the morning of his departure came, it took all of her strength to keep herself from breaking down.

Papa kissed Mama—who still was too far gone to know that her husband wouldn't be back for supper this time—and he embraced his children. Then, with tears in all of their eyes, he rode away. As Octavia watched him go, she held on tight to Bowan to keep him from running after Papa, but it was also to give herself something sturdy to cling to so she wouldn't collapse from grief. How was this actually happening?

Her thoughts turned to King Asa Draydon and the key. What a foolish, mad, greedy man—chasing after a fantasy and forcing Rustwick's army to chase after it too. How long would the king persist in his mission to find the key before realizing it was nothing more than a myth?

Bowan shrugged out of Octavia's grasp and moved to Mama, grabbing hold of her hand. "Mama, let's go inside. It's cold out."

Bowan's eyes were rimmed with red, and Octavia had no doubt that hers were too. She suddenly felt the urge to do something to make Bowan feel better. In many ways, Octavia had taken on Mama's nurturing role since the onset of her illness. She had filled Mama's shoes because Bowan deserved to keep some of his childhood. He was still only a kid after all, and he needed someone to look after him and make him feel safe.

"Hey, do you want me to make fish fry tonight?" she offered. "I know it's your favorite. I could catch some trout from the river."

Bowan considered her for a moment. He looked like he was going to burst into tears as he clung to Mama's hand, but then he pressed his lips together firmly and took a deep breath. "That would be nice."

Octavia smiled. "Consider it done. I'll cook you the best fish fry in all of Rustwick."

"Octavia?"

"Yes?"

Bowan's voice cracked with heartache. "Are we going to be alright?"

She bit her lower lip, holding her own dam of emotions at bay. "Yes,

Bowan, we're going to be alright. Take Mama inside. I'll grab the fishing gear and catch you all the trout you can eat. We'll have a feast tonight. Sound good?"

He nodded and then led Mama inside the farmhouse. Octavia, however, headed toward the shed by the side of the barn. After gathering the bait box, the fishing pole, and Papa's fishing knife, she hoisted herself atop a saddled-up Billa and left the clearing at a brisk canter. She knew just the spot to catch a bounty.

Heading downriver, Octavia rode for twenty minutes, and all the while, the solitude of nature gave her the space she needed to finally cry without restraint. She sobbed as the wind caressed her face and the chitter of birds filled her ears. She cursed Heston Creevy again, but this time out loud. She prayed to the *gods* for Papa's safety and for some miracle to happen so that he could be with them again.

As she breathed in the crisp, pine-scented air, she finally felt like she had released enough stored-up grief to function properly. Fishing would take her mind off things, and it would help her focus on Bowan instead of Papa. She was determined to make tonight a good night for him—for his sake as well as her own. They would stuff themselves with the most delicious fish fry, and they would fall asleep to have only the most wonderful dreams.

Octavia pulled back on Billa's reins to halt the horse, and she whinnied, tossing her nose up.

"I'll be quick," she assured Billa. "An hour, tops."

The horse snorted in reply, and this made Octavia smile.

Dismounting, she took Billa's reins and tied them to the low-hanging branch of a pine that hugged the edge of the Kraven River. Then she grabbed her fishing gear and plopped herself down on the flat of a boulder that protruded into the rushing water.

Ten minutes in, and she had already caught a small trout. Hoping for at least one more—and maybe a big one this time—she cast her line back into the water. After half an hour of no activity, Octavia felt a powerful tug at the end of the line, and she dug her feet into the crevices of the rock to avoid falling forward.

"Woah!"

She battled with the fish, but after a strenuous bout of tugging, the line simply wouldn't budge. Octavia had lost the creature, but her hook, unfortunately, was wedged under something, and no matter how hard she pulled, it wasn't coming free.

She swore under her breath and grabbed Papa's fishing knife to cut the line. She would have to tie on a new hook and bait it again.

She tucked the fishing pole between her legs, reaching out to grasp the clear wire, but when she brought the knife down, it slipped, and the tip of it sliced open her left palm. Octavia gasped in pain, dropping the knife and clutching her hand. She sucked air in between gritted teeth, and stars momentarily danced along her vision.

Blood was now dripping down her wrist, speckling the rock below her.

"*Gods of old*," Octavia muttered bitterly.

She stood, cradling the injury and putting pressure on her palm to try and staunch some of the blood flow. She needed to find cloth to wrap it in. Hopefully Billa's saddlebag would have something she could use.

Gingerly, she stepped off the large boulder, returning to the damp earth of the riverbank.

Crack.

An unearthly, cannon-like noise broke the quiet of the forest, and Octavia's eyes snapped to the trees. Then a sustained, wild, groaning scream pierced the air, causing all of the hairs along her arms to stand on end. Billa perked her head up at the sound and pawed the dirt in a nervous manner.

Octavia scoured the trees. She could see nothing but nature. However, this didn't calm her. Her heartbeat was thrumming in her chest, and dread as thick as smoke curled in her belly. She had the most horrible feeling. It was tangible. Monstrous. She couldn't fully explain the sensation, but something evil was in the forest, just past the tree line.

For a few seconds, her body refused to comply with her desire to flee. She was frozen in place, staring at the evergreens, too afraid to move . . .

Billa let out a whinny, and this snapped Octavia out of it. She didn't go back to the boulder to grab the fishing pole or Papa's knife or the trout she had already caught—she sprinted straight toward her horse.

She reached Billa in a few strides and launched herself atop the animal, the stinging in her sliced-open left palm now significantly less painful due to the hysteria pumping through her limbs.

Crack.

The cannon noise boomed again, and another drawn-out bellowing scream shattered the trees, only this time, the sound seemed to come from all around her.

Octavia's breath hitched in her throat.

"Let's go!" she urged Billa, ramming her heels hard into the horse's sides.

Billa moved along the river at a gallop, and wind whipped across Octavia's face, but their ride was short-lived, as something blood-covered and feral emerged from the trees, blocking their path. Octavia barely had time to gasp before Billa reared up on her hind legs with a frightened whinny, throwing her up into the air.

A second later, her back slammed onto pine-littered dirt, knocking the breath from her, and Billa took off up the river, leaving her behind.

Octavia's brain didn't even have time to register what had just happened before the creature from the forest was upon her, straddling her and wrapping its icy fingers around the collar of her tunic to shake her. But it wasn't a creature at all. It was a man . . . with bulging eyes, grime-coated skin, and sunken-in cheeks. And he was covered in blood . . .

Deep slash marks littered his chest, torn right through his shirt.

"Help me!" he gurgled, crazed.

"Get off!" Octavia screeched, jabbing the heel of her sliced-open palm up to catch the man in the chin. The blow landed with force, and the man reeled back, giving Octavia just enough space to free herself from between the man's legs.

"You have to help me!" he pleaded in a near growl. He clawed after her on his hands and knees, seizing her again before she could stand.

The man was bleeding so profusely that it was smearing all down Octavia's front, and the stench of his unwashed body made her gag. She wrestled with his hands as he desperately clung to her clothing, grabbing her as if she were a tree and he was trying to climb up her.

"I don't—want—to die! I don't—"

"Let me go!" she cried, this time kicking out at him and slamming her foot into his groin.

The man yelped, releasing her tunic and curling into a fetal position. Octavia sprang to her feet, her limbs shaking so violently she felt like she was going to collapse.

The cannon sound split the sky for a third time, and Octavia screamed, stepping backward in her fright. Her heel caught on a root, and she fell, hitting the ground hard. The man reached out for her again, only this time, his movements were sluggish, and there was so little color left in his face that he looked like a ghost. Blood oozed through the torn folds of his shirt, and then his mouth parted as he grasped Octavia's leg.

"I'm s-sorry," he croaked.

His head fell, and his body became still.

Octavia's chest was heaving. She pulled her leg from his dead hands. For a few seconds, she simply stared at him as the panic caused by the encounter continued to thunder through her. Where had he come from? Why was he covered in blood? Why did he mean, *I'm sorry*? For what? She scanned her surroundings, but the two of them were alone.

The urge to run was overwhelming, but there was also another sensation filling Octavia's veins: Fear. And the fear came with a sense of impending doom stronger than anything she had ever experienced.

She needed to get out of here. She needed to get home. Right. Now.

She moved to stand to her feet, but the moment she did, a brilliant orb of pure white light the size of an apple shone in front of her—and it was coming from the man's right shoulder. The light was emanating from his flesh, growing brighter and brighter until Octavia had to throw her hands up to shield herself from its intensity.

A flash lit up the entire forest around them. Then the light pulled itself from the man's flesh, floating through the air toward Octavia. She gasped, backing away from it on all fours, but the light chased her, catching up to her quickly. When it reached her, the orb found her left palm and dove into her skin.

"What the—"

She shrieked, batting at it as if she could ward it off. A burning hot sensation seared her palm where the orb had tucked itself in, and after a few moments of pure agony, the light snuffed itself out.

Octavia sat there stunned, her chest spasming in an uncontrolled manner. Had she gone mad? What in the *gods' waters* just happened? Fright was coursing through her like fire, and her abdomen felt like a hollow cavity. She lifted her left hand to look at it, and what she saw nearly stopped her heart . . .

There, in the center of her palm, melded deep into her flesh, was an inch-long silver key.

4

NOT YET COLD

Octavia gaped at the key, her mind refusing to accept what her eyes were clearly seeing. It was dazzling like diamonds, and it was embedded into her flesh as seamlessly as if it had always been a part of her. She was also no longer bleeding from the fishing accident.

Octavia ran her fingertips over the key. It was smooth, with no place for her to gain purchase to pry it up, but she tried anyway, digging her fingernails into her skin until she hissed from the pain she was causing herself. The key wouldn't budge. Her palm had merged with the metal.

Abruptly, a collection of angry voices and horses' hooves made her jump. She whipped her head in the direction of the tree line and then stumbled to her feet, her heart hammering. She backed away from the spot where the dead man lay in his own blood.

"This way!" someone shouted.

Without hesitation, she pelted into the trees, throwing herself behind one of the thick trunks just as a group of men on horseback came upon the scene.

"Here he is!"

There was heavy breathing and the sounds of feet padding against the earth. Octavia peeked her head out the smallest sliver—just enough to see through the thick branches. There were six men dressed in an assortment of worn and weathered fabrics. One wore a brown cloak that seemed far too small for him, while another had a rip in his trousers that went from his shin to his knee. Two of them had already dismounted their horses to examine the dead man, pulling him up with rough hands to look him over.

"It's not here . . ."

A daunting man with dark brown skin and a trimmed beard pulled his black horse closer to the dead man. He clutched a small cracked glass vial in his hand. His voice sounded like knives when he spoke, and his cold eyes appeared murderous. "What do you mean, 'it's not here'?"

The two men holding the corpse both looked at each other before meeting the daunting man's gaze. Then the shortest one spoke.

"Look at his shoulder, Voramir. The key is gone."

Voramir dismounted to examine the dead man himself. After running his fingers over the dead man's shoulder, his attention turned toward the tree line where Octavia stood hidden.

She pulled her head back, clamping a hand over her mouth to keep her rampant breath quiet. Her back dug into the pine trunk as her pulse thundered in her ears. Did he see her? There was a full ten seconds of dead silence . . .

"There's a new Keyholder, gentlemen," Voramir said, his tone snake-like.

Keyholder.

Octavia's eyes widened at the term, and her blood ran cold. No. That was impossible. The key wasn't real. It was just a story. She glanced down at the small silver key burrowed into the flesh of her left palm.

"Whoever it is was just here," Voramir continued. "The former Keyholder's not yet cold."

There was a scrape and then a thud as the dead man's body dropped to the forest floor. A frustrated growl tore through the air, and someone's boot crunched on glass.

"Our last parcel is gone!"

"What do we do?" a new voice asked.

"We *find* them!" Voramir snarled.

Octavia's body was screaming for oxygen as she forced her breathing to stay silent. Her thrumming heartbeat was demanding that she inhale gulps of air, but she couldn't let the men know that she was standing behind a tree mere feet away.

The men pulled themselves back onto their horses, and Octavia could hear the heavy snorting of the animals' breath.

"Look! Over there!" one of them called out.

Trepidation slammed through her chest. She was caught. She knew it. Octavia nearly stepped out from behind the tree trunk, but another man's gruff voice stopped her.

"And who do you belong to?"

Horse hooves pawed against the ground, and there was a familiar whinnying noise. Then more footsteps sounded, moving farther away from the place where Octavia hid.

"Billa . . ." Voramir mused. "Where's your rider?"

Octavia felt like she was going to pass out. Her horse! Billa's name was branded onto the horn of the saddle—and her *family's* name was sewn into the blanket the saddle sat on.

"Voramir, look here," another man said.

"The Fletchers, huh?" Voramir's tone turned devilish. "I think we ought to pay them a visit. Return their horse. What do you say, gentlemen?"

A murmur of agreement passed between the six of them. Then there was a "yip" from Voramir's lips, and the group of horses galloped away. Octavia's legs felt paralyzed as she leaned against the trunk of the pine.

"Bowan," she whispered.

What would those men do to Bowan? Then a far worse thought fired through her mind: what would they do to Mama? She had to get back to the farmhouse.

Octavia took off, running up the river. It was a twenty-minute horseback ride at a walk, but possibly a ten-minute run on foot—maybe quicker if she pushed herself. She pumped her arms unceasingly, her legs burned, and her lungs felt like they were on fire, but Octavia ran like her life depended on it.

She arrived at the edge of the clearing next to the barn eight minutes later, wildly out of breath. A stitch was stabbing her side like a dagger, and blackness invaded the edges of her vision. She put her hands on her knees, trying her best not to faint, but her legs buckled, and she sank to the ground, huffing on all fours. Maybe the men hadn't found their farmstead yet. Maybe Octavia had beaten them there . . .

But as she lifted her eyes, her heart dropped. The six of them were in front of her home, and they had already dragged both Bowan and Mama from the house. Bowan was yelling, struggling against the men who were gripping him, but Mama was paralyzed—stiff and in shock.

"Let me go!" Bowan hollered, putting up quite a fight. "Get your hands off of me!"

"Does this horse belong to your family?" Voramir asked, pointing to Billa.

"Yes, that's our horse! What's this about?"

Again, Bowan tried to pull himself free, but the men held him securely in place, towering above him. Octavia's whole body locked up, and her pulse raced even faster. She tried to stand, but she simply couldn't. She was still on all fours, tucked out of sight by the side of the barn, watching the scene unfold as she fought to keep herself from blacking out.

"Check him," Voramir ordered.

The two men holding Bowan tore his shirt off, discarding it in the dust. Their eyes roved over every inch of his skin, but when they found nothing, they stripped him even further until he was only in his undergarments.

"Nothing, Vor."

Voramir hissed, coming up to Bowan, his face mere inches away. "Were you in the forest just now, boy? By the river?"

Although Bowan was significantly smaller than the man, he didn't shrink away, and he didn't appear afraid. "No."

Voramir scanned his surroundings, calculated, then his eyes landed back on Bowan. "Who else lives here?"

Bowan clamped his mouth shut, glaring at the dark-skinned man with contempt, and this only made Voramir more aggressive. He grabbed Bowan's chin and dug his nails in.

"Don't test my patience, boy. Who else lives here? I know someone else does. You don't have the key."

"The key?" Bowan's eyes grew wide, but then he narrowed them again, putting up a brave front. "What are you talking about?"

Voramir's cruel gaze landed on Mama, and he appeared to mull something over. "It couldn't possibly be her . . ." His voice trailed. "She doesn't look like she's in her right mind." He walked over to Mama and cupped her chin, staring at her face intently.

"Hey!" Bowan yelled, struggling anew. "Don't touch her! Let us go! We don't have your stupid key!"

"Tell me who else lives here."

"No one! It's just us."

Voramir considered Bowan for several seconds, then said, "You're lying. You're hiding someone, aren't you?"

"Rot in the darkness!" Bowan spat. "I'm not hiding anyone! Get off our property!"

"Hmm," Voramir mused. "I think this might loosen your tongue."

In a flash of movement, Voramir withdrew a dagger from the sheath at his hip, but he didn't threaten Bowan with it. He stuck the tip of the blade to Mama's throat instead, digging it deep enough to bead blood from her neck. Mama cried out with a whimper.

It was then that Octavia was finally able to push herself to her feet. Her limbs had gained back a bit of strength, and the feeling of nearly blacking out had subsided. She launched herself around the edge of the barn and held her hands up, specifically making sure her left palm was visible.

"Don't!" she cried. "Here I am! I have the key! It's right here!"

Voramir's attention snapped to her, and he lowered the dagger, a pleased look befalling his frightening features. "There you are, Key-holder," he breathed in a dangerous sing-song.

He gave his men a curt nod, and they threw Bowan and Mama to the ground. Voramir prowled up to Octavia and grabbed her left hand with such ferocity that she gasped. He ran his thumb over her palm, directly over the key. Then his gaze cascaded over her blood-soaked appearance, and his mouth split into a cruel smile.

"Well, well," he murmured, his putrid breath warm on Octavia's face. "Looks like someone's gotten herself into a *world* of trouble." His dark brown eyes lit with satisfaction. "Take her."

Immediately, Voramir's men grabbed Octavia and promptly bound her wrists together in front of her.

"No! Octavia!" Bowan cried.

"It's okay, Bowan," she said, forcing her voice to remain steady. She would not break down in front of her brother.

"Leave her alone!"

Bowan charged forward, and Voramir turned with uncanny speed to backhand Bowan across the face. He hit him so hard that Bowan dropped to the ground with a yelp.

"STOP!" Octavia screeched. "Don't hurt him! I gave myself up! I'm going with you!"

Bowan's upper lip had split open against his teeth, and he spat blood onto the dirt. He looked like he was about to leap up for round two.

"Stay down, Bowan!" Octavia pleaded. "You have to take care of Mama, okay? Remember what Papa said." Bowan and Octavia locked eyes, and she could see that he was on the verge of tears. She gave him an encouraging nod, even though her resolve had shattered. "I'll be fine. It'll be okay."

Voramir mounted his black horse, and the men holding Octavia pushed her forward. Then Voramir extended his hand down to Octavia, his piercing eyes indicating that she needed to get on. She raised her bound hands, and he gripped her fiercely, hauling her atop the animal with surprising strength until she was seated in front of him. Voramir clutched the reins, his arms encircling Octavia, then he bowed his head ever so slightly toward Mama and said in a razor voice, "I apologize for the intrusion."

With that, the rest of Voramir's men pulled themselves onto their horses. Then the seven of them began to ride—and the last glimpse Octavia caught of her family as the men stole her away from her home was Bowan bleeding in the dust and Mama's petrified lucid eyes.

5

Flesh and Blood

The rope bit into Octavia's wrists as Voramir urged the black horse onward, and tears burned in her eyes. She allowed herself a single minute—just one—to give in to the overwhelming feeling of terror before gritting her teeth and resolving that she would do everything in her power to survive this. Whatever these men had in store for her, it wasn't going to be good, and she knew that her chances of getting out of this alive were slim at best.

After only five minutes of riding through the forest, Voramir pulled hard on the reins, halting his horse. He fished into his pocket and pulled out a handkerchief. Folding it hastily, he tied it tight around Octavia's eyes, blindfolding her. Then his chilling grip wrapped around her upper arm, and his lips brushed against her ear. "I don't need you finding your way home. You're with me now, lovely."

Octavia shuddered and clutched the horn of the saddle with her numb fingertips. She could feel Voramir's body pressed up against her own, and it made her feel sick. Voramir prodded his horse forward again.

She silently cursed herself as a thought occurred to her. Why didn't she try to jump off the horse earlier? She could have timed it strategically. They had slowed since first taking off, and even with bound hands, she could have run. Sections of the forest were also thick enough to prevent a horse from following. But now that she couldn't see, she couldn't risk something like that. She'd break her neck.

As they rode on, Octavia tried to pay attention to the turns they took and the length of time they headed in a particular direction, but after an hour, she simply gave up. She couldn't track their movements.

Three hours in, and her body was starting to hurt from being jostled by the horse. On top of that, her hands were as cold as ice from the lack of blood flow, and she was starving. She hadn't eaten anything all morning, and the fish fry was a long abandoned thought. The only thing that was sustaining her was the idea of escape. The moment Voramir stopped this horse, she was going to run . . .

Voramir let out a shrill whistle that made Octavia jump.

The ride had finally come to an end, and her heartbeat picked up significantly. She felt the pressure behind her vanish as Voramir dismounted, and then his abrasive hands dragged her down. She stumbled, losing all sense of balance because of the blindfold, but he held her firmly. Then Voramir made her sit by shoving her down and pushing her back up against what felt like a tree.

She could hear water rushing in the distance as the other men got off of their horses. If they were still by the Kraven River, Octavia felt confident she could find her way home. She was just about to tear off her blindfold and make a run for it when Voramir's hands grabbed her legs. Rope wound tightly around her ankles as he bound them together, and dread settled into her stomach. She wasn't going anywhere . . .

When he pulled the blindfold off, Octavia sucked in a sharp breath through her teeth. His face was inches from hers as he crouched at her level. His whole demeanor was that of a feral animal about to devour her whole—but it was his savage eyes that scared her most.

"I'm going to make this *very* simple for you," he stated, pulling out his dagger and twirling it between his fingertips. "Tell me how you got the key, or I'll make you bleed." He gestured to the dense forest around them with the tip of the blade. "And no one will be able to hear you scream."

Octavia's breath fled her lungs as her eyes traced the weapon, and then her mind raced with confusion. Voramir didn't know how she got the key? But how was that possible? He seemed to know that there was a new Keyholder when the previous man died—and he also seemed to know that the key had melded into the new person's flesh. That was evidenced by the way his men had searched Bowan. How could he know so much and so little at the same time? Before today, she hadn't even believed the key to be real, let alone thought about how one might obtain it. How was she supposed to answer his question?

"I—I don't know. I—" she began.

Voramir pressed the tip of his dagger into the top of her thigh, and a piercing pain shot all the way up to her hip. She screamed. It felt like fire was burrowing into her flesh. Her chest heaved, and she sucked in a pained breath, gritting her teeth and locking eyes with Voramir.

He smiled a soulless smile void of any compassion—one so wide that his yellowed teeth showed in full. "Let me ask you again. How did you get the key?"

"It just—it came out of his shoulder and went into my hand. I don't know how I got it!"

Voramir took the dagger and sliced into her forearm.

She screamed again and tried to pull away from him, but he grabbed her bound hands and yanked her forward so that her back left the trunk. Her butt slid across the dirt a few inches. Then Voramir rested his hand against the tree above her head.

"HOW DID YOU GET THE KEY!?" he bellowed. "I need you to be more detailed with your words, or I'm going to do more than simply *cut*. Tell me *exactly* what happened!"

Octavia let out a whimper. She was doing her best to remain calm, but she was more scared than she had ever been in her life. Voramir's men were loitering just past their leader, some wearing amused looks and others wearing curious ones. But none of them said a thing to stop Voramir's cruel behavior. She couldn't run, and she couldn't fight—not bound hand and foot. The only thing she could do was tell Voramir everything she saw and hope it would satisfy him.

"The man—he came out of the woods. He spooked my horse, and I fell off," she said, her voice quivering. "He was bleeding, and then he attacked me. He was on top of me, and I wrestled him off. He kept asking me to help him, and then he just . . . died." She swallowed, her throat parched. "Then there was this light. It came from his shoulder. It was small—the size of my fist maybe—and then it just . . ." Octavia stalled, realizing how insane she sounded, but she pushed herself to finish. "The light chased me, and then it went into my hand. And when it disappeared, the key was there."

Voramir's eyes narrowed. She could see that he was working something out in his mind.

"Did you cut him with anything?" he asked. "Did you try to reach into his shoulder and pry it out?"

"No!" Octavia shook her head. "It just came out. I didn't do anything to him. I didn't even know the key was there!"

"Are you absolutely sure?" His stare skewered her.

"Yes! I swear to the *gods.*"

Voramir let out a growl. He stood to his feet, raking his hands through his black curly hair. His brown skin was glistening with sweat, and he looked like he was on the verge of some kind of fit.

"The lengths I had to go for this—the price I had to pay to find the Keyholder before anyone else did—all for him to die mere *days* after capturing him! Leaving me with *nothing* and no answers!" Voramir crouched again, getting in Octavia's face once more. "How is it that *you*, a simple farm girl, were able to extract the key from his body when my dagger couldn't cut it from his flesh?"

Octavia's stomach churned, and vomit threatened to come up her esophagus. So that's why the man had severe cuts on his body when he stumbled out of the trees . . .

"What else did you do!?" he roared, his spit landing on Octavia's nose and cheeks.

"I don't know!" she cried. "I didn't do anything! Please—"

Voramir's blade dug into the skin just below her left collarbone, and she shrieked. He had only pierced her a quarter of an inch, but the agony was unbearable.

"Stop! Stop!" she pleaded. She was crying, the tears freely flowing down her cheeks. She had to say something. Anything to get Voramir to stop. "I—I remember something else!"

Voramir pulled his blade back. "Go on."

Octavia's chest spasmed, and her breath came out shaky. "I cut my hand! When I was fishing, I cut my palm! Right where the key is. I was bleeding when the man attacked me!"

Voramir's mouth parted in surprise. Then he exchanged a few quick glances with his men before murmuring, almost to himself, "*Gods of old* . . ."

Abruptly, he stood and began to pace, but he stopped after only a few seconds. Then one of Voramir's men spoke up, a slight tremor in his tone.

"You don't think it's . . ."

But the man seemed unable to finish his own thought. Whether it was from fear of Voramir or fear of uttering the thing aloud, Octavia didn't know. She couldn't even guess at what the man was going to say. But it wasn't long before Octavia had her answer, because Voramir finished for him.

"Blood magic—a magic beyond the Wells of Power. *Ancient* magic," he said with a hungry smile. It hooked his mouth, again revealing all of his teeth, as if he were a beast. He put a hand to his filthy chin, pondering something. "Perhaps that's why I couldn't cut the key free. I didn't offer my own blood in return."

Voramir prowled up to Octavia anew, and with an experienced hand, he cut the rope binding her wrists together. Before she could even massage them out, he grabbed her left hand, examining the silver key. All of Voramir's men huddled closer, keen to get a look at the thing.

Voramir took the tip of his dagger and pressed it into the heel of Octavia's left palm.

"Hopefully only one more cut, lovely," he crooned.

Then he sliced open her skin until blood dripped down her wrist. She hissed, the pain horrendous, but she gritted her teeth, hoping against hope that whatever Voramir's plan was, it would work. She didn't want this key, and he was clearly willing to torture her to get it. Maybe, if the key melded into him instead, they would let her go.

Voramir took the tip of the knife to his own flesh next, digging a jagged line into the heel of his palm. Blood seeped from the wound, falling down onto the forest floor. Then he pressed his sliced-open palm to hers.

All of them waited with bated breath. No one dared to say a word. The only sound around them was nature herself. Octavia prayed to the *gods* that the light would appear and the key would leave her, but after a full minute had passed and there was no show of any kind of magic, Voramir pulled his hand away from hers.

"Why isn't it working?" he demanded of his men, as if any of them had the answer.

"I have a suggestion," someone offered.

Octavia's attention turned to the man who had spoken. He was short and fat, with a balding head and a pig-like face. Dirt caked his skin, and he carried a sadistic gleam in his eyes that made her skin crawl.

"I know you couldn't cut the key out of the man's shoulder, but why not cut the girl's hand off? It's much easier to remove a hand than part of someone's torso."

Octavia's whole body doused itself in sheer panic, and even though her feet were still bound, she pushed herself up without thinking and tried to flee. She fell to her stomach, her wrists slamming against the pine-littered ground, but that didn't stop her from trying to crawl away.

Laughter filled her ears as the fat man grabbed her, hauling her back across the dirt.

"And where do you think you're going, pretty thing?" he lilted with pleasure.

"Get off of me!" she screeched, now contorting her body. She kicked her bound feet together like a battering ram, landing a blow on the fat man's knee, and he cried out in pain, dropping her and falling to the ground. This was enough to prompt the rest of Voramir's men to join in. The four of them grabbed every inch of her, and they dragged her back to Voramir, who simply looked amused by her struggle.

"You're a feisty thing, aren't you?" Voramir mused, coming up to Octavia.

The fat man clutched his knee and swore aloud, growling. "Well, Vor? I say we try it!"

Voramir considered him for a moment before nodding. "Yes, let's try. Put her on the ground."

The four men holding Octavia shoved her onto her stomach, and her chin dug into the dirt. Terror seared through her veins, and she fought harder, screaming and begging them to stop, but no matter what she did, she couldn't outmatch four grown men.

She felt one of them straddle her and put his hand on the back of her head, pushing the side of her face into the dirt. She also felt hands pinning her legs and right arm. Then her left arm was stretched out against her will. She couldn't move—she could barely breathe—and then Voramir's terrifying face appeared right in front of her.

He took a strip of leather and shoved it between her teeth, smiling wickedly as he ran his tongue along his top lip. "Bite down, lovely, because this is going to hurt."

Voramir took his dagger and moved to Octavia's arm. He gripped her elbow, but right as he was about to start cutting, there was a violent snap that sounded from deep within the trees. Voramir's entire body tensed, and she could feel the men holding her tense as well. Voramir scanned the forest and cocked his head, listening intently.

The sound didn't happen again, but Voramir remained on guard.

"I think we have company, gentlemen," he hissed, teeth bared. "Weapons out."

At this, the men abandoned Octavia, getting off of her quickly to draw their swords. Octavia gasped, her chest able to expand now that the crushing weight was gone. Voramir rolled her onto her back with his boot and then stepped onto her chest—it wasn't with his full weight, but it was enough to hurt. His cruel tone sent shivers through her. "If you scream, I will go back to your farmhouse and gut your little brother like a pig when this is over."

Voramir removed his foot from her chest and tucked his dagger away, pulling out his sword instead. The six men took a defensive stance all around Octavia—even the fat man, who had finally managed to get to his feet. Each of them was standing at the ready, looking outward toward a different patch of forest.

Octavia's heart was beating so violently that stars were beginning to twinkle across her vision. She felt a scream building in her throat as she continued to lay flat on her back, but she bit down against the leather that was still between her teeth to keep quiet. She would not make a sound for fear of Voramir following through with his threat.

Snap.

The noise cracked through the trees once more, and all six men turned toward the source. They formed a group with Octavia now behind them. Then a *whoosh* broke the air, and the next thing Octavia knew, an arrow was sticking out of the fat man's chest. His pig-like face lit with surprise, and then he crashed to his knees, a horrid gurgling coming from his throat.

"Show yourself!" Voramir shouted, now placing himself strategically between his men and the trunk of a tree so that it blocked the direction the arrow came from.

Zip.

Another arrow found its place in the next man's chest, and he thudded to the ground, dead before his body ever touched the earth.

It was then that Octavia decided to act. Voramir and his three remaining men were distracted, and this was her chance. She sat up and spat out the leather material in her mouth, then her jittering fingers attacked the knots of the rope binding her ankles.

"I said show yourself!" Voramir cried again.

For a moment, Voramir's razor voice made Octavia freeze, but he hadn't noticed her yet—none of the men had. They were still all facing the mysterious source of arrows.

Her fingertips pulled the last knot loose, and she unwrapped her bindings. She was free at last. Now all she had to do was run. With her heart in her throat, she stood slowly, not daring to breathe. Once she was on her feet, she began to back away.

Swish.

A third arrow embedded itself into another man's forehead, he fell straight back, and that's when Voramir saw her . . .

"THE GIRL!" he screamed.

Octavia took off, sprinting through the pines. She heard shrieks and what sounded like more arrows, but she didn't stop. She pelted through the forest, leaping over roots and ducking under branches. Footsteps pounded behind her. There was a clash of metal upon metal. Shouting. More thuds.

Octavia fled—with all the strength left in her body, she fled—and in her spirit, she prayed to the *gods* that they would help her get away. She kept running until all sounds of the scuffle behind her were long gone. When she finally slowed, she hid behind a thick pine and leaned up against it, panting furiously. She nervously chanced a glance back the way she had come, but she didn't see anyone.

"Thank you," she whispered to the *gods*.

She clutched her chest, unable to believe what had just happened. She opened up her left palm to gaze at the key. Those men were about to saw off her arm to get this thing. She shuddered at the thought, and then, without warning, she fell to her hands and knees and vomited in the dirt.

Her stomach heaved up what little contents it had, and a burning sensation filled her nose and throat. After her body was done, she wiped her mouth with the edge of her tunic and got to her feet. She needed to keep moving. She had no idea if Voramir was still on her trail—or if whoever fired those arrows was chasing her too—but she wasn't about to linger around and find out.

All she could see was dense forest. She had no idea where she was, and as she stopped to listen, even the faint sounds of water from before had vanished. If she was close to the Kraven River, she wasn't sure where it was. Right now, the smartest thing for her to do was to keep heading in the same direction she had been going—away from those horrible men.

Octavia took a measured breath, preparing to run once more . . .

Something huge and dark launched itself from the trees, and a cloth was pressed over her mouth and nose. Octavia fought against a pair of arms that held her tight, but to no avail. The hand that muffled her screams was strong and vicious. Then an overpowering, putrid, burning scent filled her nostrils, and she drifted away into the inviting arms of oblivion.

6

THE BOUNTY HUNTER

When Octavia came to, she was once again bound hand and foot, sitting on the forest floor, leaning up against a tree—and her head was killing her. Her breathing turned shallow as she caught sight of a black horse tied to a pine tree a dozen feet from her. It was Voramir's horse. He had captured her again . . .

She couldn't help how her body shook as she surveyed her surroundings. She didn't see anyone—just the horse—but she feared that, at any moment, Voramir would appear, keen for a second round with her flesh.

She attacked the top knot of the rope binding her hands together with her teeth, trying to pry it loose, but it wasn't budging. She twisted her wrists, hoping that she could slip out of the rope with sheer force, but that proved useless too.

"You're awake," a voice to her right said. "Good."

Octavia yelped, turning toward the sound, but instead of Voramir's crazed face, there was a man she'd never seen before. He stood tall and broad-shouldered, with light brown skin, long black hair that came to his shoulders, and coffee-colored eyes. He was also incredibly fit, the muscles along his arms visible under his sleeves. He wore a brown leather vest and dark fabrics from head to toe, and his jawline was sharp, coming to a rather pointed chin that carried just a hint of stubble.

Part of her panic diminished. At least he wasn't one of Voramir's men. But the small moment of relief passed quickly as she remembered that she was still tied up.

The man approached her, crouched in front of her, and pulled a dagger from his hip, bringing the tip of it to her chin and digging it in hard enough to hurt but not hard enough to break skin. Fear attacked her, and she sucked in a labored breath, unable to move away from the blade because of the tree behind her. She stared into the man's fierce eyes.

"I only have one rule," he said evenly. "Don't make this difficult for me, and I won't make it difficult for you."

Octavia's heart rammed itself against the inside of her chest. No. Not again. He was going to ask her about the key. Her mind searched for something she could offer him—any piece of information that would spare her from the weapon—but nothing came. She was going to get tortured again . . .

But then the man pulled the blade away from her chin.

The way he was looking at her . . . it was unlike anything Octavia had ever encountered. His expression was untamed and calculated. It pierced her, making her want to turn away from him, but at the same time, something hid underneath—something pensive that drew her in. The manner in which his eyes narrowed and his mouth pursed . . . she could only describe it as hatred, but it wasn't cold. There was gravity behind how his attention cleaved to her. *Every inch* of her.

The man stood, now tucking the blade back into the sheath at his hip. He scanned the trees, his body tense, his lower jaw working like he was chewing on something.

"Who are you?" she asked shakily, a little relieved that he wasn't immediately going to take the dagger to her left palm.

"Azariah Ronan," he replied in a smooth voice. "Bounty hunter."

Octavia stared at him, her mind reeling. Bounty hunter? Her words came out with a tremor. "There's a bounty on me?"

Azariah's upper lip curled as he pointed to her hand. "There is now."

Her stomach seized. The key. The stupid *gods*-forsaken key.

Her mind filled with questions. How is it that, all of a sudden, everyone seemed to know about this? She'd had the key for less than half a day. What in the *gods' waters* was going on here? A nervous jolt ran through her, but she pushed past it and decided that she was going to ask this bounty hunter as many questions as he would answer.

"How did you find me? How did you know I had the key?"

Azariah pulled on the hem of one of his leather gloves, adjusting it as if readying himself for a fight. He was still looking around, like he was expecting someone to emerge from the trees. "I was tailing those men. They were after my bounty. But when I came upon the poor man and he didn't have the key, I knew it had changed hands."

Octavia's eyes roamed the forest, and Azariah seemed to read her mind.

"They won't be coming for you," he stated. "They're dead."

The stone-cold edge he said this with made her stomach flip. There was no remorse there—no hint of kindness—and it made her afraid of him. A horrible feeling settled in her just as it did when Voramir first took her away from her home. She was now at the mercy of a new man, one who seemed just as intent on his mission as Voramir had been. Only this time, it seemed he wasn't in this for himself. If he was a bounty hunter, as he said, then someone had sent him. Which meant . . .

"You're not going to try and cut the key from my hand?"

Azariah raised an eyebrow. "No, I'm not going to cut the key from you."

Without warning, he turned and walked away from her, stalking over to the black horse and fishing for something in the saddlebag.

Despite her best efforts to temper it, anxiety stormed her body, and she strained her hands against the rope, desperately trying to pull herself free. She even wriggled her legs, but her bindings were expertly tied. Octavia suppressed a whimper and leaned her head back against the tree, fighting the urge to burst into tears. How was she going to get out of this?

Azariah's dark eyes snapped in her direction, and the look that curled his mouth sent shivers down her spine. "You're not getting out of those."

She swallowed against a parched throat, licking her dry lips. Her tongue felt like sandpaper, and her stomach was a pit. She hadn't eaten anything or had a drop to drink all day, and the sun looked like it was less than an hour from setting. She must have been unconscious for a few hours after this man had caught her.

"Can I have some water?" she asked.

He ignored her. Then she watched him take out a waterskin from the saddlebag and down several hardy gulps, tipping his head so that his long black hair cascaded down his back. Octavia wanted to curse at him, but she bit her tongue to curb the impulse. Her eyes stung from the way they watered. *No.* She would not give in to her body's desire to fall apart.

Get more information, she urged herself. "What's King Asa paying you?"

Azariah stopped drinking and let out a loud scoff. "You assume Asa Draydon sent me? That fool is so deluded in his confidence of gaining the key that he's decided to ready his army to march up to the darkness without first *securing* it."

Octavia's pulse quickened, and sweat collected against her hairline. If King Asa didn't hire this man, then who did? Azariah's mention of marching up to the darkness without the key sparked another thought in her mind—one that made her blood run cold. How many other kingdoms were going to do the same?

"Then who sent you?"

"Bastian Jasper."

"The King of Zoharth?"

Azariah dipped his head. "The very same."

Octavia sat there in silence, taking a few deliberate breaths to keep calm. The Kingdom of Zoharth oversaw the Well of Prophecy. Its *waters* had been giving people predictions since the dawn of time, but it had never offered humanity anything earth-shattering. It was used as a source of fortune-telling. When someone wanted to find out more about their future, they went to Zoharth. The Well provided cheap and meaningless divinations. But maybe the *waters* had changed? Could that be part of this nightmare? It certainly would explain how different parties were suddenly privy to the key's existence.

On top of that, Azariah's statement unnerved Octavia for another reason. King Bastian Jasper had a reputation for being a cruel and quarrelsome man. He was power hungry—plain and simple—and five years ago, he had nearly started a war between Zoharth and the rest of the kingdoms because of his decision to heavily tax non-Zoharthian use of the *waters* from the Well of Prophecy. Parceling to other kingdoms became scarce during that time, but thankfully, the conflict fizzled out when Bastian's advisors pleaded with him to allow equal access to the *waters*, lest the *gods of old* curse their kingdom too.

Octavia remembered Papa commenting that King Bastian had probably introduced the tax as a means of making Zoharth "important" again—because it was generally thought that Zoharth's

Well of Power was less useful than the other kingdoms' Wells. Papa said the tax forced people to pay attention to Zoharth, upping the desire for its *waters*.

Octavia plucked up the courage to speak again. "So, you're taking me to Zoharth."

"Yes. And now that you're awake, we need to get moving."

"Can I please have some water?" It was hard to keep the desperation out of her voice because she was so thirsty.

Azariah huffed, as if annoyed, but he walked over to her. The whole time, his eyes were searching the trees. Then he knelt and offered her the waterskin. Octavia snatched it up with her bound hands, putting it to her lips and downing the whole thing. It only partially satisfied her ravenous thirst.

She handed the waterskin back to him.

It was only then that she noticed the bandages around her thigh. She blinked a few times to make sure she wasn't seeing things, then her gaze fell on her forearm. That was wrapped too—even the heel of her left hand and the skin below her collarbone were doctored.

"You dressed my wounds?" She peered at him, confused. Why would he do that?

"Yes," he replied with an air of annoyance. "The wound on your thigh was particularly nasty, and I can't have you bleeding out on me or dying from an infection."

"So, I'm wanted alive?"

Azariah's eyes narrowed. "Very much so."

She gnawed on the inside of her cheek, mulling over an idea.

"We're leaving now."

Abruptly, Azariah stooped down, grabbed her wrists, and hauled her to her feet with alarming force. She nearly fell straight over because of her bound feet, but he steadied her. Just as he was about to hoist her up over his shoulder, she blurted out, "I need to pee!"

His eyebrows climbed his forehead. Then he gestured with an open palm. "There's nothing stopping you."

"I'm not going to wet myself!" she bit back. "Let me pee. I'd appreciate it if you didn't treat me like an animal. Didn't you *just* say you wouldn't make this difficult for me if I didn't make it difficult for you?"

She hoped that invoking his one rule would be enough to make this work . . .

There were a few seconds of silence as he appeared to mull over her request. Then he pushed her down into a sitting position against the tree and went back to the black horse. She waited, curious to know what he was grabbing, but when he came back with more rope, her heart sank.

He strode over to her and knelt on the ground. "Lean forward."

"What are you—"

"Lean forward!" he growled.

She moved her back away from the tree, and Azariah looped the rope around her waist, tying it like a belt and knotting it several times. She watched him like a hawk, noting the way he secured the rope. It was complicated, but she felt like she could undo it if her hands were free.

Then Azariah moved to her ankles, untying the tangle of bindings, and he did the same with her hands.

"Stand up," he said gruffly.

Octavia got to her feet, gently massaging out her wrists. There was about four feet of rope from her waist to his hands. Even though she knew it wasn't wise to say anything that might provoke him, she couldn't help the retort that tumbled from her lips. "Great, now I'm a dog on a leash."

"It's the best you're going to get," he snapped. "You can go behind the tree."

"This trunk isn't thick enough to give me any privacy."

"I don't care."

She folded her arms. "Well? Turn around. I'm not undressing in front of you."

His eyes darkened, but then he relented, gripping the rope tightly and turning his back to her. "Make it quick."

She stepped behind the tree and shuffled her feet, making just enough noise to pretend to be pulling her pants down. All the while, she was viciously working the knots at her waist. She knew she only had seconds before the lack of urination would give her away, but with one last dig of her thumb, she was able to loosen the final knot. She carefully looped the rope on a branch so that it wouldn't drop to the forest floor, and then she backed away from the tree to create some space between them. This was going to be a chase, but she was ready to do whatever it took to escape.

Taking a steadied breath, she turned and sprinted.

Immediately, she could hear Azariah curse aloud. Footsteps thudded after her, but she had a decent lead. She pelted forward, ducking around pines and leaping up the face of a boulder. She climbed higher, entering a rocky patch with underbrush. She hopped from rock to rock, and when she got past the semi-treacherous section, she continued through a new tangle of pines.

Water rushed in the distance, and she made a beeline for the noise. If she had to, she would jump into the river. She'd rather take her chances with the rapids than be handed over to King Bastian Jasper.

The fast-flowing water was just ahead, so she pushed herself to speed up. Her lungs were screaming, and her muscles were dead, but freedom was only a few seconds away—

Strong hands caught her around the middle, and she tumbled to the dirt. In an instant, Azariah was on top of her, pinning her under the weight of his body. She screamed, twisting herself, and this was enough to get her left hand free, but he grabbed her wrist and slammed it down with so much force that she cried out. Then his dagger was to her throat, and his face was inches from hers.

"You are *not* going to escape me, Keyholder!" His rapid breath was hot on her face, and his voice was dangerous.

She tried to push him up with her hips, but he was too heavy. She was thoroughly pinned.

"Stop fighting me!" he growled. "I will give you one last warning. You can either come with me willingly, or I will make the next few weeks *extremely* unpleasant for you. Either way, I'm going to deliver you to the King of Zoharth—whether that's riding atop a horse of your own volition or bound and gagged in the back of a wagon."

She ground her teeth, feeling completely overwhelmed. Her escape attempt had failed, but she wasn't giving up. She simply needed to play along and look for a better opportunity.

"Fine," she gritted out, panting. "You win. I'll behave."

"That remains to be seen."

He got off of her and pulled her to her feet in one sweeping motion. Octavia would have taken the chance to run again had the bounty hunter not maintained a crushing grip on her forearm. Sheathing his dagger, he took the rope that was still in his hands and tied her wrists together. Then he tugged on the knots, checking their strength. The instant he finished the bindings, he yanked her up against his body and got in her face, speaking in low, menacing notes.

"I have a bounty to collect and a reputation to uphold. And *you* have a job to do. There are *dark* things on the horizon. This is *far* bigger than your freedom!"

Octavia's breath shuddered. She was keenly aware of how close they stood, and she had to fight the urge to strike him. That wouldn't end well now that she was tied up again. But it wasn't Azariah's invading presence that frightened her most, it was his words. What was he talking about? What dark things? What job?

"Walk!" he barked, pushing her forward.

Azariah kept his grip firmly on the end of the rope that trailed between them as they traveled back the way they had come. They didn't speak. Only the sounds of birds and insects filled the silence . . .

This was going to be a long game, but Octavia silently vowed to the *gods* that she would get away from this man. Her nerves jumped a bit, and her stomach flipped as she decided to try his name on her tongue. "Azariah?"

He stopped walking—and this forced her to stop too. His entire demeanor became as stiff as stone. It was clear that Octavia's use of his name had just made him *very* uncomfortable.

"Yes?"

"What do you mean? What dark things are on the horizon?"

He stared at her with a look of confusion. His expression furrowed, and for several seconds, he didn't speak. It was like he was trying to work out if she was being serious.

"What dark things?" she repeated, this time more insistently.

Still, he gazed at her like he couldn't believe what she was asking.

He pressed his lips together, and his hands gripped the end of the rope until his knuckles turned white. Then his face morphed into something bone-chilling, and the danger behind his eyes turned her skin to ice. "The darkness around the Kingdom of Hritza is expanding past its borders for the first time since the *gods of old* created it."

7

Play Along, Dear

If the bounty hunter had said the earth was going to swallow her up where she stood, it would have been a less shocking statement. Numbness spread through Octavia's limbs, and she gaped at him, terror momentarily paralyzing her.

The darkness surrounding the Kingdom of Hritza was a void. No man's land. A pit of pure evil. It shrouded the Well of Eternal Healing from more than just humanity's eyes. Anyone who so much as reached out a finger to touch the thick, swirling, tar-like substance immediately died—and in the most horrific ways. Octavia had heard the stories from Papa. Each generation passed down the gruesome descriptions to the next. Boils bursting from people's faces and chests. Blood pouring from their mouths and ears. Their eyes sucked back into their skulls. Bodies reduced to ash or emaciated beyond recognition in a matter of seconds. Flesh ripped clean from bone . . .

It killed so destructively that many believed even a person's soul could not survive it. The darkness was a monster with no mercy, and no *waters* from all the Wells of Power could do a thing to temper it. It simply stood as a sentinel over humanity. A warning. An omen of death from the *gods of old* themselves.

"The darkness is moving?" Octavia's voice was hoarse.

Azariah could not hide his look of bewilderment at her question. He nodded slowly. Grimly.

"Papa . . ." Octavia felt like her soul had been torn from her body. Papa would be marching up to the darkness in a week. What if he got caught in it? She swallowed hard, a million questions racing through her mind. She needed more answers from this bounty hunter. "How do you know this? Did you go up to the darkness yourself? When—when did it start moving? What is going on—"

Azariah held up a hand, and she stopped talking. He simply stared at her. Then his eyebrows creased together with concern, along with something *far* deeper. His words came out barely above a whisper. "May the *gods of old* help us all . . ." He placed a palm to his forehead and let out a low throat-clearing noise. Then he studied her face carefully. "You really know nothing about this?"

Octavia laughed. It was more out of panic than humor. "Does it *look* like I know what's going on? Why would you assume that? I'm not even supposed to be here! I'm supposed to be at home, taking care of my sick—"

She promptly stopped herself. She couldn't risk telling this man any personal information. He could use it against her. She didn't know how much he already knew about Bowan and Mama—maybe some, considering he had followed Voramir and his cronies—but she needed to protect them. No matter what happened to her, she vowed to the *gods* that she would not let it get back to Bowan and Mama. They were not a part of this.

"Can you please tell me what is happening?" She bit her lower lip. Tears were forming in her eyes, so she closed them. She did not want to cry in front of him. After a few deliberate breaths, she opened them again. "I need to know what's happening to me."

There was a long pause where Azariah didn't say anything. Then he pulled her forward.

Octavia's heart fell. Was he really going to keep her in the dark? "You're not going to tell me anything?"

"We need to go."

"But—"

"It's not safe for us to linger," he cut across her sharply. "There are more people after you. People like those men who almost cut off your hand."

She tugged against the rope he was clutching, her wrists aching from how long she had been tied up today. "Who were those men?" There was an edge to her tone now. She was fed up with this. Why couldn't he just tell her? He clearly knew more than she did. What was the point of keeping it from her?

He dragged her along, now marching at a relentless pace. "We need to leave this place. We've already spent too long here."

"Here?" she repeated. "In an endless forest in the middle of nowhere?"

He stopped walking so abruptly that she collided with him.

"Do you want your flesh carved up? Do you want someone else to come along and torture you for information you are apparently too ignorant to give them?" She gasped as he pulled her closer to his body. "I am not so uncivilized. But I am also only *one* man. I can't fight off an army. So, I suggest you shut your mouth and follow me before you find yourself at the end of someone else's blade."

His head was tilted down over hers, and his imposing stature made her feel small.

"Fine," she relented.

Octavia followed him without any further resistance. He was on high alert. She could tell from the way his eyes swept the trees, and dread seeped into her. How many people were trying to find her? And how many of them would not hesitate to treat her the way Voramir had? A shudder ran through her body at the thought.

When they returned to the black horse, Azariah helped her mount. Then he hoisted himself up behind her, and the two of them took off through the forest. She gripped the horn of the saddle, feeling the invading presence of Azariah's body against her own. This felt like the moment Voramir had stolen her away—bound hands and a sense of impending doom—but at least this time she wasn't blindfolded, and she was certain Azariah wouldn't take a knife to her flesh.

The sun was beginning to fall behind the horizon, and her heart felt like it was being squeezed to death. She held back her tears and mouthed a silent goodbye to the Kingdom of Rustwick—her home—for she did not know if she would ever see it again. And in the same utterance, she mouthed "I love you" to Bowan and Mama. This last phrase broke her, and for a few minutes, it took a considerable amount of self-control not to sob aloud.

They rode on—dusk falling all around them—and she wondered if they would be traveling all night or if the bounty hunter had plans to stop and rest at some point. She wanted to ask but decided it was best to keep quiet.

Her stomach made a horrid roaring noise. She desperately needed to eat. She was just about to ask Azariah for some food when she caught sight of his starkly alert expression. His eyes panned back and forth over the shrouded trees, his expression strained and his shoulders taut. The way he was acting scared her. She didn't feel safe with him, but at the same time, right now, she absolutely didn't feel safe *without* him. A chill crawled down her spine. She had the feeling that they were being watched, and as they continued to weave through the dark at a canter, the feeling only grew stronger until Octavia's stomach was in knots. Her hunger diminished, replaced by fear instead.

Every little sound the forest produced seemed magnified, and she found herself leaning back against Azariah's body just to feel some semblance of protection. The ominous presence of the dark forest was like that of a monster waiting to devour them.

Her heartbeat ticked faster as the ride continued, and she sent up a prayer to the *gods* to protect her. Over and over again, she prayed. It was the only thing keeping her from falling apart.

An hour later—or maybe even three—she had no idea how long they rode—she felt her eyes beginning to droop. She fought to stay awake. But the horse was now moving at a walk, lulling her into a stupor with its rhythmic gait. Every parcel of self-preservation she owned was screaming at her to stay alert, but eventually, the strain of the day caught up with her, and she drifted off into a fitful sleep.

Strong hands startled her awake, and she opened her eyes with a gasp.

Azariah was dragging her down from the horse, and her vision spun as he forced her to stand up and wake up all in one jarring moment. It was morning, and the early light of the sun was streaming through the pine trees, hitting her in the face like a battering ram.

She squinted, throwing her bound hands up to shield her eyes. Her fingertips were so numb she swore they were going to fall off, and she was freezing. Her teeth immediately began to chatter.

"W-where are we?" she asked, strained. She could still only see trees, but there were the faint sounds of something else she couldn't quite pinpoint. People? Cattle? Music?

Her stomach, which was only a void yesterday, was a monstrous pit today. She was starving, and she felt significantly weaker.

"Hold out your hands," Azariah said.

When she didn't immediately respond, he grabbed her and yanked her forward a few steps. She winced, her wrists now bruised from being bound for so long. To her surprise, Azariah worked the knots quickly and untied her.

A split-second urge to run flashed its way through her mind. She was free from her restraints. She could do it. But her body felt like a flimsy blade of grass, and she was so hungry that she knew she wouldn't get far before being tackled. On top of that, yesterday's events were already producing bruises all over her body. This wasn't the time to escape. She wasn't strong enough.

"Wrap your left hand in this," Azariah instructed, offering her a long strip of dark cloth.

She took it and then gazed at her left palm. The silver key shone in the sunlight. It was brilliant. Eye-catching. There was no way she could be around anyone without drawing their attention to it unless it was well hidden.

With an unsteady breath, she wrapped the cloth around the key until it was sufficiently covered.

Then Azariah handed her a damp rag. "Clean yourself up."

She took the rag shakily. Although she didn't have a mirror, she could feel the dirt on her face. She brought the rag to her skin and scrubbed. She also wiped off dried blood from her forearms, and when she was done, Azariah took the rag back.

"Now your hair. Redo it."

She stared at him, confused. But then her mind quickly caught up with why he was asking her to do this. He didn't want her to appear like she had been kidnapped. She begrudgingly obeyed him, working her thick brunette hair free from its frayed trio of braids. She combed through it swiftly with her fingertips and then rebraided it.

"There. Happy?" she muttered.

"Put this on," he said, handing her a thin black cloak from the horse's saddlebag.

She took it gingerly, peering down over her torn and crusted-over tunic. The blood that had smeared all over her front during her scuffle with the previous Keyholder had dried overnight. She looked and smelled awful . . .

"I said, put the cloak *on*," he growled impatiently.

She obeyed him, sliding her arms into the garment and fastening the front of it so that it covered her bloody clothing.

Azariah took her by the wrist and started marching forward. The ache from the ropes felt like it went down to her bones, and his cruel grip was crushing. She whimpered, and his eyes flashed to her for the briefest moment. He didn't let go, but he did loosen his hold slightly.

Hunger pains stabbed at her stomach. "Can I eat something?"

He said nothing. He simply continued to move at a persistent pace. After another minute, he stopped and then pulled Octavia to his chest so that their bodies were practically flush against one another. He tightened his grip on her wrist to the point where she felt like her bones would break. Then he spoke in an aggressive tone.

"If you try *anything*, I will not let you eat. Do you understand me?"

She nodded, but this did nothing to temper the force with which he held her.

"Welcome to Omari, Keyholder," he breathed. "Play along, dear. Let's see if you can behave. And keep your hand *hidden*."

He released her wrist and hooked his arm over her shoulder, sauntering them both around a bend in the trees.

As they emerged from the forest, a bustling town came to life in front of her eyes. Octavia's breath hitched as she took in the colorful streets of the Kingdom of Omari, home to the Well of Fertility. Nearly every structure was decorated with orange, red, and yellow scarves. The rich fabrics clung to windows and doorways. They covered vendors' stalls and twisted together in strands that hung over the streets, weaving between houses and businesses alike.

Octavia felt like she was entering a grand tunnel as she stepped onto the cobblestone.

In addition to the scarves, flags with virility prayers woven into them were displayed on nearly every storefront, and the tavern just ahead of them was covered in the most vibrant paints she had ever seen. It was so visually overwhelming that Octavia lowered her gaze to her feet as Azariah ushered her along.

She had never visited another kingdom before, though she knew of each Well of Power—and which kingdom oversaw what. This was so starkly different from her rustic and charming hometown that it immediately made her feel homesick.

The layered scents of decadent perfumes hung in the air: myrrh, styrax, cinnamon, and rose. And hints of honey and olive oil seemed to cling to everything. The streets were crowded, and as Azariah led her forward, she bumped into a woman—a very visibly pregnant one.

"I'm sorry," Octavia murmured.

A big smile lit the woman's face, and she gave Octavia a quick dip of her head. "Nothing to worry about, love." The woman's hands immediately went to Octavia's stomach. "May the *gods* bless your womb."

Octavia was so startled by the woman's touch that she couldn't form words. She didn't need to though because Azariah quickly pulled her away. The small exchange made Octavia aware of the number of pregnant women walking the streets—they were everywhere—and as she scanned her surroundings, she noticed that the people of Omari all wore fabrics of orange, red, and yellow. Nearly everyone's garb matched the vibrancy of the scarves that were hanging about. It was an oversaturated sight to see.

The next thing she knew, Azariah was steering her into a darkly lit tavern, and the smell of salted pork and amber mead hit her nose like a wall. Her stomach roared, and her entire mouth filled with saliva. She was so hungry . . .

"What can I do for you, handsome?" a young woman asked in a sensual tone.

She was standing behind the long oak bar in the back of the tavern, eyeing Azariah like he was a meal. She ran her pinky finger over her luscious bottom lip. A flowing, layered skirt was cinched over her thick hips, her heavily lidded eyes were painted with a shimmering teal powder, and dark red curls framed her face.

Azariah donned a charming smile, sliding his arm around Octavia's waist as he leaned over the bar. The feel of his hand against her hip made her squirm, but she didn't let the discomfort show on her face.

"My betrothed and I need a room," he said smoothly. "Just for the night."

Betrothed? Octavia nearly wrenched herself from his grip. She wanted to scream for help. She wanted to get away from him. Surely the people in the tavern would help her if she yelled that this man had taken her against her will? But the key burned in the back of her mind, and this deflated every ounce of fight she possessed. She could not let anyone know about it . . .

"Your betrothed?" The young woman soured as she looked Octavia up and down, her mouth curling with displeasure, then her face donned a flirty pout as her attention went back to Azariah. "Too bad." Her fingers slid up his arm. "I could have showed you a good time."

"Setka, the patrons! More mead for the patrons!" an older woman snapped in a gravelly tone, shooing the young woman away.

"Of course, Madame Shayla." Setka winked at Azariah as she shimmied around the bar, grabbing his arm again and murmuring, "If that scrawny little doe doesn't work out for you, you know where to find me."

Two days ago, a comment like that would have ended with Setka bleeding on the floor and Octavia back in jail, but she was far past giving in to those kinds of urges. She was in survival mode. Play along, Azariah had said—and that's exactly what she was going to do.

"A room?" Madame Shayla repeated. "And did I hear the word 'betrothed'?" Her age-spotted face flowered into a brilliant smile as she took in the two of them. "Oh my! Are you in Omari for a parcel of the *waters*?"

Azariah opened his mouth to speak, but Octavia beat him to it. "Yes, we pray that the *gods of old* will bless us with many children." She hooked her arms around Azariah's waist, and she could feel him stiffen.

The woman reached across the bar and brushed Octavia's cheek like a grandma would a granddaughter. "With your beauty and his charming good looks . . ." She seemed like she was going to burst with happiness. "Your children will be strong, handsome, and blessed!" Madame Shayla's face turned devilish as she plucked something from Octavia's braided hair. It was a sprig of pine needles. She rolled it between her knobby fingers, wiggling her thin eyebrows up and down with a grin. "I see you've already gotten started. Had a quick tussle in the woods, did we?"

Octavia could feel her cheeks burn with a fire that reached all the way up to her ears.

Azariah chuckled. His hand went to Octavia's chin, and he lifted her face to look up at his. "We've been anxious for our little one to come."

She wanted to dissolve into the tattered floorboards. She had never done anything with a man before—especially not pretend to want his babies. The amount of control it was taking Octavia to keep her expression light and playful nearly caused her mouth to twitch. Once more, the impulse to cry for help clawed its way up her throat, nearly spilling from her lips. Azariah seemed to sense this, because his eyes narrowed slightly in warning, and the hand that wasn't to her chin tightened around her waist.

Octavia's will to speak died.

"Well, let me see what we've got here." Madame Shayla turned and sashayed to the very end of the bar where a big book sat open. She perused it before grabbing a large bronze key from one of the hooks on the back wall. Then she scurried back to them, handing the key to Azariah. "You're in luck. I have one room left."

He set a large handful of coins onto the oak bar. The woman's eyes grew, and her mouth dropped. Azariah had clearly given Madame Shayla much more than the cost of the room.

He then handed her a folded piece of parchment. "See to it that these items get delivered to our room immediately."

"Of course! Right away, sir!" She snatched up the coins and the parchment, bowing to him. "Enjoy the blessings of the Well, my dears. Your room is just past the bar, up the stairs, and at the very end of the hall. There's a crescent moon carved into the door. You can't miss it."

Octavia's stomach clenched as Azariah directed her forward, keeping his hand firmly at her waist as they ascended the steps. She wanted to run, but there was no foreseeable way of doing that. She was completely trapped.

Why were they even here? What did a trip to Omari accomplish? She was supposed to be his bounty—a prize to be delivered alive to King Bastian Jasper. But what if he was going to do more to her than simply bring her to Zoharth? Her pulse quickened at the thought, and her head began to swim. She couldn't fight him off if he decided to have his way with her. She was too starved and exhausted to do so.

Apprehension coiled like a thread around her throat. She had a sick feeling that Azariah Ronan was about to do something far worse to her than use his blade.

8

Vow

The room had one bed, a side table with candles, a closet, and a small round table with two chairs. It was cramped, and a musty smell clung to the blankets and walls.

"Sit," Azariah said.

To Octavia's great relief, he pointed to the chair at the round table instead of the bed. She still had no idea what was about to happen, but at least he wasn't going to bed her immediately. She walked over to the rickety wooden chair and dropped down into it. He took the seat opposite her and stared at her, a curious expression pursing his lips. It looked like he was fighting an odd sort of smile. "You were rather convincing downstairs."

"Can I eat now?" she snapped. "I'm starving, and I behaved."

She immediately regretted her tone. What if he decided to starve her longer simply for her attitude?

He cleared his throat and then folded his hands together, tilting his head so that a lock of his long black hair fell across his shoulder. He was studying her in such a focused manner that she didn't know what to do or say next.

After a few more seconds, he fished in the folds of his vest and pulled out a cloth, unwrapping it to reveal strips of dried meat and a handful of nuts. He pushed the cloth across the table, and she snatched up the morsels, ravenously tearing into the meat with her teeth. It had a smoked, savory flavor that melted across her tongue, and her stomach cried with happiness. She tossed the nuts into her mouth next and barely chewed them before swallowing.

"Better?" he asked.

She scoffed, still ripping into the strips of dried meat. "Are you going to keep me starved like this until we get to Zoharth?"

"That depends on you," he replied candidly.

Anger boiled up in her, but she bit back her next retort, opting for another bite of meat instead. "What are we doing in Omari anyway? I thought you said it wasn't safe for us to 'linger' anywhere for too long. But you got us a room for the night?"

"We won't be staying the night."

"Then what are we doing here?"

"I'm here for a parcel of the *waters*."

Octavia's eyes widened in horror, and she nearly threw up what she had just eaten. There could only be one explanation for that. She stood, backing up against the wall, and her voice came out with a whimper. "No, please don't! Please. I'm begging you!"

Azariah's dark brown eyes widened. He spoke quickly—and with a hint of disgust. "I'm not going to get you pregnant! That's not why I need it."

Octavia's panic diminished, but she didn't move from her place against the wall. "Then why . . . ? Why do you need the *waters*?" She stared at him. Did this man have a girl back home? Wherever home was for him?

"I'm hoping to hinder the others who are after you. Once you're in

Zoharth, you're no longer my problem, but until then, I'm going to do everything I can to keep you safe and pray to the *gods* that I can get you to King Bastian intact."

He was speaking like all the kingdoms of the land were coming after her at this very moment. She clenched her hands into fists, plucking up the courage to try and get more information from him. She strode back over to the chair and sat, pushing as much boldness into her tone as she could muster. "Tell me what's going on. How would anyone even know I have the key? How could they *possibly* find me? And how do you know the darkness is moving?" When he didn't respond, she added, "I'm the Keyholder. I deserve to know!"

Whatever Azariah was thinking, he didn't show it on his face. It was hardened and closed off. But then . . . he took on an expression of pity. It shadowed his complexion like a mistake, lingering long enough for Octavia to notice it before it vanished. She pressed her lips together, a horrible feeling chilling her. Why would this bounty hunter be looking at her like that? Didn't his profession prevent him from caring about her?

"What do you know?" he asked in a cautious tone. "Did anyone teach you about the *gods* growing up? Or about the Keyholder?"

"I've been taught," she said evenly. The insinuation that she hadn't been taught about the *gods of old* was insulting.

"Then tell me what you know."

He was challenging her—speaking to her like a child—and she wanted to snap at him, but she held back, deciding to recite what she had told Bowan instead. "Only the Keyholder can walk through the darkness without perishing and restore the Well of Eternal Healing to its previous state. The Keyholder will be the one to redeem humanity in the eyes of the *gods*."

"Well, yes," he said, as if that were obvious. "But do you know anything else?"

She simply stared at him.

He sighed. "I'll take that as a 'no.'"

She gripped the material of her cloak with both hands, digging her nails into the fabric. "Okay, enlighten me."

Azariah leaned forward to rest his elbows on the table. "Do you know anything about blood magic?"

Octavia's stomach dropped. That was something Voramir had mentioned when he was torturing her. She shuddered. Any magic beyond that of the Wells of Power was considered taboo magic—evil magic tied to the darkness itself. She knew that dark magic existed, however, she had never learned anything about it. Growing up, she had shunned the idea, as any pious, *gods*-fearing person would.

"No, I don't know anything about blood magic."

"It's a magic that dates back to the creation of the darkness itself, and it works only through blood sacrifice—specifically death, in its most common application. The previous Keyholder must die for the key to meld to a new master, and an exchange of blood must occur."

Octavia's heart pounded as understanding lit her mind. The pieces of her encounter with the dying man fell into place: his gushing wounds, her sliced-open left palm, traces of their blood mixing together during the tussle, and then him falling dead in front of her with a haunting gurgle of "I'm sorry."

Azariah's brow furrowed. "Those men who took you, I'm assuming they asked you how you got the key?"

She nodded, words momentarily lost on her.

"Fortunately for you, very few people understand the true nature of blood magic. Had those men known the cost, you would be dead, and the key would belong to another."

"Fortunately for me?" she repeated weakly.

Octavia couldn't hold back the trembling that had entered her limbs. Voramir's blood had mixed with hers... Had he succeeded in cutting off her hand, she likely would have bled to death, and then the key would have been transferred to him.

"So, the people who are after me want to kill me?"

"Some of them, yes," he replied. "Others may simply want to capture you and deliver you to the paying party. I'm not aware of how many bounties are out for the Keyholder right now, but at this point, I'm likely not the only one."

Her head spun as she tried to process everything. She could feel her heart race and her joints tingle. She was slipping into a panic attack, but she dug her nails into her palms and took a few intentional breaths. "Okay, but you still haven't answered my questions. How do people know where to find me? How would anyone know I'm the Keyholder? Until yesterday, it was some other guy."

Azariah's jaw tightened. He looked like he was fighting with himself over whether he should answer. After nearly a full minute of silence, he shook his head. "I think we've talked enough for today. I'm tired. I'm going to bind you again so I can sleep."

Octavia got to her feet, and in her desperation to know the truth, she said something very stupid. "If you tell me, I swear to the *gods* that I won't try to escape you. I won't fight you! I will go with you to Zoharth. I vow it! And if I don't, may the *gods of old* strike me down where I stand."

Azariah's face paled significantly, and perspiration glistened against his light brown skin. He stood, coming up to her so that he towered over her. She didn't back away as his untamed eyes searched hers. "You would make a vow to the *gods* over this?"

Her brain was screaming at her to back down—to rescind the offer so she could continue to look for an opportunity to get away from him—but her desire to know the truth about her predicament was winning out. If she did this, there was no taking it back. Vowing something aloud to the *gods* was unbreakable.

But the longer she mulled it over, the clearer her decision became. If she were to run away without knowing *how* people were tracking her, what would be the point? How could she keep herself safe? She would likely fall into the hands of someone far worse than this bounty hunter—and if he was willing to tell her what was going on in exchange for her compliance, then she was willing to give it.

She locked eyes with him. "Yes, I will vow it."

Azariah held out his hand, and she placed hers within his. He gripped her tightly. "Do you, Keyholder, vow to *gods of old* to willingly come with me to Zoharth if I share with you what I know?"

"I do."

"And do you accept the penalty of breaking this vow?"

Her breath hitched. "I accept. May the *gods of old* strike me down where I stand if I try to escape you."

"Then as the *gods* are our witness, you are tied to me." Azariah let go of her hand, and with a stiff nod, he gestured for her to sit back down at the table. "Very well, Keyholder. I will tell you what I know."

9

Twenty-Seven Days Ago

The foreboding look on Azariah's face made Octavia's skin crawl. As she waited for him to begin, she fiddled with the strip of cloth that was hiding the key, all the while keeping her gaze firmly fixed on him.

"Twenty-seven days ago, the Well of Prophecy in Zoharth gave a parcel of its *waters* to a woman named Zara Mattocks. And with that parcel came the words of a prophecy that surpassed the vain fortune-telling of its antiquity. This was a parcel directly from the *gods of old* themselves."

Azariah's arms visibly tensed, and he swallowed hard.

"Being a pious woman, Zara didn't keep the prophecy to herself—for it was a warning meant to be shared. So she sought an audience with King Bastian. She told him the words she had spoken after drinking the parcel, and she urged him to help her deliver the message to the other kingdoms. He agreed. But when Zara turned to leave the throne room, Bastian drew his sword and cut the woman down in order to keep the prophecy from leaving Zoharth. In her dying moments, Zara called a curse upon Bastian, and with her last breath, she said she had told another the words that the *waters* had produced."

Azariah cleared his throat, now furrowing his brow.

"There were seven other men present in the room when Zara delivered the prophecy—Bastian's inner council—and after witnessing the king's actions, there was an uproar. A fight broke out, and Bastian tried to cut down his councilmen too. Three escaped him. Four died by his sword."

Horror stirred in Octavia's belly. How could King Bastian defy the *gods of old* so blatantly? What an evil, horrid man. He would bring destruction with his greed. Had he not learned a thing from Hritza? Whatever Zara had cursed him with, he deserved it. She wanted to ask how Azariah knew all of this if King Bastian had gone to such extreme lengths to keep the prophecy a secret, but she stayed silent.

"In a rage, King Bastian sent his guards to Zara's home, but the person who had learned the words of the prophecy had already fled. It was on that very night that the darkness began to move past its boundaries for the first time in a millennium."

Azariah's voice grew more gruff and burdened.

"Shortly after that, King Bastian hired me to complete two tasks. First: find the three councilmen who had escaped him and kill them. And second: find the Keyholder and bring them to Zoharth."

Octavia swallowed uneasily. "And did you . . . find the three councilmen?"

"Yes. I brought their heads to King Bastian," —Octavia sucked in a harsh breath— "but not before getting all three of their accounts of what happened in that throne room. I needed to know what was worth killing them over . . ."

"Do you know the words of the prophecy?" she whispered.

Azariah looked disappointed. "Not in full. The three councilmen wouldn't tell me. They all took it to their graves. I suppose it was to protect you from King Bastian."

A shiver ran down Octavia's spine as Azariah's expression darkened.

"But their silence didn't matter in the end," he said, folding his hands and resting them on the table. "King Bastian told me what I needed to know to find you: 'Seek the one who can walk through the darkness, all the *waters* will allow it.'"

Octavia could feel her entire face blanch. There was a crushing silence after this statement, and it took her a moment to find her voice.

"Are you telling me that any parcel of *waters* from any Well of Power has the ability to find me?"

He nodded grimly. "Yes. Anyone can hunt you—anyone who knows. The *waters* have changed. Twenty-seven days ago, the Wellminders in every kingdom reported a strange disturbance. All of them had the same account: a light shone in their *waters*, then blackness swirled within the depths of their Well. The *waters* are still providing the same gifts they always have, but now . . . they can also find you."

Octavia felt like she had been plunged into an icy lake. This was so much worse than she thought. How was she going to survive this? How could she possibly escape a magic so widely accessible? The tension in her body built like a storm.

"Who knows about this?" she asked. "How many people are after me?"

"I don't know. From Zara's one mysterious runaway, to the three councilmen who escaped Bastian before I cut off their heads . . . they could have told anyone. Anywhere. That band of men who took you is only the beginning of this. How they learned of the *waters*' tracking ability and who they learned it from . . . I cannot say."

Azariah opened up the inside flap of his vest and pulled out a glass vial the size of a finger, setting it on the table between them. It was a parcel of *waters*. Octavia stared at it, drawn in by the soft blue glow. Parcels had always been a beautiful thing to her—a gift to be thankful for. But now, it terrified her to know that something that could fit in anyone's pocket could find her.

"You don't know who sent those men after me?"

He shook his head. "They were likely an independent party, keen for the glory the key might have offered them."

"Glory?" Octavia repeated weakly. She wanted to burst into tears. "What is glorious about this?" She ripped off the cloth covering the key and held her left hand up. "This thing is evil! This key has tied me to the darkness itself! I either have to walk through it or die by the hands of someone else who will have to do the same! What possible glory is there in this?"

"Oh, come now," Azariah tutted, tilting his head to the side and narrowing his eyes. "You seem like a smart woman. Why do you think there is glory in this?"

The answer came to Octavia even before Azariah had finished asking the question, and trepidation filled her to the brim. "Whoever gets me is going to use me to end the darkness and claim the Well of Eternal Healing in the name of their kingdom."

"Very good, Keyholder." His tone was venomous, and it sent a spike of nerves through her.

She shook her head, horrified. "You can't take me to King Bastian. He's evil! Zoharth can't gain control of the Well in Hritza!"

Azariah's mouth curled into something that wavered the line between frustration and anger. "And which kingdom, Keyholder, do you believe should have the *right* to unlock the Well of Eternal Healing? Which kingdom deserves to claim that *they* halted the darkness to save humanity? Hmm? Rustwick? Just because that's where you were born?"

Octavia was momentarily unable to speak. Azariah's question had pierced her, and she didn't have an answer. But she knew one thing for certain, and she was not afraid to say it.

She stood from the table. "King Bastian Jasper doesn't deserve this! And you shouldn't be taking his side."

"I don't take sides," Azariah countered coldly. "I take jobs."

She got more aggressive with her stance, placing her hands on the table and leaning forward. "And what happens if King Bastian does something horrible with me? What if the darkness consumes everything because of it? You *can't* remain impartial! Not with this!"

Azariah stood, and his chair skidded back a foot. He stalked up to Octavia with lightning speed, and she gasped as his face came within inches of hers.

"Watch me," he sneered.

He was so close to her that she could smell hints of pine and sweat on his clothing. His hand went to her chin, lifting it slightly, and a quiver passed through her skin at his touch.

"Even if I wasn't impartial, it wouldn't matter," he breathed. "You just swore to the *gods* that you would come with me to Zoharth. You made a vow, and now you are bound to it."

He pulled his hand back from her. It was hard to tell—maybe it was her imagination—but he looked . . . sorrowful?

"You're a part of this now. You carry the key. I only hope enough people remain ignorant of the *waters*' new ability long enough for me to deliver you safely. You *must* stay alive. The key *must* stay with you."

She gave him an odd look. What? Of all the things she thought he would say next, it wasn't that. Why did it matter that *she* was the Keyholder and not another? Octavia didn't want to die by any means, but his statement confused her. If she died, couldn't Azariah just deliver the next Keyholder to King Bastian? The man before her had died and left her with the key. What difference did it make?

Octavia's lips parted, and she very gently took a hand and placed it on Azariah's chest, pushing him away from her. He backed up a few paces in response. She peered at him, her mouth turning dry. A sense of doom so thick she felt like she couldn't breathe descended upon her.

"Why does it matter that *I'm* the Keyholder?"

His face turned starkly grim, and for a few seconds, he didn't speak. Instead, he stared hard at the wooden floorboards.

"Azariah," she pressed. The use of his name caused his lips to purse, but it also pulled his attention back to her. "Why does it have to be *me*?"

Octavia stared at him. Impatient. Waiting. She folded her arms together.

He exhaled slowly, and then his eyes locked with hers. "There's another part of the prophecy I know. It says that every time the key changes hands, the darkness will expand faster. Even the key changing its allegiance to you has caused the darkness to progress. I *must* keep you alive. I already failed the previous Keyholder. He wouldn't have died if I'd gotten to him sooner." Azariah put a hand to his tired face, and then he murmured something so quietly that Octavia barely caught it. "I think the *gods of old* have finally run out of patience with us . . ."

His comment surprised Octavia. Everyone believed in the *gods*. Everyone had faith to some degree, but not everyone held genuine reverence. This bounty hunter couldn't truly fear the *gods of old*, could he?

But the thought fled her mind as Azariah's eyes shadowed over with a dark glint. He spoke with conviction, drawing her attention back to the danger of her predicament. "You are the one who has to stop the darkness, or the *gods of old* may simply choose to end all of humanity at the next change of the key."

10

A PARCEL OF *WATERS*

A jarring knock on the door caused both Azariah and Octavia to stiffen. Octavia's breath caught in her chest, and Azariah moved to her quickly, grabbing her upper arm, but his touch wasn't harsh. It was surprisingly gentle. He put a finger up to his lips, and then his eyes flicked over to the closet by the side of the bed.

Octavia nodded, and he released her.

She strode across the room and tucked herself into the cramped space. The closet was barely big enough to accommodate her, but she managed to close the slats of the door. She could still see into the room, but someone would have to intentionally peer through the slats to spot her.

Azariah walked to the door. He had slipped his dagger out and was holding it discreetly at his side, right behind his leg. Carefully, he took the handle and cracked the door a few inches. Immediately, his stance eased up, and he pulled the door open. There was a scrawny boy about Bowan's age standing there with a large brown paper package in his arms.

"Madame Shayla told me to bring this to you," the boy said. "It's everything from the list you gave her. She told me to say that if there's anything else you need, just ask."

Azariah sheathed the weapon without the boy noticing and took the package from him. "Thank you."

The boy bowed. "Of course, sir." Then he scampered off down the hall.

Azariah shut the door, and Octavia breathed in a sigh of relief. She opened the slats of the closet and stepped out, thankful to be free of the tight space. Cramped areas always gave her the sensation that she would suffocate.

Octavia watched as Azariah set the package on the table and undid the brown paper wrappings. Inside, there were four items. The first was a vial with a parcel of *waters* in it, the blue hue as mesmerizing as ever. The second was a small, sheathed dagger with a tag wrapped around the hilt. The third was a single brown leather glove with the fingers cut off and hemmed to keep the edges from fraying. And the fourth was a black tunic.

"Here." Azariah handed her the glove. "To keep the key hidden."

She took the glove, examining it. It was exquisitely made. Colored threads of orange, red, and yellow were sewn into a crescent shape on the back, and the leather was soft to the touch. She stared at her left palm, once again noting the brilliant shimmer of the silver key, and then she slipped her hand into the glove, covering the horrid thing from sight.

"This is for you as well." He held out the black tunic. "So you can change out of your bloody clothing."

She stared at the tunic. Was this an act of kindness? Or simply a means to keep her appearance in order so that no one would suspect she was his captive? Octavia grabbed the delicate black fabric, holding it to her chest.

Then her eyes landed on the parcel of *waters* lying on the brown paper wrappings, and fear physically twisted around her throat like a snake. In the past, a parcel had never given her anything other than wonderful feelings. Whether it was a parcel to be consumed or a parcel to be mixed with a vat of river water to feed the ground and yield bountiful crops, Octavia had always marveled at the incredible piece of magic. Now the sight of it made her tremble.

"Can you show me?" she asked, pointing to the small vial. "How does it work?"

Azariah grabbed the *waters* and backed away from her a few feet. Then he held it out in front of him like one might hold a sword. He pointed the parcel at the doorway and then slowly panned it across the room. When it was pointing toward Octavia, the natural blue glow of the *waters* intensified and flashed. But then as he continued to pan away from her, the *waters* went back to normal.

"As long as someone has the intent to find you, they only need to point the parcel like a compass and follow its light."

Octavia took a step back. She could feel the bed behind her legs, so she sank down into it before gravity could take her to the floor. Her limbs felt useless and fragile, and her stomach was a pit. The dried meat and meager handful of nuts she had eaten earlier hadn't been enough, but right now, she couldn't eat even if she tried. She was completely overwhelmed.

How was this happening to her? A few days ago, the worst thing she had to think about was when Mama might pass on. But now, not only was her own life at stake, the lives of everyone in all the kingdoms were at stake. The idea of the darkness swallowing everything whole laced fear all the way down to her bones. But the most chilling part about this was . . . *she* was the one who would have to walk into the darkness to put a stop to it. Would the key protect her like legend said it was supposed to? Or would she perish the moment she touched the black swirling substance? What was she even supposed to do upon entering the darkness? It's not like there were instructions written out for her. Of course, none of those questions mattered if someone were to actually succeed in killing her for the key. Maybe being delivered to King Bastian Jasper wouldn't be as bad as she was imagining. At least he had the resources to protect her—even if he was going to use her to claim the Well of Eternal Healing in the name of Zoharth.

"I need to sleep before we leave," Azariah said, breaking her out of her spiral of thoughts.

He walked over to her and grabbed her hands, pulling out a length of rope. Octavia stood from the bed abruptly and pushed him away. "You don't need to tie me up. I'm not going to run. I swore it to the *gods*."

Azariah did not look happy. His upper lip curled, and his nose crinkled. He stared at her with a menacing demeanor, contemplating.

"Besides," Octavia added hastily. "I'm better off with you anyway. If someone else were to capture me, who knows what they would do. At least with you, I'm safe. Given what you've told me, it seems like you're my only chance of making it to Zoharth alive. And I'd really, *really* like to stay alive."

Azariah didn't seem convinced, but he also didn't move to bind her hands. He took a deep and uneasy breath before saying, "May the *gods of old* hold you to your vow, Keyholder."

He tossed the ropes onto the chair, and they landed with a thud. Abruptly, he took her by the wrist. His grip on her was fierce, and she tried not to wince.

"*Do not* leave this room."

With that, he let go of her and plopped himself onto the bed, closing his eyes in exhaustion. She gazed at him, relieved and a little stunned. She could not believe she had gotten him to lower his guard so quickly, but she also knew she could not defy her vow. She would stay. She had promised the *gods*, and that was sacred to her. Plus, what she'd said to him was true: right now, she was safer with him.

Still, her heart ached with sadness for Bowan and Mama. She already missed them terribly. They had no idea what was happening to her or if she was alive. But even if she could run away from Azariah, she knew she couldn't go home. Not with so many people hunting her. That would put her family in danger, and she would never do that to them.

Octavia took off the cloak Azariah had given her, hanging it over the back of one of the chairs. Then she inspected the black tunic. She eyed the bounty hunter, not wanting to change in front of him, but he was fast asleep, so she quickly threw off her old tunic and donned the new one. It felt so good getting out of that crusted, smelly garment.

She sat at the rickety wooden table once more, putting her head in her hands. Her body ached, and her stomach rumbled. Maybe she should close her eyes too . . .

"Wake up."

Azariah's voice coaxed Octavia from her slumber, and she lifted her head from the table. She could feel impression marks on her face from sleeping on the hard surface. By the angle of the sun and the orange colors it cast on the walls of the room, it was maybe an hour from sunset. She groaned. Her joints felt stiff, and her stomach was roaring with hunger again. But beyond that, she didn't want to leave the tavern. In a strange sort of way, she felt safe in this bedroom, and the idea of going back out onto the cobblestone streets frightened her.

"I need to pick up a few more things around town, but after that, we're leaving Omari. I got what I came for."

The parcel of *waters* . . .

It was the reason Azariah had brought her to Omari in the first place. She stood, stretching her shoulders out a bit. "You said you were trying to hinder the people following me? How would a parcel of *waters* help with that?"

"I've acquired a protection spell from a witch," Azariah answered. "But it requires the *waters* from all six Wells to work."

Octavia blinked several times. She tried not to let the fact that he said "witch" bother her—he was trying to prevent her from being tracked after all—but witches were known to deal with dark magic. And dark magic was something she never wanted to discover the cost of. Unfortunately for her, this key changed things. She was already tied to the darkness. Wouldn't it be prudent to take another layer of protection?

Pushing past her discomfort, she asked, "Would that actually work?"

In a way, the idea that she could somehow be magically protected from the very magic that was helping people hunt her seemed absurd, but at the same time, she hoped it was true.

"It can't shield you entirely, but it will temper the potency of the *waters'* ability to find you," he said. "In other words, if you're too far away from someone seeking you, their *waters* won't glow the way I showed you."

"Do you have all the parcels you need?"

He shook his head. "I only have five."

"Which one are you missing?"

"The *waters* from the Kingdom of Urtha."

Octavia's stomach clenched. Urtha had a reputation for its wild festivities and lavish living. It was sensual. Eclectic. And dangerously addictive. It was the kingdom people visited to piss away their money and forget about their problems. Urtha housed the Well of Euphoria, and there were plenty of people who would do anything to keep drinking its *waters*.

"Is it . . . safe there?" Octavia asked hesitantly.

Azariah gave a dark laugh. "It's safe nowhere. Not for you, at least."

"Right. Dumb question," she murmured. She could feel her cheeks turning scarlet.

"If nothing hinders us, we should be able to reach Urtha in four days," Azariah said. "Thankfully, it's on the way to Zoharth." His eyes bounced to the window, where the sunlight continued its path to join the horizon. "We need to go."

Octavia's stomach rumbled. "Can we eat something in the tavern?"

He gave her a sideways glance but then nodded stiffly. "Let's be quick about it."

Octavia followed Azariah from the room, down the stairs, and into the busy tavern below. Madame Shayla immediately spotted them and sauntered over, a gleam in her eyes. "I hope that parcel of *waters* did the trick!" She gave Octavia a wink.

Her stomach did a somersault as Azariah put his hand around her waist and pulled her close. "We pray for the *gods'* favor. Thank you for delivering the items on my list so promptly. Would you get us some stew? We're both quite famished."

Madame Shayla wagged her finger knowingly. "I'm sure you are from all that tussling. Have yourself a seat, and I'll be right along with two meals. On the tavern—for your generosity." She gave Azariah a deep bow.

The bounty hunter steered Octavia into a booth in the back corner of the tavern, then his hand left her waist. Promptly, Madame Shayla arrived with two steaming bowls of pork stew, a pitcher of amber mead, and two honey cakes. Octavia's entire mouth filled with saliva. She started eating immediately, and in five minutes, her bowl was empty and her honey cake was gone. With actual sustenance in her belly, Octavia finally felt a little less physically on edge.

Azariah did not delay. The moment he finished his meal, he pulled her from the tavern to walk the bustling cobblestone streets of Omari.

"Stay close to me," he warned, relinquishing his rigid grasp on her wrist.

Instantly, Octavia experienced the urge to run away from him. She could do it. Now that she had enough strength in her body, she could sprint, but that simply wasn't an option . . .

As they visited different vendors to stock up on food for their journey, the women around Octavia blessed her womb. It was as common a greeting as "hello," and by the time Azariah had purchased dried fruits, salted pork, honey cakes, potatoes, and some raw vegetables, Octavia's womb had been blessed one too many times for her liking.

Then they returned to the black horse in the falling light. Octavia was relieved their shopping trip was over. At least they wouldn't be around people anymore.

Azariah had Octavia mount first, and then he hoisted himself onto the horse behind her, but instead of leading the horse further into the trees, he took them back onto the cobblestone streets.

"Where are we going?" she asked.

"To Urtha. We'll ride through Omari and follow the Kraven River from the other side." Azariah said this as if it were obvious, but Octavia was shaky with her geography. She only knew the general location of each kingdom in relation to each other, not the direction they needed to travel in to get to the next one.

"Okay."

After feeding and watering the horse, their ride through the town seemed to last forever. The sunset-colored scarves hanging from every window and door made everything look the same. She didn't know why Azariah took a left at the bakery or a right at the tanner, but she trusted that he knew where they needed to go. The whole time she felt like every person who looked at her *knew*, and it drove her to clutch the horn of the saddle and lean back against Azariah as she had done the night he had captured her.

She could feel his warm breath on her neck and his thighs against her own. Despite the discomfort of being so close to this man, she craved the feeling of safety his body provided. He put a steadying hand at her waist, as if sensing the unease that coiled in her. When he had done this back in the tavern, Octavia had wanted to pull away from him, but now she didn't mind it for the sense of security alone.

By the time they reached the end of Omari, the sun had long set behind the horizon, and stars were twinkling above them. The bustling activities of the town had moved indoors, and very few people were still out on the streets.

At long last, Octavia spotted the end of the road where the cobblestone meshed with the dirt in the moonlight. The ominous forest laid ahead. It was strange that a dark mass of trees could give her peace, but she felt a knot of tension release in her abdomen at the sight.

The horse's hooves clopped on, but right as they were about to exit the street, a hooded figure stepped out onto the road a dozen yards from them. Octavia's whole body froze, and she could feel Azariah stiffen too. He pulled back on the horse's reins, and the animal stopped. The hooded figure held up a hand, and then there was a flash of something distinctly blue that lit up the stranger's toothy grin.

Abruptly, a dozen more figures stepped from the shadows all at once, surrounding the horse. There were the sounds of swords leaving their sheaths. Then the hooded figure walked forward a few paces.

"I'll make this simple," he said in a voice that sounded like nails scraping against wood. Octavia clutched Azariah's arm as the black horse pawed nervously at the ground. "Give us the Keyholder, and we'll let you live."

Azariah's voice cut through the nighttime air, strong and unrestrained. "And I'll make this even simpler—let us pass, or every one of you will die by my sword."

Amused laughter flitted through the group of strangers as they closed in on the horse.

Once again, there was a flash of blue that came from the hooded stranger's hand. "It's her alright." He let out a sharp whistle. "Take the girl. Kill the other."

The group leapt toward the horse from all sides, and Azariah urged the animal forward with a swift kick. Panic shot through Octavia's veins as the horse let out a frantic whinny, but then its cry turned into a shriek as several men cut the creature down by hacking at its front legs, causing both Octavia and Azariah to pitch forward onto the cobblestone street.

Octavia's hands slammed into stone as she skidded on her stomach, sending pain radiating up to her shoulders, and before she could even move, hands grabbed every inch of her. She screamed, kicking out at the strangers, but there were too many of them for her to stand a fighting chance.

Her arms were wrenched behind her back, and rope snaked around her wrists. Then her ankles were bound, but even still, she fought them, yelling and contorting her body. She felt a few hands slip away from her in her efforts, but they returned with force, digging their nails into her skin.

"Keep her quiet!" one of them hissed.

More hands attacked her, and someone forced a wad of cloth between her teeth and cinched a length of cord around her mouth to gag her.

She could hear metal clashing and people shouting. Someone huge and strong picked her up and slung her over his shoulder like a sack of yatchka. She wriggled and screamed, but she couldn't get free, and the gag muffled her cries.

"Quickly!" someone shouted. "Into the cart!"

The man holding Octavia threw her through thick canvas flaps into the back of a wagon. Unable to catch herself, she slammed her right shoulder into straw-strewn wood and slid, scraping her chin. Then a new person grabbed her. It was a woman, and she yanked Octavia into a sitting position by her braids. Octavia yelped, still screaming through the gag, but when the tip of a blade touched her neck, and the woman's lips snarled against her ear, she stopped.

"If you keep screaming, I'll start slicing."

There was a "yip" and the flick of a rider's crop, and then the wagon lurched forward. The woman held Octavia there—both of them sitting on the floor of the tented wagon—while the noises of the fight faded.

Octavia's chest was heaving, and stars flickered across her vision. She was having a hard time breathing, and the gag was tied so tight that it was digging into her cheekbones. Tears formed in her eyes as she tried to remain calm, but it was proving impossible. She let out a whimpering cry.

"Shut up!" the woman hissed, pressing the tip of the dagger harder. She turned her head, calling up to the driver. "Faster! Get us out of here!"

The wagon sped up, and the thundering of the horses' hooves pounded in Octavia's ears. She was going to die. They were going to kill her. Her panic increased tenfold, and before she could even think it through, she twisted in the woman's grasp, rolling out of her grip and sending her bound legs slamming into the woman's face. The woman reeled back, clutching her nose, which was now spouting blood, but after only a few seconds, she recovered, and Octavia had no countermove. The woman crawled over to her in a rage.

"You bitch!" She took her dagger and sliced into Octavia's calf.

The scream that left her mouth was strangled, and the pain in her leg was blinding. A sharp blow landed on her ribs, causing her vision to swim. Then the woman's hand weaved back through Octavia's hair, and she was once again pulled into a sitting position—her back against the woman's front. The blade returned to Octavia's neck . . .

Wham.

A violent shudder shook the entire wagon, and the woman nearly lost her grip on Octavia from the force of the cart stopping in its tracks. The woman's breath shuddered.

"Rodric! What's going on out there?" she yelled. There was squelching noise and a gurgling gasp. "Rodric!" She sounded completely panicked. She clutched Octavia even tighter, keeping the tip of the dagger to her throat. Octavia could barely move an inch, even breathing was causing the weapon to bead blood down her neck. "Rodric, what are you—"

Azariah Ronan, covered head to toe in blood, leapt into the back of the wagon, his sword drawn. He towered over the two of them.

"Stop!" the woman screeched. "If you move, I will kill her!" She practically pulled Octavia onto her lap in her fervency. Octavia sucked in a pained breath from the pressure of the ropes binding her limbs at awkward angles.

Azariah paused, but it was only for a moment, and then his blade moved so fast Octavia could barely see it. The tip of the sword slammed straight through the woman's neck, and she went limp, her dagger clattering to the wooden floorboards.

Octavia fell onto her side, unable to rescue herself from the momentum of being released so suddenly. She hit the wood hard, pain jabbing into her shoulder. Then Azariah knelt next to her, and he cut the bindings at her wrists. Once he freed her hands, he moved to her feet, cutting those bindings as well.

Octavia's trembling fingertips clawed at the gag, but she was so shaken up that she couldn't loosen it. Azariah moved quickly, and with gentle hands, he undid the knots on the cord. Octavia spat the wad of cloth onto the wood, gasping and coughing on all fours. She sucked in mouthfuls of air and began to cry. She couldn't help it. Tears spilled down her face as she fought to take control of her rattling breath.

When she looked up at Azariah, he was wild-looking and eerily calm all at once. Blood was splattered on his face and neck, and his long black hair hung in curtains around his face.

"Are you hurt?" he asked, peering over her carefully.

"I—just h-have a cut—on my calf. S-she—" Octavia's eyes landed on the dead woman, and sick rose up her throat. "I'm f-fine."

"Let me see," he said.

She shakily extended her left leg. Blood was seeping from the gash.

"It doesn't look deep. I'll have to properly clean and dress it later, but we need to leave."

Azariah tore a strip of cloth from the dead woman's tunic and wrapped Octavia's leg. She winced from how tight he tied it. Then he got to his feet.

"Can you stand?" he asked.

She nodded, but when she tried to get up, her legs gave out on her. She was experiencing a strange sort of body high. Her face felt like pinpricks were dancing all over it, and her limbs felt heavy and useless.

Azariah didn't wait a moment longer. He scooped her up into his arms and jumped from the wagon. She tensed. She didn't want him to carry her, but when she attempted to tell him this, her brain swam into a fog that rolled in like the tide. The last thing Octavia remembered before her head fell against his chest was the feeling of sticky blood pressing up against her skin.

11

A Knife Lesson and a Nightmare

When Octavia's eyes fluttered open, a soft breeze tickled her face as warm rays of sunshine filtered through the evergreens around her. She was lying on her back on a blanket, and her whole body was aching. She sat up quickly but regretted it as her head began to throb. She slammed her eyes shut, letting out a groan and massaging her forehead with gentle circles.

What happened? As the pounding in her head calmed, it all came screaming back to her. The hooded figure standing in the street. The flash of blue light. The strangers surrounding the black horse. Her struggle to escape her assailants as they dragged her away screaming. And Azariah Ronan's blood-covered face as he launched himself into the wagon to rescue her . . .

Her eyes flew open, and she gasped, clutching her chest. She jerked her head around to look for her attackers, but she was alone, so she forced herself to take a few intentional breaths to settle her raging pulse. She was miraculously alive, and it was all thanks to the bounty hunter who was tasked with kidnapping her in the name of King Bastian Jasper of Zoharth.

She scanned the trees, noting that a new horse stood nearby. It was a chestnut color. And on the ground next to the animal, there were a few different saddlebags and an assortment of weapons. Where was Azariah?

Slowly, Octavia got to her feet, peering through the pines. Rushing water sounded in the distance, and when she approached, she could see the Kraven River past a sloping section of earth and roots. Azariah stood shirtless, waist-deep in the water, dunking down under the flow to wash the blood from his muscled body. When he surfaced, his light brown skin glistened with drops that caught the sunlight, and Octavia felt a severe heat in her face. She quickly cast her eyes away from him, not wanting to see something she shouldn't.

Then her gaze fell over her own body. Her clothing was once again covered in blood, a layer of grime coated her skin, and her trio of brunette braids was a rat's nest. She also smelled awful. With a sigh, her fingers worked her braids free, and she did her best to comb through her hair with her fingertips. She wanted to jump into the river to clean herself too, but there was no way she was going to do that with Azariah down there. She would just have to wait.

It was curious that the bounty hunter had left her alone . . .

Did he really trust her that much? Octavia supposed that if she were a less *gods*-fearing woman, she might have fled despite making the vow, but perhaps Azariah had sensed the sincerity of her faith when she had promised not to run away. Whatever the reason, Azariah had extended a show of trust by walking down to the river to bathe himself instead of keeping an eye on her.

She turned away from the Kraven River and went to inspect the saddlebags, rifling through them to find something to eat. They must have lost some of their food in the altercation, because Octavia couldn't find the salted pork. Only the dried fruit, honey cakes, raw vegetables, and potatoes remained. There was also a loaf of stale bread. She tore into the fruit, tossing several dried apricots into her mouth at once. She took a chunk off of the loaf too. It was as hard as a rock, but she worked it with her teeth until it became malleable. She wanted to eat one of the honey cakes, but saving them for later would make for a more bearable journey to Urtha.

"Hungry?" a deep voice asked.

Octavia spun around, jumping up at Azariah's presence. He was still shirtless, and his hair was dripping, but at least he had pants on.

"I . . . yes. I was just—I was—" She stumbled over her words like someone caught in the act of stealing. But she wasn't stealing anything. This was her food too. She swallowed and pushed more confidence into her tone. "Yes, I'm hungry."

"That's a good sign." He peered at her. "How's your leg?"

"Sore, but I'll live."

If she was being honest, she would have said that her leg ached down to the bone. The knife wound Voramir had given her on her thigh felt like fire, and now the one on her calf added to her discomfort. A pang of nerves fluttered through her as her mind flashed back to the previous night. She looked around as if expecting someone to pop out of the trees.

"Are we safe here?"

"Not for long."

Octavia stuffed another dried apricot into her mouth to avoid staring at him. She couldn't help the stupid thought, but Azariah was . . . attractive. His toned muscles, his long dark hair, his fierce eyes and chiseled jawline . . . . She wished he would put on a shirt. She took a deep breath, flickering her gaze back to him. "Thank you . . . for saving me."

It felt strange to express gratitude to a man who was still very much her captor, but just thinking about what could've happened if those people had successfully stolen her away made her insides roil.

"It was my job," he replied in a tone void of emotion.

"Right."

She didn't know why, but the way he said that pricked at her. She silently scoffed at herself. He didn't care about her. He was a bounty hunter. He didn't even know her name. The only thing he cared about was delivering her alive.

"You should get yourself cleaned up," he said. "We have a lot of riding to do today."

She walked away without responding, heading down the slope toward the river. Her clothes felt crusty and her hair was a mess, so the idea of rinsing herself off spurred her feet faster. When she reached the river, she walked straight into the gentle flow fully clothed. The icy feel of the water on her aching body momentarily stole the breath from her lungs, but it also felt refreshing because the early heat of the day was already beginning to creep across the land.

It took her ten minutes of dunking and scrubbing to finally feel satisfied. The cuts all over her body stung, but it was worth the discomfort to finally feel clean. She trudged out of the river, sopping wet, then she pulled her hands through her hair, squishing out the excess water. Taking her hair to the side, she braided it into one long strand. She was shivering slightly, but the sun felt good on her skin, and when she had slicked most of the water from her clothing, she went back to their camp, damp but feeling oddly rejuvenated.

Azariah was packing up the horse, and she watched him for a minute. All over again, she felt overwhelmed by her circumstances. Even in the calm of the morning with the tranquil sounds of nature around her and a battle-hardened bounty hunter to protect her, she tensed. The daylight and the solitude of the forest did little to dampen her fear.

As she continued to air dry in a patch of sunlight, a thought occurred to her, and she wrinkled her brow in confusion. In the whirlwind of getting kidnapped twice—which had been immediately followed by the events in Omari—Octavia had forgotten something very strange. When Azariah had captured her, he had asked her a question that seemed wildly out of place. She stared at the bounty hunter—who still had not put on a shirt.

"When you captured me," Octavia began, "you asked me if I knew anything about this." She held up her gloved left hand. "But . . . it's like you expected me to already know about the darkness and the blood magic and the *waters*." She approached him, and he stopped working. "Why would you think that?"

Azariah gazed at her with a look that was conflicted. She could tell he was trying to decide if he should say anything. She could even detect a hint of despair in his face. "It doesn't matter. We need to leave."

She shook her head. "I'm not leaving unless you talk to me."

Immediately, Azariah grabbed her wrist and growled, "That's not up to you. We're leaving."

"Don't dismiss me!" she shot back, gripping his wrist in return. She tried to pry his fingers up, but his hold was ironclad. She glared at him, stuck. "Why did you think I knew what was going on? I had the key for less than half a day when you took me."

When he didn't say anything, she pulled against him.

"Let go of me."

Azariah exhaled a long breath, then his fierce features softened a bit. He released her, and she backed up a few paces.

He spoke quietly. Pensively. "I thought that the Keyholder would be enlightened by the *gods*. I thought that since you possessed the key, you would already know everything you needed to know to end the darkness. When the key melded to a new master, I assumed all the knowledge would come with it. You're supposed to be the one who will unlock the Well of Eternal Healing. You're supposed to be the one to save us." His expression hardened, and so did his tone. "But I see I was mistaken in my understanding. The *gods of old* clearly haven't enlightened you. You're nothing but a simple farm girl—and you don't know how to save *anyone*."

His last statement felt like a slap in the face. Her lips parted, and anger stirred in her belly. "Do you think I asked for this? Do you think I *want* to be the Keyholder? To be responsible for the darkness itself? To be hunted and used?" She could feel her cheeks turning crimson. She ripped the glove from her hand, exposing the key. It glinted in the sunlight like a knife. "If I could give this to another, I would! I don't want to save the world!" Tears threatened her eyes, but she pierced her nails into her palm to staunch them. "You're right. I'm not enlightened. I don't know how to save us. The only thing I know about being the Keyholder is what everyone else knows! Maybe the *gods* were supposed to enlighten me and they didn't. Maybe I'm not worthy of it . . . but I'm the Keyholder now, and I don't have a choice. I don't want to die, but I also don't want to see all the lands perish. I *will* walk through the darkness . . . and maybe when I do, the *gods of old* will help me."

There was a full ten seconds of silence, and Azariah's grim demeanor made the silence feel loud. "I hope for the sake of all that you are right. It's time for us to leave."

He turned toward the horse and grabbed his dark black shirt, pulling his arms through the sleeves and slipping his head through the opening. Then he put his belt and vest back on and checked the straps of the saddlebags, making sure they were secure.

"After you," he murmured.

She slipped the glove back on and went to the horse, sticking her foot into the stirrup and grabbing the horn of the saddle. Azariah moved to help her on, but she pushed his hand away, snapping at him. "I know how to mount a horse! I'm not totally useless!"

He didn't respond. He simply swung himself over the horse behind her once she had situated herself. Then they were off, riding along the Kraven River toward the Kingdom of Urtha. She hated how physically close she was to him. In Omari, she didn't mind it because he had made her feel safe, but now he had made her feel small. *You're nothing but a simple farm girl—and you don't know how to save anyone.* Those words made her want to slip off the horse and walk instead, but Azariah would likely not allow her to do that.

As they rode, Octavia noticed how alert Azariah stayed. He was constantly scanning ahead and occasionally turning over his shoulder to glance behind them.

For the next few hours, neither of them spoke. Azariah's harsh words replayed in her mind like a never-ending nightmare. In a way, she couldn't fault him for believing that the Keyholder would have all the answers. She herself would've believed the same thing if she had believed the key to be real in the first place. But she was just as clueless as the rest of the kingdoms, or at least as clueless as Azariah, given that she now knew what he did. She didn't know why the darkness was moving. But maybe King Bastian did. Whatever that prophecy said would help her, she was sure of it.

The weight of the key seemed to grow heavier the longer she possessed it. The knowledge that she would have to save them all or die before getting the chance was spiraling her mind into a pit of despair. It felt impossible. Ridiculous. Unfair . . .

Once more, she pulled the glove off to stare at the key. She traced her fingertips along its smooth surface. She angled her palm back and forth, watching the shimmering fragments reflect the sun. Maybe if she concentrated hard enough, something would come to her. Maybe the *gods* would speak to her and tell her what to do. But after focusing on the key and meditating on trying to make it do something, she gave up. She felt silly.

The truth was she had no idea what she was doing, just like Azariah said. And for the first time in her life, the *gods* felt as far away from her as the moon and the stars.

A deep ache settled into her heart. She had always felt so connected to her faith. The parcels of *waters* she had grown up using, the stories Papa would tell, the prayers she would send up . . . all of it was so sure and tangible to her. But now it felt . . . uncertain. And that thought scared her more than any dagger pressed against her throat.

When the sun started its descent toward the horizon, they finally stopped. They were still in an endless stretch of trees, but Octavia felt like they had moved far enough away from Omari to avoid another attack. Granted, she could still be tracked, but at least with the isolation of the forest, she felt more shielded than she ever would in a town setting.

The Kraven River flowed in the distance, filling the air with its churning melodies, and birds and bugs alike joined in.

"We'll rest here for a few hours, then we'll continue. We may be able to reach Urtha sooner if we keep this pace."

Octavia groaned. Her hips and legs were sore from being on the horse for so long, but she didn't say a word. Instead, she grabbed a rolled-up blanket while Azariah pulled open one of the saddlebags. He got out two onions and tossed one to her. Then he sat on the ground and bit into his like it was an apple. Her upper lip curled. A raw onion wasn't the most appetizing thing in the world, but she knew Azariah would protest them building a fire to boil water and actually cook something. It would make them visible in the dark.

"I'd rather eat one of the honey cakes if it's all the same to you."

Her comment was met with only silence.

"I could catch us a fish," she offered, but the moment she said it, she knew that wouldn't work either. A fish would require a fire to cook as well. Her stomach growled, and the loss of the salted pork made her want to cry.

She gazed at her onion and sighed, bringing it to her lips and taking a bite. It was sharply bitter and earthy, and Octavia nearly spat it out, but she forced herself to chew the piece and swallow it. She was just about to search the saddlebag for one of the honey cakes when Azariah spoke.

"Do you know how to use a blade?"

Once again, the word "useless" pricked at the back of Octavia's mind. "No. Not in the way you can. All I'm good at is cutting vegetables. But apparently not good at cutting fishing line . . ." She mumbled the last part to herself.

"I would like to show you how to handle one so that you—"

"Aren't totally useless?"

"So that you can defend yourself," he finished calmly. He pulled out a dagger with a tag wrapped around the hilt. It was the same dagger the boy at the tavern had brought them. "I'd like to give this to you."

Octavia stared at the thing, a little taken aback. He was going to give her a weapon? But she was his prisoner. Why risk that? Why extend another show of trust? Especially with something as dangerous as a dagger. She could use it against him if she were clever enough *and* quick enough. It didn't make sense. This was so unexpected that, for a moment, she thought he might be playing a joke on her to be cruel.

But he simply sat there expectantly, like he was waiting for her to come over to him.

An uncomfortable sensation zipped through her. Octavia didn't know what this bounty hunter was playing at, but she figured she might as well learn something useful from him since he was offering it. People were after her. Dangerous people. And she was woefully unprepared to deal with them. The idea of stabbing someone didn't sit well with her, but just as with the witch's protection spell, she would have to get over her discomfort in order to survive.

"I suppose," she muttered.

She walked over to Azariah and sat down next to him, taking the dagger from his hand to examine the metal work on the hilt. The design swirled like the darkness, and a small lion's head was carved into the top.

"Don't cut yourself with it," he said in a serious tone.

She gave him a dark look. She hadn't even unsheathed the thing. "I'm not going to cut myself!"

She went to pull the blade free from the sheath, but Azariah put a hand on hers, stopping her attempt. He shook his head.

"We're not going to practice with this dagger. It's for you to keep on your person. Somewhere accessible."

"Why aren't we going to practice with the blade I might actually use?"

"It's been dipped in poison," he replied candidly.

"Oh . . ."

Wouldn't it be a fiendish joke from the *gods* for Octavia Fletcher, the Keyholder and savior of all the lands, to die by accidentally cutting herself with a poisoned knife?

"Okay, show me," she said, setting the sheathed poisonous dagger down and standing to her feet.

For the next half hour, Azariah taught her a few basic stances as well as how to hold a blade so that she wouldn't injure her wrist or jam her fingers. He also showed her the proper way to thrust and where on the human body to hit to get a kill. She paid close attention to him as he spoke. He was so calm and direct. The way he held her arm aloft, the way he nudged her wrist back to proper form, the way he corrected her footwork . . . all of it was so focused and intentional. Once more, Octavia had to push away the thought that he cared. He was only showing her this to increase her odds of making it to Zoharth alive.

"Again," he said.

Octavia thrust the blade into a pine trunk and pulled the weapon back quickly, causing a splinter of bark to chip away.

Azariah nodded. "Better. Your aim is improving." He took her wrist and corrected the positioning of it. Then he placed a finger against her thumb, tracing a path all the way up her forearm. His touch sent skitters across her skin, and her stomach flipped. "In line with your arm," he reiterated. "You keep bending your wrist down. Think of the blade as an extension of yourself rather than something disjointed."

Octavia stared at Azariah as he drew his hand back. She didn't know what to make of him. Teaching her this was a gamble on his part. Did he truly carry such confidence that she wouldn't try to hurt him? Was this because of her vow? Perhaps she had given away too much of herself with that kind of promise. The vow certainly carried weight for *her*, but maybe it did for him too, because she couldn't conceive of another reason for this kind of trust.

Maybe he had faith like hers. But then, why would he be a bounty hunter? It was a profession soaked in blood and secrets, paid for by the pockets of the powerful. It wasn't the profession of a *gods*-fearing man.

Whatever the reason, it was clear that Azariah wasn't worried about her stabbing him in his sleep.

After the lesson finished, she felt a little more capable, and as the sun fully hid itself behind the horizon, she sat back against a tree with a blanket wrapped around her shoulders. She should get some rest. Azariah said they would need to keep riding soon.

Octavia's eyelids felt heavy, and even though the nighttime air was chilly against her skin, she was able to drift off...

The next thing Octavia became aware of was the scent of decaying earth.

She was lying flat on her stomach with her face pressed into the dirt. Abruptly, a trembling overtook the ground, and wind gushed over the landscape. Octavia pushed herself to her hands and knees with a burst of speed, feeling the rumblings beneath her fingertips.

What was happening?

She looked up, and the sight before her sliced a deep, primal fear right through her flesh. A torrent of wind whipped her braids back as she got to her feet.

The darkness was towering over her. Its deep obsidian blackness swirled like it was made of a thousand snakes of smoke, and it thundered like a giant monster, creeping slowly toward the place where she stood. Octavia couldn't move. She couldn't speak. She could barely breathe. The monstrous height and massive width of the inky substance was astounding. Horror-inducing. She couldn't even begin to describe the feeling of certain death that wrapped itself around her body.

Abruptly, the key burned in her left palm, and she cried out, holding her hand up to get a look at the thing. The silver metal shone like it always did, but pain riddled her skin. It felt like the key was trying to rip itself from her flesh.

The wind howling all around Octavia grew in strength as the darkness came closer, and then a roar came from its depths, shaking the earth so that she couldn't keep her footing. She fell to her knees as a tendril of black shot from the wall of darkness like a bolt of lightning.

Octavia screamed as the prong of blackness snaked out across the dirt, heading directly for her. The key seared with an agonizing pain, and before she could leap up to try and run away, the strand of darkness swallowed her whole.

Octavia screamed awake. Azariah was in front of her in seconds, firmly grasping her shoulders. His strong grip was overpowering, and for a second, she fought to push him away, still caught in the clutches of the nightmare.

"What happened!?" he demanded, his voice harsh and his eyes alert.

She steadied herself by clinging to his forearms, panting in an unrestrained manner. Her heart was beating out of control, and sweat clung to her skin. "The darkness!" she gulped. "It was here. It was—" She looked past Azariah through the trees. The tranquil peace of night lit by a crescent moon and a burbling river was all that laid ahead.

Azariah released her shoulders, irritated. "It was a dream."

With her chest still heaving, she got to her feet, shaking out her jittering hands. The crisp air tickled her face, causing strands of her dark brunette hair to dance across her forehead. She peered around again, so sure of what she had just witnessed. But there was nothing but nature.

"It's time to go," Azariah grumbled under his breath. He moved to the horse, quickly making sure all of their things were secured and fastened down in the saddlebags. "Come."

She moved to him shakily, getting on the horse, and as Azariah took his place behind her, she glanced back at the spot where she had fallen asleep. A dark and horrible feeling wound its way through her veins, and she knew deep down . . . that wasn't a dream at all. It was a warning.

12

The Turquoise Drops

The next three days slugged by. It was exhausting and frightening. Octavia was constantly on edge, and it wasn't from the knowledge that more people might come upon them to steal her away. It was because of that dream. It had scared the living soul from her, and she couldn't shake it off. The darkness had felt so real that Octavia had convinced herself that it would spring upon her at any moment, forcing her to walk into its depths.

She had thought about bringing this up to Azariah multiple times, but every time she was about to, she couldn't get the words to come off her tongue. Maybe a part of her was scared that if she said the words out loud, it would make it true. The darkness wasn't just moving, it was growing like a weed, shooting extensions of itself out to slither across the earth. What did that mean? How much time did they truly have left before it started swallowing the kingdoms nearest it? The only solace she carried was that Rustwick was the farthest kingdom from Hritza, and that meant it had the most time left.

When Octavia thought of home, it made her crumble. She couldn't help how her mind went to Bowan over and over again. He was all alone to take care of Mama, and a part of her wondered how long he would be capable of doing that. He was only eleven. Octavia desperately hoped that Bowan had gone to get help. The townspeople knew their family well. Surely *someone* would be there for them?

And then another thought trickled through her mind. Was anyone from Rustwick looking for her? Would anyone come after her? Octavia's heart fell even as she considered the possibility. Only those who knew the *waters* could track her would be able to find her. No one was coming to save her, and accepting that was the best and only way to move forward. So, Octavia turned her mind toward Urtha.

She couldn't wait to get there for the sole purpose of eating a real meal again. The honey cakes and dried fruit were long gone—and they only had a few potatoes left. She had managed to catch one fish from the river a day ago, but the meager meal roasted on a stick over a small fire didn't do much to ease the constant ache of hunger in her belly.

Urtha was wild and dangerous because of its euphoric *waters*, but it was also where she hoped their journey would take a smoother turn. One last parcel left—that's what Azariah had said—and then she could drink the witch's protection spell. After that, she prayed that they could make it to Zoharth without anyone else trying to kidnap her.

Luckily, they hadn't run into anyone since their skirmish in Omari, but there were still people after her. In all honesty, she didn't think she would truly feel safe again until the darkness was vanquished.

At long last, on a late afternoon on the fourth day since leaving Omari, a grand city flitted into view in the distance. Octavia was so excited that she gave the tired horse a few swift kicks to prod it forward.

Azariah pulled on the reins, slowing the animal once more.

"I'm starving. Let's go," she said, unable to help the annoyance in her voice.

“Have you been to Urtha before?” Azariah asked, keeping the horse at a walk.

“No, I haven’t been anywhere before. I’ve never left Rustwick.”

“Do you know what the *waters* of Urtha do?”

Once again, Azariah was addressing her like she was an ignorant child, and it frustrated her to no end.

“Yes! The Well of Euphoria,” she replied with an edge. “It makes you feel wonderful. It gives you a sort of high, like you could do anything. It also lowers the inhibitions—but enough Rustwick beer will do the same.”

“It makes you never want to leave,” Azariah stated.

Octavia glanced over her shoulder. “What are you talking about?”

“If you drink enough *waters*, you won’t want to leave. Haven’t you ever wondered why Urtha is the most densely populated kingdom? Or why there are so many stories of people traveling to Urtha only to never return to the kingdom they came from?” He paused and waited. Then he shook his head. “Given your silence, I suppose not . . .”

Octavia had to bite her tongue to keep it. It wasn’t her fault she was so inexperienced with other Wells of Power or their associated kingdoms. She grew up helping Papa manage the workers who tended to the wheat fields and caring for Bowan and Mama. Her whole world had always been her family and her charming town that produced bountiful food for all the lands. She had never traveled before because there was never a need to—and she hadn’t had the desire.

“We need to be careful. Almost everything in Urtha has a parcel of *waters* mixed into it. The drink, the food, the clothing.”

“The clothing?”

“It’s washed in it,” Azariah explained. “Everything in Urtha is designed to ensnare.”

Octavia’s stomach cried out in hunger. “Are you saying we can’t eat anything in Urtha or we might be . . . trapped there?"

"No, I'm saying we need to be careful. Ingesting some of the *waters* is fine, and honestly, nearly unavoidable, but we can't linger. One, for your sake, but two, because of the *waters*. It's when you give yourself away to it that you become trapped."

"Well, then we just won't give ourselves away."

Azariah gave a jaded laugh. "Words said by many and followed through by few."

As they approached the edge of Urtha, immense architecture rose up from the ground. The rounded structures were made entirely of white marble reeking of grandeur, and high stone arches flew to the heavens at every doorstep. It was so breath-taking that Octavia couldn't tear her eyes away—and the towering city only got taller toward the center of it all. It was as if the *gods* themselves had pulled the marble from the earth to fashion together a masterpiece.

Upon riding in, Octavia noted that the road was smooth and paved—a drastic change from the bumpy cobblestone streets of Rustwick and Omari. She inhaled deeply, and a burst of happiness pushed its way through her body, strengthening her resolve and straightening her posture. The air itself felt enchanted—invigorating—like the *waters* hung in the breeze that caressed her face.

Laughter, music, and boisterous singing filled the streets. It was beautiful. She had never heard music like this before, and she was convinced that nowhere else would she ever hear music like it again. People were jubilant. Everywhere she looked, there was an excitement and vibrancy to their voices, to their movements, to their energy. And everyone was wearing white garbs embroidered with different patterns of gold thread.

Tantalizing smells hit Octavia's nose as Azariah prodded the horse farther into the city. Spiced ciders. Herb-crusted veal. Smoked fitcha—

a tricky fish to catch from the Kraven River, but a much sought-after delicacy. Vegetable broths. Creamed coffee. Buttered pastries with fruit jams smeared over the top. And coska—a rare bird cooked for its mouth-watering and tender breast meat.

Octavia ached to scarf down a hot meal—anything but tasteless potatoes—but every time they passed a tavern, they didn't stop.

"Where are we going?" she asked, staring longingly at a roast coska a barmaid was carrying on a platter to a pair of patrons who were sitting just within the open doors of a tavern called The Turquoise Drops.

"To the Wellminders," Azariah said. "It's nearly impossible to find a parcel of *waters* in Urtha that hasn't already been mixed with something. We're going to get one drawn straight from the Well. The witch's protection spell requires—"

"Can't we eat first?" Her stomach felt like it was going to consume her whole, and the thought of having to wait any longer for food made her want to leap off the horse. When Azariah didn't respond, she pressed the issue. "Come on, you have to be starving too. Plus, the witch's protection spell can wait one more hour. If anyone in Urtha is planning on kidnapping me, they're probably already here."

She said the last statement as if she didn't care about the kidnapping part. In truth, she cared deeply, but her hunger was clouding all other thoughts from her mind, and her hands were beginning to shake for sustenance.

"Fine," he said begrudgingly.

Azariah led the horse a bit farther down the road before stopping between the junction of two taverns. There was a small gap between the curved marble structures, one of which had a pillar supporting the corner of the patio area. After they both slipped off the horse, Azariah tied the reins to the pillar.

"There's not a place for horses?" Octavia questioned. In her experience, it was odd for a tavern to not have a place to tie up a horse.

"Not here," he replied. "This is where people come to eat and drink. Animals interfere with the atmosphere." He cleared his throat. "Let's not delay."

The sounds of music and laughter grew louder as Azariah ushered Octavia back toward The Turquoise Drops, where she had seen the roast coska. When they entered the lavish and lively space, Azariah kept close to her, always vigilant, and he directed her to an open table in the back corner of the room just as he did in Omari. The white marble interior of the tavern was stunning. Everything in here was glossy and polished, from the tables to the chairs to the long bar where barmaids scurried about pouring drinks and readying food. It was packed to the brim, and the delicious scents that hung in the air drove Octavia crazy.

A barmaid with golden curly locks of hair stopped at their table, her cheeks flushed. Her face lit with a welcoming smile, and her voice sounded smooth and sweet. "What can I get you, loves?" She was carrying a tray that had two glasses filled with foaming turquoise liquid in them, and she looked out of breath from the hustle of serving so many people.

"The coska—two of them," Azariah said. "And two pastries with a pitcher of mead."

"And the smoked fitcha," Octavia added.

Azariah's gaze flickered to her. He was about to open his mouth when the barmaid said, "Of course, loves. I'll bring that right along." She scurried off, dropping the two foaming turquoise beverages at the table next to them, where two men sat—clearly drunk—conversing loudly with one another.

Azariah's face soured as if he were about to tell her off for ordering the fitcha, but she spoke before he could.

"What?" Octavia did not hide the edge to her tone. "You've kidnapped me. The least you can do is treat me to dinner after four days of bland potatoes. I know you have enough coin."

"Fitcha is expensive," he murmured.

"So am I," she shot back. "I'm sure you're being paid more than enough for me. You can afford the fish." She paused, scrutinizing him, and the question that had been gnawing at her ever since the unexpected knife lesson finally slipped out. "Why are you doing this? Why are you a bounty hunter? You seem . . ." But she didn't know how to finish her statement.

Azariah raised an eyebrow and leaned back in his chair. He was . . . somber. Or maybe he was annoyed? "I do this for the money."

Octavia didn't know how to respond. She also didn't know what to say to get him to open up. Over the last four days, she had barely been able to get Azariah to talk about anything. He had spoken to her only with short replies and stilted words. He had been kind, but in a professional sort of manner. Nothing more.

Octavia let out a slow breath, unable to help the feeling of utter loneliness that settled in her chest. But she shoved the feeling away. At least she wasn't being hauled to Zoharth bound in ropes . . .

Music and frivolity filled the tavern to the brim, and it also filled the silence between them as they waited for their food. The barmaid with the golden curls didn't take long. She brought the two coska, which were browned to perfection, and then did a second pass to bring the pastries, mead, and smoked fitcha.

It all looked incredible, but before she could lift a bite of the fitcha to her mouth, Azariah's voice stopped her. "Remember what I told you about giving yourself away."

"Right," she murmured.

Then Azariah tore into his own meal, practically swallowing an entire coska leg in a few bites. Octavia placed a flake of the fitcha on her tongue, and the most incredible sensation flew through her body. Not only was the fish the most delectable thing she had ever tasted, but it was also euphoria-inducing. Her brain seemed to overload with pleasure at the complexity of flavors that danced across her palate. This was the most delicious food in all the lands.

She shoveled more of it into her mouth at a breakneck speed, finally able to soothe the ache in her stomach. This was incredible! Nothing could compare to it, and she immediately found herself imagining what growing crops with the *waters* of euphoria could do. Maybe when this was all over, she could take a parcel back to Rustwick. She would come back here. She could stay here. Maybe she could even bring her family so that—

"Ground yourself to something real," Azariah said gently. "Repeat to yourself where you are, who you are, and where you're going."

Octavia blinked several times, staring at Azariah. She had completely forgotten he was there. The meal had so totally consumed her senses that she had finished her fitcha and her pastry, and when she looked down, there was a mug of mead in her hand—and she didn't even remember pouring it.

Octavia gasped, pushing the mug away. "Woah . . ."

"Look around," Azariah told her. "Look at them. Look at their faces."

Octavia peered out across the tavern, her attention moving from one person to the next. Melodies played, and chortling floated through the air. Everyone was so joyful. So eager. So . . . empty. Her lips parted as she finally noticed . . . It was something in their eyes. When she focused, she could just make out the smallest hue of blue, as if the *waters* had nestled into their brains and shone through their irises—every person she looked at.

An uneasy feeling wormed through her, and suddenly, the fitcha didn't sit well in her stomach.

"If they would only stop for a moment to remind themselves where they had come from, they might get up and leave," Azariah said softly. "But they won't. They'll simply continue to consume the *waters* as the *waters* consume them . . ."

He was taking pity on them—she could see it in his face. It was the way his gaze landed on each stranger with such intention. An inexplicable tenderness peeked through his hardened exterior, and Octavia found herself wondering what Azariah's story was. He was fierce and intimidating, to be sure. He had killed over a dozen people in Omari—and many more by his own admission—but there was also a subtle tenderness to him that felt so out of place for his profession. She was curious about him. She couldn't help it. She wanted to know more, particularly because it seemed like he carried a deep faith in the *gods*—something atypical for someone who killed and kidnapped for a living.

A cacophonous, deep laugh from the table next to them made Octavia jump. The two drunk men from before both stood to leave the tavern, foaming turquoise liquid in hand. But the man nearest Octavia stumbled, and he fell straight into her, spilling his drink all down her front.

She gasped, pushing him off of her and standing up. "Watch where you're going!"

The man straightened up, clutching the edge of the table to steady himself. He had brilliant olive skin, rich curly black hair, and vibrant blue eyes. It was shocking—the way the blue stood out against his sun-kissed complexion. The euphoric *waters* had clearly taken their toll on this man. His face slid into an eerie smile that made Octavia's skin crawl, and his perfect white teeth dazzled.

"And what's your name, beautiful?" His words sounded surprisingly un-slurred for how drunk he appeared. "You don't look like you're from around here." His gaze fell across the dark colors of her outfit, which stood out starkly against the white clothing everyone else was wearing.

"My name is none of your business," she shot back, looking down to examine herself. The sticky, sweet foam from the turquoise drink had soaked her tunic, and it reeked of alcohol. "Great," she muttered.

"I'm sorry," he said in a honeyed tone. "I didn't mean to spill on you. Can I make it up to you? I'll buy you a drink." He took a step toward Octavia, getting offensively close, and his reeking breath got in her face. "I know how to show a beautiful woman like you a *euphoric* time."

Azariah stood from the table, but before he could do anything, Octavia forcefully shoved the man away, and he stumbled.

"Back off!" she snarled.

This only seemed to amuse him, and his mouth curled with pleasure. "Mmm," he breathed. "Beautiful and spirited."

"Be on your way, sir," Azariah said, taking a step forward to place himself between Octavia and the man.

The man's piercing blue eyes snapped to Azariah. "Is she yours?"

"*Yes*."

Azariah's tone was dangerous—possessive—and it seemed to quell some of the man's amusement. But it didn't stop him from raking his eyes over Octavia's body. Her stomach did a somersault of anxiety.

"Leave," Azariah warned.

For a moment, it looked like the man might start a fight. But the bounty hunter's intimidating stature and well-built frame seemed to deter his itch to quarrel. The leering smile never left the man's lips as he held up his hands in surrender. "I don't want any trouble. Apologies for the spilled drink. I'll leave you to your girl."

Once more, his invasive gaze went to Octavia, but then he turned around and walked briskly out of the tavern with his friend.

Octavia flicked bits of foam from her fingertips onto the floor, peering over her clothing again. "This stuff is disgusting."

"Oh my!" the golden-haired barmaid chirped. She was back, taking in Octavia's appearance. "Poor dear. You're a mess!" Patrons called to the woman, and she craned her neck. "One moment!" She turned to face Octavia. "There's a lady's washroom. Just back there. You can get yourself cleaned up." She pointed to a door across the crowded tavern next to the end of the bar.

Octavia gaped at the woman. "There's a washroom *indoors*?"

She donned a charming smile and giggled. "You're in Urtha, love. Of course there's a washroom indoors."

With that, she scurried off, weaving her way around tables to attend to more people.

The sticky foam from the turquoise drink had splashed as high as Octavia's neck, and it felt gross against her skin. She started to walk toward the washroom, but Azariah caught her wrist. She met his gaze.

"You're not going to let me clean myself off?" she asked pointedly.

"You shouldn't be alone."

"I'll only be a minute. I'll be fine."

He didn't let go.

"Let me wash the foam off," she insisted. "I'm not going to run away."

"That's not what I'm worried about."

"I'll come right back."

Azariah pursed his lips, his eyes roving over the tavern to search the faces of everyone present. The atmosphere was electrifying, and people were absorbed in their own conversations. Azariah finally released her, but he didn't look happy about it. "Return quickly."

Octavia strode across the tavern, approaching the washroom. As she entered through the door, another woman shuffled past her, and once inside, Octavia found herself alone. The room was breath-taking. Three private stalls lined the back, and the entire right wall looked like a waterfall. Water streamed down carved rocky outcroppings in the stone, spilling into a trough structure that drained the excess out through a hole in the floor. Octavia had never seen anything like it. Nowhere in Rustwick were there washrooms *indoors*—let alone ones as exquisite at this. She was used to an outhouse, not a throne room.

Octavia approached the waterfall, cupping her hands under the flow and splashing her face and neck. She repeated this a few more times, soaking her front a bit in the process, but the sticky foam was coming off easily, and the pungent alcoholic smell was now less severe.

The door behind her opened and then clicked shut.

She went back for one more splash of water over her face, closing her eyes to soak in the crisp feel. It was intoxicating—just like the food—and she could feel it tugging at her mind, trying to spiral her thoughts into an addictive pattern. But she remembered what Azariah had said, and she held fast to her identity, thinking to herself: *my name is Octavia Fletcher, I am the Keyholder, and I am going to Zoharth.*

"Hello, beautiful."

Octavia's eyes flew open, and she spun around. The man who had spilled his drink all over her stood in the washroom, his eyes lit with desire. His olive skin glistened with sweat against his hairline, and the stench of alcohol dripped from him as if it were coming from his pores.

"You know, you were rather rude to me earlier," he leered with a dangerous smile. "I was only offering to treat you to a drink." He stalked forward a few steps. "And maybe show you what it's like to be with a real *Urthan* man."

A sinking feeling claimed both her heart and stomach. While

Octavia knew the *waters* of Urtha caused euphoria and happiness, she had no doubt they also opened up the mind to the possibility of darker pleasures—and this man seemed like he was going to give into them . . .

Octavia's eyes darted to the exit. She didn't hesitate.

With a burst of speed, she pushed past the man to grab the handle of the door, but he caught her upper arm and swung her around, pinning her up against the wall opposite the waterfall. Before she could even scream, his hand curled around the back of her neck, and his lips crashed into hers.

Panic exploded through her chest, and she wrenched herself out of his grip, pushing his face away. Then she slammed the heel of her palm upward, catching his nose with force. The man immediately cried out, his hands flying to the injury, and Octavia made another break for the door, but before she could reach it, he grabbed her around the middle and yanked her backward with vicious strength.

"You're going to get it now, bitch!" he growled. He slammed his hand over her mouth as she screamed, pressing his body up against hers. Then his free hand went between her legs.

Once more, the sheer terror of her situation gave her the strength to push him off, but this time, she couldn't make an attempt for the door. He shoved her down to the floor and was on top of her in seconds, his hands pulling at her clothing while she frantically slapped and pushed and writhed under him. She screamed again, and a horrible thought clawed through her mind: it was more than likely that no one could hear them. The tavern beyond the washroom doors was already so loud . . .

The man was trying to undo his belt while still gripping her, and she twisted to reach her right ankle. The sheathed poisonous dagger Azariah had gifted her was lodged in her sock, but it was just out of reach. She couldn't contort her body enough to grab it, and the weight of the man on top of her was crushing.

Octavia was beginning to see stars from how hard she fought him, and still, she kept screaming and screaming. A blow landed on her right cheek, and it stunned her, momentarily paralyzing her limbs. Her arms fell from the man, limp at her sides, and her vision swam. She could feel his hands below her waist, and a horrible feeling swept her body. This was going to happen. He was going to violate her, and there was nothing she could do about it . . .

A violent bang issued from the doorway, echoing off the walls of the washroom, and immediately, the pressure on her body vanished as the man was wrenched to his feet.

Azariah slammed him against the wall, bracing him there with his forearm, and the growl that left his mouth was the most terrifying sound Octavia had ever heard. It was like he was a completely different person—different even from the person who had cut down the strangers who had tried to kidnap her in Omari. He was *far* beyond wild and dangerously past reason.

"You *dare* touch her?" With a flash of silver, Azariah drew back his arm and plunged his dagger upward into the man's chest cavity just below his sternum. He held the blade there and then twisted it as the man's eyes bulged. "I told you. She is *mine*."

With a gurgling noise, the man's mouth parted, and he sputtered, but no coherent words came. Azariah released him, and he crashed to the floor, dead before his head hit the stone.

Abruptly, Azariah seemed to come out of his rage like coming out of a fog. He quickly knelt next to Octavia, examining her. Her hands were trembling and her head was throbbing, but she was too stunned to cry, though she felt the well of it bursting at her core.

Azariah's gaze moved to her left palm where the glove was still covering the key, and she could see it in his eyes . . . he knew this wasn't about the key at all.

He seemed to hesitate extending his hand out to her, almost like he was afraid to touch her—and that was when Octavia noticed that he was trembling too. It was slight and subtle, but very much present, and when she looked into his eyes, she could see that they were watering. Octavia couldn't begin to name the emotions that stormed behind his dark gaze. She didn't know a thing about this bounty hunter, but what she *did* know was that he was *not okay*.

His touch was exceedingly gentle as he helped her to her feet, and when she wobbled and grabbed onto his arm to keep from falling, he held her steady.

"Are you alright?"

She wanted to say "No." She wanted to scream it. She was nowhere near alright, but she *was* relatively unscathed—and still fully clothed. She could feel the lingering touch of the man's hands between her legs, and she shuddered. Peering up at Azariah, she said in a shaky voice, "Please, l-let's just get out of h-here."

He nodded then quickly escorted her from the washroom. As they left the tavern, Octavia was shivering so badly that she felt like she was going to pass out. The altercation sliced through her mind in flashes, like she was reliving it. The man's alcoholic breath, his horrible hands, the way he had thrown her to the floor, how he had struck her, grabbed her . . .

Octavia's face throbbed from the blow, and she wanted to scream, but her voice was gone. The only thing she could do was cling to Azariah like a promise. And so she did, because she feared she would collapse otherwise.

Azariah had saved her—thank the *gods*—but it wasn't the act itself that made Octavia's mind reel. It was his intense, overwhelming, rage-filled protectiveness. She didn't understand it. Yes, she was his bounty, but this went *far* deeper than that. It was like he wasn't fully present when he had killed the man. Something about seeing her on the floor like that had pushed him *way* over the edge.

He kept his arm around Octavia all the way back to the horse, and once more, she wondered what Azariah's story was—because now she was fully convinced—he was definitely not a bounty hunter for the money alone.

13

Omens and Visions

They rode through the smooth and luxurious streets at a brisk pace, moving farther into the white marble city. Azariah kept taking turns at seemingly random places, likely keen to get as far away from The Turquoise Drops as possible before the dead body was discovered.

Night was creeping upon Urtha, and this only fueled its exuberant atmosphere.

The enticing smells and sounds that had captured Octavia's attention and charmed her senses now seemed like poison. The music no longer uplifted her ears, the laughter no longer made her feel joyful, and the wild and carefree parties of every tavern they passed made her feel sick. This place wasn't beautiful at all. It was a trap, full of drunkenness, self-indulgence, and debauchery—its promises pretty, its snares deadly.

"The Wellminders live at the center of the city," Azariah said. "We'll collect a parcel there, and then we'll leave. Hopefully the witch's protection spell will grant us safe passage as we continue to Zoharth."

She nodded, holding fast to his words like a prayer.

The ride through Urtha took them past more sweeping architecture and marble artistry, but the closer they got to the center of the city, the more Octavia started to notice the people around them. They weren't the same as the vapid and vibrant partygoers on the outskirts of Urtha. They were dirty, discarded, and starved. They sat in rags on street corners. They stood in alleyways, isolated and alone, filth coating their white garbs.

The city had sucked them dry, drained them of money and hope, and left them desolate. And the scariest part about it was . . . if Octavia had not been intentionally looking, she wouldn't have seen them at all. She could feel the deceptive pull of the euphoria in the air tickling at her mind to ignore them, but she didn't. She looked fully into their faces as they rode by. She could see the *waters* behind their eyes and the desperation in their expressions. One ragged man even approached their horse, begging them for coin, his eyes bulging and his mouth sagging.

"Just a piece!" he pleaded. "Just so I can get a parcel! I only need one parcel! Please!"

Azariah moved the horse ahead swiftly, breaking away from the stranger.

Octavia's heart broke for the man, but she knew there was nothing she could do for him. He was spent and trapped . . .

Upon reaching the inner circle of Urtha, the white marble architecture continued, but it towered taller than it did on the outskirts of the city, and the dome at the very center was completely gated off. The grandeur once more stole Octavia's breath away as she gazed upward at the massive heights. The Well of Euphoria sat guarded somewhere beyond the gate, and an excitement stirred in Octavia's chest.

She had seen the Well of Power in Rustwick many times before. Papa had taken her to collect the *waters* on various occasions, and it had always been an invigorating and spiritual experience. She loved gazing at the beauty of the Well with her own eyes. Peering into the *waters* and soaking in the blue hue of the magic had always made her feel close to the *gods*.

All the Wells of Power looked the same, but Octavia was certain they wouldn't *feel* the same. What would gazing upon the *waters* of euphoria feel like? Her imagination craved the idea of a new spiritual experience, but the gates encircling the dome gave her pause. Rustwick's Well wasn't closed off from the community like Urtha's Well was. How was Azariah going to get them in?

They approached the wrought-iron gate, and the man guarding the innermost section of Urtha gazed down from his watchpost. "State your business."

"We are here to see the Wellminders," Azariah said. "We need a parcel of *waters* drawn straight from the Well."

"Do you have an appointment?"

"No."

The guard pursed his lips, scrutinizing the two of them. "We don't normally parcel out *waters* without knowing ahead of time who needs them."

"I have more than enough coin to pay," Azariah stated. He dug into one of his pockets and tossed a gold coin to the guard.

The guard caught it and examined it, biting the edge between his teeth. Then he faltered, and his attention fell on Octavia. He didn't say anything for an uncomfortable amount of time, but then he looked back at Azariah and gave him a stiff nod. "Very well. You may enter."

He opened the gate, and the metal hinges squealed, causing the hairs on the back of Octavia's neck to stiffen. The chestnut horse walked in, the squealing shrieked once more, and the gates closed behind them. Octavia nervously glanced back, sending up a prayer to the *gods* that they hadn't just trapped themselves.

This witch's protection spell better be worth it . . .

Beyond the gates, there was a large courtyard filled with trimmed hedges, beautiful fountains, and stone walkways. It was peaceful and gorgeous, lit by lamp posts that stood at intervals around the space. The evening air and dancing starlight above made the courtyard feel enchanted.

Azariah dismounted and Octavia quickly followed suit, keeping next to him as he handed the horse's reins to an attendant who greeted them with a sweeping bow. Her white robes swished about her ankles.

"Urtha welcomes new travelers," the girl said in a melodious voice. "Are the Wellminders expecting you?"

"No," Azariah said. "We're just passing through and hoped to collect a parcel of its famous *waters* to bring back home."

"And where is home?"

"Xadia," Azariah said.

The Well of Costly Metals . . .

Octavia glanced at him. If this was true, then it was the first tangible piece of information she had learned about him—besides his name and the fact that he was a hired bounty hunter, of course.

"Ah," the girl mused with a daring smile. "You must be a wealthy traveler, no?"

Azariah pulled another gold coin from his pocket and handed it to the girl. Her eyes widened, and she quickly snatched the coin and pocketed it.

"See to it that our horse is fed and watered," Azariah said. "We will return shortly."

"Of course, sir!" she said, once again bowing low.

"Can you direct us to the Well?"

The girl pointed across the courtyard to a grand temple structure. "Just through there."

Azariah gave her a stiff nod, and then he took off, marching across the neatly trimmed grass toward the temple. Octavia stayed close to him. The attendants that hurried about kept staring at her the way the guard had done before allowing them entrance. Nerves skewered her insides. She kept telling herself that they were only staring at her because of her dark clothing, but she couldn't shake the feeling that they *knew*. The glove sat snugly against her left palm, hiding the key that could get her killed.

"I don't like this," she murmured to Azariah, covertly glancing about. "Everyone is looking at me. We should leave."

"We'll leave after we get the parcel," he stated, striding down one of the walkways of the courtyard.

Her stomach jolted, but she didn't argue. Instead, she asked him something else. "Is what you said to that girl true? Are you from Xadia?"

Azariah's eyes met hers for the briefest moment. "Yes."

Octavia decided to press her luck to see if he would answer anything else. "Do you have family there?"

His nostrils flared nearly imperceptibly, and his mouth twitched. He did not answer her. He simply continued ahead toward the temple.

She sighed, disappointed, although she wasn't surprised he didn't respond to the question.

Once they stepped from the courtyard path to the grand marble entrance, two attendants dressed in white robes approached them, barring their access to the inside. It was a man and a woman, and they looked at each other like they were trying to figure out if they had forgotten if someone was supposed to be there.

"Do you have an appointment?" the woman asked.

"No," Azariah said. "But we wish to speak with one of the Wellminders and collect a parcel."

Azariah pulled out more gold coins, handing one to the woman and one to the man. His money was doing a lot of talking, because they both bowed, and then the woman said, "One moment please."

The man stood there silently, watching Azariah and Octavia while the woman dipped into the depths of the temple. She was only gone for a few minutes before she returned, but when she did, a second man accompanied her. He was wearing sweeping robes of pure white and a pointed white hat. Along the cuffs of his sleeves and the neckline of his tunic, gold thread wove in an exquisite pattern. Octavia didn't have to ask who he was, because only a Wellminder would be dressed so richly.

"I am told that two rather wealthy individuals want a parcel drawn straight from the Well?" he inquired.

Azariah nodded, and without hesitation, he pulled a small bag of coins from the inside pocket of his vest and handed it to the Wellminder.

The man's striking green eyes lit with enthusiasm, and he gave a quick bow. "Please follow me."

When Octavia walked over the threshold of the entryway to the temple, the magic in the air and the cavernous height of the dome astounded her. The room was huge and open, the walls lined with tall carved pillars and the floors covered in glossy white marble. In addition to this, the entire ceiling was swathed with shimmering gold, silver, and white paint. It depicted the *gods*, adorned in glory, sitting in the clouds, playing on the winds, and walking the earth. But the most breathtaking part of the temple was the Well of Power that sat at its center. It was made of dark sparkling stone blacker than midnight, and it stood three feet high and measured five feet across. Its shimmering *waters* cast blue reflections across the vaulted ceiling so that the art above it looked like it was swimming in a vast and vibrant ocean.

Octavia was struck by a strong desire to run to the Well. It radiated through her core. The tantalizing, incredible, mystic pull of the Well of Euphoria was so strong that she could feel her mind slipping back into the spiral of deception she had experienced while eating the fitcha. However, this time, there was something more.

The draw of the *waters* was beyond captivating. It was irresistible, and it brought tears to Octavia's eyes. She needed to gaze into its depths, but she held herself back, not wanting to cause the Wellminder alarm. The longer she ignored the pull, however, the stronger it grew. Something about it felt off—like it wasn't coming from her admiration of the *gods* alone. It was as if the Well had reached out and hooked an invisible string around her waist to entice her forward.

She had to stop herself from charging toward it.

But . . .

She had to look within. She *had* to.

No.

She couldn't just run up to a Well of Power.

The Wellminder's white robes billowed behind him as he led Azariah and Octavia forward. Octavia was only ten feet away from it now . . .

"Please stay back," the Wellminder instructed, withdrawing a small vial from a divot in the outer rim of the black sparkling rock. He leaned over the edge of the Well and dipped his hand into the *waters*, drawing out a parcel and examining it thoroughly before capping it off.

The blue glow of the Well intensified, and Octavia felt a rushing sensation pass through her body. The urge to peer into the *waters* hit her like a violent wind. It was overpowering and insistent—a tug that came from her core and filled her to the brim.

She *had* to look over the Well's edge . . .

It was a compulsion that ran as deep as her blood.

There was no stopping it.

She started walking forward. Azariah said something to her, but she couldn't hear him. A powerful instinct was guiding her, and she couldn't ignore it.

The Wellminder straightened up, vial in hand. "What are you doing? Please stand back!"

But his voice was oddly muted.

Octavia placed her hands on the edge of the Well, leaning over to gaze within. The *waters* shone brightly, dancing off her face, and then the key began to burn. It was sudden and intense. Octavia gasped, but she was unable to tear her eyes away from the *waters* below. Deep within the Well, a swirl of black coiled. At first, it was small, but then it grew, consuming the shimmering blue and replacing it with a tar-like substance.

Abruptly, Octavia's vision clouded over. She was still staring into the Well, but it was like gazing into a thick fog. Through the haze, two figures appeared. She couldn't see their faces, but she could hear them. Two distinct male voices spoke—a desperate one and a hardened one.

"You have ruined us all! Look at what you have done! Look at Hritza—how she burns in the darkness!"

"The gods cannot compel me to do this, Tarrick. They will not force my hand."

"Father, repent! There is nothing left for us. You have gone too far, and the gods themselves have punished the entire kingdom for it. You were wrong. And STILL, they have given you the chance to undo this. Please, I beg of you. Listen to them."

"I will not! I have done nothing but strive to make Hritza great. From the onset, I have proven that Hritza is deserving of power. I was going to create the greatest kingdom on earth! But the gods . . . they are hateful. Controlling. Undeserving of our worship and adoration."

"You would blaspheme them so openly? So brazenly?"

"YES! Humanity has outgrown them. I was about to be a god among men—and Hritza the jewel of the earth—and they saw my greatness as a challenge."

"The blood of our brothers and sisters cries out from the ground to testify against you, Father. You have done a wicked thing!"

"The gods are the wicked ones. THEY have brought this destruction. Not me! And I will NOT bend my knee to the tyrants in the sky, Tarrick."

An anguished, desolate, wailing cry reverberated through Octavia's skull like someone had taken a drum and beat on it from the inside of her head.

She gasped as if surfacing from a deep dive. Azariah's strong hands were clamped over her upper arm, dragging her away from the Well of Power, and she stumbled back, panicked. Her heart was racing, and her left palm was still burning beneath the glove. Azariah was in front of her, saying—something? She couldn't understand him. It was like her ears were full of cotton. His mouth was moving, but it was muffled and incoherent.

After another few seconds of spastic breathing, her hearing returned full force, and she became aware of her surroundings once more.

The Wellminder was staring at her, horror etched across his face. He was so pale that he didn't look alive, and when his lips parted, he spoke in a hoarse whisper. "Are you sent from the *gods*?"

"Am I—what?" She didn't understand his question.

"The *waters* . . . they rose up out of the Well at your touch. They were black like the darkness. What . . . what did you do?"

She looked at Azariah, whose face was also drained of blood. She was unsure of what to say. She had no idea what the Wellminder was talking about because she hadn't touched the *waters* at all. She had only peered into its depths . . .

Her gaze darted to the Well, and the shimmering blue color was the same as it had been when they entered the temple.

"I . . ."

"Who are you?" the Wellminder demanded, his voice now commanding. He looked between Octavia and Azariah, but then his attention fixed firmly on Octavia. "Never in all my life have I seen the *waters* rise up out of the Well!" He clutched his chest. "Are you an omen? Tell me! Why have you come here?"

The Wellminder's words were scaring her, and she backed away from him.

"We should be going," Azariah said firmly, placing his arm around Octavia. "May I have the parcel?"

The Wellminder still clutched the small vial in hand, but instead of extending it to Azariah, he held it close. He pointed at Octavia. "You have brought darkness. I demand that you leave at once!"

"We will," Azariah said calmly, now releasing Octavia to step toward the man. He held his hands up as if to signal a surrender. "But not until you hand us the parcel of *waters* we paid for."

The Wellminder shook his head, backing away from them, and Octavia felt her stomach drop. It looked like he was about to start shouting for help. Azariah sensed the same thing because he moved so quickly that the man couldn't even gasp. Azariah hooked the Wellminder's neck and applied enough pressure to cause him to pass out. He slumped against Azariah's body, and Azariah carefully laid him on the white marble, pulling the vial from his hands and tucking it into his vest.

"Follow me quickly!" he urged her. "And wipe that stunned look off your face!"

Octavia jolted into motion, and the two of them jogged from the temple. When they reached the entryway, the woman attendant who had brought the Wellminder out tried to say something to them, but Azariah brushed her aside, charging back into the spacious courtyard.

The night sky above them was littered with stars, and a slight wind whipped about them.

For the entire walk back to the gates, Octavia's heart was in her throat. What had just happened back there? Why didn't *she* see the *waters* turn black and rise up from the Well? All she remembered was hearing voices. Did Azariah hear them too?

"This way," Azariah said, pulling Octavia down a new path.

Ahead, she could see stables and more attendants.

Panic now clawed at her. What if they couldn't get out? What if the guard didn't open the gate? What if they discovered she was the Keyholder? They would be trapped, and who knows what would happen to her as a result.

The attendants they passed gave them strange looks, but Octavia hoped it was only because they were moving so quickly. When they got to the stables, Azariah called to the same girl he had asked to attend to their horse, and she approached them with surprise.

"Leaving so soon?"

"Yes. Our horse, please."

"I have only just started to feed him, sir."

"Our horse, please!" he said again, this time more forcefully.

"Very well." She gave him a nervous bow, walking back into the stable. It only took her a minute, but she returned with the chestnut animal, handing the reins to the bounty hunter. "Here you are, sir."

Azariah pushed Octavia up onto the animal before she could even attempt to mount herself, and then he swung himself over the top of the creature. With a hard kick, he prodded the horse down the path toward the gate. The creature's hooves thudded against the stone, and when they reached the guard, Octavia felt like she couldn't breathe.

Were they actually going to get out of this?

A woman's voice shrieked from behind them, her words echoing off the stone, and Octavia's heart sank all the way to her toes.

"STOP THEM! DO NOT LET THEM GO!"

14

Lost

The guard's attention snapped to the two of them, and he drew his sword. Then Azariah's hand grabbed Octavia's upper arm. He spoke against her ear in a way that spiked her fear. "Ride and don't look back. I will find you."

Was he about to—?

Abruptly, Azariah leapt off the horse, leaving Octavia atop the animal. He charged the guard, climbing up the watchpost and ducking out of the way as the guard swung his sword. Azariah pulled the man down by the front of his tunic, and he crashed to the stone below, sword clattering.

Clang.

A lever slammed against metal, and the gates opened up, the wrought-iron squealing in protest. The horse whinnied and reared up, causing Octavia to cling to its neck for dear life. Then Azariah's forceful gaze met hers, and he shouted, "GO!"

She didn't hesitate.

She kicked the horse into a gallop, flying through the gates and leaving the bounty hunter behind. Wind whipped through her hair, and the sounds of shouting slowly drifted into non-existence as she moved away from the temple.

She pushed the horse as fast as it would go, and the animal charged down the smoothly paved streets. Her pulse thundered through her limbs, her hands shook, and complete chaos took over her mind. She couldn't think, she just rode.

It was only when Octavia felt sure that no one had followed her that she pulled the horse back from its gallop and stopped. She took several heaving breaths, clutching her chest to steady herself. The horse was panting heavily as well.

Octavia took a quick assessment of her surroundings. She had no idea where she was, and it didn't help that all the white marble architecture around her looked the same. On top of that, it was harder to see in the dark. The street lamps that lit the way were dim. Only the insides of taverns were lively and shining bright.

She swallowed hard, unable to believe her fortune. For the first time since Voramir stole her away from her home, she was alone. She was free. The bounty hunter wasn't with her anymore. But right as the thought thrilled her, a deep sense of dread replaced the high as she realized this "fortunate" turn of events was not so fortunate after all. There was no "being free." Not as long as she had the key. The darkness wasn't going to stop moving—she was tied to it—and she couldn't run away. Besides, where would she run? She couldn't go home. People were hunting her, and they would not hesitate to hurt her family to get to her. She had also vowed to the *gods* that she wouldn't escape Azariah, but she never anticipated losing him like this. Surely the *gods* wouldn't punish her for this unforeseen circumstance?

Anxiety laced her veins as her brain continued to reel. Suddenly, not having Azariah by her side made her feel as directionless as the wind. As much as it pained her to admit it, she needed him. She turned to glance behind her, as if simply looking around might pull the bounty hunter from the shadows, but all she saw were Urthans meandering the streets . . .

Octavia nudged the horse into a walk. "What do I do?" she whispered to the *gods*.

A slew of horrible thoughts assaulted her. Azariah said he would find her, but . . . what if he couldn't escape the temple? What if he had been captured? Or killed? What would she do? She wasn't safe here—or anywhere for that matter.

Should she go to Zoharth alone and present herself to King Bastian Jasper, as was the plan all along? He knew the words of the prophecy in full—words she was sure she needed to know to walk through the darkness. But could she even make it there on her own? She couldn't defend herself. Sure, she was someone who could put up a fight, but she wasn't trained in weaponry or practical self-defense. And Azariah's one knife lesson didn't make her an expert. She didn't even have the witch's protection spell yet. What would happen if she came upon a group of people intent on kidnapping her? Or worse, killing her? How would she get away from them?

Maybe she could simply go up to the darkness itself, since that was the endgame of all of this anyway . . .

The idea of that squeezed the breath from her, and she clutched the reins of the horse so tight that her hands hurt. The night in this unfamiliar city of pleasure and destruction seemed more menacing than ever, and for a moment, she fought a sob. It lodged itself in her throat, keen to choke the life out of her.

"Just think," she said aloud. "Breathe and think."

Logically, she should stay in one place to give Azariah an easier time of finding her, but where would be the safest place to stay? After a few minutes of thinking it through, Octavia reasoned that she should move toward the outskirts of the city. One, to get away from the temple in case the attendants or Wellminders were searching for her, and two, to provide herself with the opportunity of escaping Urtha if she needed to. Realistically, she couldn't wait for Azariah forever. But she would wait for him as long as she could.

A breeze caressed her face, and delicious smells captured her attention. Then the sounds of bleating reached her ears. Was that sheep?

She strained her eyes in the dark, moving past another tavern and coming upon a set of stables. What had Azariah said? Something about the outskirts of the city not having a space for animals because it didn't match the atmosphere? She was definitely still in the center of the city.

Even here, where the taverns were rowdy, Octavia noticed that they were less plentiful, and not all of them were playing music. On the outskirts of Urtha, however, she distinctly recalled that nearly every structure was a tavern, and nearly every tavern had music.

"I suppose I should follow the music. The louder the better," she said to the horse, pulling it around to start down the street in the opposite direction.

Over the next half hour, she kept vigilant, walking the horse through the city and turning down street after street. Sometimes she would get hopeful upon entering a section that seemed more boisterous and music-filled, but her hope would soon crash as she moved on to find more stables housing livestock and horses.

She was starting to wonder if she should ask someone for directions *out* of Urtha, simply so she could get to the outer rim of the city—she hadn't up to this point purely out of fear. She didn't want to interact with anyone if she didn't have to, but she was lost.

Octavia sighed in frustration. At this point, she should just stop and wait . . .

She turned down another street, keen to find an isolated place to dismount, but just as she was about to prod the horse into trot, two drunken women stumbled out in front of her. One was laughing, and the other was talking way too loudly. They didn't even notice Octavia pulling hard on the animal's reins to avoid hitting them.

"Liska, shut up a moment! I'm serious!" the shorter woman said to her laughing friend, pulling on her arm. "We need to stay together! You shouldn't go by yourself."

"Nonsense," her friend replied, giggling.

"The barmaid said someone had been murdered in the washroom at The Turquoise Drops, Liska! I'm not joking! Urthan guards are swarming the tavern, but they haven't found the person who did it. Maybe we shouldn't be out tonight."

Octavia's pulse jumped up a notch. The women were walking away, still oblivious to her presence, so she directed the horse to stay behind them as they crossed the street, keeping just within earshot.

"The Turquoise Drops? But that's . . . that's so close to here!"

The short woman nodded vigorously. "Let's go back home. I don't feel safe right now."

The two women scurried down the street, disappearing from sight.

The Turquoise Drops? A pit formed in Octavia's stomach. Of all the places in Urtha to stumble upon . . . She shouldn't be here. With her horse and her dark clothing, she clearly stood out. What if someone recognized her? The barmaid that served her earlier might . . .

Octavia peered down the dark street, unnerved. Her stomach was in knots. She needed to get away from this place, so she ushered the horse forward quickly, but when she took the animal around the next corner, she found herself directly in front of The Turquoise Drops. The tavern was swamped with activity, and over two dozen Urthan guards stood outside—with even more inside.

Panic thundered through her, and she cursed under her breath, pulling the horse away and retreating back the way she had come. Octavia scanned her surroundings, spotting a secluded and dark alleyway between two taverns. Without hesitation, she took the horse there, hiding herself in the shadows and taking a few deep breaths to calm her racing heart.

Octavia dismounted and led the horse even further into the recesses between the structures. Then she leaned her back up against a marble wall, closing her eyes for a moment to take some calming breaths. She had to talk herself down from the panic threatening to overwhelm her mind. It had been less than an hour since she and Azariah had parted ways, but Octavia had a sinking feeling that something horrible had happened to him.

Still, she would wait for the bounty hunter, and if he hadn't found her by morning, she would reassess her options.

Octavia rubbed her eyes and pushed herself off the wall. Leaving the horse in the shadows, she crept forward to peer out into the street. Music and frivolity charmed the air along with the waftings of delectable food. The city seemed as lively and ensnaring as ever.

She sighed. This was simply the wrong place for her to wait. Octavia was just about to slip back into the alleyway to retrieve the horse when a distinct flash of blue lit up somewhere to her left. She froze, whipping her head in the direction of the light.

Fear turned her blood to ice. Had she imagined it?

Her eyes scoured the dark crevices across the street, but she could see nothing. Only the light spilling from the taverns was visible in the night. Maybe it was Azariah? Her heart leapt in hope for a moment, but then it quickly faded. If it were the bounty hunter, surely he would announce his presence? Wouldn't he simply walk across the street and join her?

Suddenly, the fact that she was alone felt ten times worse. The people who had tried to kidnap her in Omari were a team. She might stand a chance if it was only one person, but there was no way she could fight her way out of a group intent on taking her.

Octavia shook herself out of her frozen trance, digging her hand into her boot and retrieving the poisoned dagger. She unsheathed the weapon, held it aloft, and backed away from the street, tucking herself just between the taverns. She couldn't help the intense feeling of being watched. Her palms were sweaty, her stomach squirmed, and her jaw tightened. It was unnerving, feeling *this* afraid of people, but she was certain she saw a flash of blue.

For the next minute, all she could do was stand there in the dark with the horse at her back and the street at her front. She kept the dagger at the ready, clutching it firmly and standing in the fighting stance Azariah had taught her during the knife lesson.

A second minute passed . . .

Then a third . . .

Maybe she had imagined the flash of blue?

"I need to get out of here," she whispered to herself.

With jittering fingertips, she sheathed the dagger, stuffing it back into her boot. Then she turned away from the street, moving toward the horse, which stood a dozen feet from her.

Abruptly, a huge hand pressed over her mouth, and a strong arm wrapped around her waist, pulling her deeper into the alleyway. She screamed as she fought with the figure who had grabbed her, but the stranger kept her thoroughly pinned.

Then a familiar voice spoke into her ear. "It's me. Stop screaming."

Her panic, which was a moment ago wild and unrestrained, calmed considerably, and the force of the arm wrapped around her waist slackened. She yanked Azariah's hand away from her mouth.

"Why did you do that!?" she hissed, angry, although she was extremely relieved to see him. "I thought I was getting kidnapped again!"

But Azariah didn't answer her question. Instead, he countered with one of his own. "Why are you back here? I murdered a man just around the corner, and you returned to the scene of the crime? There are Urthan guards crawling the streets, and they're looking for us. The man's friend gave them our descriptions. I overheard them talking."

"I was lost!" she retorted. "I didn't know I was back here until I was!" She glared at him, but then her demeanor softened. She truly was glad he had found her. "You got away from the temple, I see."

"There weren't many guards," he replied. "I escaped soon after you—and thankfully, I didn't have to kill anyone." Azariah shot Octavia a disapproving glance. "When I didn't find you close to the temple, I thought you had run." He pulled a parcel of *waters* from his pocket, and its blue glow shimmered in the night. "But I suppose I found you quick enough. I just wish you hadn't strayed so far."

"I didn't try to run away from you!" she snapped. "I just—I thought it would be best if I wasn't close to the temple. I thought—if the attendants came after me, or if they had captured you—I—" Octavia stopped talking. She didn't blame Azariah for thinking she had run, but she also couldn't help but feel frustrated by his words. She let air pass slowly between pursed lips. "I can't run from this . . . or from you."

The intensity of the bounty hunter's gaze was piercing as he narrowed his eyes. He was silent for a few beats, appearing to weigh the truth of her words. "I suppose you truly are a woman of faith."

There it was again—another comment that sparked Octavia's growing curiosity about Azariah and the nature of his belief.

"I *am* a woman of faith," she said. "But my vow to the *gods* is not the reason I didn't run away from you."

His expression now took on an intrigued curiosity. "Then why?"

An odd fluttery sensation swept Octavia's stomach. Why was she all of a sudden nervous? She fidgeted with the glove that covered the key as the complicated flurry of reasons for why she didn't escape him crowded her mind, but she simply summed it up with a single statement. "Because . . . I need you, Azariah."

15

Magenta Powder . . .

Azariah's expression was hard to discern. Maybe it was the cover of darkness, or maybe it was the fact that she had said something so brazen and absurd, but he appeared miserable, like her words were a physical blow. The subdued look quickly fled his face, and his fierce exterior returned. He cleared his throat.

"We need to buy some food, and then we need to leave."

She nodded, a tangle of emotions settling into her stomach at his response. "Right."

What was she even feeling? Affection for him? She violently rejected the idea in her mind. Absolutely not. He was a means to an end for her just like she was for him. There was nothing between them but business. He was her enemy of circumstance. End of story.

"It's only a matter of time before our description circulates this city. We need to blend in and get out of Urtha."

Azariah swung a satchel out from behind his hip, opening the flap to reveal white garb with golden thread.

"Here, put this on," he said, throwing her a silky shirt that was nearly as long as a dress. He pulled out a white vest and jacket and donned the clothing quickly. Octavia did the same. She adjusted the fabric around her waist, admiring the finery. It fit rather well, and she was surprised that he got her size correct.

After dressing, Azariah motioned her to follow him. "Let's make this quick. Keep by my side and don't draw any attention to yourself. Avoid eye contact with people. That will help."

With that, they left the horse in the shadows and strode into the light spilling from the nearest tavern. Octavia kept close to him, nerves jutting into her stomach. The loud music and lively conversation stuffed her ears to capacity, and as they entered the tavern, the smell of coska and mead attacked her. It was quite the abundance.

They walked straight to the bar at the back, which looked nearly the same as the one in The Turquoise Drops, and Azariah waved down a barmaid, who shuffled over to him with two pints of mead in her hand.

"What can I do for you, sir?" she asked breathlessly.

"Do you have any dried meats and dried fruits available?"

"Sure do."

"Can you wrap up enough for six days?"

"Of course, sir. Give me a moment. I'll need to go back to our storeroom. Any particular meats?"

"Anything is fine."

The barmaid walked out from behind the bar, delivered the two pints of mead, and then shimmied back around, striding through what looked like a stockroom door.

The coska once more tugged at Octavia's sense of smell, and the pull of the *waters* enticed her, causing her to ponder the idea of sitting down on a barstool and ordering some food. And maybe a drink? It would be lovely to drink away the evening and not worry about anything or anyone. Maybe they could stay for one round of drinks?

Hadn't she earned it after all she had been through?

She shook herself, forcing her thoughts back on the right track. *My name is Octavia Fletcher, I am the Keyholder, and I am going to Zoharth.*

Keyholder . . .

The word turned in her mind like a storm, and the voices she had heard from the Well of Euphoria drifted back to her. Who were the two shrouded figures she had seen in the fog? Why had the key burned? What had even happened? In the hurry of their escape, she hadn't been able to talk to Azariah about it. She yearned to ask him about the incident, but now was not the time. She would have to wait until they were out of Urtha.

"Here you are, sir."

The barmaid was back, handing Azariah a hefty package wrapped in brown paper. He gave her money, and then the two of them left the tavern, returning to the horse and securing their food into one of the saddlebags.

In the cover of darkness, it was easy to slip away. Azariah took them far from The Turquoise Drops, traveling along the outskirts of the city. As they rode, Octavia swore she kept catching glimpses of someone following them. Her eyes would dart, and her head would snap around, but each time, she saw nothing but shadow. Still, she couldn't shake the feeling that they were being tailed.

"Why do you keep looking back?" Azariah asked after the fifth time of her doing so.

A chill swept her skin. "I think we're being followed. I keep seeing . . . I don't know what I keep seeing . . ."

Azariah encouraged the horse into a trot as they continued down the streets. "We'll be out of the city soon."

"Not soon enough," she muttered to herself, still nervously glancing into the shadows between every tavern.

"Vrelia is a six-day journey from here."

Octavia's stomach clenched. It was the last kingdom they would pass through before Zoharth. A flash of movement caught Octavia's eye once again, and she whipped her head to the side, desperately trying to catch sight of the person she swore was right behind them. But still, there was nothing there.

"Get us out of here," she whispered. "And get that witch's protection spell on me."

Azariah nodded, pushing the horse even faster, and to her great relief, ten minutes later, Octavia said goodbye to the city of pleasure. She hoped she would never visit it again. The dark forest stood ahead, and like a welcome embrace, the trees cloaked them.

Octavia looked back one last time, and still seeing no one, she decided that perhaps the *waters*—along with her tired mind—had been playing tricks on her.

They rode at a decent pace, following the Kraven River for half an hour before Azariah pulled up on the reins. "Let's rest and eat. The poor horse needs rest as well."

"And the witch's spell?" Octavia pressed.

"Yes."

The moonlight shining overhead made it easy for them to see their surroundings. The river rushed a dozen yards away, and Azariah led the horse through the trees to the flow. Then the two of them dismounted, and the animal dipped its head into the water, drinking heavily. Octavia did the same, kneeling and cupping her hands to bring the cold liquid to her lips. It was refreshing to drink something without her mind having to fight entrapping thoughts.

"Come here."

Octavia got to her feet and walked over to Azariah, who was sitting on the ground cross-legged. She sat in front of him, watching him as he pulled out six shining vials of blue *waters* from the inside of his vest.

"Remember, this isn't going to stop the *waters'* ability to track you. It will simply dampen the effect. If people are still close enough, there's nothing we can do."

Octavia nodded. "I'll take what I can get."

Azariah set a tin cup down in the dirt and began to uncap the vials. One by one, he poured them into the cup, and as each vial was added, the blue glow intensified. Then he withdrew a vial of magenta powder, and when he emptied the contents into the *waters*, the color changed from blue to pink, and smoke began to rise up like it was boiling.

Octavia grimaced. It looked magical but extremely unappetizing. "I'm assuming I drink it?"

"You would be correct," Azariah said with a nod. He picked the tin up off the dirt and handed it to her. "Every drop."

Octavia brought the cup to her lips and drank. It tasted like soot—earthy and bitter—and she nearly spat it out, but she forced herself to swallow all of it, and when she finished, her stomach gurgled in an unpleasant manner. She pressed a hand over her mouth and repeated viciously in her head that she would not throw up, despite the violent urge to. Once the sensation settled, a new one followed, and for a moment, the key tingled in her palm. It warmed but didn't burn, and then, as quickly as it had started, it stopped.

Azariah peered at her. "How do you feel?"

"Exceptionally normal," she responded. "Well, at least as normal as I can feel with this stupid piece of metal stuck in my flesh."

He grunted in reply.

She folded her arms across her chest. "Do you know the range of the protection?"

Azariah shook his head.

She ran her thumb over the glove, feeling the soft leather. Part of her felt hopeful now that she had taken the potion, but another part of her scoffed at the idea that they wouldn't run into any more trouble. Zoharth was still quite a journey from here.

She glanced at Azariah, her mind now turning to a new subject. "What happened at the Well of Euphoria?"

Azariah paled. Even in the dim moonlight, she was able to see how her question shook him.

"I could ask you the same," he replied. "What were you thinking, looking into the Well?"

"I didn't do it on purpose!" she countered. "I just . . . it was like this overpowering force drawing me to look in."

Azariah's brow arched upward, unconvinced. "But, what did you *do*?"

"I don't know," she admitted. "The key started to burn. And then—" She stopped herself. She was about to say she heard voices, but the words felt stuck on her tongue.

"And then?"

She gnawed on the inside of her cheek. "Does the name Tarrick mean anything to you?"

Azariah simply stared at her.

"I'll take that as a no."

He rubbed the back of his neck. "Are you going to elaborate?"

She sighed, deciding there was no benefit in keeping the incident to herself. "I heard voices coming from the Well."

"Did the *gods* speak to you?" His tone grew more hopeful. "Did they enlighten you?"

Octavia felt a hollow pit form in her stomach, and she shook her head. "It wasn't the *gods* speaking. And I don't know. I don't feel enlightened. I heard two men talking. They were arguing about Hritza and about the *gods* giving them a chance to undo things." She peered at him, feeling utterly useless again. Desperation laced her voice. "What happened to me?"

"You walked to the Well, you looked over its edge, and then the *waters* began to rise to the ceiling of the temple at your touch, but they were black like the darkness. You were in a trance. You wouldn't respond to me. Then the *waters* sank back into the Well when I pulled you away." He paused, considering her for a moment. "You didn't see any of that, did you?"

She clasped her hands together. "No. All I saw were the two men arguing. Well . . . not really. They were standing in this thick fog. I couldn't see their faces." She buried her head in her hands for a few seconds, unease curling her stomach into knots. Then she looked up at Azariah. "What does it mean?"

The bounty hunter scratched his chin, maintaining his steely gaze. "You're the Keyholder. You tell me."

Once more, Azariah's harsh statement about her not knowing how to save everyone from the darkness slashed through her mind. Were the *gods of old* playing with her? Deep down, she knew that the conversation she had overheard in the Well held great importance, but she had no clarity in her mind to be able to decipher its meaning. How could she be the Keyholder and be *this* ignorant? Frustration burrowed deep in her brain, and she let out an incoherent noise. "I'm exhausted. I need to sleep."

She got up from the ground and walked to the horse, grabbing one of the rolled-up blankets and swinging it around her shoulders. Azariah didn't protest. In fact, he didn't say anything at all. Part of her wished he would. She longed for words of comfort or solace—anything to keep her mind from falling into the abyss of fear and self-doubt. If only Papa were here. He would know what to say to her and how to encourage her. But Papa felt as far away as the *gods*, and she knew that dwelling on him would only make her feel more miserable. He was with Rustwick's army right now—wherever they were.

She sat down at the base of a tree and leaned up against it, closing her eyes and focusing her mind on trying to think through the conversation she had heard from the Well. But the fragments escaped her.

She prayed to the *gods*. *What am I supposed to do? What were you trying to show me?*

But no answer came. Only the rushing river and the singing bugs sounded around her.

She sighed in frustration and attempted to tuck away the events of the day. But this proved fruitless because the incident in the washroom vividly returned to her, making her whole body shudder. Her eyes cracked open from a spike of apprehension.

"It's done. You're fine," she whispered to herself. "You're safe."

Her gaze landed on the bounty hunter. He was sitting in the dirt, facing the Kraven River, and he was . . . praying? He was hunched over with his head bowed into his clasped hands. She couldn't see his face, but his posture looked defeated. Crushed. And for the next few minutes, Octavia observed him silently.

The longer she stared at him, the more she felt like walking over to him to see if he was okay. She wanted to ask him . . . ?

She didn't know what . . .

No, she shouldn't disturb him. Whatever this moment was, Octavia felt like she was prying simply by watching him. So instead of getting up, she prayed—and this was the first time she prayed for the man who had kidnapped her. She thanked the *gods* for how Azariah had intervened at The Turquoise Drops and how fervently he was protecting her. He may be her enemy of circumstance, but *gods* was she was grateful for him. She wasn't going to survive this nightmare without him.

"Sleep," she told herself. "Just sleep."

With anxiety in her chest and confusion in her heart, she forced her eyes closed, hoping to get a few hours of respite before having to continue on toward her fate in Zoharth.

Octavia was walking in a golden wheat field with Bowan in the late afternoon sun. He was running, and she was chasing him, laughing. The breeze blew against her face, light and playful, as the two of them raced along, huffing madly.

She was gaining on him, and soon, she caught him by the upper arm, wrestling with him as he giggled. He pushed her away, but she snatched him around the middle and hugged him tight, refusing to let go even when he protested.

"Stop it, O!" he said, chortling. He kept pushing at her hands, but she wouldn't budge.

"Nope! Not a chance!"

The wheat around them stood tall, hiding them from view, and the breeze picked up with a big gust, tossing the stalks around so that they slapped into them.

"O! Stop it!" Bowan's voice now sounded much deeper. It was gravelly and distorted, and when she looked into his face, his mouth was split into a bone-chilling smile that was way too wide for his eleven-year-old features. His eyes were unnaturally wide too, boring into her.

Octavia gasped, releasing him from the bear hug. Bowan's head tilted, but then it kept going until it was upside down—though his body remained upright. His neck elongated, his teeth sharpened, and his voice dropped another octave.

"Keyholder!" he rasped, crouching on all fours like a beast, his movements jerky and wild.

Octavia screamed, stumbling back from him. She tripped over the uneven ground and fell, her wrists slamming against the dirt.

Bowan, his black eyes fixed on Octavia, lunged from his crouched position, his mouth gaping open as if to swallow her whole. She threw her arms up to protect herself and slammed her eyes shut . . .

But nothing happened.

She simply lay there in the dirt of the wheat field. No pain came. No attack ravished her body. Nothing.

She tried to open her eyes, but they were stuck shut. And then her limbs became heavy. She weighed so much. Her arms were glued to the earth. Her legs were made of stone. And no matter how hard she fought, there was nothing she could do to unstick herself from the ground below . . .

"Cassia! Are you sure?" a voice hissed.

"Yes, he'll meet up with us."

"This wasn't the plan."

"It is now!"

Octavia tried to open her eyes, but they felt like they were a hundred pounds each. Thick fatigue flowed through her body, and her head felt like a boulder. Was she still dreaming? She must be dreaming . . .

"We'll wait by the hook, like we said. And if he doesn't show by dawn, we'll leave."

There was a frustrated grunt.

Octavia tried again to force her eyes open, but they simply wouldn't budge. It was like fighting a deep sleep. The more she tried to wake up, the further she slipped into the fog. Darkness surrounded her, and her mind drifted, falling in and out of nothingness. She didn't know how much time passed or if it was passing at all . . .

"Did you check her?"

"She's still out."

"Are you sure?"

Octavia's mind latched onto the words, and her heartbeat quickened. She still couldn't open her eyes, and her body was still unimaginably heavy, but this time, she could feel something else. She was lying on her side on something hard, and her arms were behind her back. As her brain furiously worked to pull itself out of the haze, more sensations came.

Rope. Her wrists were bound. But her ankles weren't.

Panic momentarily choked her. No. Not again. This couldn't be happening again! Her lungs threatened to spasm, but every ounce of her self-preservation told her not to move a muscle. She had been drugged. Heaviness clung to her like a cloak, but she wasn't unconscious anymore. Feeling was slowly returning to limbs and face, and she had to stifle the urge to let out a groan.

She wanted to move—to open her eyes—but her mind screamed at her to keep absolutely still. A singular and all-consuming thought took hold of her: assess and survive.

"He still hasn't returned!" a harsh male voice whispered. "We need to leave!"

"No! It's not dawn yet!" a woman's voice responded.

"Does it matter? We have the Keyholder!"

Shuffling footsteps sounded by her head. There was more whispering, but she couldn't make any of it out. Octavia continued to take stock of her surroundings without opening her eyes. Her face felt like it was pressed into dirt, water trickled somewhere behind her, and a pine scent lingered strong in her nostrils. She was definitely still in the forest, and from the voices present, it sounded like she only had two captors. Was she still at their camp or had these people taken her somewhere else?

Her brain slipped into a rapid fire of panic-inducing thoughts. Where was Azariah? How had these people captured her without a fight? The only logical conclusion she settled on was that he was dead. Otherwise, why wouldn't he be here? Dread throttled her. Somehow, some way, these people had snuck up on them in the forest as they slept. She *knew* they were being followed out of Urtha. She had felt it in her gut. How desperately she wished she had listened to her instincts and persuaded Azariah to continue their travels.

Tears threatened her eyes, but she stayed still, coaxing her mind to stay on task. Stay alive. Escape. She would do whatever it took to survive. She would not let them take her without a fight. A lump built in her throat as she continued to sense what was around her. Her two captors were both pacing right next to her.

There was a slew of curses, and then the female voice said, "Check her again!"

Rough hands grabbed Octavia's face, and she forced herself to remain limp. Then the hands went to the rope that bound her hands together behind her back. There was a tug.

"I told you. She's still out."

The hands left her. The pacing continued.

Octavia felt an odd pain against her right ankle, and she tried to decipher what was causing it. Her heart leapt in hope. It was the poisoned dagger. If she could somehow free her hands and get the weapon out from the sheath inside of her sock, she might stand a chance of catching these two off guard.

The footsteps sounded like they were getting farther away now, and Octavia cracked her eyes open the smallest fraction of an inch. Through her eyelashes, she could see a man, a woman, and a white horse a few yards away. Her two captors had their backs to her, still conversing in low whispers, so she flexed her hands, feeling the strength of the rope. It was tied tight, but it didn't travel very far up her wrists as Azariah's ropework had when he had captured her. These people were clearly not bounty hunters . . .

She kept her eyes open, but only as slits, making sure the man and woman didn't turn around as she shimmied her wrists in the rope. Her skin was starting to rub raw, but she could feel her left hand slowly slipping through the bindings. All the while, she kept the rest of her body still—her legs sprawled in the same position, her hip biting into the earth, and her shoulder and cheek pressed down into the dirt. She worked silently and furiously, and with another minute of twisting her wrists, her left hand slid free.

The small moment of triumph was quickly overtaken by anxiety as she calculated her next move. The man and woman still stood by the white horse, and they still hadn't noticed her, but any sudden or large movements would give her away, and she didn't have the dagger in hand yet. She slowly crept her hand toward her ankle while carefully sliding her ankle closer to her butt. The movement was painstaking.

The groggy sensations from the drugs were still lingering, but not to the degree they had been before. She felt like she was fully capable of springing up to her feet once she had the weapon in hand.

"We've waited long enough! Gregor is probably injured. Or dead. We're leaving!" the man said in a raised voice.

Octavia's pulse spiked as heavy footsteps thudded against the dirt. The man was coming back to where she lay, and there was no hiding her unbound hands. This was it. She had to act.

In a flash of movement, Octavia's hand dove into the sock under her boot, and her fingertips grasped the blade. She yanked it free and sat up just as the man came upon her. His wide eyes and open mouth were all she saw before plunging the dagger deep into his thigh.

He let out a blood-curdling scream, dropping to his knees and falling over the top of her. She pushed him off, wrenching the blade free from his skin and leaping to her feet. Her head sloshed, and her vision tunneled, but she didn't let that stop her. She launched herself at the woman, tackling her to the ground and bringing the knife down to slash her shoulder. But the woman seemed more prepared than the man.

She shrieked, grabbing Octavia's wrist to stop the blade before it pierced her. She rolled around until she was on top of Octavia, and Octavia, in her panic, did the first thing that came to her mind. She sank her teeth into the woman's arm.

A wild yowl split the forest air, and Octavia was able to slash the blade into the woman's chest. It wasn't a deep cut, but it was enough. The woman crumpled, and Octavia shoved her off. Once more, Octavia sprang to her feet, and then she bolted, sprinting to the horse. Laced with the high of panic, she grabbed the animal's saddle, swung herself up, and kicked at the creature's sides, spurring it into a gallop.

She didn't look back. As she rode, her vision slopped from side to side, and her heartbeat pounded all the way up into her ears, so she clung to the horse's neck with all her might, fearing that, at any second, she might fall off.

Once she was sure she was a fair distance away, Octavia slowed the horse to a walk, simply to calm herself down. The first rays of dawn were peeking over the horizon to light the sky, splashing it with vibrant color. Ordinarily, it would have been a spectacular sunrise, but it was marred by the reality that she was once again alone and unprotected. And this time, she had no way of meeting up with the bounty hunter—or even knowing if he was still alive.

16

. . . And White Powder Too

"I survived."

Octavia repeated the words to herself incessantly as she led the horse along the Kraven River. She took stock of her surroundings, noting that the place where she and Azariah had camped for the night was nowhere in sight. In fact, Octavia had no idea how far those people had taken her.

Her breath came and went like a rampant wind, and it made her head spin.

She was desperately trying not to panic because she knew that wouldn't help her situation in the slightest. She had stabbed two people. She had actually *stabbed* them—and that meant she had killed them. The poison from the dagger would do its work. Maybe it would be quick, or maybe it would be slow and agonizing. She didn't know. All she knew was that she had escaped. So why did she feel guilty?

She shook herself, shoving the feeling down. No. At least she wasn't a captive. At least she wasn't at the end of someone else's blade. Her eyes scoured the trees as the horse continued its walk, and all the while,

Octavia forced herself to take slow intentional breaths. She wanted to scream Azariah's name, but that would be as dumb as succumbing to the panic budding in her abdomen.

There could be more people in the forest . . .

Abruptly, her mind clung to pieces of the conversation she had overheard between the man and the woman. There was a third accomplice. Someone they were waiting for. Someone named Gregor. Had he been the one to deal with Azariah? Is that why Azariah hadn't come for her? Maybe they were both injured. Or maybe they were both dead . . .

Octavia pulled up on the reins to stop the horse so she could think. She needed to find their camp. She had to try and figure out what happened to Azariah before moving on. But how was she going to find her way back? She racked her brain for something to latch onto—any marker or identifier that would help her find the spot where she had slept. The only thing she knew for sure was that Azariah had made camp by the Kraven River.

"Think!" she scolded herself. There had to be more than that.

Her mind replayed the previous night, and she focused on when they had left Urtha. They had rode for thirty minutes along the Kraven river, and they had traveled . . . against the flow of the water. In all likelihood, her captors probably took her farther away from Urtha, which means if she rode *with* the flow of the river, she might find their camp again.

Maybe the blanket she slept with would still be there? She sent a prayer up to the *gods* that it would be. She turned the horse around and rode in the same direction as the water—back toward Urtha.

The entire time, she kept her eyes and ears sharp. In all honesty, she didn't know what she would do if she came upon more strangers. Probably spur the horse into a gallop, but if they had horses too, they could catch her.

"Stop it!" she snapped. "Just find the camp."

The minutes turned into an hour, then the hour turned into two, and the longer she searched, the worse the pit of dread in her stomach got, until she was absolutely certain that Azariah was dead.

She felt like she was going to throw up, so she quickly got off the horse and strode to the water's edge. Plunging her hands into the icy liquid, she splashed some of it onto her face to clear her mind.

Octavia went over her line of reasoning one more time: if Azariah was unharmed, he would have found her by now, so either he was hurt or dead. She had done her best to find him, but this forest was endless, and people were still after her. The fact was, she was now going to have to do this alone.

Fear physically choked her, and she splashed more water onto her face. It was an unbearable realization—and the worst part about it was the decision she would have to make. Should she go to Zoharth or should she go straight to the darkness itself?

She groaned, raking her hands through her hair. She didn't know how to get to Zoharth . . .

The only thing she knew was that if she kept following the Kraven River against the flow, it would lead her straight to Hritza. She laughed aloud. Was her lack of geographical knowledge really going to make the choice for her?

She got back onto the horse, pulling the creature around to start heading in the opposite direction of the flow. But right as she was about to kick the animal forward, something gave her pause. It was a deep gut feeling that had nothing to do with logic and also nothing to do with the key. It was almost like the *gods* themselves had whispered in her ear, though she heard no audible voice.

Octavia's eyes traveled across the pine-littered ground. Then her heart leapt. There, deep within the trees, nearly obscured from view, was the knit blanket she had fallen asleep on. It was dragged back into the forest, far enough away from the edge of the river where she could have easily missed it.

With a newly found focus, Octavia leapt from the horse, unsheathing the poisoned dagger from the inside of her boot. She crept forward, examining the ground. Blood was speckled into the dirt, and there were footprints. Enough to show that there had clearly been a fight.

She continued into the trees, leaving the white horse at the edge of the river. Every few steps there was more blood, and as she walked farther in, the blood grew copious. She felt like she couldn't breathe. Any second now, she was going to come across Azariah's body. She was sure of it. How could he possibly survive losing this much blood?

She stepped past a particularly thick pine trunk, and when she did, she had to stifle a scream. Two men lay motionless on the ground. It was Azariah and a stranger. She approached cautiously, her eyes raking over the scene. The stranger's chest was littered with stab wounds, and dark blood was smeared down his chin and over his neck. The empty look in the man's eyes told her he was dead.

Distress clawed at her chest, and she forced herself to look at the bounty hunter. His eyes were closed, and as she knelt to examine him, she didn't see any wounds. She sheathed the dagger, and then her hands crept over his chest, searching for an injury. She found none, and when the subtle movement of his chest rose and fell under her touch, she gasped.

He was alive . . .

Her fingers went to his neck, and a strong heartbeat pulsed beneath her touch.

"Azariah!" she said, now shaking him gently. But he didn't move.

It was then that she noticed white powder on him. Traces of it were in his long black hair and caked against his upper lip. Her mouth parted as her fingertips brushed the substance from his face. He had been drugged, and by the looks of it, the excess powder directly under his nose had been keeping him out.

But then . . . How had he fought and killed the man?

Octavia glanced down over her own clothing, and she found that residue powder was stuck to her as well. She swept it away, taking care not to breathe any of it in. Then she scoured her surroundings, checking to make sure they were alone. Once more, she examined the bounty hunter for any injuries—this time more thoroughly—but again, she found nothing.

"Thank you," she whispered to the *gods* in relief. She bowed her head over Azariah's chest, feeling his even breathing. She had woken up from the drugs, so it was only a matter of time before he did too. She would just have to wait. He was far too heavy for her to lift onto the horse.

Octavia pulled her dagger out again, standing to her feet. She would stay here and guard him until he woke up. He had protected her, and now she would protect him.

Two hours later, Azariah began to stir. At first, his eyes fluttered open. Then he started to twitch his fingers, and soon he was able to move his limbs. Octavia's heart ran wild with relief, and she crouched by his side, peering at him intently.

When he locked eyes with her, confusion lit his face. She gently helped him sit up, and his breathing became labored. He rubbed circles against his forehead, and then he tipped forward onto his hands, almost face-planting into the dirt.

"Woah!" she said, steadying him. "How are you feeling? Is the world still sloshing back and forth?"

All he did was groan.

"I'll take that as a yes."

She stood, walking to the white horse, which she had tied to a tree branch next to them as she had waited for him to come to. She dug through the stranger's saddlebag and pulled out a waterskin. When she returned to Azariah, she handed it to him.

"Drink."

He took the waterskin, tipping his head back to empty it. Then he wiped his upper lip, panting like a dog.

She stared at him, and then her eyes fell on the dead man who was still sprawled in the dirt. "What happened?"

Azariah blinked rapidly, and then his eyes closed for a moment. He looked like he might fall over, and even though he was still sitting, she put her arm against his back to keep him upright.

"Just breathe. It will wear off soon enough," she encouraged.

"I was keeping watch," he said, his voice cracking with gruffness. "There was a noise that came from the trees. Like a twig snapping underfoot. So I drew my sword . . . when . . ." He clutched his head within his hands. His words sounded slurred, the drugs still very much apparent in his mannerisms. He cleared his throat. "A man charged at me. We fought. He threw a powder in my face. I . . . I stabbed him, and then I saw more people. They took you, and I tried to . . ." His face pinched with frustration. "And then I woke up here."

Octavia let out a long and slow breath. How Azariah had managed to kill the man while falling under the influence of the drugs without getting a scratch on him was an honest miracle—and it only pointed to how experienced of a fighter he truly was.

"How did you escape?" Azariah asked. "Did they drug you too?"

She nodded, and she recounted her tale briefly, holding up the poisoned dagger as she finished telling the story. "Thanks for this. I don't know if I could have gotten away without it."

The way his brown eyes fixed on hers made her stomach squirm. He was still fighting the lingering effects of the drugs, but he had this focused energy in his expression that was undeniable. It was almost like he was thanking her for coming back for him with his gaze alone, though he didn't say a word.

"I almost couldn't find you," she said. "I followed the river back toward Urtha, and I nearly gave up, but right as I was about to leave, I felt . . ." she paused. She wasn't sure how to explain the overwhelming urge she felt to search the forest. She wanted to say the *gods* had led her back to him, but that sounded crazy. More and more, this deep unexplainable pull was welling up in her heart when it came to this man, and she didn't understand it. Octavia felt bonded to Azariah just like she felt bonded to the key—albeit in a completely different way.

"I just . . . I had to look one more time," she finished hurriedly.

"Well, thank the *gods* that you did. I would've had to collect another parcel of *waters* to find you."

Once more, it wasn't the words he said but the way he said them that pricked at her. His tone had settled back into business, and the grateful look on his face had vanished. What was wrong with her? Why was she feeling this stupid sense of disappointment? Why did she care how he looked at her?

"Are you hurt?" he asked.

"No."

"Good."

Azariah got to his feet unsteadily, and Octavia almost reached out to help him, but she held herself back.

"You stole a horse," he mused, nodding to the white animal.

"I also killed two people," she shot back.

A slight smile curled Azariah's mouth. "So you did. Do you know where our chestnut horse is?"

"No."

Azariah groaned, saying something about losing the dried meat, and Octavia's heart fell as well. If they didn't have any food, how would they make the journey through the long stretch of forest between Urtha and Vrelia?

But as the *gods* would have it, their provision abounded, because after a quick search atop the white horse, they found the chestnut one a mile down the river, and soon both Octavia and Azariah had their belongings in order and a horse each.

It felt strange. Having her own animal gave Octavia a new sense of freedom. But as Azariah turned them toward Vrelia and started their journey anew, Octavia had to remind herself that she was not free at all. And whatever she was feeling for this bounty hunter didn't matter, because their journey still had only one end for her: the darkness.

17

My Name Is Octavia

Their first day of travel was long and arduous. Azariah had them fill all of their waterskins to the brim because they were headed away from the Kraven River. The next body of water they would come across, according to Azariah, was Ash Lake, but that would be a three-day journey through the evergreens.

They rode at an alternating pace: a canter, and then a walk. Azariah was careful not to wear the horses out, but he was also keeping them moving. Always cautious. Always scanning the trees. But for the first time since the key melded to her palm, Octavia felt at peace. The people who had captured her had followed them out of Urtha. They had been close enough for the *waters* to work, but Octavia was sure that she would finally have a few days of rest. She and Azariah were far enough away from the kingdoms for the witch's spell to shield her. And although she didn't know the range of the protection, she felt it in her gut. For now, she wouldn't be kidnapped. Thank the *gods*.

As they traveled, Azariah kept quiet and focused. Octavia wanted to talk to him, simply to pass the monotonous hours of silence, but she couldn't think of anything to say.

Once more, loneliness swallowed her whole. Her heart ached for Bowan and Mama. She hoped Bowan was doing okay caring for Mama all on his own. The hardest part about this was the knowledge that Bowan probably thought she was dead. As for Mama? She had no idea if she was lucid enough to remember that Octavia had been captured by those evil men. And Papa . . .

She closed her eyes for a moment as tears stung them. She wanted to curse King Asa Draydon and Heston Creevy all over again. With the darkness moving, who knew what dangers Rustwick's army would come across—or who would perish as a result. She felt anger bubbling up in her chest, but Papa's words came to her mind: "Even though you can't control what happens, you *can* control how you react. You can."

She pressed her lips together, staunching her emotions as she continued to follow Azariah through the trees. So far, this whole experience had been one big test of Papa's words. Her circumstances were entirely out of her control, but she had done her best to navigate them. She *had* exercised control, despite everything, and in her heart, she had resolved to do what she must to end this.

After a grueling day on horseback with only a few quick meal breaks, Azariah finally had them stop in a small clearing with large boulders surrounded by dense trees. Octavia slid off the white horse, drained, and she stretched out her sore legs and hips.

The light of the sun was receding fast, and shadows were creeping across the forest.

"I can keep watch," Octavia offered upon noting the dark circles under Azariah's eyes. He looked like he was about to collapse from exhaustion.

"No, it's fine. You rest."

"No, it's not fine," she countered. "You look awful. Just sleep. I'll be okay." She folded her arms across her chest, staring him down. He looked like he was about to argue with her, so she continued. "I'll wake you if I need you. Besides, I don't think anyone can find me this far away from Urtha. I took the spell, remember? I'm fine."

To be honest, she was a bit nervous keeping watch, but she also knew that if Azariah didn't get some rest, then he wouldn't be able to protect her effectively. Even someone as skilled as him wasn't invincible.

Azariah combed a hand through his long hair, letting out a sigh, but then grunting in reply. "Fine. Don't fall asleep."

"I won't."

He strode to the chestnut horse, grabbed a rolled-up blanket, and sat against the flat face of a nearby boulder, leaning back against it and closing his eyes. He was asleep within minutes, his mouth slightly ajar and his breathing deep.

For the next two hours, Octavia killed time by pacing and eating a few strips of dried meat. She felt tired but awake enough. Azariah was the one who really needed the sleep anyway. After wearing her legs out, Octavia finally sat down with a blanket wrapped around her shoulders. She gazed at Azariah's face, studying him in the moonlight. He looked like he was at war with himself: a furrowed brow, a tensed jaw, crinkled eyes. Even in sleep he was on edge, like he could never truly rest.

A cool breeze tossed strands of Octavia's brunette hair across her forehead, sweeping a chill through her skin. She wished they could build a fire, but that wasn't going to be a possibility during the night. For now, the blanket would have to suffice in warding off the cold. The idea of her bed back home made her want to cry. How lovely would it be to go home? To have a hot meal, a full belly, and a soft pillow to lay her head on? To hug Bowan and Mama? To wake up to the sound of their voices again? To . . .

Octavia closed her eyes, pressing a fist firmly against her forehead. "Stop dwelling on them," she whispered to herself. "It's only breaking your heart."

Azariah stirred, but he didn't wake. The expression on his face now seemed more dire, and his breathing became labored. For a moment, Octavia wondered if she should wake him because it looked like he was having some kind of awful dream. Sweat clung to his hairline, and his lips moved, like he was repeating something.

Octavia stood and walked over to him. She nearly reached out a hand to gently shake him, but his murmured words stopped her.

"Rebekah." His brow furrowed deeper. "Rebekah . . ." Azariah's face had paled a considerable amount, and he was even more distraught. He was calling after someone, desperate for them. "Please don't do this! I can . . ." His words became mumbled and incoherent, but then they returned with force. "Don't take her. I beg you! Please!" Azariah's closed eyes were moving back and forth rapidly, and his body shuddered.

Octavia was momentarily paralyzed, watching the bounty hunter, unable to reach out her hand to wake him.

"Rebekah!" he cried out.

The way he said that name caused frisson to burst out across her entire body. Her heart jumped up into her throat, and she broke out of her hesitancy. Grabbing Azariah's vest, she shook him. "Wake up!"

Azariah startled awake, jumping to his feet so quickly that Octavia fell backward from her crouched position. Her wrists slammed into the dirt as she caught herself, and the blanket slipped from her shoulders. She winced.

"What happened!?" Azariah checked his surroundings frantically, but then, seeing nothing, he knelt in front of Octavia, wide-eyed and aggressive. His tone now turned demanding, and he shouted at her. "What happened? Are you hurt?"

She shook her head, a little stunned by his outburst. "No."

There was a beat of thick silence.

"Then why did you wake me?" He sounded annoyed.

"You were having a—" She almost said "nightmare" but decided against it. "You were dreaming. You seemed distressed. So, I decided to wake you."

Azariah swallowed hard, letting out a shaky breath. He rubbed his fingers against his right temple, closing his eyes for a few seconds. Then he extended his hand toward Octavia, who took it, and he helped her to her feet. His sudden gentle touch sent a spark zipping down her arm, and when his hand left hers, the lingering sensation gave her goosebumps.

"I'm sorry," he mumbled. "I didn't mean to raise my voice like that."

"It's fine," she said, brushing herself off. She peered at him in the dark, his face barely visible in the shrouded moonlight. She probably shouldn't ask this question, but it was burning in her like a fire. "Who's Rebekah?"

Azariah looked like she had slapped him, and immediately, she regretted saying anything at all. He took a step back, and his lips parted. She couldn't tell if he was angry or frightened or something else entirely. If anything, he looked like he might shout at her again.

She continued quickly. "I'm sorry. I . . . You were saying her name while you slept. You were—"

She stopped talking because Azariah seemed beside himself. He ran both of his hands through his long black hair, and then walked away from her, scuffing the dirt underfoot. He stayed quiet for nearly a minute . . .

When he spoke, it was barely louder than a whisper.

"It doesn't matter who Rebekah was."

Was? Octavia couldn't help but notice the tense—and she also couldn't help but notice the deep anguish that clung to Azariah's words. She felt an odd sort of desire to say something comforting, but she had no clue what she could possibly say.

When she first met this man, she had been scared of him, but now, he seemed more human to her than ever before. There was no denying it. Something haunted him. Whoever Rebekah was, Azariah had lost her. Maybe she was the reason he was a bounty hunter? Octavia wanted to know more.

She proceeded cautiously, steering the conversation in a new direction. "How long have you been doing this? Bounty hunting?"

Azariah's eyes snapped to her, and she could feel heat crop up in her cheeks from the intensity of his gaze. "Why does it matter?"

"Because you just . . . you don't seem like the kind of person who would be a bounty hunter," she replied.

There. She had found it—the words she had been searching for in The Turquoise Drops when she had first started this line of questioning.

"You don't know anything about me," he said stiffly, now striding back over to her and towering above her. He was so close that his breath tickled her face.

"You're right. I don't," she admitted. "But . . ."

Octavia hesitated. Her mind moved back to the man in the washroom. How he had grabbed her, how he had tried to have his way with her, and how Azariah Ronan had flown into a blind rage and killed him with the declaration of "She is *mine*." She remembered the way Azariah had trembled afterward, the way he had stared at her with watering eyes . . .

She had to ask.

"Back in the washroom at The Turquoise Drops, you said, 'she is mine' when you stabbed that man." Octavia spoke softly, now fully giving in to her curiosity. "Why did you say that? What happened to you back there?"

"I was protecting you. That man was going to violate you. You're my bounty."

She shook her head. "It was more than that. You became someone different. Like you were out of your mind with the thought of him touching me. Like you . . ." Her breath hitched. "Like you care about me."

Azariah snatched her upper arm, and she gasped.

"It doesn't matter what happened in the washroom," he growled.

Octavia wrenched herself from his grip, now abandoning her soft tone for a fierce one. "I think it does. I'm not just some bounty to you, am I?"

Azariah seemed unable to respond, but then his lower jaw stiffened, and he gritted out his retort. "Yes, you are."

"There's something more," she insisted. "Something you're not telling me."

Azariah moved with uncanny speed. In a flash, he grabbed her wrist with iron force and pushed her back a few paces. Then he spoke with a dangerous venom. "You are nothing more than a package to be delivered to King Bastian Jasper. Do not mistake my kindness or leniency for affection. I don't care about you, I care about *delivering* you." His mouth pursed, and she could feel him shaking. "I don't even know your name, Keyholder. Nor do I want to. You don't get to talk to me as if we're equals. You don't get to question me. And you don't get to make demands of me. I am not obligated to tell you *anything*!"

Octavia's chest was heaving. Defiance curled in her stomach while anger and frustration stormed in her chest. He had reduced her to an object—a package, not a human being. And it cut at her emotions in a way that stung far worse than any physical blow. He still clutched her wrist so hard it hurt, but she gritted her teeth through the pain. Then she said something she thought she never would . . .

"My name is Octavia." Her eyes stung as she glared at him. "Now maybe you could look at me like I'm a person instead of a package. I'm not simply the key!"

Once more, she wrenched herself free from his grasp, and this time, she walked away from him. She stooped to the ground, picked up her discarded blanket, and then marched to the boulder where Azariah had been sleeping.

"Now, if you don't mind, I think I'll get some rest. You can keep watch."

She slammed her eyes shut, leaning back against the stone. She didn't want to sleep. In fact, she didn't think she *could* sleep because of how angry she felt. But she also didn't want to engage in any more conversation.

Azariah didn't say anything more for the remainder of the night, and soon, despite the coiled up threads of anxiety from their heated exchange, Octavia was able to catch a few hours of rest. Azariah gently woke her an hour before dawn, murmuring how he would like to get more sleep as well before they left, to which she begrudgingly agreed. Then he curled up and slept until the sun was fully risen above the horizon.

The morning chill had seeped into her from the long night, and she had taken to pacing back and forth again to keep her body warm. Once Azariah was awake, they both ate a quick meal of more dried meat and dried fruit, then they mounted their horses to continue on their way.

It was another strenuous day full of riding and silence. Azariah didn't want to talk, per usual, but the way he ignored her was more poignant this time. Their conversation had clearly disturbed him down to his soul, and Octavia wished she understood why, but she knew she wasn't going to be able to pry more information from him. Rebekah had been someone he cared for deeply—that much was apparent—and Azariah had lost her. What her fate had been? Octavia had no idea.

She couldn't wait to get to Ash Lake, simply for the pleasure of taking a bath. Octavia was beginning to smell, her skin was salty with sweat, and she had started her monthly flow. She had never freely bled before, but she had no rags to use, so blood had soaked through her pants. Thankfully, the fabric was dark and thick, but it was uncomfortable. Octavia also thanked the *gods* that she wasn't sharing a horse with Azariah.

Even though they had one more day to go before reaching the lake, she kept her complaining to herself. She tried to occupy her mind with the beauty of nature, but her thoughts would spiral in the silence of their travels.

Azariah's words were playing on a loop in her head. She did her best to try and staunch them, but all she could hear was him saying: "I don't care about you. I care about *delivering* you."

Stupid. Stupid. Stupid . . .

Octavia viciously reprimanded herself for caring about what he said at all. It shouldn't bother her. It would be smart of her to carry the same cold exterior that he did, even though deep down, his words made her want to cry.

This was puzzling. She couldn't comprehend why she felt any sort of attachment in her heart toward this man. Perhaps it was because she had been forced into spending so much time with him. Or maybe it was because he had saved her from real danger more than once. Whatever it was, Octavia knew she had to shut these inadvisable feelings down. Azariah had made himself perfectly clear: she was a job to him. Nothing more. And whatever sentiments she carried for how he viewed her didn't matter. They were a fabrication of her circumstances, she told herself. That was all.

Still, the way he had put her in her place so harshly twisted loneliness into her like a knife . . .

The key burrowed deep into her left palm made her feel less human. It was a glaring truth to confront, but the reality was, from here on out, people would see her only for what she carried and not for who she was.

It wasn't fair. She was no longer Octavia Fletcher, daughter of Theodin Fletcher, Rustwick's wealthy and fortunate wheat overseer. She was Octavia Fletcher, Keyholder, savior of all the lands—or at least, she would be if she survived long enough to get to the darkness.

On the final day before reaching Ash Lake, Azariah stopped them for a midday meal. Octavia desperately wanted to use some of the water in her last waterskin to clean off her pants and legs, but drinking it was more important than being clean. She would just have to wait for the lake.

They sat down on the ground and ate in silence, but this time, Azariah kept glancing at her over and over again. He seemed perturbed—and possibly even a little upset. She was about to snap at him to stop staring when he finally spoke.

"It was unfair of me to say what I did," he murmured. "You're right. You're not simply the key."

Octavia's eyes met his, and she stopped chewing on the handful of raisins she had thrown into her mouth. Was he . . . apologizing?

Her heart leapt in hope at the thought. Maybe he would actually *talk* to her now. It would certainly make their travels more bearable. Octavia never knew how badly she craved basic human connection until this experience had deprived her of it. She waited, desperately hoping he would continue, but he seemed at war with himself.

A furrowed brow, tightened lips, stiff shoulders . . . All of this made him appear deeply troubled—like speaking to her was unimaginably painful. She didn't understand it. What was wrong with him? Why couldn't he just *say* something?

Octavia waited for a few more seconds, but when Azariah

remained quiet, she got to her feet, a fresh skewer of frustration digging at her. It riddled her body like an illness.

She couldn't take his silence. She couldn't *take it*!

Letting out an exasperated hiss between clenched teeth, Octavia turned her back on the bounty hunter and stormed away. She left her horse behind. She left everything behind. She didn't have the intention of running away from Azariah, but she *did* want to get space from him—if only for a few minutes to slap some sense back into herself.

He was her captor. Her *captor*.

He didn't owe her anything, and she shouldn't expect—

A strong hand clamped over her upper arm, and Octavia spun around to face Azariah, who had gotten up from the ground to come after her.

"I'm not trying to escape you!" she yelled, pulling against him sharply. "Let go of me!"

To her surprise, he immediately did. Octavia didn't wait for a reply. She promptly continued storming away from him. She needed a moment. Just a minute to—

"Octavia."

Hearing her name from his lips stopped in her tracks so suddenly that her breath caught in her throat. A bolt of nerves shocked through her insides, and her mouth parted. With clammy hands and a falling feeling in her stomach, she turned toward him. Slowly. Hesitantly. And when their eyes met, it caused her chest to tighten.

Azariah wore a look of deep reverence and remorse. Even his posture was respectful.

He let out a few long breaths, and then said, "Please."

The word was so soft that it broke something in her. It felt desperate. It was a plea that begged her to listen. A beat of silence passed between them, but this time, Azariah didn't succumb to his quiet and withdrawn nature. He spoke. And he did so deliberately.

"I'm sorry for what I said. I don't know how you became the Keyholder, but what I *do* know is that you hold a sacred position—one that I do not take for granted. I am a man of faith, just as you are a woman of faith." He gave her the smallest dip of his head as if to acknowledge her. "You are blessed by the *gods.*"

Octavia didn't know what to say. She didn't feel blessed by the *gods*. She felt cursed.

He continued with a sober and courteous tone. "Yes, I am taking you to Zoharth, but I also understand that this is bigger than King Bastian claiming the Well of Eternal Healing. *You* are the one who will save us. Not him."

He paused, seeming to gather himself.

"Please forgive me for reducing you to nothing more than the key. I shouldn't have done that."

Octavia blinked, wondering if she had just imagined his apology, but by the regretful expression on his face—and the fact that he had come after her—she knew that this was very real.

Azariah's tone softened even more. "I'm sorry we had to meet under these circumstances, Octavia. I truly am."

Once again, the use of her name stole her breath away. Azariah's vicious words from the night before came rushing back: "I don't even know your name, Keyholder. Nor do I want to."

Her name.

She had finally given it, and he had finally chosen to use it.

Hearing it broke through some of the loneliness in her spirit, filling her heart with something she couldn't decipher. It shattered the feeling of being reduced to an object, and it gave her strength.

For a moment, she didn't know what to do with herself, but then she plucked up the courage to speak. With her heart in her throat, she decided to use his name also. "I'm sorry too, Azariah."

18

Reputation, Masks, and Other Such Strings

On the third day after Urtha, when Ash Lake slunk into view in the distance, Octavia spurred her horse into a gallop, overtaking Azariah. The instant she got to the water's edge, she flung herself in. The cold felt refreshing on her grimy skin, so she dove under the surface, feeling her hair soak through to her scalp. The dried blood from her flow began to flake off under the water, and Octavia itched to tear her clothes off. She swam farther from shore, peeling her pants off under the water and scrubbing them out to clean them. She also dunked her head again and again until she felt like her hair was sufficiently rinsed.

After struggling to get her pants back on underwater, she swam back to shore, sopping wet, but clean. She strode over to Azariah, who had dismounted, and the feel of the crunchy pebbles beneath her feet made her wobble a little.

"Can I borrow your dagger?" she asked.

Azariah raised an eyebrow. "What for?"

She could feel her cheeks flush with embarrassment even though she had no reason to feel embarrassed. "I'm going to cut a few pieces of fabric off my blanket. I can't use my poisoned blade for this. I'm tired of bleeding through my pants, and now that I'm clean, I'd like to stay that way."

He handed her the hilt of his dagger, and she took it, moving back toward her horse. She carefully cut a few strips of fabric from the end and then returned the blade to Azariah. Then she strode off into the trees that hugged the lakeside to put a strip of cloth into her undergarments in private.

The sun was setting, and even though she was still soaking wet, Octavia was so happy to be clean that she didn't mind bearing the chill of her damp clothing.

When she returned, she saw that Azariah had set up their camp at the edge of the trees, situating their saddlebags by a clump of gnarled roots. The horses were both drinking from the lake, and when they were done, they took to grazing along its border, ravenously eating the mossy plant life. The poor creatures . . .

Octavia sat next to Azariah, huddling in her blanket, and as he stared out at the lake, so did she. It was beautiful in the falling light. Peaceful and quiet. And for a moment, Octavia didn't feel like she was on a dangerous quest.

"Do you know the story of how Ash Lake got its name?" Azariah asked, not tearing his gaze away from the glassy surface.

He sounded pensive, and Octavia was surprised that he had initiated the conversation.

Since he had apologized to her, Azariah hadn't been talkative, but he also hadn't completely shut down her attempts to converse. It was a welcome change, and she would take what little interaction he was willing to offer her.

"No," she replied. "How did it get its name?"

"They say the Kingdom of Hritza burned so badly as the darkness swallowed it that the ash from its destruction carried on the winds all the way down to this lake. And its waters turned black like tar, killing all the life in it. The ash here was so thick that it covered the lake and buried all the trees. Death. That's what this place was."

Octavia searched the lake, and the beauty of it seemed to sharpen. The way the trees reflected off the water, the way the air smelled so fresh and crisp, the way fish bumped against the water's surface, causing tiny ripples to form . . .

"It's so beautiful here now," she said. "I don't see any trace of death."

"A thousand years is a long time," Azariah commented. "Time has a way of healing all things. But I suppose time is now the enemy, isn't it . . ."

The darkness crept to the forefront of her attention, and Octavia recalled the nightmare she had prior to entering Urtha. In her mind's eye, the tendrils of black shot across the earth toward her. Octavia shivered. She had felt certain that the nightmare had been real, but she had held herself back from telling Azariah. Now she felt the urge to share it.

"Before Urtha, I had a dream," she said. "The darkness was growing across the ground like a weed. It wasn't simply moving as a wall." Her stomach clenched. "I have a bad feeling that things are about to get much worse. For everyone. I don't know how much time we have left before the darkness reaches the nearest kingdom. Zoharth, Vrelia, and Xadia are all close to the darkness, and . . . what if . . ."

She swallowed hard, dread filling her to the brim. Then, an idea came to her—a wildly frightening one, but a logical one nonetheless. She locked eyes with Azariah, and even though she didn't want to say the words aloud, she did anyway.

"Take me to Hritza. We don't have to go to Zoharth to stop the darkness. I can walk through it on my own, and not in the name of any kingdom as their prisoner."

Azariah's eyes lit with something she couldn't decipher, then his gaze hardened. "No. I'm taking you to Zoharth."

She felt her stomach drop. "But . . . don't you want to stop the darkness? Isn't that the point of all of this?"

He didn't respond.

"Is it the money? Is that what you care about? Getting paid for me?"

She could see his lower jaw working, like he was grinding his teeth, but still, he said nothing. She stood, and the blanket fell from her shoulders. Irritation was now coursing through her as she peered down at him.

"You said that you understood this was bigger than King Bastian. You know *I'm* the one who will have to save us! Why draw this out? The end is the same. I have to walk through the darkness to try and stop it, so why waste time? What if we can't even get to Zoharth before the darkness starts killing people? What then?"

Azariah stood. "You swore to the *gods* that you would go to Zoharth."

"Don't turn this around on me!" she shot back. "Answer the question."

"I am *nothing* if not my word. I am bound by it, just as you are by yours."

Octavia scoffed. "So you made a vow to King Bastian that you would bring him the Keyholder?"

"No."

"Then what?" She threw her hands up. "Why can't you take me to Hritza?"

Azariah's composure snapped, and his cheeks darkened. "I have a reputation to uphold, and I will not let *you*, of all people, destroy it!"

"And what *is* your reputation, Azariah? What do people know of you? What do they expect from you?"

Azariah appeared to restrain himself from grabbing her, like it was taking all of his willpower not to lash out. His voice grew more dangerous. "I have never failed in capturing a bounty or carrying out a kill, and I am not about to start with *you*."

Octavia glared at him. "So this is about keeping a perfect record?" She laughed out loud, and she couldn't help the mocking intonations of it. "The darkness is going to start swallowing kingdoms whole, and you're worried about some stupid tally of keeping score?"

Her words ignited a fire in him, and this time, he *did* grab her. His fist clamped over her upper arm. "You are *dangerously* close to overstepping my tolerance, Keyholder! I do not have to explain myself to you, and if you don't shut your mouth, I will not hesitate to treat you like the prisoner you are."

Anger boiled in her like a storm. She knew she was still his prisoner—and he knew she would not run away—so threatening her with that felt like a slap in the face. So much of her wanted to yell at him. To push him further. To demand answers. But her gut was telling her stop, and this time, unlike the Rebekah incident, she listened.

She clamped her mouth shut and glowered at him. His grip on her upper arm slackened, and then he released her altogether.

Silence hung between them. They were both still staring at each other, and she resolved to not look away until he did. It was her way of still arguing even though he had forced her to stop. Finally, Azariah broke her gaze, turning away from her to sit back down in the dirt.

Octavia did the same, settling down criss-crossed and tracing a pattern into the dust with her finger just to give herself something to do. But in her mind, she was wild with wondering about the mysterious bounty hunter who clearly had a secret he was unwilling to voice.

Like a bad habit, Octavia's mind replayed Azariah's words. *I will not let* you, *of all people . . .*

Her? Who was she to him? Certainly she was more than simply the Keyholder. His retort felt personal, and the mystery dug at her conscience like a branding iron. She was so frustrated she wanted to scream.

"Can I sleep first?" she asked, her voice barely audible.

Azariah nodded, but he didn't look at her.

She chewed on her lower lip, snatching up her blanket from the ground. She threw it around her shoulders and then picked a spot by the base of a pine not too far off.

This was going to be another extremely long night.

The remaining three days of travel between Ash Lake and the Kingdom of Vrelia passed in a blur of riding, sleeping, and acutely sparse conversation.

Unfortunately for Octavia, her decision to question Azariah had prompted him to stop speaking to her all over again. And it just felt so . . . personal.

It wasn't worth the struggle.

Octavia had resolved to put away her curiosity concerning Azariah, because once she got to Zoharth, they would part ways, and it wouldn't matter anymore. It was simple, really: the more she made herself care, the worse that moment would be. From the beginning of this forced partnership, she had known that it would end with Azariah handing her over to King Bastian. She wasn't sure what delusion had come over her to think that Azariah would ever deviate from his mission, and it was foolish of her to try and get him to.

Dwelling on the puzzle that was Azariah Ronan would do nothing for her. Instead, she should be dwelling on the fact that she was about to belong to a far crueler man—one who likely wouldn't release her even after she walked through the darkness. She needed to think about what surviving *without* this bounty hunter would look like.

It was this depressing line of thought that filled Octavia's mind to pass the time, and when she and Azariah finally came upon the outskirts of the kingdom that housed the Well of Beauty, Octavia stopped thinking about King Bastian Jasper and turned her mind to the task at hand.

Azariah slowed his horse so that he rode next to Octavia. She glanced at him, noting how tired he appeared.

"We're going to make this visit quick," he said. "I'd rather not stop in Vrelia at all—for your sake—but we don't have enough food to make it to Zoharth. We'll restock our supplies, feed and water our horses, and be on our way. I can buy you a new blanket, if you wish."

Octavia had been cutting pieces from her blanket for days while she finished bleeding, and now it was much smaller and didn't keep her as warm as she would like.

"Yes, that would be nice," she said quietly. "Thank you."

He dipped his head ever so slightly. For a few moments, the only sounds between them were the horses' hooves pawing the dirt, but then Azariah cleared his throat. "Do you know in Vrelia, people wear masks."

He didn't make the statement with an insulting tone, but Octavia could feel her face grow hot with annoyance anyway. She felt like a child, being quizzed on general kingdom knowledge—like when Azariah had asked her if she had been taught about the *gods* growing up.

"Yes, I know they wear masks."

"Do you know why?"

She ran her tongue along the inside of her teeth. She didn't, but she also didn't want to admit it. "A cultural thing?" she offered half-heartedly.

Azariah's mouth curled with a slight smile. "Well, yes. But in Vrelia, it's the law."

Octavia raised an eyebrow. "It's the law to wear a mask?"

He nodded.

This piqued more than a few questions in her mind, and she asked the first one that came to her—albeit, probably not the most important one. "Do you have masks for us to wear?"

"No, but upon entering the kingdom, Vrelia's watchmen provide travelers with them. We will each put our own unique markings on our masks."

"Why is it the law?"

"It's so people can tell each other apart."

Octavia was so confused. She stared at Azariah, wondering if he was playing a joke on her, but if he was, he didn't break the facade. If anything, he was as serious as ever. "Doesn't a mask do the opposite of that? A mask hides someone's identity. By definition."

"It's because of the Well of Beauty," Azariah explained. "Do you know what happens to someone when they consume the *waters*?"

Octavia frowned, feeling exasperated at the seemingly obvious question. "They get more beautiful."

"Yes, they do. But like everything, beauty has its limits *and* its price. For those who consume the *waters* over and over again, they've chosen to sacrifice themselves at the altar of appearance, and in the end, it costs them their face."

Octavia's alarm increased, and sweat gathered on her palms. "What does that mean?"

"Most of the people who live in Vrelia all have the same face. The Well of Beauty has converged their features into perfection. Perfect symmetry. Perfect eyes. Perfect jawlines. Down to the smoothness of their skin. All of it is the same. And that's why it's the law to wear a mask, because everyone must be able to be differentiated. The markings a person chooses for their mask is what makes them unique—and not their actual face."

An uneasy feeling settled in Octavia's stomach. The idea that the Well of Beauty could steal a person's features over time was both horrifying and fascinating, and it intrigued her more than she cared to admit.

The two of them approached the outer wall of Vrelia. Unlike the previous kingdoms, the entrance was guarded. Masked sentries dressed in rich golden fabrics stood in front of a tall golden metal gate. It was an incredibly beautiful sight to behold, and as Azariah brought his horse to a halt, two men walked forward to greet him. Their masks covered only the upper half of their faces, and immediately, Octavia could see how their mouths and jawlines were identical. Even their stature and build were nearly the same. The only thing that set them apart was their masks. One man's mask was painted with intricate swirls of ruby and bejeweled with deep red stones as dark as blood. The other man's mask was adorned with blue feathers, silver rhinestones, and royal blue silk sewn into a ruffled pattern around his nose.

"Do you wish to enter Vrelia?" the man with the blue-feathered mask inquired, peering up at Azariah.

"Yes."

"Do you and your companion need masks?" His dazzling eyes landed on Octavia, and she was immediately struck by their stunning beauty. They were gold like the sun itself. She had never seen such eyes. And when she looked at the guard with the bejeweled ruby mask, she noted that his eyes were also gold.

"We do," Azariah said.

With a deep bow, the blue-feathered man nodded to the ruby man, and the gates swung open. Azariah and Octavia followed the blue-feathered man into a small courtyard sectioned off by high white walls that blocked the city of Vrelia from sight.

To the left of the courtyard, there were a dozen golden tables with cream-colored eye masks—hundreds of them all set out into neat rows. And to the right, there were more golden tables, but these held every decoration, paint, and fabric a person could wish for. Rhinestones, feathers, gems, powders, costly metals, silk flowers, linens, inks, sharp-tipped quills, ribbons, twine, glues, colored parchment, needles and thread . . . it was an abundance to feast the eye upon.

The blue-feathered man cleared his throat. "Before entering the city, you must make a mask. Your mask is your identification and must be worn at all times. Failure to do so will result in your arrest and expulsion from the city. Every mask is cataloged—even for travelers passing through. Please," he said, sweeping his hand in a grand gesture. "Select a mask and create your unique markings."

Azariah dismounted, and Octavia followed suit. They led their horses to the far side of the courtyard and then approached the golden tables that held the eye masks. They were all the same, so Octavia selected the first one she saw. It was made of a malleable substance that felt like rubber, and fabric straps were attached to either side.

"It is customary to take your time creating a mask," Azariah murmured to her. "Vrelians see it as a sign of respect, because something beautiful cannot be rushed. I will not ask you to hurry, but bear in mind that our stay here will be short."

With that, he walked away from her to select a mask of his own.

When Octavia approached the tables of decorations, she went straight to the paints. She wasn't an artist by any means, but all she could think about was home, so over the next thirty minutes, Octavia took a paintbrush and carefully inked yellow stalks of wheat onto her mask. It was a bit messy, but when she was done, she felt quite proud of it, and a pang of homesickness pricked at her. The fast-drying colors set quickly, and Octavia put the mask over her eyes, tying it behind her head and double knotting the straps to ensure it wouldn't fall off.

She had been so consumed with painting the wheat that she had momentarily forgotten about Azariah, and when she looked for him, he was standing by their horses, already wearing his mask. He had painted it silver, and on the forehead, there was a twisted band of gold outlined in black. It looked like a ring. The design, while simple, was stunning, and she couldn't help but stare at it. It was the kind of looped symbol that looked like it had taken practice to perfect.

The blue-feathered man took note of each of their masks, writing on a scroll that he had slipped out of his garments.

"Both simple yet elegant designs," he said.

He motioned to an attendant who was standing nearby. The girl hurried forward, her golden skirt swishing about her ankles. Her mask was sunset orange and looked like a cat's face with whiskers and pointed ears.

"Please see to it that these travelers' horses are boarded in the stables."

"Yes, sir," the girl said with a bow.

She took the reins from Azariah and promptly led the two horses across the courtyard to a door in the outer wall. It opened to reveal a cavernous stone hallway, and then the girl disappeared within, taking the animals with her.

Octavia glanced at Azariah questioningly.

"Animals aren't allowed inside," he replied. "The streets in Vrelia are kept clean. Cleanliness is a virtue in Vrelia. We will retrieve the horses when we leave."

"Oh," Octavia said with a nod. She was about to ask why Azariah hadn't grabbed anything from the saddlebags, but just as she opened her mouth, she spotted a bag slung over his shoulder, so she said nothing.

"The Kingdom of Vrelia welcomes you to its *waters*," the blue-feathered man said. "May the beauty of the *gods* bless your eyes and bless your bodies. Safe travels."

And with that, Azariah and Octavia walked past the high white wall blocking Vrelia from view. When they rounded the bend, the sight that met Octavia's eyes was overwhelming.

The streets were glassy and shone so brightly in the morning sun that they appeared to be made of gold. The rich beauty of the symmetrical architecture was stunning too. Everything was sharp and right-angled, piercing to the eye and alluring to the spirit. The structures were made of a sheer reflective material so that everywhere a person looked, they could see themselves.

Fountains made of citrine—a golden-yellow crystal—were interspersed down the grand street, and weaving in between them were glass sculptures of faces. Each sculpture emphasized a different feature: the lips, the eyes, the nose, the jawline, the cheeks . . .

It was bizarre yet enticing.

Everywhere Octavia looked, charm and glory filled her senses. From the golden garb that people wore to the shimmering reflections of the glassy street to the myriad of intricate masks, Vrelia dripped in glamor. This truly was the most beautiful kingdom of them all. Vrelia was like walking on the sun with the stars dancing around you—and she thought Urtha had been a sight to behold.

"Octavia."

Azariah's voice snapped her out of her wonder. He had walked ahead down the glassy street and was a considerable distance from her.

She hadn't even noticed that she had stopped in her tracks to gape at everything.

"Sorry," she said, jogging to join him.

"Stay with me. It's easy to get distracted by this place."

That was quite the understatement. Octavia felt like she could sit here and stare at *this* street alone for hours on end and not get tired of its beauty.

She kept by Azariah's side, but this didn't stop her from taking in the kingdom. The people walking the streets glanced up at them as they passed, their golden eyes dazzling, and Octavia couldn't help but stare. Their masks—which were decorated in every conceivable way—made each of them stand out despite their eerily similar physiques.

And there was another thing she noticed about them. Nearly everyone's skin was shimmering. Once Octavia was able to get a closer look, she discovered why. Sand-sized flecks of gold were glittered across people's forearms and necks, as if it had been applied with a salve. It made them look as glorious as the *gods*.

"Let's stop in here," Azariah said, gently brushing Octavia's arm. He pointed to a shop called Famous Fabrics.

When they entered the small boutique, the scent of soap and citrus hung in the air. A woman with a black and white flowered mask approached them, her golden eyes flashing with delight.

"Welcome! What can I help you with?" she asked sweetly.

Azariah peered around the racks of decadent clothing. "Do you have a warm blanket we could purchase?"

"Of course." The woman directed the two of them toward the back wall where racks of woven fabrics were stacked as high as the ceiling.

"Are you two visiting Vrelia to get away? A little break from life?" she asked, eyeing Octavia. "I can recommend some of our must-see sights! The Fountain of Gold in front of the palace is a marvelous place to start. And you can get gold-dipped figri at the Glamours Bakery there!"

"Figri?" Octavia repeated.

"Oh, it's a type of cookie, dear," she said warmly.

"We're just passing through," Azariah said. "But thank you."

"Ah, I see." The woman slid a delicate finger over her black and white flowered mask. "Well, if you ever plan to stay here in the future, the figri is to die for! I highly recommend it."

"Sounds amazing," Octavia replied. The idea of actually visiting here again temporarily distracted her from the reality of her situation. It would be lovely to take a break from life and bask in the glory of Vrelia, but unfortunately, that wasn't something Octavia could do . . .

She slid past Azariah and approached the back wall. The first blanket that caught her eye was silver. It was stunning, and she was drawn to it, but it wasn't the most practical blanket. So she opted for a thick amber one that was soft to the touch.

Azariah paid for the blanket and then escorted her from the shop.

"Are the fabrics washed in the *waters*?" Octavia asked. For a moment, she imagined sleeping with the amber blanket and waking up the next morning with smooth and rejuvenated skin. She had never been the kind of girl who obsessed over her appearance, but the idea of getting a boost from the Well of Beauty teased at her sense of vanity.

"Probably, but it's not the fabrics that carry the beauty that consumers seek. It's the creams," Azariah said. "Vrelia sells a cream called Balm. It's one of their most coveted products. A parcel's amount of Balm costs the same as a hundred bushel's worth of wheat back in Rustwick."

Octavia nearly choked. She stared at Azariah, aghast. "A parcel of Balm costs more than six thousand pounds of wheat? Why would it cost so much?"

"Balm is made by distilling the *waters* from Vrelia's Well into a concentrated form. It's a highly effective cream, and when applied to the skin, it helps mitigate aging. Youth is beauty, and beauty is youth. And that's something people will pay for. Balm is one of the reasons that Vrelia has maintained its relevance in trade despite its small size. That, and its geographical position between Zoharth and the other kingdoms. Travelers from Zoharth pass through Vrelia often because no one wants to travel over the outlet that extends from Jagged Gulch Lake. They would be too close to the darkness of Hritza in that direction."

Octavia tried to picture the locations Azariah had mentioned. All she knew was that Zoharth was almost completely surrounded by water.

Something about this felt comforting to Octavia. The loud silence of the past few days was now forgotten, and Azariah had slipped back into his more conversational self, which, Octavia realized, only really happened upon entering a new kingdom. It was like he took joy in teaching her.

After stopping by a few more shops to gather food, they were ready to leave the dazzling Kingdom of Vrelia behind. They had only been there for a few short hours, but it was enough to make Octavia wish she could spend more time exploring the golden sights. Everyone here had been so welcoming and so kind . . .

But the key underneath the glove weighed heavy on her heart, and she knew that delaying their journey wasn't an option. Perhaps it was the witch's protection spell, or simply provision from the *gods*, but no one cast a suspicious eye toward Octavia, and no one seemed threatening. Maybe she and Azariah truly *would* have safe travels all the way to Zoharth.

Octavia whispered a quick prayer of thanks up to the heavens for their continued safety, and as they walked along the glassy streets that shone like the sun, a strange peace filled her heart.

It didn't take any time at all to reach the other side of Vrelia. Compared to the immense size of Urtha, Vrelia was a blip—a beautiful little jewel in the vast forest that surrounded it.

Azariah directed them toward the stables, where they collected their horses and packed up their things. Then the golden gates at the exit of the city swung wide, and the golden-eyed people masked in shades of exquisite beauty bid them farewell.

Once more, Azariah and Octavia rode side by side in the afternoon sun. Azariah kept staring at her. She could see him out of the corner of her eye. He held a sort of somberness that hadn't been present when they had entered Vrelia.

"It's another five days to Zoharth," he said softly.

Anxiety twisted in a coil around her stomach. She didn't want to go, but she also didn't have a choice, and she knew that bringing up the conversation of traveling straight to Hritza wouldn't be a good idea.

"I suppose you'll be glad to be rid of me," she commented.

Azariah didn't respond, and when she looked at him, he appeared miserable. It was an expression she was coming to know well, for he had borne it a few times along this journey, and it drove her mad with wondering. She simply couldn't shake the feeling that there was so much more to this man when it came to *her* than she would ever know. Why would he look at her like that? She almost opened her mouth to ask him another personal question—to prod him for answers—but she stuffed the desire down.

It didn't matter.

It couldn't matter.

It shouldn't matter.

More and more, Octavia felt an invisible string tugging at her heart, tying her to Azariah, pulling at her emotions in a way that was confusing and frustrating . . .

Whatever she was feeling concerning the idea of parting ways with him was something she was going to have to snuff out.

She gave her horse a swift kick forward, hoping that by creating some physical distance between herself and the bounty hunter that it would help to create a distance in her heart too. But just as the white horse began to canter, a wild rustling sounded from the trees all around them. Abruptly, dozens of people on horseback emerged from the pines, surrounding them.

19

Two Bounties for the Price of One

Octavia pulled hard on the reins, her heartbeat slamming against her ribs like a cannon. These people had to be soldiers—she could tell from their dark red garb and their metal breastplates. They continued emerging from the trees until there were easily sixty men, and all around them, swords were being pulled from sheaths. Azariah drew his own sword, bringing the chestnut horse in front of Octavia's white horse, but deep in her heart, she knew he could do nothing to protect her. There were simply too many men.

A bald man with a thick gray mustache and a terrifying scar cutting across the right side of his face rode forward from the small army. His piercing gray-blue eyes landed on Octavia, and then his lips split into a cruel smile as he pointed a parcel of *waters* directly at her chest. There was a violent flash of blue. Then he tucked the parcel into his crisp dark red vest.

"Hello, Keyholder," he crooned. He gave a quick nod to his men. "Restrain them."

The horde on horseback closed in, and though Azariah attempted to fight them off, it was of no use. Octavia's horse was pulled away from Azariah's, and then hands grabbed her, sliding her off of the animal. She screamed, twisting and kicking, but she was quickly subdued.

Two men firmly gripped her upper arms, pulling her hands together in front of her. Metal cuffs with heavy chains clamped over her wrists, and her stomach dropped as panic overwhelmed her. Then they searched her for weapons and found the poisoned dagger in her boot, confiscating it.

There was grunting and shouting. Octavia's eyes landed on Azariah.

He was still putting up quite a fight, but the skirmish ended abruptly as a heavy blow landed on the back of Azariah's head, causing him to crumple to the ground. The moment he fell, the men around him swarmed, kicking him over and over again.

"STOP IT! STOP! Don't hurt him!" Octavia shrieked, straining against her captors, but they were incredibly strong and held her in place.

The bald man's attention snapped to Octavia, and he held up a hand. His voice came out loud and harsh. "I said restrain him, not kill him!"

The mob dissipated at the command, and the brutal beating stopped. As the soldiers hauled Azariah up, Octavia could see that his lower lip was split open and bleeding profusely. He was also gasping, as if he couldn't get a deep breath in. Chains clinked around Azariah's wrists, and two large men forced him to stand, holding him steady as the bald man dismounted to approach the scene. He walked up to Azariah with a strange look on his face that caused the deep red scar to pull taut. It was bone-chilling. Then his lips parted, and his gray-blue eyes grew unnaturally wide.

"Take his mask off," he instructed.

Azariah's mask was torn from his face, and the deafening silence that followed this made Octavia's skin turn to ice. For several seconds, the bald man couldn't speak. He simply gaped at Azariah. But then a sick pleasure crept over his features, replacing his shock.

"Azariah Ronan," he said in a slippery voice. "As I live and breathe."

Azariah launched himself at the bald man, and the soldiers restraining him nearly toppled to the ground. They managed to keep their grip, however, and a few sharp blows landed on Azariah's ribs, causing him to double over and gasp.

One of the men holding Azariah nodded up to the bald man. "Pierre, you know him?"

Pierre traced his fingers over his thick gray mustache, a frightening look of pleasure befalling him. "Yes, I know him. We're rather well acquainted. Aren't we, Azariah?"

Azariah gritted his teeth with a rage Octavia had never seen before. He looked like he would enjoy nothing more than to rip into Pierre's neck with his teeth.

"*You* have the Keyholder?" Pierre mused, glancing back at Octavia. "In the name of what kingdom, may I ask?"

Azariah spat in Pierre's face, and once again, he nearly pulled himself free from the soldiers restraining him. More blows landed, and Azariah fell to his knees in the dirt. Pierre slowly wiped the saliva from his face, peering down at Azariah with an amused smile.

"Let's see what we've got here," he said.

He strode over to Octavia, and his rough hands yanked the mask away from her eyes. She gasped at the force he used, and when her mask was gone, there was once again a look of pure shock that radiated his face. Pierre stared at her like he was unable to believe his eyes, then his gaze landed back on Azariah. He looked between the two of them several times.

"*She's* the Keyholder?" An impish grin split his mouth so wide that all of his teeth showed, and a dark laugh escaped his lips. "Oh my . . . this must be absolutely *killing* you, Azariah. The *gods of old* are surely playing with you."

Octavia's heart was pounding so hard she was starting to feel weak. What was Pierre talking about?

"Well, well! This is my lucky day, boys!" Pierre shouted, causing Octavia to jump. "Two bounties for the price of one: Azariah Ronan and the Keyholder." His cruel eyes roved over Octavia, and he grabbed the chain that linked her wrists together. Pierre yanked her forward roughly and turned her around, pinning her up against his body so that her back was to his front. His right arm snaked around her waist, and his left hand curled across her neck. Octavia gasped as Pierre gripped her in the invasive embrace. The sudden and forced closeness caused her to freeze up. She did her best to hold back a whimper, but this man was scaring her *far* more than any of her previous captors.

"What do you think, Azariah?" Pierre buried his nose in Octavia's hair, inhaling deeply. "Shall I have my way with her too?"

"If you touch her—" Azariah began with a growl.

Pierre gripped Octavia tighter. "You'll do what? Kill me?" He chuckled, pulling Octavia back a few paces, his nose still lingering against her hair. "You already had your chance, Ronan. You won't get another."

Abruptly, Pierre released Octavia and shoved her back toward the soldiers who had held her before. They clamped their hands over her arms. Pierre's frightening gray-blue eyes bored into Octavia's, and he cupped her chin.

"In the name of King Joda Akoni, you now belong to the Kingdom of Xadia, Keyholder."

Octavia's heart seized. This was the bounty hunter's home

kingdom—the one that housed the Well of Costly Metals. Azariah had a bounty on him? For what?

Pierre's gaze landed back on Azariah, and an evil smile split his face. "As for you, Azariah. You now belong to *me*."

Pierre gave a sharp whistle and threw his pointer finger up in the air.

"Let's move, boys! Back to camp. And keep your eyes *sharp*. We don't want to lose our precious little Keyholder." Pierre took his hand and slowly stroked the side of Octavia's face. She shrunk back at his touch, a shudder running across her skin.

Azariah let out a strangled yell. "Pierre, I swear to the *gods*—"

One of the men struck Azariah full across the face, and the blow echoed through the trees. Azariah grunted, spitting blood on the ground from his split-open lip.

"Gag him," Pierre instructed. "Put him in the wagon. I want four men guarding him at all times. Do *not* underestimate him!"

More men surrounded Azariah, and they hauled him away through the trees until Octavia couldn't see him anymore. Her breath came out rapidly, her hearing turned fuzzy, and stars flickered around the edges of her vision. Her body felt numb as Pierre issued another set of instructions to the soldiers surrounding her.

Then Pierre's face was in front of hers, and her hearing turned sharp again.

"And you, my dear," he crooned with a delighted grin. "You'll be riding with me."

Pierre swung himself over the top of his red-brown horse, and the two men holding Octavia hoisted her onto the creature so that she was sitting in front of him. Pierre hooked his left arm around her waist, and with his right hand, he gripped the reins. With a swift kick, the horse launched into a gallop, spurring them through the trees and away from Vrelia.

Complete panic swallowed her whole, and tears welled in her eyes. She sucked in a jagged breath as wind whipped at her face. Pierre didn't relinquish his fierce grip on her, and all around them, dozens of horses thundered in a chorus. There was no getting out of this. Whatever was about to happen—whether they planned to kill her or use her—she now belonged to the Kingdom of Xadia.

Her mind whirled, not only from the peril of her situation, but also from the exchange she had witnessed between Pierre and Azariah. How did the two know each other? What dark history was coming into play here? What could Pierre have possibly meant by the *gods* playing with Azariah? Her stomach clenched as her mind turned to another part of the conversation: Pierre's threat of having his way with her.

The very idea spiraled her panic deeper. She felt ill, and stomach acid pushed its way up her throat. She nearly turned her head to the side to vomit, but a hard swallow held the sick back.

They rode at the breakneck pace for nearly twenty minutes before slowing, and even then, Pierre kept the entourage moving. Octavia couldn't count how many soldiers were around her, and though she searched the group, she didn't see Azariah. There was, however, an open wooden cart pulled by two horses bringing up the rear—and given Pierre's instructions, Azariah was probably within.

She felt like she couldn't breathe. The thought of Pierre doing something horrible to Azariah scared her just as much as the thought of him doing something horrible to her. The way her heart beat wildly within her chest, the way her mind went crazy with anxiety, the way she felt like she wanted to scream Azariah's name . . .

Never in her wildest imaginings did she think she would actually care about the bounty hunter. But she did. Somehow, through all of this, Azariah had made her care. And that scared her to death.

It took all of her self-control to keep from falling apart. She knew she needed to calm down, think, and keep her head on her shoulders if she was going to have a chance of surviving this. And so, despite every effort of her body fighting against her, she slowed her breathing, grounded herself in her mind, and resolved to somehow escape.

They rode for hours, the sun hot overhead. Octavia's tongue grew dry with thirst, her stomach rumbled with hunger, and her wrists ached from the chains. Eventually, the trees began to thin out, and in the distance, Octavia could see an open expanse of desert with an encampment. There were hundreds of tents set up, horses penned in corrals, and fire pits burning everywhere. Smoke rose up into the air in wafts.

Octavia's heart dropped into her gut. There was no denying it. This was Xadia's army, and even though she didn't know exactly where she was, she was sure that the darkness itself was close by. Why else would all these people be camped here if it wasn't for the purpose of claiming the Well of Eternal Healing in Hritza?

"Welcome to your new home, Keyholder," Pierre whispered in her ear. A sharp chill flew down her spine at his grating voice. "Xadia will forever be in your debt soon." Pierre then called back to his men in a loud voice. "Secure our extra guest at the stake. Keep him guarded!" His lips returned to Octavia's ear. "As for you, my dear. I have somewhere *special* in mind."

Pierre led them into the encampment down a long row of tents. Upon entering, all eyes were on her. Some were curious, while others were leering. Octavia kept her chin held high and didn't let the fear she was feeling show on her face. Her expression remained cold and hardened even though inside she was a mess.

Up ahead, past another two dozen canvas tents and three fire pits, there was a much grander tent, and it was dark red. It looked like it belonged to the commander. It was easily four times as large as the surrounding tents, and out front, there was an awning propped up by wooden poles that had been dug into the ground.

Pierre led his horse up to the dark red tent and dismounted. He grabbed Octavia's chained hands and pulled her down after him. A teenage boy with curly black hair and dark brown skin hurried from the tent.

"Commander Zarqel," he said with a bow.

"Take my horse to the corral," Pierre instructed.

"Yes, sir."

The boy grabbed the reins of the red-brown horse and scurried away. Pierre, keeping a firm grip on Octavia's chains, marched her into the tent. The inside was lavish, furnished with a deep red settee, six wooden chairs set around a wooden table, a woven red rug, and a cot. In the back right corner of the tent, there was a large metal stake sticking out of the dirt, and attached to it, there were more chains. Wrist cuffs just above waist level. Ankle cuffs at the base. With barely any chain length from the stake to the cuffs to allow for much movement.

Octavia swallowed hard as Pierre led her to the stake. His gray-blue eyes never left her brown ones as he unlocked her current cuffs and then pushed her up against the stake so that her back was touching the metal. He shackled her wrists first and her ankles second. His stare was so piercing that it stole Octavia's breath away.

Just as in the forest outside of Vrelia, Pierre gazed at her like he couldn't believe his eyes. He ran his fingers over his gray mustache, scrutinizing Octavia from head to toe. Then he got close to her. Uncomfortably close. And a disgusting smile crept across his mouth.

"Let's start with something simple," he said. "My name is Pierre Zarqel, commander of Xadia's army. What's yours, Keyholder?"

Octavia didn't answer. Instead, she turned her head away from him, but this didn't stop the rot of his breath from trailing into her nostrils.

"Oh, come now," he cooed softly. His hand went to her chin, forcing her face back toward his. "What's your name?"

"Rot in the darkness," she hissed.

Pierre's smile only deepened. "My, my . . . this truly is *uncanny*." He relinquished his grip on her lower jaw, backing up a few paces to examine her again. She felt so vulnerable simply because of how fiercely he was staring at her. Octavia also had no idea what he meant—and she was too afraid to ask.

"Where is the key? On your body?" When she didn't answer, he raised an eyebrow and swept his hand forward. "I could undress you to check."

"My left hand!" The chains that bound her to the stake gave her just enough room to grasp the glove on her left hand and pull it off.

Pierre grabbed her palm to gaze at the key. It was dazzling to behold, and it reflected like the sun even in the shelter of the tent.

"I'll make you a deal, Keyholder." His eyes lit with desire. "You answer my questions, and I won't kill the bounty hunter."

Her lungs felt like they had been stabbed, and her hands began to shake. She pushed a false confidence into her tone.

"I don't care what happens to the bounty hunter. He was my captor."

"You didn't look like his prisoner," Pierre commented.

"Well, I was."

"I think you're bluffing." He cocked his head to the side, his scar pulling at an odd angle with his toothy grin. "I think you care. In fact, I'm *betting* on it." He withdrew a curved dagger from his hip and twirled it between his fingertips. "How did you get the key?"

Octavia's heart pounded, and her eyes traced the edge of the blade. Why would Pierre ask her something like that unless he wanted to take the key for himself? If she relinquished the information, there would be nothing to stop him from killing her, and the thought of dying terrified her.

"Very well," Pierre said, striding away from her toward the tent flaps. "I'll return with the bounty hunter's finger. I can draw this out as long as I need to."

"Wait! Don't!" Octavia was unable to hide the desperation in her voice.

Pierre turned, a wicked look flashing across his face. "That's what I thought. Tell me how you got the key."

Octavia's mind moved quickly. She knew she was going to have to come up with something to survive this—and fast. Then an idea came to her. A stupid, stupid idea. She tried to come up with another one, but her mind had already latched onto it, and so, with her heart in her throat, she ran with it.

"Can I make you a deal too?"

Pierre laughed. "You are at *my* mercy, dear. There is no deal but my terms and mine alone."

Octavia held up her left palm. "But I am blessed by the *gods*. Surely you know that. You wouldn't be foolish enough to pass up an opportunity to gain the wish?" She looked at him like he was stupid, and she hoped that he would buy it.

Pierre faltered for a moment, then his eyes narrowed. "What wish?"

"The one that only the Keyholder can grant," she said as if it were obvious. "I am enlightened by the *gods*, and because of that, they have given me a wish to bestow on anyone I choose." She again peered at him as if she were shocked that he didn't know this information.

From his expression, she could tell that she had piqued his interest . . .

He approached her cautiously. "What deal, Keyholder?"

"In exchange for the wish, a question for a question," she said. "Only the truth from both of our lips—and if you harm the bounty hunter, I will not grant it to you."

He seemed to ponder the offer and displeasure visibly curled his lips, but then a power-hungry look replaced it—one that turned Octavia's stomach. He slipped the dagger back into the sheath at his hip, and a small moment of relief flooded her. She had ensnared him with the lie.

He pulled up a chair so that the back of it faced Octavia, and then he straddled it, his imposing stare skewering her. She could scarcely believe her luck.

"Very well, Keyholder. Let's talk."

20

A Question for a Question

The air in the tent was stifling and thick with tension. This was a dangerous game, but she would play it to save them both.

"I'll start." Pierre ran his tongue over the top of his lip like he would love nothing more than to ravish her. "What's your name, Keyholder?"

She couldn't staunch the shiver that flew down her spine. Deep in the pit of her stomach, a horrible feeling dug at her. This man was probably going to do a lot more to her than simply ask her questions . . .

"My name is Octavia."

"Octavia," he repeated lustfully. "How pretty."

"How do you and Azariah know each other?"

Pierre scratched his chin and gave a dark chuckle. "That's quite a question in exchange for your name."

"You're the one who chose to ask for it," she asserted coldly. "A question for a question. That's the deal."

Pierre's upper lip twitched in agitation, but he relented, giving her a stiff nod. "Indeed."

He stood from the chair and turned his face to the side, displaying the thick scar in full, which went from his chin, up his cheek, to the back of his skull. Pierre then unbuttoned the front of his red vest and pulled up his dark shirt to expose his chest. Three deep slash marks ran from his collarbone, down his abdomen, to his hip.

Octavia sucked in a hasty breath at the sight. It was ghastly.

Pierre dropped his shirt down to cover the scars. Then he swept his hands out, palms open to the ceiling of the tent. "Azariah Ronan was once Xadia's finest metalsmith. He crafted weapons using the costly metals mined with Xadia's *waters*. King Joda Akoni gave him three months and a thousand parcels worth of costly metals for a large custom order of weapons. I was in charge of the pickup, but when I arrived with my men, I discovered he had stolen the costly metals instead of using them to fulfill the order. He had traded the metals for an impressive stock of *waters* from all the kingdoms. When I confronted him about it, he gave me these scars. That's how we know each other."

Octavia's stomach churned. Azariah had stolen from King Joda and attacked Pierre when confronted about it? She immediately wanted to ask him more.

"My turn," Pierre said, now buttoning up his vest. "How did you get the key?"

Octavia's heart began to race. Giving him the full answer to that question would be a death sentence—she was sure of it. The hungry look in Pierre's eyes said it all. She clenched her teeth, resolving to avoid the root of the question for as long as possible. "A man came out of the woods while I was fishing and attacked me. He was . . ." She stopped herself. Mentioning blood might lead Pierre to ask her about blood magic—if he knew anything about it at all—so she decided to keep that to herself. For now. "He died in front of me. Then there was this bright light, and the key came out of his shoulder and went into my palm."

Pierre didn't look satisfied with her answer, but just as he was about to open his mouth, Octavia spoke again.

"Back in the forest outside Vrelia, you said there was a bounty on Azariah. For what? Stealing costly metals from King Joda?"

Pierre's upper lip curled with anger. "For murder. Azariah murdered all of my men that day. He's wanted by the king." Pierre's hand went to his face, and his fingertips traced the horrific scar. "And by me as well. I survived. Barely. It's been a *long* three years." His last statement sounded savage, riddled with bitterness and wrath.

Octavia's eyes widened. She didn't know Azariah well, but something in her spirit told her there was more to this story than Pierre was letting on.

"Tell me about the wish," he said, a creeping excitement in his voice. "What may I wish for?"

"There are only three things I cannot grant," Octavia replied quickly. "I can't bring back the dead, for they belong to the *gods*. The wish cannot touch the darkness. That is also the prerogative of the *gods*. And finally, there is only *one* wish. You cannot wish for more." She tilted her head, looking at Pierre, and then pulled enticement into her tone. "But anything else is within my power. Money. Fame. Prestige. Even a long life."

Pierre chuckled. "I don't want any of that."

Octavia almost asked him what he *did* want, but she couldn't waste a question like that. This was a match of wits, and she had to keep her edge. "What did you mean when you said the *gods of old* must be playing with Azariah? That this must be killing him?"

Pierre's already toothy grin widened, and he leered at her. "So many questions about the bounty hunter. How *interesting*."

Abruptly, he approached Octavia and slid his right hand behind the base of her head, gripping her hair. She sucked in a harsh breath, but she couldn't back away from him. The thick metal stake and the chains wouldn't let her. Pierre then put his mouth up to her right ear slowly, his nose brushing up against her temple. He whispered with a vile glee. "You look *so* much like her."

Octavia tried to push Pierre away, but the chains pulled taut at her attempt, and this only seemed to fuel his fun. He tightened his grip, keeping his body pressed up against hers.

"You have her fiery spirit too."

She stifled a whimper. She could feel Pierre's hot breath against her face as he gripped her. "I look like who?"

"Rebekah," he whispered. "Azariah's dead wife."

Octavia's mouth parted, and Pierre pulled back to gaze into her eyes. He seemed to relish in her shock. The hand that he had hooked behind her head slid away, and then he brought it to her chin, his thumb tracing her bottom lip.

She shrugged her face away from his touch, her heart pounding all the way up into her ears. The revelation was like a physical blow radiating through her body, and so many of the pieces from this insane nightmare fell into place. The way Azariah looked miserable when he stared at her. The way something about this had always felt personal. The way he had fiercely protected her over and over again . . .

His wife. His dead wife. She felt like she was going to be sick.

"I believe it's my turn again," Pierre mused. "Six days ago, something strange happened. The *waters* I was using to track you went dark. Our hunting party lost the blue glow at Urtha. How is that possible?" He peered at her intently. "Something Azariah did?"

She had to force herself to breathe because she was still so shocked from Pierre's previous answer. "I took a protection spell from a witch. Azariah collected a parcel of *waters* from each Well for the potion, and six days ago, I drank it." She was careful not to give too much away. She needed to prolong this conversation for as long as possible so she could think of a way out of her lie. Because once Pierre realized the wish wasn't real, she would be in serious trouble.

"But the *waters* clearly still work on you," he commented. "Explain."

She shook her head. "It's my question now."

He sneered at her, still maintaining his intrusively close stance.

"How did Rebekah die?"

At this, Pierre's already devilish countenance morphed into something bestial, and pleasure splayed across his face. "Azariah was too *weak* to protect her from me. Just like he's too weak to protect *you*."

Octavia's lungs constricted. What did that mean? This conversation had now turned far darker than she had bargained for. A deep, primal urge to run overtook her, and she pulled at the chains even though she knew it would do her no good. Every part of her being was screaming at her to get away from this man. Her legs started to shake. She felt like she was going to burst into tears, but she couldn't show Pierre any weakness. He seemed to feed off it. She had to maintain some level of control.

"Now, explain the witch's protection spell. How does it work?"

She pursed her lips. "When I'm close enough to a vial of *waters,* it will shine blue. But if I'm too far away, the spell shields me. I don't know the distance. But that's why you couldn't track me."

Pierre furrowed his brow. "Clever."

"What are you going to do with me?" she asked. There were so many more questions she wanted to ask, but if she was going to continue to lie her way through surviving this, she needed to know outright.

"That depends," Pierre said.

"On what?"

He let out a long breath, and his covetous gaze landed on her left palm. "How do *I* get the key?"

Octavia swallowed hard. She knew it—he wanted the key for himself. But if he killed her, the darkness might kill them all. No matter what, she could not tell him about the blood magic and how it worked. For the sake of everyone in the lands, she had to come up with something compelling to explain why he couldn't take the key. An unnatural calm descended upon her even though her body was still working hard to push her into panic.

She was the Keyholder. She was blessed by the *gods*. And maybe she didn't believe that when Azariah had said it to her, but she had to believe it now. She didn't have a choice.

"You can't get the key. I am the last Keyholder."

Pierre's expression darkened. "Do not play me for an ignorant fool! The key *can* and *will* have a new master, and you will tell me what I need to know to gain it, or I will gut your precious bounty hunter like a pig and make you watch!"

"You will not touch him!" she snarled, pulling at the chains again.

Pierre scrutinized her, cocking his head to the side. "Tell me, Octavia, if you were Azariah's bounty—his prisoner, as you say—then why are you so protective of him? Why do you care?"

Her heart felt like it was being squeezed to death. Her lips parted, but she didn't know how to answer his question . . . because it was the same one she had been asking herself through all of this.

"Surely you don't have feelings for him?" Pierre offered.

A spike of anxiety drove its way through her chest, and the silence between them stretched on.

Pierre's mouth widened with cruel delight, and he raised an eyebrow. "Or do you?"

She shook her head. "I don't."

"Oh my . . ." Pierre simpered, now pulling the chair back toward himself and straddling it again. He peered up at her, and the amusement in his expression was bone-chilling. "Oh, but this is *too* good. You have feelings for him?" He threw his head back and laughed. It was a mocking, mirthful laugh that made her skin crawl.

"I don't have feelings for him," she said, but the confidence in her voice was gone. "I just don't want you to hurt him."

"DON'T LIE!" Pierre barked. He threw the chair out of his way, and it toppled over on the dirt. He approached her, getting in her face, and she gasped. "You yourself said it, Keyholder. Only the truth from both our lips!"

Her heart was ramming itself mercilessly inside her chest. She needed to calm down. She had to keep her head. Once more, an unnatural calm swept over her. She needed to placate him, even if she wasn't sure if the words she was saying were true or not.

"Fine," she gritted out. "I have feelings for him. But I couldn't tell you why even if I wanted to."

Pierre looked beside himself with glee. It saturated his face. "Oh, the *gods* have surely favored me today!" His eyes raked over her body, then his hand caressed her chin. He spoke softly, but with deep hatred in his voice. "He will *never* reciprocate those feelings. You know that, don't you?" His stare pierced her. "Rebekah broke him."

Octavia tried to pull her face away from Pierre's touch, but he dug his nails in. "Now, let's continue our little game, shall we, Octavia? How do I get the key?"

"It's not your turn!" she snarled.

He growled at her, moving his hand down to her neck and squeezing. It wasn't tight enough to choke her, but it was tight enough to pin her up against the metal stake. "You're avoiding the question, and my patience is wearing thin! I'm going to ask you one last time, Keyholder. How do I get the key?"

Octavia locked eyes with Pierre and sneered. "You can't. I already told you. I'm the last Keyholder." Her brain moved quickly, and in her heart she sent a prayer up to the *gods* to give her the strength and cunning to pull this off. "*I* am the one who must walk through the darkness, or there will be no one to walk through it at all. That's why it's moving—it started when *I* got the key."

Pierre paled significantly. His mouth parted, his eyes grew wide, and his grip on her neck vanished. He backed away from her. "*You* caused the darkness to start moving?"

"Yes!" She pulled a bit of history into her lie. "The *gods of old* are tired of humanity's greed, and they've decided to take back all the Wells of Power with the darkness. If something happens to me, or if I choose *not* to walk through the darkness—which I *can* do—then everyone will die. The *gods of old* are ending this with me."

Pierre looked like he had been stabbed. The fear on his face was palpable, and for a few moments, he was unable to speak. Octavia's heart was racing in her chest. Pierre clearly didn't know the timing of the last key transfer—and he clearly also didn't know the words of the prophecy—because he was buying this. On top of that, Octavia had no idea *why* the darkness had started moving in the first place, but it was close enough to her gaining the key for the lie to work.

Pierre took a hard swallow. Then he seemed to pull himself together, his demeanor turning sinister once more. He stayed quiet for nearly a full minute as his fingers brushed his mustache. His lower jaw tensed and relaxed repeatedly. Octavia could tell he was working something out in his head. It was almost as if she could see the glory he craved falling through his fingertips—the imagined fantasy of being the Keyholder himself, the savior of all the lands, gone. Her lie had scared him, and for now, her lie had saved them all.

"Very well, Keyholder," he breathed. "Here's what's going to happen.

The rest of Xadia's forces will arrive by the end of the week. And when they do, we will march up to the darkness, and you will walk through it in the name of Xadia."

She could scarcely believe her luck. She had gained herself some time. And somehow. Some way. She was going to use it to escape Pierre. With all that burned inside her, she wanted to walk through the darkness in the name of no one. The Well of Eternal Healing, if she was able to unlock it at all, shouldn't belong to one kingdom. It should belong to them all. But she needed to be careful to appease the man who held her captive.

"And now," Pierre continued. "My wish?"

Octavia's stomach dropped. The wish. The stupid wish. Her brain worked furiously to latch onto another lie. Time. That's all she needed.

"What is it that you wish?" she asked, peering at him, now donning false confidence like a cloak. "You said you don't want prestige or money or fame? What do you want, Pierre?"

A wicked smile played on his mouth. "Revenge."

A jitter flew through her body at the way he hissed the word. She pressed her lips together to hide how her mouth quivered. "On whom?"

His evil delight deepened. "On Azariah Ronan."

It took all of her self-control not to react to this. She schooled her features, keeping her face passive. "What do you wish?"

Pierre approached her again, and his hands went to her waist. He pulled her up against his body until the chains yanked taut, and he crooned into her ear. "I wish for Azariah to relive his wife's death. Over and over again. Like a waking nightmare. Until he *begs* me for death himself. And right before I grant him that, I will tell him *you* were the one who allowed him to relive it."

Sick threatened to push its way up her throat at the vileness of his statement. She locked eyes with him, still playing the part of the all-knowing Keyholder blessed by the *gods of old*.

"To bestow the wish, you, being the vessel, must purify yourself. First, you must fast for two days, emptying your body of earthly sustenance. It shows your willingness to rely on the spiritual sustenance of the *gods.* And you must commit your mind to prayer, emptying it of earthly ties and seeking after the things that are from above. At the end of your fast, you must drink a parcel of *waters*—any parcel will do. Only then may I bestow the wish."

Everything in Octavia wanted to shove him away from her. His hands against the back of her waist, his invasive presence, his foul breath . . . it made her want to vomit. But she didn't shrink away. She took a centered breath and said in a commanding voice, "You will do nothing to the bounty hunter, even after the wish. I swear to the *gods*, if you kill him, if you even *touch* him, I will not walk through the darkness in the name of Xadia."

Pierre's eyes gleamed with lust, and he licked his lips. He let out a long breath, like he couldn't believe her gall. "You are quite a force, aren't you? I do enjoy my women passionate." Octavia shuddered in his grip, now starting to panic. He was getting far more aggressive with his hold on her. His fingernails dug into the clothing at her hips. Then his mouth went to her neck, and he kissed her, his teeth nipping at her skin.

"You are to remain pure for two days, or I cannot grant the wish!" she gasped. "Purifying yourself is not just about fasting. It's about the body *and* the mind. The wish is sacred. Do not think you can mock the *gods* and still receive it! You must commit to this. Two days. That is all."

Pierre looked like he wanted to yell at her, but he gritted his teeth, restraining himself. His hands left her waist, and he backed away, giving her a sweeping bow, though his eyes still feasted on her like he wanted to rip off her clothes.

"Very well, Keyholder. I will do the fast and purify myself. Then you will grant me my wish, and I will enjoy every minute of it. Azariah deserves to rot in the darkness, but all your fighting for him has made me realize something, Octavia." His terrifying grin grew. "Keeping him alive is going to be much more satisfying than killing him. You have my word. As the *gods* are our witness. I will not harm him. And you, my dear, will walk through the darkness in the name of Xadia."

"As the *gods* are our witness," she repeated. "So shall it be."

Pierre's gaze pierced her one last time, and then he turned his back and strode out of the tent, leaving her chained there in a stunned silence.

21

Absalom

Immediately, Octavia began to hyperventilate. She sank to the ground, and her arms were pulled above her head by her wrists, the chain length not long enough to permit her to comfortably sit. Stars danced across her vision, her lungs hurt, and her tongue was so parched that it felt like sandpaper. She had done it. She had bought herself two days. And she had saved Azariah.

Tears formed in her eyes, and she was unable to stop them. One slipped down her cheek and into her mouth. For a few minutes, all she could do was cry. She did it silently, her chest shuddering and her body shaking, and when she had calmed down enough to see clearly, she pulled herself up to a standing position again to allow the blood to flow back into her numb hands.

How was she going to escape this? What would Pierre do to her when he found out that the wish was a lie? Would he have his way with her? Kill her? Would he torture Azariah? The horrible thoughts flew through her mind at unsettling speeds, and the urge to vomit returned full force. She turned to the side and threw up in the dirt. Barely anything left her stomach because she hadn't eaten all day, but the burning sensation was strong in her throat and nose.

What chilling nightmare had she found herself in? Bargaining for the life of the man who had kidnapped her, falling between Pierre and Azariah's dark and deadly history, bearing the resemblance of Azariah's dead wife . . .

So many pieces collected in her mind like a storm. She didn't have the whole story—she was sure of it—and she wished she had asked Pierre more. Why would Azariah attack Pierre and kill an entire group of King Joda's guards? What was Rebekah's true role in this?

Octavia inspected the cuffs at her wrists, pulling at the chains to test them. She tried to slip her hands out, but the metal dug into her skin. Even if she could get her wrists free, her ankles were chained too, and there was no way her feet were going to fit through.

She didn't know what to do. The noises of the encampment wafted through the tent flaps: the low murmur of conversation, the occasional clank of metal, the crackle of fire pits, the snorts of horses . . .

Octavia stood there, numb. Time passed like molasses, her mind ran weary with escape plans that had no merit, and the tent grew hot underneath the desert sun.

When late afternoon hit, abrupt and cacophonous cheers roared through the camp, causing Octavia to jump. It sounded like the voices of at least a hundred soldiers. Jeering. Cursing. She couldn't make out anything intelligible, but it was clear that something was happening beyond the tent flaps.

Octavia's stomach plunged all the way to her toes. Azariah. What was Pierre doing to him? Pierre swore he wouldn't harm the bounty hunter, but she had a twisted feeling that he had lied.

The taunting and shouting lasted for only a few minutes longer, and she strained to hear something of use, but she couldn't. She felt helpless.

"Please, protect him," she whispered to the *gods*.

It was the only thing she could say . . .

As night approached, the sunlight that shone through the canvas material of the tent dimmed. Her stomach ached with hunger, and her mouth now felt like the desert. Still, no one came in to see her. Pierre hadn't returned, and she wondered how long he would leave her here. Her legs were shaking, not only from hunger, but also from the strain of standing for so long. She wanted to sit, but every time she had attempted to, the pain in her arms and wrists from being forced above her head was too much to handle for more than a few minutes at a time.

Soon, it was completely dark, and with no lamps to light the tent, Octavia couldn't see. The only thing she could keep her eye on was the tent flaps because the light from the fire pits beyond was filtering through the slit.

She kept telling herself: don't panic. But the hungrier she got, the weaker she felt, and panic began to creep in anyway.

With a parched throat, she plucked up the courage to call out. "Hello?" Her voice came out strangled. She needed to be much louder if she was going to get anyone's attention. She tried again. "Hello?"

Octavia waited a few seconds and then tried again, raising her voice even higher. Footsteps scuffled from beyond the tent, and then a figure silhouetted by firelight peered through the flaps. She couldn't see their face, but from their outline alone she could tell it wasn't Pierre.

"Can you get me some water?" she asked the stranger. "Please? I haven't had anything to drink all day. Or anything to eat."

The stranger stood there a moment longer, but then the flaps of the tent closed back to a sliver, casting her into the dark.

"Wait!" she called out. "Come back!" She yanked the chains in her frustration, and tears welled in her eyes.

She let out a shaky breath. How long could she keep herself together under these conditions? Escape wasn't going to be an option for her mind to ponder if all she could think about was how famished she felt. She stood there in the dark, feeling the beat of her heart in her chest. It was like a booming drum. She wanted to dissolve into tears. She felt the build of it in her throat—the desire to scream.

The tent flaps opened again.

The stranger was back, and Octavia's spirits leapt in hope. There was a flash of flint, and then a lamp was lit. Octavia stared at the newcomer. It was the teenage boy she had seen earlier—the one who had taken Pierre's horse from him when they had arrived. The lamp light flickered off his dark brown skin, dancing through his curly black hair. He set the lamp on the wooden table and then walked up to Octavia.

She retreated a step, feeling the metal stake at her back. The teenage boy was staring at her with a sense of wonder. The gleam in his deep brown eyes was reverent and marveled. He gave Octavia a deep bow and spoke to the ground at her feet.

"You are truly blessed by the *gods*. It is my honor to meet you, Keyholder. To stand in your presence."

He raised his gaze up toward her, and she blinked several times, unsure of what to say to such a formal greeting.

"I . . ." she faltered. "Can I have some water?"

He gave her another bow—this one smaller than the first—and then he walked over to the table. He grabbed a metal pitcher and a tin cup, pouring her some water. Then he returned to her and offered her the tin. Octavia took it and downed the whole thing in a few seconds.

"Can I have more?"

He obliged, filling her cup again. She emptied every last drop. Then he took the tin from her, placing it back on the table with the pitcher. The way he was staring at Octavia was focused and poignant. From his face alone, she could tell that he was truly awed by her.

"Can you get me a chair?" she asked, nodding to the one Pierre had knocked over earlier in the day. "The chains won't let me sit on the ground."

The boy approached the chair, pulled it upright, and then dragged it over to her. Octavia did her best to move out of the way so he could place it against the metal stake, and when the chair was situated, she dropped into it, relief flooding her shaking legs. Her wrists were still pulled up to a degree, but they were at her shoulders now instead of pulled up above her head.

"Thank you," she murmured, peering up at him. "What's your name?"

"Absalom," he replied. "Is it true? Are you going to walk through the darkness in the name of Xadia?" He seemed unable to hide his excitement. "The soldiers say that we might have all perished if Commander Zarqel hadn't found you when he did. Praise the *gods* we have you."

Octavia swallowed uneasily. "Yes, it's true."

Absalom's eyes were wide. Innocent. Even though he looked older than Bowan, there was something about his spirit that reminded Octavia of her little brother, and a deep ache for home tore through her.

"What is it like to be enlightened by the *gods*? You must feel so close to them."

Octavia nodded. "It is truly wonderful." The lie tasted foul in her mouth, but there was no room for morals trapped under Pierre's thumb. With all her heart, she wished she *was* enlightened by the *gods*. At least then she would understand what was happening with the darkness.

Maybe this boy could be the key to her escape. They had only interacted for a few minutes, but she could already sense his dedication to the *gods*.

"Where's the man Pierre brought here with me?" she asked. "The bounty hunter."

"He's chained to a stake at the center of camp," Absalom said.

"Is he—" Octavia's tongue felt stuck to the roof of her mouth, choked out by fear. She collected herself with a slow breath. "Is he unharmed?"

Absalom nodded.

Relief flooded her limbs, and she rested her head back against the stake. Pierre had kept his word. For now.

"Will the Well of Eternal Healing truly belong to humanity again?" Absalom's face lit with hope. He seemed to burst with joy at the very thought.

Octavia peered at him gently, and the ache in her heart grew stronger. What was this pious boy doing in the service of such a cruel and wicked man? "That is the hope."

Absalom lowered his eyes to the dirt at her feet. He clenched his hands together and spoke in a wavering tone. "May I see the key?"

He lifted his gaze to hers sheepishly. Octavia took her left hand, which had been balled up in a fist, and opened it wide, showing off the sparkle of the key.

Absalom's mouth parted, and he stared at it with wonder. The look of amazement in his face was so pure—so undefiled and selfless. Then his eyes shone with tears. "I never thought . . ." he began, his voice thick with emotion. He wiped his eyes and cleared his throat. "Forgive me."

Octavia couldn't help the nurturing nature that rose up in her. "It's okay."

Absalom ran a hand through his curly black hair, pressing his lips together. "I never thought there'd be a chance for me."

Octavia tilted her head. "What do you mean?"

He smiled, and his eyes glistened. "I am dying," he whispered. "And now, because of you, I might be able to drink from the Well in Hritza."

Her chest tightened. She stared at him, and he stared back. There was so much hope in his face that it made her tear up with sorrow. He looked so young—too young to be worrying about death. Octavia was already having a hard enough time imagining Mama dying, but if Bowan were dying too? This poor boy. Had he also endured insults like "*Hritza*" for being sick?

Octavia blinked away her tears. "How old are you?"

"I'm fifteen."

She felt overwhelmed. Thoughts of the Well of Eternal Healing turned to thoughts of Mama, and in her heart, Octavia yearned for the outcome of this to be access to the *waters*. But if Xadia controlled the Well, would they allow someone from Rustwick to drink from it? She could ask the same question of any kingdom. Would the controlling party treat the *waters* as they were meant to be treated, sharing it equally among the lands? Or would they horde it? Tax it? Squeeze every coin from the hands of those who were desperate to use it?

In truth, Octavia had no idea what the outcome of this would be, but she didn't have the heart to look Absalom in the face and crush his hope of living.

"May the *gods* truly favor you," she said.

He smiled once more, a grand and hopeful smile that reached his eyes. "They already have. You are here. I have seen the key with my own eyes, and now my faith is stronger than it has ever been."

Octavia's belly rumbled with hunger, and her head began to throb. "Please, can you bring me something to eat?"

Absalom's eyes darted to the tent flaps, and he lowered his voice. "I'm not supposed to feed you. But you need your strength for the darkness." He pulled out a piece of cloth from his pocket and unwrapped it to reveal some cheese. "Here, eat it quickly."

She snatched it up and ravenously devoured the small block. It tasted nutty and had hints of honey and salt, taking the edge off of the discomfort in her stomach.

"I will bring you more when I can," he whispered.

"Thank you."

Absalom gave her a bow of respect. "I'm sorry. I must go now."

He scurried from the tent, leaving Octavia alone. With a chair underneath her, a small morsel in her stomach, and a few tins of water to quench her thirst, she felt like she wasn't losing her mind anymore. She whispered a prayer of thanks for the dying boy who revered her as much as he revered the *gods.* Now, she could continue to mull over how to escape.

The only option she could think of was Pierre unlocking her chains. She was not going to get out of them otherwise. But what would make him do that? She wracked her brain for an answer. None came.

She was exhausted from the day, both physically and emotionally, and so she decided that the best thing to do was to try and rest. She needed to keep up her mental strength. Octavia had outwitted Pierre once. She could do it again.

Her lie would only last her so long, and when it expired, death likely awaited her.

She closed her eyes, centering her mind, and in the quiet of the tent, she whispered, "I am Octavia Fletcher, Keyholder, savior of all the lands, and I *will* survive this."

22

The Commander's Wife

Octavia awoke to Pierre sitting in front of her with a dagger held lazily in his hand, and on the tip of it, there was an apple slice. She gave a start, stirring from her slouched position in the chair. Her neck had been lulled to the side, resting on her right arm. Her wrists and hands were numb, her body was stiff, and she was cold from the early morning chill that had swept the tent.

"Good morning, Octavia," Pierre lilted.

Her eyes landed on the knife. "You're supposed to be fasting."

"I am," he said. "This isn't for me. It's for you. You must be hungry, right?"

She pursed her lips, wanting to refuse the apple simply because Pierre had offered it, but she was once again starving. The meager block of cheese from the previous night had not been enough.

"Yes, I'm hungry."

"Open up," Pierre crooned, sticking the tip of the dagger to her mouth. Octavia moved her hand to try and grab the slice, but Pierre pulled it out of her reach. "Ah, ah! Let me do it."

She glowered at him, balling her hand into a fist, but she opened her mouth to comply. Pierre brought the apple to her lips, and she pulled it off the knife with her teeth, biting into it. The sweet juices ran down her throat, and her belly rumbled for more. Pierre, however, didn't have any other food in sight. A single apple slice? He was taunting her with the idea of food and not really here to feed her.

"How did you sleep?" he asked.

She simply glared at him, refusing the question.

"You know, I'd really rather not take that chair from you," he said in a slippery tone, hand to his thick gray mustache. "But if you refuse to talk with me, I will. That chair is a privilege, not a right."

"I slept fine," Octavia lied. The truth was, she had barely slept at all, only nodding off late into the night. She had probably gleaned two hours at most.

Pierre's eyes lit with amusement. "There's a good girl."

"Can I have more to eat?"

He looked her up and down, clearly reveling in her discomfort. "If you behave."

"I need my strength," she countered. "For the darkness."

"Oh, don't you worry about that. I'll make sure you have plenty of strength when the time comes."

Pierre stared at her, and Octavia felt helpless under his intense gaze. It was violating. The way his attention latched onto her, the way he studied her face, the hungry gleam in his eyes . . .

"What is going on in that pretty little mind of yours?" Pierre inquired, fingering the flat side of the dagger. He twirled the blade a few times as he continued to stare at her. Then he took the tip of the weapon and placed it to her chin. Her stomach twisted, and she sucked in a harsh breath. "Are you afraid of me, Octavia?" He lingered on her name like he was savoring every syllable of it.

Though her pulse raced and perspiration formed on her brow, she clenched her teeth and looked him dead in the eye. She spoke slowly and deliberately. "No."

Pierre chuckled, shaking his head and pulling the dagger back. "You really are something else."

Octavia remained silent. She didn't feel brave, but just as with pretending to be enlightened by the *gods*, she would fake this too. This man fed off of fear, and she would not give that to him.

"I truly cannot get over the resemblance," Pierre continued. "It's like looking into the face of a ghost."

"You killed Rebekah. Didn't you?" There was a long beat of silence. "Why?"

He gave a toothy smile. "I'm done talking about Rebekah. I'd rather talk about you. Where are you from?"

Nerves jumped through her body at the question. She could not tell this man any personal information. She wouldn't put it past Pierre to use her family to get her to behave. The bounty hunter was one thing, but her brother was quite another. A pit formed in her stomach as a new thought occurred to her. Bowan knew the timing of the last key transfer. He had seen Voramir kidnap her because of it. Mama possibly knew it too, but she was likely too far gone to recall it.

Pierre could never know she was from Rustwick.

"I'm from Omari."

He pressed his lips together in pleasure and inhaled slowly. "The Well of Fertility." His eyes went to her stomach and then between her legs before returning to her face. "Tell me, Octavia, have you ever been with a man?"

Her lower lip began to tremble, so she locked her jaw in place. Her limbs felt weak, her stomach roiled, and the apple slice she had eaten a few minutes ago threatened to come back up her esophagus. She couldn't bring herself to speak, so she shook her head.

The elated glint in Pierre's countenance was vile. He leaned forward in the chair, resting his hands on his knees. "After this fast, I'm going to *enjoy* you."

Tears formed in her eyes. She couldn't help it. They were completely out of her control. The physiological response tied to panic had won out, and fear was now very present on her face. She gritted her teeth harder, suppressing a whimper.

"Oh, don't cry," Pierre simpered, taking one of his fingers to wipe away the tear that had spilled down her right cheek. "I treat my women well. If you behave, you will want for nothing. I can give you a good life, Octavia."

She finally found the courage to force words out. "After the darkness, you'll no longer need me. The Well of Eternal Healing will belong to Xadia. And I will be free of you."

Pierre licked his lips. "You will never be free of me. You are *mine* now. And I never lose what's mine."

"You can't follow me into the darkness!" she spat. "No one can. I must walk into it alone. And when I do, I will not return to you."

"Not even for *him*?" Pierre raised an eyebrow, tracing his finger along the dagger. "After the darkness falls, there is nothing to stop my blade from skewering him like a dog."

"You've put too much faith into my feelings for him!" Octavia hissed.

"Have I?"

Octavia couldn't speak. It was like her voice had been ripped from her throat. She wanted to say, "I will not return to you!" She wanted to scream it. But something held her back. Maybe she would only know what to do after walking through the darkness, but her heart shattered at the thought of allowing Pierre to kill Azariah. She could do it. She could run. She would be alone and free and far enough away from any army that might capture her. Maybe that was the smart thing to do—unlock the Well and then slip away, lost to time and history, never to be heard from again. The Keyholder who saved all the lands, dissolved into mist to escape the evils of men and the ruins of a war that was sure to follow.

But Azariah . . . Could she truly leave him behind?

"Do you have any family in Omari, Octavia?"

"No. My parents are dead. And I am an only child."

Her quick response and jaded tone made the lie teeter precariously on the edge of being unconvincing, and she scolded herself in her mind for not answering more carefully. Everything about this had to be controlled, down to her attitude. She was still playing a game at the mercy of this vile man.

"An only child? In Omari?" Pierre scrutinized her, and she held her breath. "I find that *very* hard to believe."

"Well, it's the truth."

Pierre's upper lip curled in displeasure, as if he wanted to prod further, but then his face fell back into a sinister glee. "Then you have no one who will miss you."

Pierre reached out to tuck a strand of Octavia's disheveled hair behind her ear. She shrank away from him, and he smiled.

"I need you to understand something, Octavia. I've decided that I want you. A woman of your status at my side will make Xadia the greatest of the kingdoms. Xadia will control the Well of Eternal Healing, and Xadia will keep the Keyholder as our symbol of favor from the *gods* themselves. So, you should get used to the idea quickly, or your life is going to be very unpleasant. Like I said, I treat my women well. But only if they behave. And I want you to hear me when I say this: you can run from me if you like. You're right. I can't follow you into the darkness. But if you do not return, I will kill Azariah. Maybe I *am* putting too much faith into your feelings for him. Maybe that's a threat that won't get you to come back. Fine. But I vow to the *gods* that I will hunt you until I find you again. The *waters* will help me. The witch's protection spell has an expiration date—spells always do."

Cruelty twisted his expression.

"Get this through your pretty little head: you belong to me. I'm going to make you my wife, and we will seal our union before the *gods.*"

The silence in the wake of his statement was bone-chilling. Octavia felt like she couldn't take a breath. A scream built in her throat, and it took everything in her not to sob. Was this truly going to be the rest of her life? A prisoner to Pierre? His wife in decoration alone, but his slave to do whatever he pleased with behind closed doors? What nightmarish abuse awaited her at the end of his fast?

Perhaps Pierre wouldn't kill her when he found out the wish wasn't real. His motivation to use her as a symbol of favor from the *gods* for Xadia felt too strong. It was compelling. If Xadia had the Keyholder, then maybe the other kingdoms wouldn't fight Xadia for control of the Well for fear of incurring the wrath of the *gods.*

She was completely overwhelmed. The idea of escaping Pierre now seemed small and impossible. She couldn't even begin to conceptualize a way out. More tears spilled down her cheeks, and this time, she couldn't help but whimper. It was a soft cry—barely audible—but it visibly delighted Pierre.

He snaked his hand under her chin, lifting her face up an inch. "I'll see you later, my dear." And with that, Pierre got up from the chair and strode out of the tent.

Octavia sat there, completely numb. Her face felt like needles were stabbing it all over, and her knees were tingling. Her arms also felt heavy. Stars edged her vision. She couldn't breathe. She couldn't breathe!

"Help me!" she pleaded with the *gods* as she strained against her chains. Her tears fell onto her pants. "Please help me! I don't know what to do!"

She willed the key to burn. To do something. Anything. She poured all of her mind into the thought. Maybe it could disintegrate the chains that held her there. Maybe it could give her divine power to escape. Or supernatural strength. Maybe it could . . .

Nothing.

Nothing happened.

Tent flaps rustled, and Octavia yelped at the noise, fearing that Pierre had returned. But it was not him. It was Absalom. Part of her panic diminished, but her tears were still very much present.

Absalom hurried over to her, giving her a quick bow of respect. He glanced back over his shoulder. "I am here with more food," he whispered, withdrawing another cloth from his pocket. He opened it to reveal cheese, a small piece of bread, and a few grapes. "I know it's not much, but I don't need it like you do."

Octavia felt like she might throw up if she ate right now, but not eating was risky. Who knew when Pierre would decide to allow her to eat. Absalom held the cloth within her reach, and she grabbed the grapes first, chewing them furiously. Then she ate the cheese, finishing with the bread. It was all gone in two minutes, and her belly felt slightly more satisfied.

Tears still wet her face, and Absalom stared at her, his brow pinching together, like he wanted to offer her comfort but wasn't sure how.

"Commander Zarqel can be a harsh leader," he said in a small voice, like he was speaking from experience. "But he will not kill you. I heard him boasting to the camp. You are to be part of Xadia's royalty. Higher than a Wellminder. Second only to King Joda—as Zarqel is. You are to be the commander's wife."

Absalom's words, though clearly meant to be taken as encouraging, only made Octavia feel worse.

Her hands started to shake violently, and she let out another cry. She bit the inside of her cheek, closing her eyes to gain back her composure. It took a few attempts, but she finally spoke, gazing at Absalom like she would gaze at Bowan. "Thank you for your kindness to me."

Absalom dipped his head toward her. "It is my honor to help you, Keyholder."

It was only now, with the daylight slipping into the tent, that Octavia noticed the sallowness of his skin. He had discolored eye bags, and he was far too skinny for his age. His sickness—whatever it was—was taking its toll on his body. She wanted to learn more about this boy.

"Why do you serve Commander Zarqel?" she asked.

His eyebrows creased together. "I am his bondservant. I am paying off a debt my father owes." He looked like he was going to cry, but he pressed his lips together firmly and took a resolute breath.

Octavia's heart broke for him. Pierre would take a sick and dying boy away from his family to pay off a debt? Her revulsion for her captor festered deeper.

"Is your family in Xadia?"

Absalom nodded. "My parents and my little sister. She's seven."

Homesickness stabbed at Octavia's resolve. This sweet boy must be missing his family just as much as she was missing hers.

"I'm sorry."

Absalom ran a hand through his black curls. "I pray that I will see them soon. With the *waters* from Hritza, I will be able to finish my three years of service to Commander Zarqel. Then I will return home." He looked so hopeful. "I had accepted that I would die a bondservant, but now, with you . . ." He couldn't bring himself to finish the sentence.

He was overcome with emotion, and his dark brown eyes gleamed with tears. "Thank you, Keyholder." He backed away from her, peering at the tent flaps nervously. "I must go."

"Absalom, wait!"

As the boy halted, Octavia faltered. Part of her felt bad for the question she was about to ask him. From their brief exchanges, she knew how much her presence in Xadia's camp meant to him. She wanted to help him. She truly did. But she had to remind herself that Pierre was planning to do unspeakable things to her, and she was not going to let that happen without doing everything in her power to escape . . .

She locked eyes with the sickly boy and spoke in an unwavering tone.

"Do you know where Commander Zarqel keeps the keys to these chains?" She pulled her wrists until the restraints tightened.

His sickly face drained of color. "I do, but . . . I cannot unchain you. You must walk through the darkness in the name of Xadia. I need the *waters* from the Well."

Octavia's heart fell. Of course he would never unchain her. She was his only hope of living. Her chest felt like a weight had crushed it, so she said the only thing she could: "I understand."

He turned to leave once more.

"Absalom!" she said again. He stopped. "Has the bounty hunter eaten anything?"

If Pierre was starving her, she was sure he was starving Azariah too.

"I don't think so," he replied.

"Can you help him?" Her voice was optimistic. "Please?"

Absalom seemed to mull it over, chewing on his lower lip. He appeared a bit jumpy, like he had lingered in the tent for too long. "I will try, but I will have to wait until nightfall. Commander Zarqel has kept him guarded with four men even though he is chained. I don't know if I can feed him, but I will do my best."

She nodded. "Thank you."

Absalom bowed to her before slipping through the tent flaps like a wisp of smoke.

Octavia spent the day in solitude. Pierre didn't return to the tent, and all the while, she wracked her brain for a way to trick him into unchaining her. But she couldn't see him doing that until Xadia's army was ready to take her to the darkness itself.

It was torture, being chained to this stake, and she wasn't even in direct sunlight. The tent flaps shielded her. She thought of Azariah, and her stomach flipped in discomfort. He was probably far worse off than she was by now. They had only been captured for a little over a day, but at least she had eaten and had some water since then. She'd also been able to relieve herself in the dirt below the chair—thankfully in private. The idea of wetting her pants made her extremely uncomfortable, and she was glad it hadn't come to that yet.

As the sun continued its descent through the sky, she hoped Absalom would be able to help Azariah. That was all her heart could latch onto. It was all that was keeping her sane—the pious boy who had chosen to help her. Her mind was spent trying to come up with a plan. Part of her wanted to abandon the idea of escape and start working on what she could say to Pierre when he inevitably discovered that the wish wasn't real. But she still had one day left of his fast . . .

She had stood and sat repeatedly throughout the day, mostly to keep her body from going numb, but now she sank into the chair, entirely defeated from the hours of restless thought and isolation. Maybe she should try to sleep and pray that the *gods* would give her a dream or a spark of inspiration.

The tent grew dark as the sun set, and her eyes began to droop. She fought to stay awake, but she knew it was a losing battle. Her eyelids felt heavy, and so she finally shut them . . .

A piercing scream split the night. It was so loud and so violent that when Octavia's eyes flew open, she launched herself to her feet, yanking the chains taut and tipping over the chair. She was still shrouded in the darkness of the tent, barely able to see a thing. The hairs along her arms stood on end as a chorus of voices erupted into chaos. It was the men in the encampment—the soldiers—and *all* of them were screaming.

23

Deus Ex Deus

Octavia's fight or flight instinct kicked in, and she desperately strained at the chains, but they wouldn't budge. The sounds of camp beyond the flaps of the tent were deafeningly loud. Footsteps pounded against the earth. Voices shouted, and horses whinnied. Metal shrieked against metal.

Octavia's pulse spiked tenfold, and her eyes darted through the darkness of the tent. What was happening? Her body felt like it had been struck by lightning as the chaos all around her grew louder.

Thwack.

The tent flaps burst open, and someone sprinted in. Octavia couldn't see what the newcomer was doing, but then a spark ignited, and a lamp was lit. It was Absalom, and he was so pale that he looked dead. Sweat licked his hairline, and his hands shook as he stumbled away from the opening of the tent.

"Absalom, what's happening!?" Octavia demanded.

For several seconds, the boy couldn't speak. He simply opened and closed his mouth repeatedly.

"Absalom!" Octavia shouted.

Crash.

A huge rumbling shook the ground, and Octavia almost lost her footing. Absalom fell to his knees, dropping the lamp, which cracked against the dirt but stayed lit. Then Absalom's horrified eyes snapped to Octavia, and a shuddered rasp came from his throat. "The darkness!"

Octavia's stomach seized, and her veins flooded with an icy sensation as a primal fear ripped through her chest. The darkness was here? How could Xadia's army not realize that they had camped so close to it?

"Unchain me!" she cried, pulling at her restraints. She wanted to run. Everything in her was telling her to run—as fast and as far as she could.

Absalom seemed unable to move. He was still on his knees near the entrance of the tent, staring at it like it was going to eat him alive—and his eyes were so wide that it looked unnatural.

"ABSALOM!" she shrieked. "You have to unchain me! Please!"

More shouting and screeching came from outside the tent, and the ground trembled again, this time more violently. Octavia had to hold onto the chains to keep herself upright.

The tremor seemed to snap the frightened boy out of his petrified trance. He scrambled to his feet, running over to the table where the pitcher of water had tipped over from the force of the earthquake. He ducked under the surface, and for a moment, it looked like he was hiding, but then he popped his head back up, and in his hand, he held a small bronze key.

He ran to her, staring at her with trepidation. He held the key close to his chest like he was uncertain of following through . . .

A roar split the air—like the earth beneath them might open up and swallow them whole. It was so loud that both Octavia and Absalom slammed their hands over their ears.

"If I unchain you, you have to walk through the darkness in the name of Xadia!" Absalom cried. "I need you!"

"I will walk through the darkness in the name of *everyone*!" she exclaimed. "You will drink the *waters* and be healed! You and so many others!"

Absalom's trembling hands gripped the bronze key, and he started to cry. "You are going to run!"

"I am," she affirmed. "But, Absalom, you need to trust me, and you have to free me! Please! I cannot save anyone if I am chained and the darkness sweeps over this tent!"

Absalom hesitated for only a moment longer, and then he sprang into action. He started with her wrists, unlocking the cuffs, and then he moved to her ankles. The moment she was free, she held out her hand, yelling over the torrent of noise crashing through the tent flaps. "Give me that key!"

Absalom handed it to her, and she gripped it fiercely. Then she put both of her hands on either side of the terrified boy's face, and she looked him in the eye. "I swear to the *gods*, I will walk through the darkness and unlock the Well of Eternal Healing. You will be healed, Absalom. You will! May the *gods* protect you! Your bravery today will not be overlooked."

She threw her arms around him and hugged him like she would hug Bowan, and when she released him, she cried, "Run! Get away from here!"

Absalom nodded, still shaking from head to foot, and then Octavia sprinted to the tent flaps. She threw them open, and the sight that met her eyes made her go weak in the knees. At the edge of the camp, a monstrous wall of darkness crept forward. It was so vast and so wide that it swallowed the stars and blotted out the moon. A torrent of wind was coming from it, streaking across the camp like a storm. And all around her, people were running and screaming. But it wasn't the gargantuan wall of blackness that forced a scream from her throat, it was the snake-like tendrils of darkness slithering across the ground, charging ahead of the wall into the camp.

Octavia's heart felt like it was going to give out. She was still standing frozen at the flaps of the tent. It was like her nightmare, but this time, it was real. She shook herself, breaking out of her trance, and her mind honed in on one thing and one thing alone: Azariah Ronan. She would not leave him.

She scanned the chaos of the camp. Fire pits burned. Soldiers sprinted across the dirt. Tents were being destroyed in the panic. And in the center of it all, chained to a tall metal stake, she spotted the bounty hunter.

She launched herself over the earth, running as fast as her legs would carry her. No one stopped her. In fact, no one even noticed her. They were all too consumed with the creeping darkness and the threads of black shooting into the encampment.

Something huge collided with Octavia, and she shrieked. A soldier had run straight into her, and they both slammed to the ground. The soldier's eyes went wide when he saw Octavia, but right before he could call out, a prong of darkness flew across the ground, narrowly missing Octavia and latching onto his leg. He screamed, and in the blink of an eye, his skin had melted from his bones, leaving a puddle of black tar behind like he had never existed at all.

Octavia scrambled to her feet, even though the power of the collision hurt her chest. Her eyes searched for Azariah again, and she found him. There were no guards around him, and she could see him pulling at his chains, desperately trying to get away.

With a strangled yell, she sprinted toward him, weaving past fleeing soldiers who were racing in the opposite direction. She dodged another man, almost tripping over the uneven ground, but she kept her footing.

With a few more bounds, she reached Azariah and collided into him to stop her momentum. When he saw her, his bruised and bloodied face changed from desperate to shocked. "Octavia!?" he cried. "What are you doing? Escape this place!"

"I'm not leaving you! I have the key to your chains!" she yelled, fumbling with the small metal object. Her hands were shaking so badly that she could scarcely keep her grip.

Bang.

The earth felt like it had cracked open, and both Octavia and Azariah fell. Octavia landed flat on her stomach, but Azariah's arms were yanked upward by the chains, and he let out a roar of pain. Octavia spat blood onto the ground. She had landed hard enough for her teeth to dig into her lower lip. Pain riddled her bones, but she pushed herself up again, returning to Azariah.

She grabbed Azariah's waist and helped him stand, then she dropped to her knees to attack the cuffs at his ankles. She jammed the key into the keyhole, popping open one cuff, and then she freed his other ankle too, but when she stood to unlock the cuffs at his wrists, Azariah's petrified eyes and gaping mouth caused her to turn around. A tendril of black was crawling across the ground toward the metal stake, billowing like smoke and frothing like boiling water. It was less than a second from reaching them, and Octavia knew she wasn't going to get Azariah free in time.

Everything in her body screamed at her to move out of the way and let the darkness feast on Azariah's flesh. And though the feeling ran as deep as her marrow, another instinct took over, and she allowed it in fully. It was a decision made in her spirit, resolved by the glimpses of faith she had seen from him—and how her heart had attached itself to his.

She was the Keyholder, and the darkness could *not* have him.

Octavia planted her feet, standing in front of Azariah, her back against his chest. She gripped his arm with her right hand and screamed, thrusting her left hand forward, palm open to the plague. As the thread of black shot toward them, ready to devour them, the key burned bright like the stars, and the darkness halted its trajectory. The snake-like extension seemed to sniff at Octavia's palm like a snarling monster contemplating the attack, but then it dove to the right, diverting its path around the metal stake to claim a soldier who was limping away. The man screamed as the blackness wrapped around his torso. Blood burst from his eyes and from his mouth, and he gagged on it as he died.

Octavia's whole body shook as she shoved the bronze key into the cuffs at Azariah's wrists. After a few seconds, she was able to pry them loose, freeing him from his bonds.

She locked eyes with him, unable to believe what had just happened. Azariah grabbed her hand, squeezing it tightly in his own. His face was layered in a sheen of sweat, the terror in his eyes still very much present.

"Run!" he said.

The two of them took off through the chaos of the camp, and as they sprinted, Azariah's hand never left hers. They darted around fire pits and leapt over discarded canvas material from fallen tents. The rumbling of the earth continued, building like a storm of death.

Azariah stumbled, nearly falling, but Octavia kept her grip on him, helping him continue. It was clear from his physique that his imprisonment had been more brutal than hers. He appeared to be running off of sheer panic and a dose of self-preservation instead of actual stamina.

The open expanse of desert before them was dotted with trees in the distance. If they could get into the forest, they might have a chance of escaping. A wild cry sounded from directly behind them, but Octavia didn't look back. From the squelching sound alone, she knew the darkness had claimed another victim.

Hundreds of feet slammed across the ground. Hundreds of people fled for their lives.

Wham.

Octavia's hand was wrenched from Azariah's, and in the mayhem of the stampede, someone shoved her. She fell and threw her arms up above her head to shield her face from someone's foot.

The kick landed hard against her arms, and a man toppled over her, falling to the dirt. More people tripped as a result, creating a dogpile. Octavia gave a strangled cry, the weight of multiple men now on her legs. She wriggled free, gulping the air madly in her efforts, and as she did so, the eye-catching brilliance of the key pulled at the attention of the men around her.

"KEYHOLDER!" one of the soldiers yelled, pointing at Octavia. He screamed to the men who had fallen with him. "It's the Keyholder! She cannot escape! Grab her!"

The man lunged at Octavia, and she shrieked, scrambling to her feet, but he caught her wrist, yanking her back toward himself. She kicked wildly as his arms wrapped around her waist to drag her away. More men joined now, lifting Octavia from her feet to hasten their flight away from the darkness.

"Azariah!" she screamed, struggling to twist free. In the pandemonium that surrounded her, she couldn't see him, but she screamed for him again. "Azariah! Help me!" She yanked her legs back, putting up so much of a fight that the men carrying her all fell to their knees. "Get off! Let go of me! AZARI—" A huge hand pressed over her face, and she was lifted from the ground once more.

But very quickly, the group toppled, pulled apart by the bounty hunter. Azariah's fists flew again and again, knocking the men down. Then his strong hands clamped over Octavia's arms, pulling her upright. He grasped her hand again.

"Run!" he urged.

They made a beeline for the trees. The packed density of the mob was starting to disperse now as some people peeled off to the left and others to the right. Azariah kept them running straight, and though Octavia's lungs were on fire, she pushed her legs to move faster, keeping pace with him.

Hurtling into the trees felt like a miracle from the *gods* above. The pines sheltered them as they continued to flee, and now that they were gaining some distance from the immense wall of darkness slowly creeping across the land, the sounds of the groaning and quaking earth began to lessen.

Still, they did not stop. Azariah pulled her forward with relentless force. They ran and ran until Octavia felt sure she was going to die if she didn't stop. There was no one else around them now, and the trees had grown thick.

"Wait!" she cried. "Stop! I—can't—breathe—I—"

She yanked her hand out of Azariah's, collapsing to the ground on all fours, her chest heaving like it was going to explode. Her ears muffled out the sounds around her, and her vision tunneled to black, but she didn't lose consciousness. She could still feel the dirt under her fingertips and a hand on her back.

After a minute, her vision and her hearing returned, though her heartbeat did not give up its frantic charge to pump blood through her veins as fast as it could.

She peered up at Azariah, and he grabbed her hand, hauling her up again. "We must keep going," he said. "We cannot stay here."

He looked wildly beside himself and completely out of breath, but there was something else in his eyes that was awed. Dumbfounded. His cracked and bleeding lips were parted as he stared at her. It was like he was fighting with himself to say something, but the only sounds between them were their rapid breaths.

Abruptly, Octavia's knees buckled, and she fell into him, her hands grasping his shirt. He steadied her, keeping a firm grip on her upper arms until she could gain back her footing.

"Can you keep running?" he asked.

She peered up at him. "Yes."

He gave her a resolute nod, and then held out his hand. She took it, and together, they continued to flee through the night, away from Xadia's scattering army, and away from the rattling clutches of the darkness.

24

The Greatest Metalsmith In All of Xadia

By morning, Octavia barely had any strength left in her body, and Azariah looked like he was on the verge of collapse. All night they had fled, avoiding pockets of Xadia's soldiers as they slipped through the trees, stopping to hide, communicating in silence, and then running until their legs could scarcely carry them.

Now, with the sun rising above the trees, Octavia's desperation built. They had no food and no water, and if they didn't find some soon, they would be in big trouble. At least they were finally alone. They hadn't stumbled across soldiers for the past two hours, and although Octavia's nerves were on high alert from expecting the darkness to spring itself upon them again, it never came . . .

She wanted to stop and give up. Her feet hurt, her tongue was crazed with thirst, and her forehead pounded with a splitting headache, but something in her spirit told her to keep going. Just a little while longer. It was like the moment when she had almost given up searching for Azariah after those people had drugged her. She couldn't explain the sensation, she just knew they had to press on.

Five minutes later, like providence was smiling down on them, Octavia spotted the smooth surface of a lake in the distance. Both Azariah and Octavia bounded forward, a renewed vigor in their steps, and when they reached the water's edge, they ran straight into it until they were waist deep. The lake felt refreshing against her skin, and she cupped handful after handful of water into her mouth. Azariah did the same, gulping the liquid as if he was on the brink of death.

They drank until they were satisfied, and then they both dunked under the water to rinse themselves clean. Immediately, Octavia felt like she wasn't going to pass out anymore. She was still starving, but quenching her thirst pulled a new thread of energy into her limbs. She could fish. She would fashion together something and catch them some food. Now that her brain wasn't screaming at her for water, the threat of death wasn't as dire.

When the two of them trudged out of the lake, Azariah collapsed on all fours. He was shaking, and Octavia knelt beside him, placing a hand on his back.

"Are you okay?"

She hadn't really had time to assess him thoroughly since their escape because they had been moving for hours through the dark in silence to avoid capture. But now, in morning's light, having finally found a place to rest, she saw how weak and beaten he was. A ghastly bruise had formed in the right corner of his mouth, his lips were split open in several places and crusted over—even after the wash in the lake—and there was another bruise on his cheek with a nasty cut just below his right eye.

"Did they feed you anything?" she questioned. "Or give you any water?"

He shook his head.

Her stomach clenched with sympathy—and she felt like *she* was going mad with hunger. Because of Absalom, she had eaten a meager meal twice since Pierre took her. She couldn't imagine how hungry Azariah must be.

"I'll find you something," she assured him. "Just rest here in the shade."

Immediately, Octavia set to work. She marched into the trees, searching the ground for a stick long enough to fashion into a spear. She found one a few minutes later and broke the edge of it off with her boot so that it splintered. It wasn't particularly sharp, but it would do the job if her aim was true. Then she waded into the lake. She was so desperate for food that the idea of fish flaking through her teeth drove her crazy.

"Please." The prayer left her tongue like a habit. "We need food."

Octavia stood in the lake for nearly an hour. She kept checking for the darkness while hunting for fish, still certain that it would sweep into sight without warning, but the sky remained blue and clear, so she focused her efforts on catching a meal.

She kept still, carefully eyeing the clear water. Fish would occasionally swim by her legs. She would position the stick above them, then plunge it into the lake, but each time, the creatures were too quick. Octavia let out a frustrated growl after attempt seven, but then centered her mind again, determination filling her to capacity. She was not about to escape the darkness *and* Pierre Zarqel only to starve to death.

Her eyes scoured the water. Swimming along the bottom, a huge fish slinked into her view, and she held her breath, not daring to move a muscle. The tip of the stick was positioned just under the surface, and when the creature got close, she slammed the splintered end down. There was a mighty wriggling motion, and Octavia shouted in victory. She had skewered the creature, and though it fought, it quickly died from the wound in its flesh.

Octavia dunked her head under the water, grabbing the fish and hauling it back to shore. It was heavy and filled her arms, and she thanked the *gods* for it.

Azariah was leaning against a tree with his eyes closed, and he did not look good. His breathing was uneven, and his brow was furrowed—probably due to pain. He likely had more injuries than the ones on his face.

She set the fish in the dirt, and then hastily set to work building a fire. She hadn't built many, but Papa had shown her how. After another thirty minutes of collecting kindling and vigorously applying friction using a stick against wood, Octavia had a decent fire going.

The smell of the fish cooking was the most maddeningly delicious scent she had ever encountered, and she knew it was because she was famished. When the creature was crisp and slightly blackened, Octavia took some to Azariah.

"Here. Eat," she said, offering him the meal.

He tore into it, ravenous in his hunger, and before long, they had consumed about half of the animal, with plenty to spare for later. Finally, Octavia's belly felt satisfied, and the two of them sat there by the lake in silence, soaking up the sun and reveling in the satisfaction of having full stomachs at last.

With her basic needs met, Octavia was unable to stop her brain from jumping to the next task at hand. Which was . . . ? She didn't know. She peered at Azariah. Would he still insist on taking her to Zoharth? Was her decision to save him going to result in the same situation she had been in for the past two weeks? Was he even still her captor?

The thoughts swirled in her mind, tangling together into a mess. She opened her mouth, but Azariah's soft voice beat her to it.

"You came back for me." His deep brown eyes lifted to her face. He had always gazed at her so fiercely, but the way he was looking at her now was different. It was softer. It carried more depth, like he was finally allowing himself to feel something real and raw. "Why did you do that?"

"I . . ." The word snagged on her tongue.

Something new was stirring in her soul. Before their imprisonment, she had done her best to staunch feeling anything at all for him. But when Pierre had captured them—when it became personal—all of that came crumbling down.

She had protected him without hesitation.

The way Azariah had reacted to seeing Pierre, the vile threats Pierre had made toward him, the revelation regarding Rebekah . . . All of it had pushed Octavia to realize something she hadn't been able to articulate before: the mystery and misery of this man had drawn her heart to his in a subtle, yet powerful way.

She had feelings for him. As crazy and scary as that sounded, she had feelings for him. And it was only now that she understood why.

He was a man of faith—a *good* man that she had misjudged because of her circumstances. She didn't care about the story Pierre had spun. Whatever truth there was to Pierre's scars—however Azariah had been involved—she was certain that Pierre had twisted the tale. The clues that Octavia had gathered along the way concerning Azariah only confirmed his faith and good nature. Whether intentional or not, he had allowed pieces of himself to slip through the cracks of his battle-hardened exterior.

It was present in the trust he had extended to her during the knife lesson. It was there in the aftermath of the washroom and apparent outside of Urtha when Azariah had bowed his head to pray by the Kraven River. It was woven into his sorrow when he had apologized to her for reducing her to nothing more than the key. It was in his words of encouragement, even as he was taking her to Zoharth—that *she* would be the one to save them, that *she* held a sacred position. It was in the way he had said her name for the first time. So softly. Like it broke him. And it was in the kindness he had chosen to extend to her—despite his profession, despite his charge to bring her to King Bastian, despite Rebekah, despite everything . . .

Though she did not know the extent of how he had suffered, Octavia knew Azariah had suffered greatly. And Pierre's evil intentions for him had pushed Octavia's heart even further. Nothing Azariah had done to her warranted leaving him behind. Not there. Not with Pierre.

So many thoughts stormed through her, but all she could get herself to say was: "I couldn't leave you there."

It was an impossibly insufficient thing to say.

Azariah's expression grew more pensive—even a little somber—like he couldn't put the pieces of something together in his mind. "You could have run, but you didn't. You stood in front of the darkness for me."

Nerves jumped through her stomach. The memory of the tendril of black shooting toward Azariah was seared into her brain—as was the sound of her own scream as she shielded him . . .

It was the fuel of nightmares. She had diverted the darkness away because it had recognized the one who could vanquish it. It was something she hadn't fully processed yet.

"I wasn't going to let you die," she said. "I couldn't do that."

Azariah put his head into his shaking hands. He took some intentional breaths—deep and slow—as if he was trying to avoid having a panic attack. He didn't speak, and neither did she. She simply stared at him as he stared at the ground between his hands, and the chorus of nature filled in the gaps.

When Azariah raised his head up, he had tears in his eyes. Octavia was taken aback. From all she had observed from this man, she had never expected something like this. He had faithfully kept his serious and unbreakable exterior, but now he looked damaged, like something had been taken from him.

"How did you escape?" he asked.

"A servant boy. He helped me. When the darkness came, he unchained me."

Azariah took his eyes off of the dirt and looked her full in the face. She wanted to say something to comfort him because he looked so overwhelmed, but everything her mind came up with sounded ill-fitting.

"Pierre told me that he—" Azariah balled his hands into fists. A mix of pain and rage attacked his features. He looked like he might yell, but his voice came out barely above a whisper. "He told me he violated you."

Octavia's stomach flipped. Given what she knew of Pierre, he had said that simply to torture Azariah. What a vile, cruel man. She shook her head, tears now forming in her eyes too. "He didn't. He didn't touch me."

Azariah's crusted lips parted. "He didn't?"

"I lied. I said I had a wish from the *gods* to give to anyone I want but that he had to fast and purify himself for two days to receive it." She knotted her fingers together, a shudder passing through her. "Pierre wanted the key for himself, but I told him I was the last Keyholder. I said the darkness started moving when I got the key and that the *gods of old* are ending this with me."

Azariah peered at her. There was so much going on behind his eyes, and he once again looked miserable. The expression seemed to leach into his resolve like poison—like nothing in the world could comfort him.

She wasn't sure what else Pierre had told him or done to him, but she needed to let Azariah know what she had learned. She could not continue another moment holding it in.

Her pulse spiked, so she pressed her fingernails into her palms and bit the inside of her cheek to pluck up her courage.

She had to say it . . .

"Pierre told me about Rebekah, and how I look like her. He said she died. He also told me about you. But I have a feeling I didn't get the whole truth."

The strain in Azariah's face heightened, and he took a shuddered breath. "What did Pierre tell you?"

Octavia gazed at him with all the comfort and kindness she could muster, but it felt impossibly insufficient to ease the suffering that saturated Azariah's face.

"Pierre said you stole the costly metals that King Joda provided you for a custom order of weapons. He said that when he confronted you . . . that you . . . killed all of his men. And that you tried to kill him too. He said you're wanted by the king."

Azariah buried his head in his hands again and stayed quiet. Octavia didn't know what to do, but she knew that if Azariah chose to tell her anything, she would believe him over Pierre.

She would ask him once, and then she wouldn't ask him again. The deep anguish that stole over his whole body was chilling, and it swept over her too. She could feel him on the verge of breaking down, even though she couldn't see his face.

"Azariah." She said his name softly, placing a hand gently on his shoulder. "What happened to Rebekah?"

He lifted his head to stare out at the surface of the lake, and so Octavia turned her gaze to the lake as well. There was silence for a long time. She didn't prod him, and she didn't ask for more. He wasn't going to tell her, and even though that drove her wild with the desperation to know, she was going to accept it. She had to.

"I loved her from the moment I saw her . . ." Azariah began. "It was her kindness that struck me most. It lit up her spirit and shone like the sun on everyone around her. No one in all my life had halted me in my tracks and captured my attention in such an astounding way. Rebekah was beautiful, inside and out. The day I met her, I remember thinking I *had* to get to know her—if she would allow it." He paused, and his voice softened. "The days of falling in love with her were easier than falling asleep, and when we vowed before the *gods* that we would spend our lives together, it was my happiest moment. For five years, I loved her." Azariah's eyes closed. "Those were the best years of my life."

His hands began to shake, so he clasped them together, resting his elbows on his knees as he sat in the dirt.

"When I met Rebekah, I was working my way up in metal-smithing, studying under one of the finest teachers in all the lands. Once I was skilled enough, I opened my own forge, seeking to earn a name for myself. And I did. All across the kingdom, people sought after my craftsmanship. *My* work."

His attention was still focused on the glassy surface of the water, like he was contemplating what to say next.

"One day, Rebekah went to town to pick up some bread, and while she was in the bakery, she met Pierre." His voice faltered, almost cracking. "Pierre immediately took to her, inquiring about her. He was aggressively forward, but she rejected his advances outright. Her refusal, however, did not deter him. He became more hostile, and the men in the bakery had to escort him out. Rebekah stayed in that shop for three hours for fear of running into Pierre outside. And when she finally came home that day, she told me what happened. She said he wouldn't leave her alone. Even when she said she had a husband, he wouldn't relent."

Azariah paused for a few beats. It was like he was falling into a trance.

"I was concerned. I didn't want her to go to town alone, and I went with her for the next few weeks, but Pierre never turned up, and eventually, we forgot about it. Then one day, a royal regiment arrived at my forge—soldiers from King Joda with instructions to fulfill a large order of custom weapons for the king's personal guard. They gave me costly metals mined with the *waters* from Xadia's Well and a contract date of three months to fulfill the order. Such a short timetable was a stretch for me, but I agreed. My skills as a weapons craftsman were well known in Xadia, and this job was from the king himself. I couldn't pass up an opportunity like that.

"So, I set to work. I crafted the order. I dedicated my days and nights to foraging the weapons, and I used every last parcel's worth of costly metals King Joda provided me. I had barely finished in time. The last blade I crafted was completed two nights before King Joda's men were set to come."

His eyes burned with tears.

"Rebekah and I celebrated that night. The pay for the order was going to change our lives. I was going to build a bigger workshop, hire some apprentices, and expand the forge. We were going to start—" Azariah stopped speaking. He pressed his quivering lips together. "We wanted a family."

Octavia's heart squeezed in her chest, and a small piece of her broke at his words.

"The order was ready, locked away in the shed behind my shop. And then the morning of the pickup came. A group of King Joda's guards arrived—thirty of them in all with three empty wagons to receive the order—but when I directed them to the shed, I found that the lock had been cut, and all the weapons were gone."

Azariah gritted his teeth.

"They accused me of stealing the costly metals. I told them I had completed the order, but they didn't believe me. Our conversation got heated. I didn't know it at the time, but the man I was speaking with—the one in charge of the pickup—was Pierre." Azariah's tone grew thick and grieved. "Rebekah came out of the house because of the commotion. She froze in her tracks. I could see recognition in her eyes. She was staring at Pierre like he was a ghost, and the cruel smile that split his face . . . it was like the darkness itself was in him."

Grief pinched his expression, and his voice broke.

"Pierre demanded I pay him the cost of the order since it was nowhere to be found, but I didn't have that kind of money. He said since I couldn't pay, he had another exchange in mind."

Octavia's stomach dropped all the way to her toes.

"Pierre gave orders to his men to take Rebekah in place of the weapons, as payment. I pleaded with Pierre not to take her, but his men grabbed her and hauled her away. I tried to stop them. I tried to get to her. But Pierre's men beat me until I couldn't stand." He sucked in a rattling breath. "I could hear her screaming for me, but I couldn't . . . I couldn't get off the ground. And then they took her away. Pierre took my wife away."

A tear slid down his face and dripped off his chin. A thick silence followed this that Octavia dared not break.

"I remember lying there in the dirt for almost an hour, trying to get up. Everything hurt. I could barely breathe. It felt like I was dying, and the sun . . . I remember the sun beating down on me without mercy. So, I prayed to the *gods* for strength, because I had to go after her. I prayed like I had never prayed before, and like a miracle, strength returned to my body, though the pain did not stop. I grabbed my sword and my knives, and I took our horse after Pierre and his men. I followed the hoofprints and wagon wheel tracks left behind in the dirt, and I found that they did not lead further into Xadia, but away from it—out into the forest."

Azariah's voice was growing more distressed by the second. He clamped his hands together, white-knuckled and tensed.

"When I came upon their camp, I . . ." He swallowed hard, and his eyes burned with more tears. "I saw the weapons I had made. All of them. Pierre's men were loading them up into the wagons, securing the order, and that's when I knew . . . Pierre had stolen the weapons so that he could frame me as a thief and take Rebekah as payment."

Octavia's small intake of breath felt like a stab wound. She placed a hand to her mouth, her eyes brimming with tears of shock.

"And then I heard a noise. *Gods* I will never forget that noise . . . a whimpering cry. I snuck around the wagons, staying hidden in the trees, and then I found her. She was on the ground, and Pierre was . . ." Azariah couldn't seem to bring himself to say it. "I have never felt anger to the depths of my soul like I did that day. All I can recall is my vision turning red, and my sword cutting through the air at Pierre's head. Over and over again, my blade flew. I killed every last man. And when my mind cleared, I wasn't standing by Rebekah anymore. I was by the wagons, and the dirt was stained crimson with blood.

"I ran to her. She was still lying there on the ground. She had been beaten, her clothes were torn, and she . . . she sounded like she couldn't breathe. She didn't seem lucid. But when I held her—when she saw me—she looked at me, and all she could do was say my name."

He cradled his head in his hands and let out a soft cry.

"I held her in my arms as she died. I just held her, and I told her I loved her. Over and over again. Even after she was gone. It's all I could say."

The melody of nature floated around them as Azariah stopped talking. Octavia was crying, feeling his story as if it were her own. The rage and sympathy she felt for this man was running through her veins like fire. She couldn't even begin to process it. She simply sat there by his side, stunned.

"I took Rebekah home," Azariah whispered. "And I buried her behind our house. I wanted to lie down in the dirt and die with her. I didn't want to leave her. But I knew that King Joda would kill me for killing his men. I knew I had to flee Xadia, and that I could never return. And so, I ran. I left everything behind. My entire life. Everyone I'd ever known. I left them. Soon after, I discovered that Pierre had survived me, and that he was hunting me. King Joda had also put a bounty out for me."

Azariah tightened his fists and ground his teeth in rage.

"But I have killed every man who has ever attempted to take me back to Xadia. There is no one Pierre has sent after me that has come back to him alive. So, I decided that I would become a bounty hunter myself, that I would be unrivaled by anyone in all the lands, that any wealthy patron who could ever want to hire a bounty hunter for a kill or a capture would know *my* name. The bounty hunter with a bounty on him—uncapturable and unkillable. Because I had nothing left to live for and no home to return to.

"And it worked. Pierre learned of my new profession and continued to seek after me, and I continued to evade him, taking on larger bounties—more difficult kills. And succeeding. Always succeeding. Always outsmarting and killing those Pierre sent my way. Until King Bastian Jasper of Zoharth gave me the biggest job of all: catch the Keyholder and bring them to Zoharth."

Azariah locked eyes with Octavia, and his brow turned upward, all the rage and roughness gone, now replaced with anguish.

"And then the Keyholder was *you*. When I saw you, I thought I was going mad. That it must be a trick from the *gods*. But there you were, my bounty to be delivered for a price. And every time I looked at you, I couldn't stop seeing her. And when it was Pierre that captured us . . ."

He fought with himself to keep speaking, his whole body shuddering.

"It was like I was reliving what he did to me three years ago."

The weight of Azariah's story crashed over Octavia like a wave, and she stared at him with glassy eyes, wishing she could say something that might mitigate his pain. But the reality was, nothing she could say would bring back the dead or stop the aching of his heart.

"I thought Pierre would kill me," Azariah murmured. "I shouldn't be alive right now."

Everything Octavia did to fight for him rushed back to her: the game of wits, the wish, the lie about starting the darkness in motion, the threat she had made of not walking through it at all . . .

All of it had been to save him.

"What happened?" He looked up to the sky as if asking the *gods* themselves, but then he turned to Octavia. "How . . . I don't . . . understand . . . I . . ."

It seemed he could not find the right question to ask, and so, for the first time since Azariah began his story, Octavia spoke.

"I bargained for your life. Pierre was going to torture you to get me to tell him how to gain the key. He threatened to kill you. He threatened to—" Octavia faltered. Pierre's heinous intentions for the fake wish came screaming back to her. No. She would not tell him that. Not after hearing his story. "I didn't relent. I told him that if he even touched you, I would not walk through the darkness in the name of Xadia. I did everything I could to protect you. I—"

Octavia's own words choked her. The moments between her and Pierre collided through her mind like physical blows, and she wanted to burst into tears. She had come so close to Pierre forcing himself on her, and Azariah had come so close to being killed.

"Thank you, Octavia." It was a whisper that barely carried over the breeze that danced across the lake. Azariah let out a long breath. "I owe you my life twice over. And I can't . . . I can't do this anymore."

His eyes met hers, and something fractured beneath the sadness in his countenance.

"I release you from your vow, Octavia. I will not force you to go to Zoharth. You are free of me, and you may walk through the darkness as a free woman not bound by any kingdom or man. As the *gods* are my witness, you are free of me."

Her heart skipped a beat, and her lips parted. Was she truly hearing this? He was setting her free? She could scarcely believe her ears, and her heart soared with hope, but it very quickly plummeted as the reality of all the evils of those who hunted her slammed down on her chest like an avalanche. She needed Azariah's protection, but it was more than that, she had finally realized that her heart needed him too. This whole experience had forged something in her that was unbreakable—a bond that went beyond the key melded to her palm.

So Octavia Fletcher said something she never imagined she would, and she took the bounty hunter's hand in her own as she said it. "I don't want to be free of you."

25

A Plan to Seek the Guidance of the *Gods*

The look on Azariah's face was hard to interpret. He no longer appeared like he was going to break, but there was still so much emotion behind his eyes—so much hurt and pain. It was visible in his posture, in the way his jaw tensed, in how he drew in breath . . .

He slipped his hand out of hers. "I can't."

A piece of Octavia's heart fractured as Azariah got up and walked away from her. He stopped at the edge of the lake and stood there in silence. Pierre said he would never reciprocate her, and he had been right . . .

She sat there, numb. In a way, she couldn't blame Azariah for not wanting her. She looked like the woman he had loved and lost. His heart had belonged to another for so long, and his heart had been shattered in the most cruel and vile way. How could he have space for her? How could she expect him to? It wasn't fair of her to want him, but she also couldn't help the way she felt.

What was she supposed to do? She had never experienced

something like this before. No man had ever claimed any portion of her heart, but Azariah had. And now she was going to have to learn to deal with his rejection. She couldn't make him care, and she couldn't make him want her back.

And so, Octavia did the only thing she could: she stuffed down the urge to cry and pulled up a toughened exterior—one that was steadied and confident, even though those two words just broke a piece of her. She stood and walked over to Azariah, looking at him with intention—though he himself didn't look at her.

"I still need you. I can't protect myself. Please don't leave me to do this alone. I know you can't walk through the darkness with me, but you can help me get there."

Her throat closed, and she had to shut her eyes for a moment to center herself.

"Pierre said he was going to make me his wife—that if I didn't return to him after walking through the darkness, he would hunt me. He told me he never loses what's his. I would rather die than be his! Please. You have to help me. I don't know if he . . ."

Octavia's emotions were threatening to take over and push her into hysteria. She didn't know if Pierre had survived the creeping wall of darkness, but if he had, she had no doubt he would come after her. The very idea of being under his thumb again was enough to spin her mind into panic.

"Please, Azariah. Don't leave me."

There was a beat of thick silence that hung between them. Finally, Azariah turned his face to look at her, his tears now gone. "I will not leave you, Octavia. I promise. I will go with you to the darkness, and I will protect you to the best of my ability until then."

Relief swept over her, and she wiped her eyes with her fingertips. "Thank you."

The reality of what she was about to do stabbed her like a dagger. The darkness. She was going to walk into the darkness. It was a terrifying idea, actively seeking it. The memory of the black, tar-like substance creeping through Xadia's camp caused her pulse to quicken and her chest to constrict. They were running out of time. Soon, it would reach a kingdom—whether that be Zoharth or Vrelia or Xadia—and when it did, the Well of Power in that kingdom would fall, and a lot of people were going to die.

Octavia peered around at the lake, which seemed much larger than Ash Lake. "Where are we?"

"This is Jagged Gulch Lake."

"Which direction do we go in to reach the darkness?"

Asking the question snatched all the strength from her body. She felt hopelessly underprepared. She didn't know what to expect, or what to do, or even where to go to find the Well in Hritza once she had entered the darkness. Did maps of the fallen kingdom even exist anymore? What if she couldn't find the Well at all? And if she did find it, what if she couldn't figure out how to unlock it and reverse the darkness? Then a new thought shadowed her mind: what if there was no reversing the progress the darkness had made over the land? Maybe her mission was about halting it and not destroying it.

The *gods of old* had not enlightened her, and all it did was make her want to run away from her fate instead of toward it. How could she possibly seek guidance? She could pray, but the *gods* might not answer her.

So many questions crashed through her that she was having a hard time staying calm. Panic was lapping at her resolve like the water along the lakeside, but she did not allow it to win out. How was she going to do this?

Azariah furrowed his brow at her like he could sense the storm of questions in her mind.

She stared at him and chewed on the inside of her lip. "Do you have *any* idea what I'm supposed to do when I find the Well in Hritza?"

Part of her hoped he would say "yes" and share something he hadn't already shared, but judging by his expression, he had nothing else to offer.

"I'm sorry, but I already told you everything I know of the prophecy—and everything I know about the Keyholder."

Octavia's mouth parted. "The prophecy . . ."

The thought hit her with the force of a storm, and Azariah's story of Zara flew through her mind. Zara drank the *waters* from the Well in Zoharth and she learned the words of the prophecy. What if Octavia did the same? Surely the *gods* would communicate with her? She was the Keyholder after all. And then another thought came to her: the Well of Power itself. Back in Urtha, she felt compelled to look into the *waters*, and what she saw was about Hritza . . .

Suddenly, a plan fell into her mind as if planted there by the *gods*. The feeling was so overwhelming and so powerful that she gasped. She locked eyes with Azariah. "Take me to Zoharth."

He raised an eyebrow and blinked several times as if he didn't hear her correctly. "What?"

"I need to know the words of the prophecy," she said resolutely. "I want to drink a parcel of *waters* from the Well, and I want to stare into its depths, just like I did in Urtha. I saw a memory in the Well at Urtha, remember?"

Azariah scoffed. "How could I forget? I had to escape the Well-minders."

"What I saw was important. It was a memory about Hritza. I saw two men arguing about *undoing* things!" Hope stirred in her chest. "Azariah, the *gods* were trying to communicate with me back in Urtha. I'm sure of it! But you pulled me away from the Well. I only saw a piece of what I needed to see."

Azariah appeared disturbed. He put a hand to his chin, contemplating. "Why risk being captured to possibly see more memories about Hritza? Or drink the *waters* to learn the words of the prophecy? Forgive me, but we don't know if that will even work. You can walk into the darkness now. Time is running out. Pierre held us captive in the desert just beyond Hritza, and the darkness has already claimed it."

"Look, if the darkness has crept upon Zoharth, I'll walk into it. But if there's *any* time at all . . . then I must try to prepare myself. I can't explain it, but there's something important I need to know. Something the *gods want* to tell me." The instinct in her gut only grew stronger with her words, like the key itself was confirming them. "Once I go to the darkness, I'll be alone. No one can help me. Why risk the fate of all the lands on a guess of how I'm supposed to vanquish the darkness if I can find that information out beforehand? Yes, I know I need to go to the Well in Hritza. But I don't know how to unlock it or how to destroy the darkness. What if I try everything I can think of and none of it works? I'll have walked through the darkness in vain. It will consume all the Wells of Power. All the lands! Everyone . . ."

The thought sank its razor-sharp claws of terror into her body. She would be the only survivor—alone in the darkness with not a soul left.

"If there's even a chance that I can learn *how* to put an end to this, then I have to take it," she said firmly. "It's not enough that this key protects me from dying. Please let me try to learn how to save us before all that's left for me to do is walk into the darkness and hope for the best. I can't go to Zoharth alone. I don't even know where the Well is. I need you."

She stared at him, hoping with everything in her soul that he would agree to help her.

Azariah let out a long breath, pinching the skin between his eyebrows. He tapped his foot in the dirt a few times, then he cleared his throat. Then he mumbled something to the effect of "What have I gotten myself into?"

"Fine. I will take you to Zoharth. But you do understand there's a real possibility of you being captured, right?"

She nodded. "I do."

"If King Bastian gets his hands on you, he will force you to walk through the darkness in the name of Zoharth."

"I know."

Again, the powerful instinct tugged at her heart, and—maybe it was her imagination—the key seemed to warm slightly. Somehow, she knew deep down that she needed to be enlightened by the *gods*.

Another strained sigh left Azariah's lips. "I will help you."

She clasped her hands together, relieved—in part because there was no way she could pull this off on her own, but also because it meant she didn't have to walk into the darkness yet. She felt invigorated by the idea of finally getting answers—of knowing what to do. Perhaps she finally *would* be the all-knowing Keyholder she had only pretended to be while Pierre's captive.

Eagerness built in her, bolstering her resolve. "Do you know the way to Zoharth from here?"

Azariah cocked his head, giving her an amused smile. "Do you think I don't?"

She wrinkled her nose, feeling slightly embarrassed. He had probably traveled the lands dozens of times over as a bounty hunter. Of course he knew where to go.

Azariah stooped down to the ground, taking his finger and tracing the outline of an elongated oval in the dirt with a downward curved hook in the right-most portion of the drawing.

"This is Jagged Gulch Lake."

Octavia studied the oval for a few seconds before Azariah continued.

"And this is Zoharth." He drew an 'X' in the dirt above the lake on the left. "We're here." He drew another 'X' on top of the hook that jutted out to the right of his drawing. "Traveling down and around the Lake would take too long. That's a four-day journey at a quick pace. But we can get to Zoharth in less than a day if we travel up to the outlet here." Azariah brought his finger toward the top of the drawing. "Jagged Gulch Lake feeds into the Restless Sea, and there is a narrow section that we could swim across." He eyed her. "How's your swimming?"

"Stellar."

"Good. It's a decent swim, but doable."

"Then let's go."

Azariah peered up at her, and then rose to his feet. It looked like he wanted to say something that had nothing to do with the plan to go to Zoharth, but she could see him change his mind, because his mouth pressed firmly shut.

"Azariah?"

"Yes?"

"Thank you. I couldn't do this without you, and I just want you to know that I . . ." She stopped herself. She didn't know how to express her gratitude properly—in part due to her feelings for him, which complicated things. But she would have to put those away if she was going to save everyone. What she felt for him didn't matter when it came to the darkness, or the prophecy, or being enlightened by the *gods*.

"I am glad to be of service to you, Keyholder," he said with a small dip of his head.

The term "Keyholder" felt so proper, as if Azariah were trying to emotionally distance himself from her through his words alone. She surveyed him with a clenched feeling in her stomach. She wasn't feeling sadness, but that's the closest thing she could call it.

"Azariah?"

The use of his name pulled a subtly strained look onto his face. "Yes?"

"Thank you for sharing your story with me."

His lips pursed, and he got very quiet.

"I know that wasn't easy for you," she murmured. "I'm so sorry for your loss." Her throat constricted. Even thinking about his tale made her eyes water, but she pushed the grief away. It wasn't hers to carry. "May the *gods* truly bless you."

He gave her the briefest nod, his eyes glistening, but then his melancholy snuffed out, and his walls rose up again—the toughened bounty hunter with the exterior of steel.

With that, Octavia and Azariah gathered the remaining cooked fish into a piece of torn fabric from Octavia's tunic and began their journey up the side of Jagged Gulch Lake toward the outlet. The only thought now turning over in Octavia's mind was . . . how in the *gods' waters* was she going to be able to look into the Well of Prophecy and drink a parcel without getting captured?

26

WHY ME?

Octavia kept pace with Azariah along the lakeside. All she could think about was the Well of Power in Zoharth, and her stomach squirmed at the idea of repeating the incident in Urtha. She had no doubt the *waters* of the Well would turn black and rise up just like last time—and that's what would likely get her captured. Especially if the Well of Prophecy was as heavily guarded as the Well of Euphoria.

"What's the plan?" she asked.

"The Well is at the center of Zoharth," Azariah explained. "Fortunately for us, it's the most openly accessible Well of Power in all the kingdoms. Anyone can walk up to it."

Octavia gaped at him. "What do you mean *anyone* can walk up to it?" She had never heard of such a thing. Granted, Rustwick's Well wasn't guarded to the same degree as Urtha's Well, but people had to get permission from the Wellminders to approach it.

"Given the cheap and typically meaningless fortune-telling nature of the *waters*, gathering a parcel straight from the Well isn't popular. Instead, people seek out those with experience in divination—those who know how to incorporate the *waters* into tea leaves or tokens or card readings. In Zoharth, fortune tellers hold a higher status than Wellminders by the very nature of how they interpret the *waters*. So, while anyone can approach the Well and drink from it, unless they know how to divine the meaning of what they've learned, they are lost. That's why it's typically the fortune tellers who gather the *waters* directly from the Well, and not everyone else."

Octavia chewed on her lower lip. "If that's the case, then why does Zoharth have Wellminders in the first place?"

Azariah slid her a sideways glance. "It's still a Well of Power gifted to humanity by the *gods*. The Wellminders look after it and ensure its upkeep. But since so few people are clamoring to get their hands on a parcel directly, the Well is more of a sight to see rather than a commodity to covet."

"Okay. That's good though, right?"

Azariah nodded. "The challenge isn't going to be getting to the Well. It's going to be ensuring that no one sees you look into it. If the *waters* behave the same way as they did in Urtha, that's quite a spectacle."

"Then we need a distraction," Octavia offered. "One that will draw everyone's attention away from the Well. You know Zoharth better than I do. What do you think would work?"

Azariah considered the question for a minute before answering. "There is a set of stables that border the Well. If I can get the horses and livestock loose, that should provide a sufficient distraction."

"A stampede?"

"Of sorts."

"That should work. I only need a few minutes."

Pebbles crunched under their feet as the shoreline turned rough, and Octavia put her hand up to shield her eyes from the sun. She peered ahead. The other side of the lake wasn't as far away anymore, which meant they must be nearing the outlet.

Abruptly, Azariah stopped walking, and his brow furrowed. "I need to ask you one more time. Are you absolutely sure you want to do this?"

"I'm certain," she said. "I have to know what the *gods* want to show me."

He exhaled sharply. "Very well."

He took off again, and Octavia had to jog to catch up to him.

"We'll need new clothes," he said. "And you'll need some kind of cloak. I don't like the idea of people being able to see your face. You need to avoid becoming recognizable."

"We don't have any money."

"Theft is one of my many skills," Azariah said, his serious tone lightening a bit.

A grin curled her mouth. "Are you going to teach me how to steal?"

He huffed, but Octavia caught the smile that passed like a ghost across his face. "I'm afraid I'm going to insist you leave that up to me. I don't need you getting caught for petty theft when you have a more important job to do."

"Fair."

As their walk drew on, both of them grew quiet. Azariah traveled at an aggressive pace, and after another hour, Octavia was completely out of breath. She understood why they were moving so quickly, but at the same time, her body was yelling at her to rest. She only wished she had time to truly do so. That, however, wouldn't be wise.

Every few minutes, Octavia's eyes scoured the trees. She still couldn't shake the feeling that the darkness would spring upon them, but the day was clear, cloudless, and beautiful. For now, they were safe, and as the sun dipped into late afternoon, they came upon the skinniest part of the outlet that fed into the Restless Sea.

"Let's stop to rest," Azariah said, glancing back at Octavia.

She was panting and sweating from the heat of the day. Grateful for the break, she plopped down by the water and splashed some of it onto her face. The crisp temperature shocked some life back into her.

After washing her face, Octavia found a small boulder that jutted out slightly over the water, and she sat down, pulling her boots off and sticking her feet into the flow. She stared across the outlet. It was beautiful here. The pines that hugged the shoreline burst with vibrant greens, and the lake water's deep blue reflected their image. Octavia closed her eyes and took an intentional breath through her nose, just existing in the rare moment of peace.

Footsteps sounded from behind her. "May I join you?"

Octavia opened her eyes. Azariah pointed to a spot on the boulder next to her.

"Sure."

He sat and copied her, taking off his boots and putting his feet into the lake. Octavia's gaze flickered to him. He was staring at her. His soft brown eyes held her there, and her stomach did a little summersault, so she cast her attention back to the water.

For a few minutes, they both sat there, letting the sounds of nature fill the quiet.

"Rustwick is beautiful this time of year," Azariah said softly. "Harvest season is nearly here, isn't it?"

Octavia glanced at him. His bruised face was contemplative.

"Yes, harvest season starts in a few weeks."

Had Azariah visited her home on more than the occasion of her kidnapping? With a comment like that, she supposed he must have. Had they ever been in town at the same time? Or walked past each other along the cobblestone streets, ignorant of the way their fates would intertwine?

"I love harvest season," she said.

Her throat tightened, threatening to cause tears. She missed her home and her family so much it felt like an illness, and her heart filled with longing for the life she once had.

"Would you tell me about it?" Azariah asked.

Octavia raised an eyebrow. He wanted to know? After his rejection, she would've thought that Azariah would strive to keep things strictly professional between them, but maybe his question was borne out of a desire to feel normal again—human. He had lost so much of that since Rebekah. She had to repeat to herself that he didn't care—not in *that* way—because thinking that he did hurt too much.

Her mind drifted back to her home as she spoke, and the ache she carried for it only grew.

"The wheat is gold like the sun—the bounty incredible to behold—and the harvest festival is the best week of the year. Everyone gathers into town to eat and drink and dance. There are betting games and pig races and bobbing for apples. There's even pie eating competitions. My mama makes the most amazing yatchka cream pie you'll ever taste."

Azariah wrinkled his nose with a smile.

"You don't like yatchka?" she asked with a teasing undertone.

"Too sweet of a fruit for me."

"Well, I bet if you tasted Mama's cream pie, you'd change your mind."

He gave a soft laugh, and Octavia couldn't help but grin. "Maybe I would."

She'd not seen a genuine smile cross the bounty hunter's face before, and it made her happy to see him like this.

Her stomach flipped as she spoke again. "Maybe you could come one year? You like beer, right? Every year there's a beer tasting where the town votes on the best sample of beer from that year's crop. Then at night, when the stars come out and everyone is too full to do anything else, we all look into the sky. All the lamps are put out, and it allows the stars to shine like diamonds." Octavia blinked, a deep sadness rushing through her. "Those are some of my happiest moments."

"That sounds truly wonderful," he replied. "So you . . . you have family back in Rustwick."

A knot of homesickness clenched her stomach. "Yes."

"You must miss them terribly." Azariah's smile was now gone. "I'm sorry you've had to be away from them."

"Me too. Perhaps I'll see them again . . . when this is over." She rubbed her face, wiping away a tear.

"I pray to the *gods* that you do," he said gently.

She didn't know what it was, but she felt the desire to share more with this man. When she had met him, she hadn't even given him her name, but now she wanted him to know her. The words that slipped from Octavia's lips brought her both comfort and heartache, healing some of her loneliness while breaking new parts of her because of the circumstance she was in.

"My brother Bowan is only eleven, and he's taking care of Mama all by himself. She's . . . sick. And we don't know how much time she has left." Her voice grew thick. "When those men kidnapped me, Bowan watched them take me away. He probably thinks I'm dead. He probably feels so alone and scared right now."

Azariah peered at her. She could feel his eyes on her face, but she kept looking out at the water instead, because she feared she would burst into tears otherwise.

"And Papa. He's not there to help them, and it's all my fault." Shame festered in her again for what she did to Mildred—for how stupid and impulsive she had been. "I punched a Wellminder's daughter in the face for insulting Mama, and then her father went to King Asa and had him conscript Papa into Rustwick's army. He's marching up to the darkness, and it's all my fault."

Octavia buried her head in her hands, overwhelmed. Seeing the darkness in person for the first time was enough to give her nightmares until the day she died, but to know that Papa could potentially meet the same fate she saw some of Xadia's soldiers meet was a horrid thought to bear.

"Papa told me not to get into any more trouble. He made me promise! Because *I'm* the one who is supposed to take care of Mama and Bowan. I should be there for them, but I'm not. And I'm in so much trouble."

She pulled her head up from her hands, frustrated with herself.

"Of all the places I could've been when my Papa rode away to war, I chose to be at the Kraven River trying to catch a stupid fish instead of being with my brother! I just wanted to make him fish fry. It's his favorite. I just wanted to make him happy, but I should've waited. He just needed me to hold him, he didn't need to eat fish fry! *Gods . . .*" She shook her head, balling up her fists. "I'm here because of a fishing accident! I sliced my palm open with Papa's knife when I went to cut the line because it got stuck on something. And then the Keyholder ran out of the woods. He was bleeding, and he attacked me, begging me for help. And when he died, the key came out of his shoulder and went into my hand. And I . . . I shouldn't be here! I shouldn't—"

Azariah's hand went to her shoulder, and his touch was so light and gentle that it sent goosebumps across her skin. His attention on her didn't waver. He seemed perplexed, as if he was considering something for the first time. "You didn't seek the key out for yourself . . ."

Octavia wasn't sure if he meant that as a question or a statement.

She swallowed, clasping her hands together to temper the shaking that had taken them over. Her voice came out with a strained whisper. "I wish I had never gained the key. I'm not in this for the glory. I never was. I'm in this mess because I was in the wrong place at the wrong time."

Azariah's brow furrowed in thought. It was like her words had cast a spell over him, and his face grew troubled. "Or perhaps you are in this because the *gods* saw something in you they've not seen in any other Keyholder."

She wiped her eyes with her fingertips, and frisson swept her skin. "What do you mean?"

Azariah placed the flats of his palms on the boulder and kept his attention on Octavia. "The history of the key is long and bloody. It is transferred through death, by murder. People seek it out on purpose and gain it with intention in their heart. It is not something won by accident. But you . . . you are different. You don't want to open the Well of Eternal Healing in the name of any kingdom, you want to open it for all. You want to end this for all of us, and it seems you do not want credit for doing so. Maybe that's why you're here."

She pressed her chapped lips together, feeling the heat of the sun on her face. "Are you saying the *gods* chose me?"

He tilted his head, compassion in his expression. "It is possible. Yes."

"Why? Why me? Who am I? I am not special. I am not a warrior or a king or a Wellminder. I can't do the things you can do. I can't fight or influence the kingdoms so that they do not war with each other over this. Things are about to change, Azariah. With the Well of Eternal Healing open—if I can indeed open it—there will not be peace that follows the fall of the darkness. How am I supposed to know what to do in the wake of this when *gods of old* haven't even revealed to me what I'm supposed to do to vanquish the darkness?"

Azariah's demeanor sobered even further. "I cannot answer you. I don't know. I'm sorry, Octavia."

Her heart fell. Her frustration was like a tangle of rope in her mind, impossible to undo. This trip to Zoharth would give her answers, she was sure of it. The Well of Prophecy would provide her guidance. She just had to trust that when she looked into the *waters*, another piece of this puzzle would reveal itself to her—and perhaps the words of the prophecy would be revealed to her too.

The two of them held each other's gaze. Azariah seemed like he wanted to offer her words of comfort. His face was so troubled, and hers probably was too. Her stomach did another somersault from the intensity with which Azariah looked at her, and she could feel heat crop up in her cheeks.

He spoke softly, but his words lit her spirit. "I don't think you have to be a warrior or a king or a Wellminder to save us. I just think you have to be you."

She didn't know what to say. He was being so kind to her, and it felt unexpected, simply because of the way he had gently but firmly refused her earlier. His words played over in her mind: "I can't."

He couldn't.

She couldn't.

Her heart couldn't handle it . . .

Octavia broke his gaze by getting up off of the boulder and grabbing her boots. She stuffed her feet in, lacing up her shoes and moving to grab the fish she had tied up in her ripped tunic.

"We should eat before we swim," she said.

He murmured in agreement. They ate the remaining portions of fish quickly, and when they were finished, Azariah stood by the water's edge.

"There's a current here. It flows toward the sea," he explained. "Just keep your sights on shore, and don't wear yourself out. Pace the swim."

Octavia looked to her right. As far as she could see, the outlet continued on.

"Well, I'm glad I got to eat before I drown," she quipped.

Azariah raised an eyebrow and folded his arms across his chest. "There's a bridge further down, but King Bastian keeps it guarded. I didn't think you'd fancy another round of being captured. I thought you said you could swim?"

"I can. I'm just tired." Her fingers went to the largest of her wounds—the one that Voramir had dug into her thigh. "These knife wounds are still healing, and I haven't slept much. I'm sure you're exhausted too. Are you not?"

Azariah swallowed, the dark circles under his eyes only confirming it. "I am."

Octavia didn't want to pry, but she also suspected that he had more injuries than he was letting on. She could only see the ones on his face, but she had no doubt that Pierre's men had inflicted more damage to him than that.

"Are you okay?" she asked. "I mean . . . physically okay?"

He took an uncomfortable breath. "I'm fine."

She nodded, not wanting to push the issue further. Her stomach was now clenching with nerves. She could see the other side of the outlet, but the flow of the water looked strong, and the swim would probably take fifteen minutes.

"Are you ready?" Azariah asked.

She shook out her hands. "As ready as I'll ever be."

They waded into the icy flow. Octavia sucked in a hasty breath, and before her mind could talk her out of it, she forced herself to begin. She pulled broad strokes through the water, kicking hard, and Azariah stayed by her side, swimming at her pace. Soon, the two of them were panting with their efforts.

The current was starting to take its toll, and it swept them farther down the outlet. Octavia sucked in huge gulps of air, the fatigue in her body working against her. She dipped her head under the flow for a moment, popping back up and gasping. The other side still seemed so far away, but she knew if she let any amount of panic into her mind, the results could be deadly.

She felt Azariah's hands at her waist.

"Float on your back for a moment," he instructed. "Just breathe. I've got you."

She turned onto her back immediately, floating there to catch her breath, and Azariah's hands gently steadied her as he treaded water. After a minute, her heartbeat had calmed considerably, and she turned back onto her stomach, pulling strokes again.

Determination dug into her, and her lungs found a rhythm along with her body as she pushed herself to finish the swim. After another grueling ten minutes, her feet finally found purchase against the muddy bottom on the other side.

Octavia's lungs were on fire, and her muscles ached down to the bone.

She flopped onto her back on the dirt at the shoreline, completely spent, and Azariah did the same. Her breath ran rampant. She could feel the strain her body had endured over the past two weeks. Even with the fish in her belly for energy, that swim took a piece out of her, and for the next fifteen minutes, all she could do was lay there, even after Azariah had recovered.

"Are you alright?" he asked.

The way he was looking at her was so focused. She held his gaze as a swooping sensation traveled through her stomach. She nodded, because what else was she supposed to say? When she finally found the strength, she pushed herself up into a sitting position.

"How far is Zoharth?"

"Three hours from here." He pointed through the trees behind them. "Back that way."

Octavia groaned. It would be nightfall by the time they got there, but that might actually help them since it was easier to stay hidden in the dark. "Let's go."

Azariah extended his hand to her, and she took it. He hauled her to her feet, and with determination in her heart, Octavia Fletcher turned her mind to Zoharth and the Well of Power that might finally give her some answers.

27

Ruin and Ruse

"Zoharth is more tent than permanent structure," Azariah explained as they trekked through the forest. "The fortune tellers prefer it. It makes moving shop easier, which means the streets are always changing. The only permanent structures are the palace, the Well of Power, and a few taverns, barns, and stables. The rest is nomadic."

Octavia couldn't help but smile at Azariah. He had always been so open with her when it came to teaching her about the kingdoms. Now that she had been traveling with him for some time, this felt routine. And the familiarity of it brought her comfort.

"Actually, there are docks to the west of the palace that are permanent too," he added. "Zoharth's main food source is fish, since it borders the Restless Sea. The seafood is quite good."

Octavia rubbed her hands together to warm them. The breeze was growing chilly as the sun began to descend through the sky.

"Well, I do like fish," she teased.

Azariah slid her a sideways glance, and she caught the smile that curled his mouth. "Well, then, you'll fit right in."

She gave a soft laugh. "Sure."

The shadows of dusk grew larger as the sun left the earth behind, and Azariah hurried them along. As they neared Zoharth, the melodious sounds of lutes and fiddles floated through the air. It wasn't as enticing as the music of Urtha, but it was welcoming. It was harder to see now that night had claimed the land, but a dim glow filtered through the pines, beckoning them to enter.

Octavia ran forward upon seeing the lights, but Azariah stopped her, pulling on her arm gently.

"I'll steal us some clothing. You wait here. I'll be quick."

She shook her head. "No, I'm going with you. I don't want to stay in the dark alone."

"You have nothing to cover the key. And you look like you've been kidnapped."

"You don't look any better yourself," she countered. "Your face is bruised, and that cut under your eye looks awful. Plus, I'll keep my palm hidden against my tunic. No one will see the key."

He gave a frustrated sigh. "Fine, but keep silent, keep your head down, and follow me."

"I will."

The two of them stepped out of the trees and onto a dirt street filled with tents of deep blue and royal purple. Some were tall and vaulted, while others were cozy and inviting. The other thing that struck Octavia were the lights. Each oil lamp had its own miniature cage with design work cut out from the metal. The shapes were that of diamonds, crescents, eyes, hands, and fish. The oil lamps were everywhere. They hung above tent openings and over the streets. It was like walking into a collage of metal stars. It didn't light the way well, but it was enough to see by, and it created a soft glimmer that was homey and welcoming.

Woven rugs of dark purple, emerald green, and sunset yellow were out front of each tent, and as they moved into the outskirts of Zoharth, the scent of burning incense filled Octavia's nose. It was so overbearing that it made her eyes sting. She could smell citrus, cinnamon, jasmine, and spice. They passed tent after tent, and more smells came to her. Frankincense, clove, and eucalyptus mixed with lemongrass, ginger, and sandalwood—the air was thick with it.

There were also vendors with carts selling filets of fish and all other manners of sea creatures. The salty smells that wafted through the air were offset by the sweet perfumes that overtook them.

She followed Azariah down the dirt street, keeping close to him. It wasn't very crowded outside the tents, but inside them, people packed together. They huddled around tables where women with thick head scarves held up cards or cups with herbs in them.

A flash of light lit up to Octavia's left, and she clutched her chest, stifling a shriek.

For a moment, it looked as though someone was holding a parcel of *waters* toward her, but it was simply a large crystal ball that caught the light from the many metal-caged oil lamps. The reflection in its glassy depths was mesmerizing.

Azariah stopped walking in front of one of the large purple tents, and Octavia collided into him. He steadied her.

"Careful," he chided.

"Sorry."

Octavia peeked inside the tent. Within, there were tables filled with folded fabrics and others filled with shoes and belts.

"Stay here." Azariah pointed to the dark shadows between two tents, and Octavia slipped out of view.

She stood there, hugging herself in the breeze that tossed wisps of hair across her face. It was chilly, and she hoped Azariah would be able to steal her something warm. While she waited, she worked her braids free, combing her hair out with her fingertips and rebraiding it so that she didn't look as disheveled. She examined her clothing. She absolutely looked like she had been held captive. Her tunic was stained and torn in several places, and her pants were no better. The only thing that still looked decent was her boots.

It took Azariah ten minutes, but he returned clutching several items: a new tunic, two pairs of black pants, two deep blue cloaks, a pair of leather gloves, and a leather bag. He handed Octavia her clothing, and then promptly turned around, facing the street.

Octavia threw the cloak around her shoulders for privacy and then peeled off her tattered clothing, donning the new outfit. She took one glove and pulled it over her left hand, stuffing the other one into her pocket. Everything fit her perfectly, and this time, unlike in Urtha, she knew why Azariah had been able to guess her size so well. Thoughts of Rebekah once more fired through her mind, but she shoved them away. She wasn't Rebekah . . .

She handed him her tattered clothing, and he put it into the bag.

"Are you ready to go to the Well?" he asked, adjusting his cloak around his shoulders.

"Yes."

"This way."

They walked back out onto the streets, pulling their hoods up. Immediately, this gave Octavia a sense of security. The fact that her face was now hidden quelled some of the anxiety stirring in her chest at the idea of staring into another Well of Power.

As they moved toward the center of Zoharth, music and chatter danced through the air, but she drowned it out. Her mind was now focused on the *gods*, and she prayed for their favor. Whatever it was they wanted to say to her, she was ready to receive it.

"Okay, here we are," Azariah whispered, stopping them at the end of a row of tents.

He pointed to the left. When Octavia stuck her head around the edge of the last tent, the blue glow from the Well of Power shone bright into the night. Surrounding the sparkling black rock of the Well, there were four stone arches. Each arch framed a side. The tents of Zoharth surrounded the Well too, although there was a respectable distance between the Well of Power and the nearest tent—about thirty feet on all sides.

Immediately, Octavia could feel the pull of the *waters*, and the key warmed in her palm. She took a shaky breath, longing to look into the Well, but there were six people standing by it. Whether they were Wellminders or fortune tellers, Octavia didn't know . . .

The pull was so strong that she almost stepped forward around the tent, but Azariah grabbed her arm.

"Wait."

He scouted their surroundings, and then his gaze fixed firmly on a set of stables across from where they stood.

"There's the stables I mentioned," he said. "Wait here until everyone leaves the Well. I'll let the animals loose, and that should cause enough of a scene."

She locked eyes with Azariah, and her breath caught. With all her heart, she hoped that this was going to be the moment she would discover how to vanquish the darkness.

"Go," she whispered.

"May the *gods of old* enlighten you."

He walked briskly around the perimeter of the Well, hugging the tents to keep in the shadows.

Octavia's heartbeat picked up a notch. She stood there, her belly curling with nerves. As she stared at the blue *waters*, the desire to go to the Well built. It was like there was an invisible hook anchored through her navel drawing her forward, like the Well itself was about to yank her from the shadows.

Seconds turned into a minute, and then a minute turned into two . . .

She could hear no disturbance in the night, and no animals were running about.

The key began to tingle, now joining the Well in its efforts to get her to walk toward it. But there were still people standing directly under the black marble arches. No one could see her do this. That was critical.

Abruptly, a smattering of hooves against the earth and a sharp squealing echoed through the night. Then a stirring of voices joined. People started shouting. Even from where she was standing, Octavia could see the commotion. Goats, pigs, horses, and sheep were all storming the street, and the people at the Well noticed. They turned away from it, hurrying in the direction of the tumult.

This was it. She had to act.

Octavia launched herself around the tent, darting up to the Well, and the key burned like a hot coal, causing her to wince. Being in the presence of another Well of Power was invigorating. It filled Octavia's heart with reverence, overwhelming her senses. She placed her hands on the edge of the black sparkling rock and peered over to look into the *waters*. The blue glow flashed so brilliantly that it blinded Octavia, but it didn't matter because her mind was thrown into the fog she had experienced back in Urtha.

Two figures appeared through the mist, shrouded and not fully visible. There was a brilliant golden glow from one of them. Then two voices spoke, but this time, they were new. One voice was feminine and ethereal, while the other belonged to a man who sounded desperate and frightened.

"You have seen, and now you know. You must make your choice."

"No . . . NO! I don't want to do this! There must be another way. Surely, you cannot think I would do this! I want out. Please!"

"There is no way out."

"I will not walk into the darkness. Give me another way! I'm begging you! There must be something else I can do. Give me something else to do, and whatever it is, I will do it!"

"Is your decision final?"

"P-please . . . you . . . you cannot do this . . ."

"You understand what your refusal means, don't you? What it will cost?"

"Please. P-please! I—I can't—I w-won't—"

"I will ask you one more time. Will you walk into the darkness?"

"Oh gods! Oh . . . I . . . it's not fair! It's . . . This isn't what I wanted! This isn't the glory promised! How could you do this to me!? To everyone before me!? You . . . you are sick! Perverted! I cannot . . . I . . . No! NO! I WILL NOT!"

"Then by your own words, you have cursed all that draw breath. From this moment forward, the darkness now moves, and it will swallow the land. The blood of every innocent man, woman, and child is now on your hands, Keyholder."

Octavia stumbled back from the Well of Power as if it had spewed her from its depths. She crashed to the ground, her wrists slamming against the dirt, and pain radiated up through her shoulders.

What? She had *just* looked into the Well. Why did it cast her out so quickly? Octavia felt like her heart was beating out of her chest. She looked around wildly, expecting to see people upon her demanding to know what they had just witnessed. Surely someone had yanked her back from the Well for the vision to have ended so abruptly?

But she was the only one there.

The commotion of livestock and horses was still rampant. Voices cried out. Tents were in shambles, and people were running about the dirt streets.

She huffed, pushing herself to her feet and trying to steady her trembling hands. She ran toward the black sparkling rock, slamming her hands down and looking over the edge again. She had to see more. But this time, nothing happened. The blue *waters* shone into the night, magical and serene. No voices came to her, no fog enveloped her senses, and the key had stopped burning.

"What? That's it!?" She lifted her head up the night sky, frustration now clinging to her. "No! You have to show me more!"

She stared into the Well, willing the memory to continue. Only blue reflected off her skin. In her desperation, she cupped her hands into the *waters* and brought them to her lips, drinking deeply. The *waters* slid down her throat, and Octavia continued to gaze into the Well, hoping that the words of prophecy might spontaneously burst from her lips. A strange sensation swooshed through her, and she felt like the words of *something* might be within her grasp, but it slipped away like the wisps of a dream upon waking.

"That can't be it!" she shouted. "Please! Show me more!"

Shrieks split the night, and Octavia turned just in time to see the spires of a tent collapse. Several horses were trampling through it, caught in the fabric of the tent as it fell. Distressed whinnying reached her ears, and she backed away from the Well, a sinking feeling curling in the pit of her stomach.

Where was Azariah? Why wasn't he back at the Well? He should be here by now. With her heart in her throat, she glanced back at the *waters* one last time before charging in the direction of the stampede. People were running between the tents. The chaos had now swept down an entire row of fortune tellers' havens.

Through the panic, someone ran straight into Octavia, and they both ended up in a heap on the ground. The man didn't even acknowledge her before scrambling up to continue on his way.

Octavia leapt to her feet, scanning the tents.

"Azariah!" she shouted over the swell of voices.

A horse charged at her, and she dove out of the way, narrowly missing the creature as it barged through the crowd. She clambered up to her feet, her body aching from the impact with dirt.

"Azariah!" she cried out again.

Strong hands grabbed her shoulders from behind, and she shrieked. No. She was not going to get taken. Not again. She threw her elbow back toward the stranger's face, but a firm hand blocked it.

"Octavia, it's me!"

"Azariah!" she yelped, relieved.

"We need to get out of here!"

He pulled her away from the frantic crowd back toward a section of tents that weren't affected by the animals. They ran, easily slipping away into the shadows of the night.

"This way!" Azariah turned right at an intersection of tents, and Octavia sprinted after him. For ten minutes, the two of them fled through the dark streets of Zoharth, passing more tents than Octavia could count, and once the shrieks of people had faded into the distance, they stopped, taking shelter between two stables.

They both stood there panting. Octavia leaned over with her hands on her knees, and Azariah placed his fists against the wooden wall of one of the stables.

"Where were you?" she demanded. "I couldn't find you. I thought that . . ." She jammed her fingers into the stitch in her side, still breathing heavily. "I thought something had happened to you."

"It took a bit of convincing to get the pigs to run," Azariah panted.

"I was on my way back to the Well when I spotted you."

The soft snort of horses and the bleating of a goat came from inside the stable they were up against.

Azariah now stared at her with iron determination, his brow furrowed. "Did you see what you needed to see? Did the *gods* enlighten you?"

Octavia wanted to scream at the sky, but she was too out of breath. She fought with herself for a few seconds before words would come. "I saw more, but not enough."

Azariah's expression fell. "What do you mean? What did you see?"

Octavia raked her hands through her hair, throwing the hood of her cloak off. "It was like last time. I couldn't see their faces, but I saw a woman talking to a young man. She kept asking him to make a choice. And he . . ." A shiver flew down her spine. "He sounded terrified. He told the woman that he didn't want to walk through the darkness—that there must be another way. But the woman said there was no other way." Sweat crept along her back as she continued. "He refused. He said he wouldn't walk through the darkness, and the woman said because of this, the darkness was going to consume all the lands. The woman called him 'Keyholder.' "

Even in the shadows, Octavia could see how Azariah's face drained of color.

"I think I saw a memory of the last Keyholder before me. He's the one who started the darkness in motion."

A sense of doom spread through Octavia's veins as she turned over the words exchanged between the woman and the young man. What could be so terrible that the young man would refuse to walk into the darkness at the penalty of spreading it across all the lands?

"What else did you see?" Azariah pressed.

"That's it. The Well spit me out after that. I tried to look into it again, but it only glowed blue like normal. I even drank the *waters*, but nothing happened."

Her lungs felt like they wouldn't function properly. It wasn't enough. She didn't know enough. If anything, she had even *more* questions now. Then something dawned on her mind, and it sucked all the strength from her body. Each Well of Power would probably show her more, but there was not enough time for her to travel back to any of them. This was it. Zoharth's Well of Power was the end of things. She would have to face the darkness, but now she was even more terrified to do so.

The young man's hysterical voice echoed in her head: *"I will not walk into the darkness. Give me another way! I'm begging you! There must be something else I can do. Give me something else to do, and whatever it is, I will do it!"*

What evils awaited her within? What was the true cost of being the Keyholder? How was she supposed to undo things? The memory she saw in Urtha seemed to suggest that was possible. So many questions overwhelmed her mind that she began to hyperventilate. She couldn't help it. She clutched her chest as stars flickered along her peripheral vision.

"I can't do this! I don't know what to do!" she cried. Discouragement throttled her. "Why are the *gods* speaking to me in riddles? Only showing me glimpses of things I cannot understand!" She looked up at the sky, yelling at the *gods* with everything inside of her. "What do you want from me!?"

The ambient night air was as peaceful as ever. No answer fell from the heavens, and no voice sounded in Octavia's mind. She had nothing. She nearly cursed aloud at the silence. She scuffed her foot in the dirt, letting out a feral growl and tugging violently at her braids.

Hopelessness consumed her like a raging fire. Azariah stared at her through the dark. It looked like he wanted to offer her some kind of comfort, but none came.

Octavia hugged herself, casting her eyes down to the ground, her mind still reeling. She couldn't believe that after risking a trip to Zoharth and drinking a parcel of *waters*, the *gods* had still given her no further instruction. No more memories. No more words. No prophecy.

No prophecy . . .

An idea sparked in her mind. A crazy, stupid, dangerous idea . . .

"The prophecy. I can still learn the words of the prophecy." She had spoken so softly that Azariah tilted his head like he hadn't heard her correctly.

"Octavia—"

"I can still learn the words of the prophecy!" she repeated, this time much louder. She clasped her hands together so tightly that the skin across her knuckles turned white. "King Bastian—he knows the prophecy in full. I need to speak with him."

Azariah's mouth fell open, and he gawked at her as if she had slapped him. Before he could argue, Octavia continued.

"Deliver me as your bounty to the palace. I'll gain an audience with King Bastian simply for being the Keyholder. I know he killed people to keep the words of the prophecy to himself, but that was only to get his hands on me before anyone else did. If he has me, there's no reason for him *not* to share the words. He'll tell me—especially if he thinks it will help me walk through the darkness in the name of Zoharth. Then I'll have the answers I need."

"Are you insane!?" Azariah countered, incredulous. "You want me to deliver you to the king? I thought you wanted to walk through the darkness as a free woman to claim the Well of Eternal Healing for everyone. If I give you to Bastian, he will force you to claim it in the name of Zoharth!"

"You can get me out."

Azariah threw his head back and laughed. It wasn't a mocking laugh—it was more out of disbelief than anything else—but Octavia felt affronted by it nonetheless.

He folded his arms across his chest. "No."

She challenged him, her tone sharp. "Are you telling me that if I had belonged to Bastian in the first place and someone else had hired you to find the Keyholder, that *you*, Azariah Ronan, the *best* bounty hunter in all the lands, couldn't steal me away?" She put her hands on her hips and raised an eyebrow, waiting.

Azariah ground his teeth together and was silent for several beats. "I—Of course I could—you—you're impossible—I—" He stopped speaking. She had never seen him this flustered. He clamped his hands into fists and took a few sharp inhales.

"Deliver me as your bounty, claim your payment, and then steal me back! King Bastian won't expect it. You'll have the element of surprise. Besides," she added as an afterthought, "we could use the money. We both have nothing but the clothes on our backs."

"Let me get this straight," he said gruffly, pinching the skin between his eyes. "You want me to *purposely* give you to King Bastian so that you can *maybe* learn the words of the prophecy, and then have me risk my entire reputation *and* career as a bounty hunter by stealing you back?"

"Yes," she said firmly.

"No." He shook his head. "I'm not doing that."

"You're already risking your reputation by *not* delivering me!" she shot back. "You're the one who said you've never failed to capture a bounty or carry out a kill. Besides, you won't have a reputation or a career to rebuild if the darkness swallows everything whole, Azariah! You'll be *dead*, along with everyone else!" Tears burned in her eyes at the thought, bolstered by her fear. "I *have* to do this! You said you would help me. You said you would go all the way up to the darkness with me! And that you would protect me to the best of your ability until then."

"I didn't know you would actively seek to put yourself in danger!"

"I'm the Keyholder!" She threw her hands up. "I *am* danger! I am tied to the darkness itself! I've told you before, but I will tell you again: there's something important the *gods* want me to know. It's a feeling I can't explain, and it burns in me like a fire! I won't ignore this! The words of prophecy are about *me*. Me! I must know them. If the prophecy contains instructions on how to find me, then it likely has instructions on how to defeat the darkness too."

"Octavia, I can't . . ."

"Why? Because you care about me?" She could not hold back the question or the force with which she asked it.

It hit him like a physical blow, and for a few moments, all he could do was stare at her. He opened and closed his mouth several times, and she waited for him to say something—anything—but he didn't, and another piece of her heart fractured. Whether it was because he was too scared to admit it or simply because he did not hold any feelings for her at all, she didn't know. But it didn't matter. She shoved her feelings down again, anger lacing her tone now.

"Fine. You may not care about me, but surely you care about everyone else? Surely you care about the fact that soon—*very* soon—the darkness will come. And just because I walk into it doesn't mean I'm actually going to be able to stop it. I have to know the words of the prophecy. Azariah, please!"

He grew more serious, contemplating her, and Octavia was sure he was going to refuse the idea again. It was, after all, a crazy idea with a ton of risk, but it might be the only way to learn what she needed to know to defeat the darkness.

Azariah ran a hand through his long black hair and spoke through gritted teeth. "You're insane. You know that, right? This plan is insane."

Octavia folded her arms. "Does that mean you'll help me?"

He let out a frustrated growl. "*Gods* . . . I . . . Yes, alright. I will help you."

A knot of tension broke in her abdomen, and she gave him a curt nod. The two of them stood there, gazing at each other, the silence between them thick with unspoken tension. She was sure he wanted to say something more, but as the seconds stretched on, he didn't. She wished he would. She wished he would stop looking at her like he was miserable. There was a longing beneath his eyes that he couldn't hide. It was grieved, but it also held concern . . . and something else.

When she couldn't take the silence any longer, she said, "Okay, then let's go to the palace."

Azariah rubbed the back of his neck. "We can't go yet. I'll need to steal some supplies, and I'll need to . . ." He shuffled his stance a bit, lowering his eyes to the dirt.

"You'll need to what?"

"I—are you—absolutely sure about this?"

"Yes!" she said, exasperated. "Just be straight with me. What needs to happen to pull off this ruse?"

"You need to look like my bounty. We can't walk up to the palace without selling our ruse."

"Okay, and?"

Azariah grimaced like the idea made him uncomfortable. "I'll need to bring you in bound and gagged like I would any other bounty. To walk in as equals would invite unwanted questions."

"Fine," she said without missing a beat. "If that's what it takes. Just get me to the king."

He seemed taken aback by her willingness to go along with this. His hand went to his chin, and he murmured something under his breath that she couldn't catch. By his expression, Octavia could tell that this didn't sit well with him. "May the *gods* help us. Let's go. I need to steal some things before morning's light."

By the time the sun had woken up to light the earth, Azariah had stolen everything he needed from the tents that scattered Zoharth. He had several daggers hidden on his person, rope, a broadsword, a parcel of *waters*, a pack with food rations, and a tin of white powder—the same kind of powder they had been drugged with after leaving Urtha. Octavia had also put back on her old and torn clothing. The two of them took shelter in the trees that lined the outskirts of the magnificent Zoharthian palace. They needed to hash out their plan one last time . . .

"I'll present you at the gates of the palace. The guards will let me take you all the way into the throne room. I'll ask for my payment, and leave," Azariah began. "But I won't leave the palace grounds. I'll take my time, and even make further demands to satisfy the full amount of what I'm owed. King Bastian was rather generous in what he promised me, but I wouldn't put it past him to try and shirk me of some of it."

"And I'll get King Bastian to tell me the words of the prophecy," Octavia said. She thought of Pierre and how she had leaned into her role as the all-knowing Keyholder. She could do this.

"I'll give you one hour before getting you out," Azariah said. "That's all I'm able to risk. And that's about as long as I'd be allowed to stay on palace grounds to gather my payment without raising suspicion. If you can't get him to tell you the words by then, that's it. It will be much harder to extract you from Zoharth's dungeon or from the center of Zoharth's army if they were to march you to the darkness."

"That's all I need."

"One hour," he reiterated.

"I understand."

"And do your best to stay in the throne room. Keep Bastian talking. Do whatever it takes. If he moves you, it will be difficult for me to steal you back. I have a parcel of *waters* to track you if I need to. You'll still be close enough to me for it to work."

"I'll do what I have to do to stay in the throne room. I'm rather experienced with lying to save my own neck now."

Octavia knelt in the dirt and rubbed her hands into it. Then she combed the dirt through her hair and pulled her braids unevenly, fraying them. Then she smeared some dirt on her face and arms, taking care to make it look uneven and not intentionally applied. "How do I look?"

"Like you've been kidnapped."

"Perfect."

Again, he appeared so conflicted—like he was going to argue with her—but he let out a sigh instead. "Hold out your hands."

She did so, and he took the thick rope and tied her wrists together in front of her. It was tight, but it wasn't as tight as it had been when he had first captured her.

"You should be able to slip your wrists out of this if you need to," he said.

She nodded.

"I'm going to be rough with you," he warned. "If we're going to sell this, we both have to play the part. You need to put on a show of resisting me too."

"I know."

The two of them locked eyes, and her stomach flipped. They were really going to do this. Determination kindled in her like a fire. One way or another, in an hour, she would know the words Zara had spoken.

She took a deep breath, and in her heart, she prayed to the *gods* for their favor in tricking King Bastian Jasper.

Azariah held a length of cloth in his hands, but he didn't move.

"It's fine," she said. "I'll be fine."

He hesitated only a moment longer before putting the cloth between her teeth and tying it tight around her mouth. The fabric was dry against her tongue, and for a second, her mind ran wild with the desire to *not* do this. She quelled the panic. She would do her part, and Azariah would do his. She trusted him, and that was the end of it.

He gave her a reassuring look, and his hand went up to the side of her face. He gently brushed her cheek with his fingertips as if to say, "We can do this," and then his hand fell away.

"Ready?" he asked her.

She nodded. Azariah's demeanor changed abruptly. He donned a calculated look, and he strode from the trees, pulling Octavia along behind him. There was about two feet of rope between her hands and his, and he held the end of it firmly.

The grand palace was ahead of them—a five-minute walk at most. Azariah had gotten them as close to the entrance as possible before starting their ruse so he didn't have to parade her through Zoharth's streets.

"Too public," he had said.

As they approached, the sheer size of the outer stone walls towered above them, and the massive silver gate reflected the sun. Guards in the watchtowers on either side of the gate spotted them, and Azariah yanked her forward. She nearly stumbled from the sudden movement. Gritting her teeth against the fabric in her mouth, she leaned into the ruse and tugged back against the rope as if she didn't want to follow him.

"State your name and your business, sir," one of the guards called down to Azariah, his eyes flickering to Octavia.

"Azariah Ronan. I have a bounty to deliver to King Bastian."

The guards in both watchtowers suddenly straightened and glanced at each other, eagerness now visible in their eyes. From their reactions alone, Octavia could tell that they knew who he was—and who she must be.

The guards quickly nodded to one another, and the gates screeched open. Octavia's pulse thudded uncomfortably. This was it. After walking through the entrance, they could not turn back. She looked back over her shoulder at the tree line where the thick pines blended together, but a tug from the rope pulled her to Azariah's side. They moved into the courtyard of the palace grounds. The gates screeched shut behind them with a clang, and Octavia took a steadied breath in through her nose. Her fate now rested in the hands of the bounty hunter.

28

From the Lips of Zara the Wise

The palace courtyard was massive, and the towering gray rock walls rose high, blocking out the early morning sun. The stone was carved with intricate arches, and at the top of each arch, purple and blue flags stuck out from holes in the rock. In the center of the courtyard, there was a grand stone fountain, and past it, there were steps that led up to the entrance of the palace. Above the entrance, a balcony overlooked the fountain, and the architecture above the balcony rose into the heavens, making Octavia feel incredibly small.

One of the guards had hurried down from his watchtower to join Azariah. "This way, sir," he said, gesturing across the courtyard enthusiastically. "King Bastian will be most pleased with your arrival." He took off, traipsing over the hand-laid stone walkway.

Azariah followed, and he dragged Octavia in his wake. She put on another show of resisting him only to have him snatch her wrists and snarl, "Stop fighting me! It's over now!"

The guard's eyes landed on Octavia and then went back to Azariah.

His brow raised ever so slightly as he studied the bounty hunter, and then amusement cropped up in his smirk. "Run into trouble, I see."

Azariah shot Octavia a disgusted look. "More trouble than I had bargained for. She was not an easy bounty to protect. I'll be glad to be rid of her, for *my* sake."

When they reached the stone steps, Azariah hauled Octavia up them, and she gasped, nearly losing her footing. Once they were at the top, the guard took hold of the ornate metal handles fitted into the carved wooden double doors, and they swung outward. Beyond the entrance, a cavernous stone hallway stretched on—as long as a city street. Arched windows stood at intervals to their left, letting in sunlight, and tapestries, paintings, and weaponry hung on the wall to their right.

Octavia had never seen a structure so large in her life. The sheer size of the space caused her to stare up in wonder at the vaulted ceiling and the decadent carvings along the stone.

"Who will handle my pay?" Azariah inquired. "Has King Bastian drawn up the list of what I'm owed?"

The guard nodded. "Yes, sir. I will handle your pay." He grew a bit quiet, and color cropped up in his pale face. "I will gather what you are owed as promptly as I can. Once King Bastian allows it."

"Allows it?" Azariah repeated, his tone turning dangerous. The severity of his voice caused the man to shrink back a step.

"Well, sir, we must confirm that this girl is, in fact, the Keyholder. You understand, don't you?"

Azariah pulled Octavia's bound wrists toward his body, grabbing her left palm and forcing her to open her fist. The key shone in the sunlight from the windows, and the guard's eyes grew wide. For a moment, it seemed like the sight of the key had petrified him, but then he shook himself out of his trance.

"*Gods,*" he whispered. "It really is the Keyholder . . ."

"Of course it is!" Azariah snapped. "Do you think I came all this way for nothing? Do you know who I am?"

"I—yes, I do—Of course—I didn't mean to suggest that—"

"But you did."

There was a beat of silence so thick that the guard gulped.

"Take me to the king," Azariah snarled.

The guard nodded and continued down the vast corridor. Octavia tried to keep her breathing steady, but a strange hum of energy filled her limbs. It wasn't quite panic, nor was the sensation thrilling. The feeling was completely new, and it stemmed from the fact that the danger she was in was quite real, even though she knew this was all an act.

Blood coursed through her veins, rushing like a storm, and her muscles tensed as she was led forward. She was going to stand in the presence of the king, and she had to keep her wits about her. Octavia bit down hard on the fabric between her teeth, mustering up all the courage she could as the guard brought them to the end of the corridor. They stopped in front of another set of double doors. These were silver, and the carved symbols on the outside matched the metal-caged oil lamps she had seen back on the streets of Zoharth: diamonds, crescents, eyes, hands, and fish.

"Please, wait here," the guard said with a nervous bow to Azariah. He pulled on the handle of the throne room door and slipped within, leaving them alone.

Azariah glanced at Octavia, asking with his eyes if she was okay. She gave him the smallest nod, and his hands tensed on the end of the rope that bound her hands together. Standing in the silence of the massive stone entryway was nerve-racking, and Octavia's stomach knotted.

Abruptly, the doors to the throne room opened wide, and the guard ushered Azariah in with a sweep of his hand. "Step forward and stand in the entryway. I will announce you."

Octavia's lungs spasmed as Azariah grew far more rough with her. He wrenched her forward, and her wrists ached from the force. Then he stood with her at the spot the guard had indicated.

The throne room was magnificent. It had a vast vaulted ceiling, carved stone pillars, a decadent velvet purple carpet, and a large silver throne at the far end. To the right of the throne, there was a long mahogany dining table set with a feast and a dozen people seated around it—both ladies and lords—and to the left, there were seven empty silver chairs set in a line—no doubt seats for Bastian's murdered councilmen. The room smelled like roast coska and mead.

The guard called out in a loud voice. "Presenting the bounty hunter, Azariah Ronan, to His Majesty, King Bastian Jasper."

Everyone seated around the mahogany table turned in unison at the guard's announcement, and the man at the end of the table stood. He was dressed in decadent robes of royal blue with a silver crown atop his head, but it wasn't his clothing that stunned Octavia, it was his ancient-looking face. Deep wrinkles entrenched his skin like canyons, wild long gray hair flowed down back, and his cold gray eyes looked like all the life had been sapped from them. He appeared well over a hundred years old.

How did she not know of Bastian's age? She thought he was a bit older than Papa, but not by much.

Octavia's gaze briefly flickered to Azariah's face. He seemed off-put by the king too, as if he couldn't believe what he was seeing. His expression hadn't quite slipped into shock, but something had clearly and starkly shifted in his demeanor. Why was he looking at Bastian like that? Hadn't he seen him before? Whatever the reason, she needed to snap Azariah out of his momentary lapse. Aggressively pulling against her bonds, she grunted through the gag and did her best to wrench herself free from him.

This jarred Azariah right back into the ruse, and he grabbed her upper arm with iron force, dragging her forward. As he strode in, confidence dripped from his tone like honey from a comb.

"King Bastian, I have brought you the Keyholder," he said, bowing low. He opened up Octavia's palm so that the key shone bright.

Every eye in the room fell on it, and wonder struck the ladies and lords. No one could speak. They all simply gawked at the key like it had stupefied them—but not the king.

"Azariah Ronan." Bastian's whispery, grating voice caused the hairs on Octavia's arms to stand on end. A malicious smile split his mouth, revealing crooked yellow teeth. "I was beginning to worry you might not come, but I see your sense of self-preservation has won out."

Self-preservation? Octavia glanced at Azariah, unsure of what Bastian meant.

"Your reputation precedes you well. I was right to put my faith in it." Bastian strode up to the two of them with the vigor and quickness of a young man, even though his body was ancient. The king searched Azariah's face intently, and he smirked. "My, my . . . look at you . . ." His cold eyes flickered to Octavia. "And who do we have here?"

She struggled in Azariah's grip again, so he snatched a hand through her braids, yanking them cruelly. "I said, stop fighting me!"

The skin along Octavia's scalp stung, and she let out a whimper, halting her attempts to get free.

"I have gone to *great* lengths to retrieve her, my King. She's yours, as promised. Now give me what *I'm* promised."

Up close, Bastian's face was alarming. He was so old it looked like he was decaying. Anxiety clawed up her throat, and Octavia felt like she couldn't breathe. Just standing in his presence was starting to make her question their plan, but there was no backing out of it.

Bastian's eyes pierced Octavia as he studied her with fascination.

He carried a power-hungry gleam beneath his deep wrinkles.

"Unbind her," Bastian whispered.

One of the ladies at the mahogany table stood, placing a hand to her chest. "But sire, she looks feral! Surely you wouldn't unbind the creature without first shackling her." She giggled like she was amused with herself. "Not with the court present."

"Get out!" Bastian hissed.

"Sire?" the woman repeated hesitantly.

"I SAID GET OUT!" he roared. "ALL OF YOU! OUT! GET OUT!"

The court jolted up as if Bastian had cracked a whip across their bodies. Chairs scraped against the stone, and their footsteps clamored to obey the king. Within a minute, the throne room was empty, save for the three of them.

Octavia's heartbeat was now beating wildly out of control. The bounty hunter still held her firmly, but he released his hold on her hair.

"Unbind her," Bastian ordered.

Azariah turned Octavia to face him, and as he worked the knots at her wrists, his eyes never left hers. A subtly strained look pinched his brow, and he visibly swallowed. She couldn't quite decipher what he was thinking, but something about this was bothering him, and something behind his eyes had changed. Azariah's hands moved to the cloth between her teeth, and he pulled the gag from her mouth.

"My payment?" Azariah reiterated, eyeing the king. His tone was borderline paranoid. "You *have* included what you promised me, yes?"

Bastian inclined his head, sweeping an ancient hand toward the throne room doors. "Indeed, as the *gods* are my witness, I have. My watchtower guards will see to it that you get everything you're owed. The Kingdom of Zoharth thanks you for your services. Now, *get out.*"

Azariah didn't move. His jaw tensed, and so did his hands, like he was questioning in his mind if he was actually going to leave Octavia alone with the king. In truth, Octavia didn't want him to leave either, but she couldn't let him blow their cover. She threw the bounty hunter a vile look filled with all the hatred she could muster.

"Rot in the darkness!" she spat at him.

This only amused Bastian, and his dead eyes snapped to Azariah. "You heard her, Ronan. Time for you to go."

Azariah pressed his lips together, then he gave the king a quick bow before turning on his heels and walking out of the throne room. The doors slammed shut, the sound echoing off the stone.

Bastian traipsed to the mahogany table and then took a seat. She blinked several times, unsettled by his lack of concern for her running away. She was not bound, there were no guards present, and the doors were a quick sprint away. Under different circumstances, Octavia would have run, but she had a job to do.

"Do you like coska?" he asked her.

She was rooted to the spot, still standing in the same place Azariah had left her.

"Come. Sit and eat." Bastian gestured to the feast set before him. "I'm sure you're hungry from your travels."

"You're not . . ." Octavia's breath hitched. It was probably stupid for her to say this out loud, but she couldn't help herself. "You're not going to restrain me?"

Bastian chuckled softly. "No. You've probably had enough of that." His white eyebrows inched up his forehead. "Am I right?"

"I . . . yes." She glanced back at the doors to the throne room.

"Thinking of leaving?" he inquired, pulling a tender piece of coska from the bone. He stuck the roasted bird into his mouth, chewing it and letting the juices dribble down his chin. "You won't get far. Come, eat with me."

Octavia hesitated, but then her determination to get the words of the prophecy compelled her forward. She took the seat on Bastian's left, and the smell of the roast coska made her mouth water. She eyed the food enviously, but a sense of caution held her back. What if he had tampered with it somehow? But then, she reasoned, why would Bastian poison her? He didn't even know she would be coming, and he also wanted her alive—that's what Azariah had said the day she met him. So, abandoning her caution, she snatched up a leg and bit into the meat. The savory flavor was incredible.

Bastian seemed pleased. A wide smile lit up his wrinkles, entrenching them so deep it was disturbing to behold.

"May I see your hand, Keyholder?" he asked in an overly sweet tone.

Octavia considered him warily. Every person who had kidnapped her for the key had been horrendous to her. But he was playing nice. Too nice . . .

She extended her left palm toward him, and he took it, examining the key with hungry eyes. His leathery pointer finger traced the shiny silver metal, and a chill swept Octavia's skin.

"Truly the *gods* have blessed me today," he murmured. His gaze shifted upward to her face. "What is your name, child?"

He was peering at her with rapt attention. She wanted to look away from him, but she couldn't. It was like he had cast a spell over her.

"Octavia," she replied.

"Tell me, Octavia. Did the bounty hunter explain to you why you're here?"

"You want me to walk through the darkness to claim the Well of Eternal Healing in the name of Zoharth."

His eyes gleamed. "Yes, I do. What do you think of that?" He tilted his head, examining her. His cold eyes did not blink. They were glued to her, unwavering.

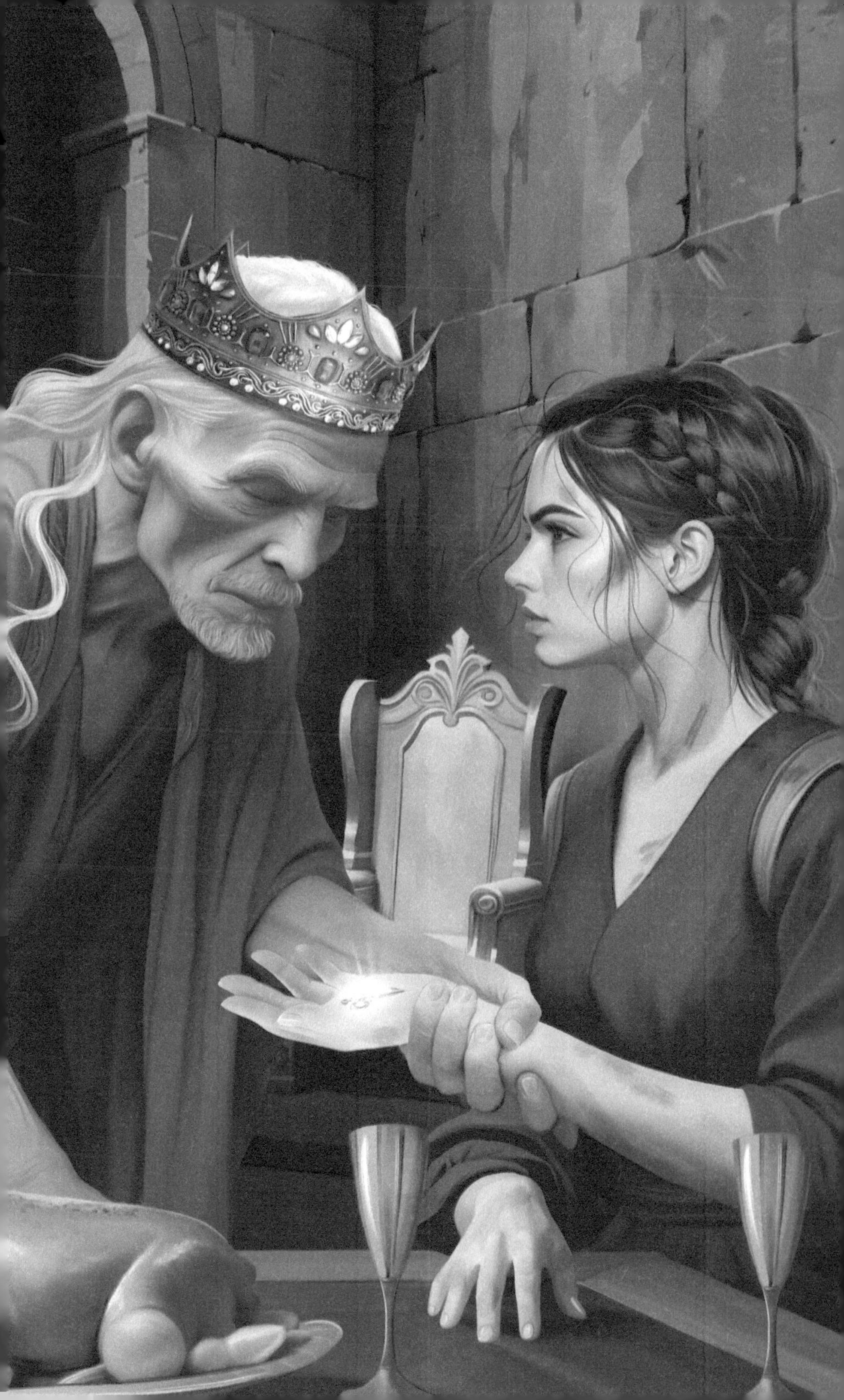

Octavia didn't know what the truth would elicit from this man. She wanted to be the Keyholder for everyone, not just for Zoharth, but she also had to play this right. She chose her words carefully.

"I think a man who would go to such great lengths to ensure he got to the Keyholder first clearly holds his kingdom in high regard."

In truth, she knew Bastian didn't care about the citizens of Zoharth. The only thing he cared about was the glory she could bring him. He was a vile beast, but she would flatter him nonetheless.

Bastian's eyes narrowed, but he did not lose his sickeningly sweet nature. "What lengths are you referring to? What else did the bounty hunter tell you?"

Octavia swallowed another bite of coska, her heartbeat ticking faster. She might as well get straight to it. She needed to steer the conversation in the direction of the prophecy, and the only way she could think of doing that was sharing what she knew.

"He said there was a prophecy about me, and that you had killed your entire council to keep the words of it to yourself. He also said you killed the prophetess who delivered the prophecy."

The king's eyes flashed, a dangerous smile befalling him. "Indeed. I cut her down. Just there."

He pointed to the spot where Azariah had brought Octavia in. The lack of remorse in his tone sent shivers across her skin, and Octavia clenched her teeth, pushing back against her body's instinct to get up from the table and flee.

"The prophecy must contain words of great importance if it was worth killing over," Octavia continued.

"Only in that it contained instructions on how to find *you*, Keyholder."

Octavia knew that was a lie. There was more to the prophecy than the part about the *waters*. She challenged him.

"Then if that's the case, share the words with me. You have me now."

Bastian's amused smile grew. "My, my . . . so forward."

"I see no reason not to be," she countered. "I must walk through the darkness. It creeps over the land, even now. Time is running out."

Bastian's sweet demeanor changed in a heartbeat. His brow furrowed and he snarled at her. "What did Azariah Ronan tell you?"

Octavia took a steadied breath. "Only that the *waters* can track me and that the darkness is moving for the first time in a millennium."

When the king did not reply, Octavia pressed forward, pulling on the threads of her role as the Keyholder blessed by the *gods of old*.

"I will do whatever you ask of me, King Bastian, but I need to know the words of the prophecy. That is my only request. If the *gods* gave the *waters* to the prophetess as a warning, then I must know them. They may help me defeat the darkness."

"Hmm, so forward *and* willing." He cleared his throat, eyeing her in a calculated manner. "I'm going to be very honest with you now. There's much I wish to discuss, but what happens to you next is entirely up to *you*. You wondered why I haven't shackled you? I want to approach this as equals first." His voice turned gravelly and threatening. "But I will not hesitate to treat you like a *dog* if I must. Do I make myself clear?"

Octavia nodded, a cold numbness dousing her veins.

"Very well," he said, folding his wrinkled hands together. "First, I want you to understand that even if you leave this throne room unbound, you still belong to me. Whatever your life was beyond these walls is of no consequence anymore, so I suggest you mourn any losses you perceive you've suffered *quickly* and then put it from your mind. I don't care about your past. I don't even care about how you got the key. You stand for Zoharth now. You will defeat the darkness for Zoharth. And you will claim the Well of Eternal Healing for Zoharth. But that's not all I want from you."

Octavia's stomach flipped, and she balled her hands up under the table to stop them from shaking. She forced a courage she didn't feel into her tone. "If you want to approach this as equals as you've said, then tell me the prophecy. Extend your favor to me, and I, in turn, will extend mine to you."

"Why so persistent in this?" Bastian probed. "Why does it matter to you so much?"

"The *gods of old* gave me a dream," she lied. "After the bounty hunter captured me, I dreamed the same dream every night. I was standing before *you*, King Bastian, and the *gods* would whisper in my ears to ask you to repeat the words of the prophecy. But every time you would begin, I would wake. It has burned in my heart like a fire ever since. I must know. That is all I can think about. That is why I've asked you. To not ask would show my disobedience to the *gods*, because why would they show me the same dream over and over again if the words were not important? You want me to walk through the darkness for Zoharth? Tell me the words. Sharing them with me can do nothing but help."

Bastian considered her, hand to his chin. His lifeless eyes seemed to stare right into her soul, but she did not relinquish her determined look.

"I suppose . . . since I have you now . . ." He seemed to struggle with the idea for a few seconds. The silence in the throne room was heavy with tension, and Octavia could scarcely believe this might actually work. In her mind, she prayed to the *gods* to tip the scales of Bastian's heart in her favor.

Bastian's leathery hands clenched and unclenched, then he flared his nostrils and opened his cracked lips.

"From the *waters* of the Well of Prophecy,
From the lips of Zara the Wise,

a millennium and not a vessel willing
unless the wrong is righted, all will perish
seek the one who can walk through the darkness
all the waters will allow it
but beware of the darkness and those who seek to conquer it
for each time the key changes hands, it will seep faster
burning, burning, all burning, all consuming
it must be paid in full
to the one the darkness calls
only by approaching it may they know
greed will be the undoing, and forfeit the gain
the path chosen will determine the fates
not but a chance left in the gods' graces is all the time that remains"

A strange sort of tingling entered Octavia's body. The feeling could only be described as divine. She clutched her head and gasped. For a few seconds, her mind swam, and her vision slopped from side to side. She clutched the edge of the mahogany table, and took a labored breath, fighting the urge to pass out. Then the sensation ended, and her mind righted itself.

"What just happened to me?" she whispered. She locked eyes with Bastian, unnerved. "What did you do to me?"

"I did nothing. It's the words of the prophecy. Once you hear them, you cannot forget. It is the doing of the *gods*."

Octavia's eyes widened, but her mind immediately confirmed the truth of his statement. She knew the prophecy perfectly. The words were paved into her soul as if she'd known them her whole life. But the meaning was something she would have to ponder. Before she could turn her thoughts to what she had learned, Bastian spoke again, his expression darkening.

"Now that that's out of the way, let's get down to business, Keyholder. I'm sure you've noticed my appearance, have you not?" He swept his leathery hands outward.

"Yes."

King Bastian clicked his tongue. "It's 'Yes, my King.' We wouldn't want you to start off this partnership with ill manners, would we?"

Octavia's jaw stiffened, but she knew she would have to placate him, so she repeated the phrase with respect. "Yes, my King."

Bastian's grin was cruel. "Good." His tongue ran over his teeth, and he grabbed another leg of coska, ripping into its flesh. After he swallowed the mouthful of bird, he continued. "I am only fifty years old. Six weeks ago, I looked my age, but the day I learned the words of the prophecy, everything changed. I am now aging at an unsustainable pace. It was the work of the prophetess . . ."

Bastian's words immediately made her recall Azariah's story of Zara, and a chill zipped through her. The bounty hunter's voice replayed in her mind: *"In her dying moments, Zara called a curse upon Bastian, and with her last breath, she said she had told another the words that the* waters *had produced."*

"I am dying," Bastian whispered. "Soon, my body will age past what I'm able to bear, but with you, I am saved. Once you unlock the Well, you will bring me a parcel of its *waters*, and I will drink it and be healed." He paused, becoming pensive. He stared at Octavia like he couldn't believe she was here in his presence. "I thank the *gods* for their favor in allowing Azariah Ronan to fall into my clutches when he did—otherwise I don't think I would've gotten my hands on you."

Octavia furrowed her brow, confused. What was Bastian talking about? She peered at him with a sinking feeling in her gut. "What do you mean 'fall into my clutches,' my King? I thought you hired the bounty hunter?"

"I did, but it was a twist of fate that brought him to me." Bastian's posture straightened a bit as he leaned back against his chair. "You see, I had some loose ends to tie up after learning the words of prophecy—namely a mysterious someone the prophetess had told the prophecy to. I couldn't have everyone after the Keyholder. So, I sent my guards to the prophetess's house. There, they captured a man and brought him to my throne room for questioning. It was Azariah Ronan. That is how I met him. Thankfully, my guards were able to collect him before he could escape the bounds of Zoharth with the words of the prophecy."

Octavia's blood ran as cold as ice, and she brought a hand up to her mouth. The horror that streaked her whole body became visible on her face. It was as if King Bastian had taken a dagger and run her through with it. Azariah was the one Zara had told the words of the prophecy to? He knew? All this time? And he had chosen to go along with her plan to trick Bastian into giving her the words of the prophecy anyway?

Panic drowned her, and for a moment, all she could do was sit there and try not to pass out. It couldn't be . . .

Why would he do that? How could he do this to her? It didn't make sense. But a terrifying possibility fell into her mind like an avalanche. Did he plan to leave her here? Somewhere along the way after escaping Pierre, had he changed his mind and decided to collect his pay? One thing was certainly clear: Azariah had lied to her. And if he had decided to leave her, she now belonged to King Bastian Jasper.

Stomach acid pushed its way up Octavia's throat, and she desperately fought to keep control of her breathing.

The king narrowed his eyes at her. "This is news to you, I see."

She opened and closed her mouth as her brain continued to process . . .

Gripping the side of the table, Octavia dug her nails into the wood. She had to know more. There *had* to be more to this—some explanation as to why Azariah would do this to her. He had seemed so reluctant to go along with the ruse. She couldn't believe it. She wouldn't. But then . . . Why didn't he tell her the prophecy if he already knew it?

Her voice shook as she spoke. "Why didn't you kill the bounty hunter? If he knew the words of the prophecy, why did you send him after me? I thought that's why you killed all of your councilmen—to keep the words from escaping the confines of the palace. To get to me first."

"I nearly did," Bastian replied. "But my sword was stayed by two things. One, I had heard of a bounty hunter from Xadia who had never failed a job, and it just so happened to be him—three of my guards confirmed his identity. And two, I knew I had the means to control him. I could make him do my bidding, so I did. To keep him from going rogue, I had a witch cast a spell on him."

"A witch?" Octavia repeated. Was it the same witch who had given Azariah the vial of magenta powder that had shielded her from those who sought the key? She felt like she couldn't breathe. "What spell?"

"The witch made a potion using my blood, and I made the bounty hunter drink it. He is magically bound to me. My fate is his. When I die, so will he." Bastian scratched his chin. "It was the only way to ensure he would come back to me and not say a word regarding the prophecy. Sharing it with others would've only made his job more difficult. But now he is free of me. Part of his payment was the antidote to the spell. Once he takes it, his fate is no longer tied to mine."

Stars danced around the edges of Octavia's vision as horror swallowed her whole. Azariah had traded her for a cure . . .

Bastian eyed her like a predator. "My army is ready to march, I've just been waiting for you. But before we go, there's a little matter we must take care of first. I can't simply trust your word without insurance, Keyholder. The truth is, there's nothing to stop you from abandoning Zoharth once you step foot into the darkness. You see, in order to ensure your loyalty to Zoharth, I must magically bind your fate to mine. That way, you cannot run off. You will walk through the darkness in the name of Zoharth to heal me, because if you don't, you will perish too."

Blinding hot panic flooded through Octavia's limbs, and her heart beat mercilessly in her chest. If Bastian bound her to his cursed illness, he would be putting the lives of everyone in all the lands at risk. How long did he even have left? By the looks of it, he was mere days from death.

"Now, this is the part that depends on *you*." Bastian's voice turned into a snarl. "Are you going to take the spell willingly, or do I need my guards to force it down your throat?"

Every piece of her mind and body was telling her to run. As much as she didn't want to believe it, Azariah had lied to her, and right now, she was alone to fight for her fate. She could not let this happen. Without warning, Octavia leapt from the table, retreating from Bastian and sprinting toward the double doors.

"Wrong choice, Keyholder!" the king growled from behind her, toppling his chair.

She burst through the exit into the cavernous hallway beyond. Part of her hoped she would see Azariah standing there, ready to rescue her, but she was met instead by a group of guards.

"Seize her!" the king cried.

Octavia darted down the corridor, narrowly avoiding three of the guards. Their fingertips snagged at her clothing as they clambered after her. More guards appeared down the hall, rushing toward her, and a sinking feeling plummeted through her gut. There were too many of them.

Hands arrested Octavia's arms, and she shrieked, fighting to pull herself free, but the men dragged her back the way she had come until she was at the throne room doors again. The king's feral eyes raked over Octavia as she continued to struggle in the guards' grasp.

"Let me go!" She threw her head back, knocking into one of the guards, who stumbled away, clutching his face in pain.

"Put her out!" Bastian snarled.

A rancid cloth was pressed over Octavia's mouth and nose. She screamed, contorting her body and desperately trying to draw breath, but the hand over her face was suffocating. Her brain cried for oxygen, and her lungs desperately fought to pull in air, but every second that passed slugged her mind deeper into the dark until her senses fell into the arms of oblivion.

29

The Pain in the Payment

Octavia awoke in the damp and the dark, lying on her side against cold stone. There was no light at all, and for a few seconds, she feared she had gone completely blind. She sat up, and immediately, she gagged as something cold and forceful yanked up against her neck. Her hands went to examine the object. It was a metal collar.

Tears sprang to her eyes as panic exploded through her body. She clawed at the collar, pulling at it with her fingers and gasping, but there was no getting it off. She scooted back a few inches to allow the pressure on her neck to diminish, and with her hands, she felt around in the pitch black. Rugged stone was beneath her, and then she felt the chain. It extended from the back of her neck to the wall, and it was only three feet in length.

"N-no. No!" she whimpered, scraping at the collar. Her lungs spasmed, and she began to hyperventilate. The sheer, terrifying horror of her situation drowned her, and she screamed. "Let me go! Please! Let me go!"

Her own voice echoed all around her. She could see nothing at all. The only sensations grounding her were the cold metal collar and the stone, and soon, her mind caught up with the reality of her situation. She was in a dungeon, probably under the palace, where the light from the sun could never reach, and Azariah Ronan had abandoned her.

A torrent of torturous thoughts bombarded her, and she sifted through them like wheat. Azariah had traded her for a cure. He had changed his mind and left her. And now she was chained like a dog, awaiting her fate. She was Zoharth's salvation now—the king's salvation. Azariah had pulled the ruse of a lifetime, pretending to go along with her desire to trick Bastian into giving her the words of a prophecy he already knew, all for an antidote he desperately needed to live. In the end, the bounty hunter had proven himself to be a survivalist, plain and simple. Whatever shred of decency he had gained at Jagged Gulch Lake when he released her from her vow and set her free was now gone. Azariah had finally rid himself of the girl who had nearly gotten him killed.

She didn't want to believe any of it, but it seemed to be unequivocally and horrifyingly true. How long had it been since Azariah left the throne room after delivering her? How long had she been unconscious? How long had she been chained to this wall?

Far longer than one hour . . .

"*I'll give you one hour before getting you out,*" Azariah had said. "*That's all I'm able to risk.*"

Betrayal dug into her heart like a dagger. How could he do this to her? She had trusted him. He had even fought against the idea of this ruse from the beginning, but perhaps it was seeing Bastian's age that finally pulled his allegiance away from her. He had gotten his cure, and the only thing it cost him was the bounty he was meant to deliver all along.

She cursed herself for pushing Azariah to take her to Zoharth in the first place. What a stupid, stupid fool she had been!

Octavia sobbed into her arms, the collar around her neck not allowing her to bend forward more than a few inches. The cries wracked her chest as her tears fell, and bitter whimpers grated her throat like hot coals.

How was she here? How had an unfortunate fishing accident turned into the nightmare of all nightmares? She was supposed to be home with Papa and Mama and Bowan. She was only a wheat farmer's daughter, not a savior. But fate and chance were laughing at her. Keyholder. Coveted prize. A means to an end for evil men to steal, control, and use . . .

She cried and cried, raking her hands through her hair and screaming at the top of her lungs into the cold silence of the pitch-black dungeon, and when she had no strength left in her body to cry anymore, she simply leaned against the wall, silent and stunned, her cracked lips parted and her parched tongue unable to utter anything more.

She stayed like that for minutes on end. Or maybe it was for an hour. Time didn't have a meaning to her anymore. She was at the mercy of the king, who would retrieve her from this hole when he saw fit. Octavia Fletcher now belonged to King Bastian Jasper.

Torment was the only thing that occupied Octavia's mind as she sat there, and the utter lack of light tormented her too. The air was stale and rotten down here, and it suffocated her. Her stomach ached for food, her mouth longed for water, and her heart yearned for this nightmare to fade. But it didn't. This wasn't a dream. This was really happening.

A clinking sound drove Octavia to jerk upright. Metal keys jingled, a door scraped open, and dim light from somewhere to her left showered the damp dungeon. She could see bars that were too far away to touch, and then two guards walked into her view—one was fat, and the other one was lanky. The lanky guard clutched a torch, and both men leered at Octavia as she shrunk back against the stone. Her eyes hurt from the light, even though it wasn't much light at all, and she stifled a sob.

"Look who's finally awake," the fat guard chortled.

"King Bastian waits for you in the throne room, Keyholder," the lanky guard announced.

The fat guard swung a ring of keys around his stubby forefinger, jamming one into the keyhole of the cell door. It screeched open, and he entered. His chubby hands went to the chain fastening Octavia to the wall, and he pushed the key into a rusty lock. Once the chain was separated from the stone, the fat man grabbed the excess coming from the back of the metal collar and yanked Octavia to her feet.

She gave a strangled squeak, her hands grasping the collar to keep the pressure off of her windpipe.

"Move."

The guard stayed behind Octavia, steering her by the neck toward the cell door. She clung to the collar, tempering the force he used to the best of her ability. Hot tears spilled down her face without mercy, burning her eyes, and she let out a soft cry as her chest jerked with breath. "Y-you're hurting m-me."

"Shut up!" the fat man snarled.

He pushed Octavia down the narrow dungeon hall, and the lanky guard with the torch followed. Next, they traveled up a set of rough-cut stone steps into another hallway.

Octavia's body felt numb with dread, and her mind fought blacking out as she was led forward. The stone corridors blended together. She had no idea where she was. But the one passageway that opened up to the sky beyond the palace shone bright with stars, confirming once again in Octavia's mind that she had been abandoned. She had entered the palace early that morning, and now it was night.

Finally, she recognized her surroundings. The silver throne room doors were ahead, and the two guards brought her into the cavernous space. King Bastian sat on his throne, and standing next to him, there was a tiny, hunched-over old woman with hair of wild purple. The witch. Her toothy grin lit her age-spotted face as she raised a bony hand, clicking her long fingernails against each other and eyeing Octavia with sickening pleasure.

In front of Bastian's throne, there was a table with metal cuffs fastened to the surface, and six more guards stood nearby. The fat man stopped Octavia mere feet from the table.

"The Keyholder, my King," he said, bowing low. "As you requested."

Bastian rose from his throne and walked around the table, coming up to Octavia. He stood so close to her that his foul breath fell across her face. Her heart beat wildly with fear. She couldn't speak even if she wanted to . . .

The king tutted, his canyon wrinkles burrowing deeper into his face as he smiled. "I'm going to offer you one last chance to approach this in a civilized manner, Keyholder. Do you see my friend here?" He gestured back toward the witch. "She's made a very special potion for you tonight. Now, my question. Again." Bastian stared at her with his ghastly, almost-dead eyes. "Are you going to drink it willingly, or shall I have my guards restrain you and force it down your throat?"

Octavia found her voice, weak and trembling though it was. "King Bastian, please. Please don't do this! I will walk through the darkness in the name of Zoharth. I swear it. I will! But you cannot tie me to your illness. If you die before I can unlock the Well, we will all perish! Everyone!"

Bastian's upper lip curled in displeasure. "Is this your final answer?"

"Please don't do this!" she begged him.

"Put her on the table."

The guards moved in unison, and the fat guard holding her neck released her and backed away, allowing the other guards to grab her.

"NO! No! King Bastian, you cannot do this!" she cried.

She flailed against the guards, but they quickly subdued her, slamming her onto the table. Her back hit the wood so hard that it stunned her, wrenching the breath from her body. Too dazed to move, the guards were able to lock the cuffs around her ankles and wrists.

Octavia's chest spasmed as feeling surged back through her. She strained against the cuffs, crying uncontrollably.

"King Bastian, p-please!"

The king strode up to her with a murderous look, and he withdrew a dagger, which caused Octavia's panic to increase even more. With a quick flash of silver, the king slit the heel of his palm and held it over her face, letting specks of his blood drip onto her cheeks. She twisted in her restraints, whimpering and turning her face to the side.

Bastian pulled his hand back and hissed, "You better walk through the darkness quickly, Keyholder—for the sake of all—because you are *mine*, and your fate is *my* fate!" His feral eyes flicked upward, and he motioned the witch forward. "The blood you require."

He held out his palm, and the old woman hobbled toward him with a vial of black liquid in her hand. She positioned the opening under the drip of the wound, collecting the blood so that it mixed with the liquid. A sizzling sound bubbled up from the vial, and smoke came out of the top.

Octavia pulled at the cuffs, contorting her body. She had to get away from them. She couldn't let this happen. Her pulse thundered through her ears, and black spots invaded her vision.

"Keep her still and open her mouth!" Bastian ordered.

A sharp blow landed on Octavia's stomach, and she gasped. Then one of the guards held her head still, while a second guard forced his grimy fingers into her mouth. She bit him without restraint, and he roared in pain, drawing his hand back.

Another guard approached. "Don't use your hands, idiot!"

The guard held up a metal clamp, and with force, he pushed it into Octavia's mouth. Then he cranked it, prying her jaw open. She screamed.

"Quickly!" Bastian roared, ushering the witch to Octavia's side.

Her eyes widened with horror. She couldn't move. She was hyperventilating to the point of seeing stars, the panic in her raging like an inferno. There was nothing left for her to do. Her brain worked furiously, weighing her options. If she didn't try to swallow the potion, she might choke on it. But if she did take it, she might die before she ever got the chance to unlock the Well.

Bang.

The throne room doors burst open with a violent crack, and every eye turned toward the newcomer. Octavia's heart leapt in her chest.

It was Azariah Ronan, sword in hand, with a black cloth mask over his nose and mouth.

"What is this!?" Bastian demanded. A brief look flashed between the bounty hunter and the king, and then Bastian yelled. "Guards, seize him!"

Azariah moved so quickly it was like he was made of wind. The guards drew their swords, and a fight broke out. Metal clanged. The guards grunted with their efforts, but each one that engaged Azariah fell to the ground within seconds as white powder was thrown into their faces.

Bastian and the witch both retreated, but Azariah was too fast for them. Before they could even cry out, the powder was thrown into their nostrils. The witch tumbled back, the black potion shattering across the floor, and in the same stride, Azariah slammed the king onto his back. Bastian's eyes nearly popped from his skull upon impact, and right before he passed out, Azariah growled, "Thanks for the antidote, my King!"

Octavia whimpered, the clamp now sending shooting pain up the sides of her face, and Azariah ran to her. He gently uncranked the clamp, pulling it from her mouth, and she stared at him, her eyes watering in disbelief.

"Did you swallow any of the potion?" he asked, panting heavily. He pulled his mask down below his chin.

"N-no." A buzzing sensation had entered her entire body, causing her to shake violently. "Get m-me off this table!"

Azariah stooped, snatching a set of keys from one of the unconscious guards. He moved to her ankles first, unfastening the cuffs. Then he freed her wrists. She sat up, leaping away from the table as if it were made of molten rock.

Her hands scraped at the metal collar around her neck. "Get t-this off me!"

Azariah moved behind her, inserting a key into the lock. Then a click sounded, and the collar broke in two, falling to the throne room floor. Octavia's feet were unsteady beneath her, and her knees buckled, so Azariah caught her in his arms. She peered up at him, her heart thrumming in an untamed manner. His brown eyes were so fierce they looked like they were burning, but not with anger. It was something else entirely. It was an expression that rivaled even the one she had seen from him in the washroom. He seemed tormented and *terrified*.

"You came back f-for me," she stammered.

"Of course I came back for you."

She buried her head into his chest, completely overwhelmed, and for a brief moment, Azariah hugged her, wrapping his strong arms around her and holding her close.

"Come on, we don't have much time," he prompted. "We must leave."

He rushed her to the throne room doors, where a covered wheelbarrow sat in the shadows. Azariah moved quickly, throwing the brown burlap fabric aside.

"Get in!" he said, pulling his mask back up over his nose.

Octavia obeyed him, climbing in and curling up into a ball.

"Stay silent!"

He threw the fabric over the top of the wheelbarrow, hiding her within. Her body was still experiencing a petrifying high from being strapped to the table and held down by the guards, so it was difficult to keep her breathing quiet, but she forced her lungs to comply, taking only sips of air, even though it made her head swim.

He had come for her. Azariah had come for her. She wanted to burst into tears. Whether it was from happiness or shock, she didn't know.

She could hear the throne room doors shut, and then the wheelbarrow flung into motion, rolling down the cavernous hallway. Azariah's pace was aggressive, and his labored breathing was strong.

Octavia slammed her eyes shut. She knew she was covered by the fabric, but even still, she felt exposed. She clasped her hands together and curled her body even smaller, wanting to disappear. Prayer was the only thing her mind could cling to. Over and over again, she prayed.

The wheelbarrow bumped along, jarring her slightly, and then it abruptly halted. She could hear a deep voice grunt, as if to call out for help, but no words came. Then the thud of a body hitting the floor sounded directly next to her.

The wheelbarrow moved again, picking up speed. It glided over the stone below, and after another minute, it stopped for a second time.

More muffled grunting. Footsteps shuffled against stone.

Thud.

The sharp screech of a metal gate caused the hairs along the back of Octavia's neck to stand on end. Were they at the gates of the palace already?

Suddenly, the wheelbarrow tilted at an angle as if it was rolling up a steep ramp. Then it jerked with force and tipped against a rough surface, nearly causing Octavia to tumble out. She anchored herself to the inside of the wheelbarrow by jamming her feet up against the wood, and she pressed a hand over her mouth to stifle a gasp.

For several seconds, everything was still . . .

Then there was a flick of a rider's crop, the pawing of horses' hooves, and the bump of wooden wheels.

Octavia didn't dare make a sound. Not yet. She waited as they rode, keeping her hand over her mouth. She couldn't believe the turn of events.

Tears slipped down her face unrestrained, and she cried silently. She had come so close to having that potion poured down her throat, and if that had happened, she never would've been free of Bastian Jasper—not until she brought him a parcel of *waters* from the Well in Hritza.

Thank you, she thought to the *gods.*

They rode and rode. Azariah kept going, taking the horses as fast and as far as he could, no doubt to put some distance between them and the palace, because the moment someone discovered the scene in the throne room, they would be in big trouble.

Octavia lost track of time, her mind drifting and her body cramping from the fetal position, but finally, the cart came to a halt, and she could hear Azariah dismount. Still, she didn't move. She didn't know where they were, and the smartest thing for her to do was wait for him.

He tugged off the burlap fabric, and the dark of night enveloped them, but the moon provided enough light for her to see. They were in the forest somewhere.

Azariah's mask was gone, his face was flushed, and he looked disheveled with his long hair hanging in curtains against his cheeks. He stared at her with relief and then extended his hand toward her. She took it, and he helped her up and over the edge of the cart, setting her gently onto the ground.

So many questions and emotions flew through Octavia's mind and heart that she didn't know which one to tackle first. It was like a wave surging through her.

"Are you alright?" he asked with concern. "We can't linger here long. But I wanted to get you out of the wheelbarrow."

Hesitantly, he lifted his fingertips to her cheek to brush a piece of hair from her face. Octavia slapped his hand aside, anger now forcing its way to the forefront of her emotions.

"Zara told you the words of the prophecy? And you led me to the palace like a pig for slaughter anyway!?" she demanded. Her heartbeat raced in her chest, and she curled her hands into fists. "You lied to me! You said you didn't know anything other than what you told me!"

Azariah's face turned ashen.

Octavia slammed her palms against his chest, pushing him away.

"You never told me about Bastian's potion either! You were bound to his cursed illness? Did you not think for one second that he might do the same to me to force my loyalty to Zoharth? If I die, Azariah, so does everyone! Why didn't you tell me you were going to trade me for a cure!?"

"Octavia—"

"I thought you had left me!" she cried. "I thought you had changed your mind and left me! How could you do that?"

"Octavia, I can explain!" he said, approaching her. He reached out like he wanted to steady her, but she shrank away from him.

"Don't touch me!"

He held up his hands, retreating a few paces.

Octavia's chest heaved. She could not hold back the spite in her tone. "Did you get your cure?"

Azariah looked as pale as a ghost. "I did."

She sneered at him. "So, you got your payment. Your *freedom*! Meanwhile, Bastian chained me in a hole in the dark like an animal! I thought I would belong to him until I died! How could you not tell me about your payment? You let me pull this ruse with you all for a prophecy you *knew* all along!"

There was a beat of silence so tense it made her want to strike him. Azariah seemed momentarily unable to form words, and Octavia's anger coursed like a storm through her veins, stirring wrath into her heart and shattering it like glass.

"What happened?" she demanded. "Why did you leave me there? You said you would give me an hour, but you *abandoned* me!"

"Bastian's guards forced me out!" he replied, distressed. "I didn't want to go, but I didn't have a choice. A group a dozen strong escorted me from the palace grounds the moment I left the throne room. That's why I couldn't come for you within the hour. I needed to wait for the cover of night to sneak back in. And I used this too."

He pulled the parcel of *waters* from his pocket. Octavia stared at the blue glow.

"Let me explain. Please!" he begged her.

She glared at him, tears falling down her face. "You better have a good explanation for this, Ronan, or I swear to the *gods*, I am done with you!"

Azariah's expression pulled taut with emotion he couldn't staunch. She could tell that this had pushed him to desperation. "I never knew the full prophecy."

"Liar!" she retorted.

"I'm not lying!"

"Bastian captured you from Zara's home!" she countered. "He told me so!"

"He did, but I'm not the one Zara shared the prophecy with! It was her brother."

Octavia's mouth quivered as she sucked in a strained breath. "What are you talking about?"

Azariah buried his face in his hands for a few seconds, composing himself. Then he looked up at her. "Before the darkness started moving, I traveled to Zoharth. I was looking for answers on what to do with my life. I hate bounty hunting! I hate what my life has become since Rebekah! And so, I sought out a fortune teller to gain the guidance of the *gods*.

"It was at a tea leaf reading that I met Zara. She was kind to me, and after the reading, she invited me to her home. She said she felt something stirring in me—a tie to the *gods*—and that she needed time to divine what it was, if I would allow her. And so, I did. I stayed at her home for three nights, and all the while, every divination she performed told me my destiny was tied to something far larger than myself. Something that would save all the lands."

Azariah took a deep breath, his hands shaking slightly.

"Zara was on the brink of discerning my destiny when she learned of the prophecy. She went out that morning, and I never saw her again. I was resting in her home. I had caught ill, and that evening, her brother burst through the door with a frightened look in his eye. He began to pack his things in a trance-like state. I couldn't get him to tell me what was going on. He just kept saying he had to leave. I blocked the exit, demanding that he speak to me. And then his frantic movements tamed for a moment, like clarity overcame him. All he said to me was: '*Seek the one who can walk through the darkness. All the waters will allow it. But beware of the darkness and those who seek to conquer it. For each time the key changes hands, it will seep faster.*' Then he left, running off into the night."

Azariah swallowed hard, sweat visible on his brow in the moonlight. He shuffled his stance in the dirt, still maintaining Octavia's harsh gaze.

"I didn't know what to do. I didn't know where Zara was. I thought I should wait for her—that she would be back soon. Then I could tell her about her brother's strange behavior." He rubbed a hand against his face, and his brow turned upward with regret. "I should have left. I knew something didn't feel right, but I didn't listen to my gut. King Bastian's guards stormed the house not thirty minutes later, and they chained me, hauling me off to the palace. I had no idea what was going on, but when I knelt before the king, he accused me of knowing the words of a prophecy. He said Zara had shared it with me."

Azariah's whole body was shaking now.

"I told him Zara had said nothing to me! I told him I didn't know of any prophecy, but he didn't believe me. He drew his sword. He was about to cut me down when one of his guards rushed forward to stop him. The guard went up to Bastian and whispered something in his ear. It was a hushed exchange, and then Bastian asked me if I was the bounty hunter from Xadia who had never failed to carry out a job."

His voice sounded strangled in his throat.

"And I knew then that something awful was about to happen to me. I told Bastian who I was simply because it was the only thing stopping his sword. I didn't want to die on that throne room floor . . . I was convinced that he knew of the bounty out for me from King Joda. I thought I was going to be delivered back to Xadia—to Pierre. But then he gave me a job instead.

"He told me to find the three councilmen who had escaped him and bring back their heads, and he told me to find the Keyholder and deliver them to the palace. But before he released me, he made me drink a witch's potion that bound my fate to his. He said the only way I would be free is if I finished the job. He told me he was cursed, and that he didn't know how much time he had left, so I should carry out the job quickly if I wanted to live."

Azariah's eyes were watering to the point of tears.

"When you suggested the ruse, I thought, 'This could be my chance.' You could get the words of the prophecy you so desperately sought, and I could get the antidote Bastian promised me. I could live."

Octavia exhaled in livid frustration. "Why didn't you tell me? What could you *possibly* have been thinking to let me go into that blind?" Hurt struck at her heart, and she let out an embittered yell, tugging at her braids. "Do you not trust me? Have I not proven myself to you!?"

The truth was Octavia would have done the ruse with him anyway, even if she had known, because her heart belonged to him. It was that simple.

"Do you want me to say it outright?" she exclaimed. "Is that what you want? I care about you, Azariah! You've made me care, and I hate that you have, because there's nothing I can do about it! You—you've—"

She approached him again, shoving him for a second time, and this caused him to stumble back.

"You have shut yourself off from me, and I know why! Let's not pretend otherwise. I've come to terms with it. I respect it, even!" Her eyes burned with more tears, and one fell down her cheek onto the pine-littered dirt. "I understand that I can't change what you've decided to do with your own heart. But how could you not trust me? After *everything*! How could you not tell me the truth about why you were taking me to Zoharth?"

"I wanted to!" Azariah replied. "*Gods,* I wanted to! I nearly did. So many times. But—"

"But what, Azariah? What?" She threw her hands up.

"I've been alone, Octavia! For three years, I've been alone!" He covered his face with his hands and took a shuddering inhale before dropping his arms to his sides. "And I have lost myself to the things I have done to survive. I don't know what it's like to trust anyone anymore . . ."

A bead of sweat trickled down the side of Azariah's face. His voice sounded so distressed that it seemed like he was having a hard time breathing. Stress riddled his posture like an illness.

"I've had no one to rely on but myself. All I've encountered since Rebekah has been the *worst* of humanity. The pit of darkness in people's souls! The way Pierre has hunted me . . . The way I've had to *constantly* live looking over my shoulder, never truly resting, never truly at peace, never a moment where I could talk to someone! About anything! Ever! I—"

He shuffled back a few more steps.

"You're right. I should have told you about the spell. And the cure. I was a coward not to, and the moment I left you in that throne room, I regretted not telling you. When Bastian's guards forced me to leave, I knew what you would think of me. And that tore me apart because—"

Azariah stopped talking abruptly. He stared at Octavia, and the storm of regret pooling in his vivid brown eyes alarmed her.

"You were a job to me. You *had* to be! When I saw your face for the first time, I wanted to curse the *gods*. What cruel game were they playing with my miserable life!? How could they do this to me when I have suffered so?" He let out a soft cry that skewered Octavia's ears. "How could the Keyholder be *you*? I wanted to hate you!"

Octavia felt her stomach plunge, and resentment curled in her. This wasn't her fault! None of this was under her control. Nothing about this was fair for either of them. She opened her mouth to spit out a retort, but Azariah continued before she could do so.

"But even as I hardened my heart against you, even though I *purposely* chose not to speak to you unless I had to, even though I kidnapped you and forced you to go with me . . . You have shown me kindness I cannot begin to understand and compassion that I do not deserve!"

He placed a palm up against the side of his tired, grief-filled face.

"And when you protected me from Pierre—when you came back for me in Xadia's war camp and stood in front of the darkness for me—I finally understood what Zara meant when she said I was supposed to help save all the lands. I was never meant to deliver you, I was meant to help you."

A layer of stone-cold silence passed between them, and this seemed to push Azariah over the edge.

"Please, Octavia, don't be angry with me!" he pleaded. "I was wrong to keep the truth from you. I was a coward, scared back into survival mode at the cost of your safety. I didn't . . . I didn't consider that Bastian might do that to you. When you wanted to do this ruse, I knew it would be dangerous, but all I could think about was that I might live. Please forgive me for my selfishness. For my cowardice. I'm so sorry."

The look of anguish on his face stole the breath from her lungs, and she stared at him for a long moment. So much emotion was charging through her body that Octavia felt like her limbs were filled with lightning.

But just as she was about to speak, a sudden realization struck her with the force of a storm—and it was because of what Azariah had said to her at Jagged Gulch Lake. Understanding crashed over her, and her mouth parted. After they had escaped Pierre, Azariah had let her go knowing full well that he would never get the cure for the spell cast over him.

"You released me from my vow," she whispered. "You freed me . . ."

Her eyes stung with more tears, though none fell down her face, and she took a step toward him timidly, peering up at him.

Her pulse was beating like a drum.

They were standing so close now . . .

"Why would you do that?"

"Because I . . ." Azariah's breath tickled her face as he gazed at her. His attention was so focused. So poignant. "I would've rather died than lived with the knowledge that I had sold you to a man like Bastian Jasper. And though I have tried to ignore it, I can't anymore because . . . I have found that I care for you, Octavia. And my heart—I thought I could never give it to another. Never." He pressed his cracked lips together, tenderness filling his features. "But you have changed my mind."

Octavia's breath hitched, and her heart fluttered as his words sank into her, showering her with a warmth that flew to the ends of her toes. Azariah swallowed hard and then lifted a hand to brush strands of hair from her cheek, and this time, she let him. His fingertips traced the side of her face as his eyes searched hers.

"And it's not because you look like her . . ." he said softly. "It's because of what you have done. It's because of who *you* are. You have been so strong. Through all of this. Through all of the evil that has tried to break your spirit, you have never wavered in your determination. You are truly the Keyholder for *all* of us. You have given me hope. And you have shown me that maybe my life doesn't have to be . . ."

He trailed off as if he was afraid of the next words teetering on the edge of his tongue.

"Doesn't have to be what?" she breathed.

"So lonely."

Tentatively, she reached up a hand, placing her palm gently against his cheek. He felt rugged under her touch, the stubble of his beard prickling her soft skin. Deep affection for him stirred in her heart. Desire took over, and, throwing out the pieces of her self-control that told her to hold back, she lifted her lips to his slowly, stopping just an inch away. She lingered there, uncertain if he would respond.

Their breath mixed together.

It was like time had stopped . . .

But then his lips moved to hers, and he kissed her, moving his hands to the small of her waist. His mouth was tender and strong, and the smell of his skin was earthy. He slid his right hand from her waist to the nape of her neck, deepening the kiss, and Octavia moved her lips in response, welcoming the intensity of it.

She clung to his neck, feeling the comfort and security of his body against her own. The most wonderful shower of acceptance flew through her, shattering the fear and loneliness that had latched itself onto her heart. The kiss pulled new threads of yearning from Octavia, so she savored every moment of his lips against hers.

When the kiss ended, the two of them stood there slightly out of breath, still holding each other. Octavia's eyes were glistening, but it wasn't from sadness.

Her heart hurt for him. It hurt for all the misery he had endured, for everything he had been forced to do because of Pierre and Bastian, and for how he had been broken down in the most cruel and barbaric ways . . .

So Octavia let it all go—all of her anger and resentment—and she offered Azariah the words she knew would help him heal a part of his crushed spirit.

Because he needed it, and she truly meant it.

"I forgive you."

30

The Bridge

Octavia's cheeks burned with heat. She wanted to kiss him again. She wanted to stay here in his arms and forget about everything. With all her heart, she wished she wasn't the Keyholder hunted by power-hungry and wicked men. She wished she could be free. Maybe after the fall of the darkness, she would be . . .

"We should go," she whispered.

At this point, the palace throne room was likely swarmed by guards, and soon, there would be more sent out after them. They couldn't stay here much longer.

Azariah's hand cupped her cheek, and the two of them took one more moment in each other's arms before breaking apart.

"Let's gather what we need," Azariah murmured. He strode over to the two cream-colored horses hitched up to the cart and got to work, undoing the horses' tethers. "We'll take the horses and what we can fit in our saddlebags."

She nodded, moving to the back of the cart to scope out anything useful she could pack. Octavia hoisted herself up, scouring the cart.

There were four large crates, and when she pried the lid off of one, she found a mountain of gold coins. Her stomach flipped uncomfortably. Were all these crates filled with gold? She pried off another lid, and sure enough, more coins.

"You certainly got paid well," she commented.

"You're the Keyholder, savior of all the lands," Azariah replied with a hint of humor. "How much did you think you were worth?"

She wrinkled her nose with a huff. "Anything we can eat back here?"

"The crate in the corner."

She pried that one open, and salted fish filled the interior. "Perfect."

Ten minutes later, the two of them were ready to go. Octavia had changed back into the new clothing Azariah had stolen for her previously, and she wore the deep blue cloak tight around her shoulders. Both of them had stuffed their saddlebags to capacity and mounted the horses, leaving the cart filled with gold behind—although Azariah did take some of it with him.

"Someone's going to get very rich by accident," Octavia joked.

Azariah gave a dry chuckle. "Indeed."

They rode through the trees, and it didn't take long for Azariah to ask her the question she was sure he had been holding on to since escaping the palace. "The prophecy, did you learn it?"

"I did."

"Are you willing to share it?"

"Once I tell you, you can't unlearn the words. The *gods* have made it so." She said this only because it was fair of her to warn him.

He nodded firmly.

Octavia mulled over the words in her mind. Now that she had the space to ponder it, she knew where she had to go, and it made her chest seize. The darkness. It had always been the endgame, and now it was the place she must go for answers too. After everything she had endured to learn the words, she couldn't believe that the answer was still one shrouded in mystery. At the very least, their trip to the Zoharthian palace accomplished one thing: Azariah Ronan's life was no longer tied to King Bastian's—and for that alone, their ruse had been worth it.

Octavia took a deep breath and recited what Bastian had said.

"From the *waters* of the Well of Prophecy,
From the lips of Zara the Wise,

a millennium and not a vessel willing
unless the wrong is righted, all will perish
seek the one who can walk through the darkness
all the waters will allow it
but beware of the darkness and those who seek to conquer it
for each time the key changes hands, it will seep faster
burning, burning, all burning, all consuming
it must be paid in full
to the one the darkness calls
only by approaching it may they know
greed will be the undoing, and forfeit the gain
the path chosen will determine the fates
not but a chance left in the gods' graces is all the time that remains"

She finished, and Azariah clutched his head as if he had a severe headache. He rubbed his temples, bending forward over the horn of his saddle and gasping. A few seconds later, he straightened up. "Woah."

"That was my reaction too."

She gripped the reins to her horse, taking stock of the lines she already knew. The *waters* could track her. The darkness would seep faster if anyone else gained the key. The wrong being righted at the penalty of all perishing was obvious, but the one new piece of information she had gleaned was the instruction specifically aimed at her: *to the one the darkness calls, only by approaching it may they know.*

She took a deep breath . . .

"All that's left for me to do is go to the darkness. '*Only by approaching it may they know*.' The answers I seek are there. Whether I must walk into it to find out what the *gods* have for me, or if I simply need to stand in its presence . . . I don't know, but this is it." Octavia's breath shuddered, and her hands shook. "Take me to the darkness, Azariah."

He looked grim, and the color in his face drained away. "We are not far from the outlet. The desert awaits us on the other side. Then it's only another day to the darkness. Or perhaps . . . less."

The fear she felt was like a physical manifestation of a bird of prey wrapping its talons around her neck. She gazed ahead, wishing once more that she didn't have to do this, but knowing in her heart that she would do it for the sake of all.

The horses rode on at a walk, and a breeze picked up, tickling her face.

"What do you think it means when it says, '*greed will be the undoing, and forfeit the gain*'?" Octavia asked.

Azariah scratched the back of his neck. "It could be referring to the greed that made Hritza burn in the first place—the greed that started the darkness. But I suppose it could also refer to the greed of present men. I mean, you've seen enough of that in the past few weeks to last you a lifetime."

She scoffed. "That's the understatement of the millennium."

"As for the part about forfeiting to gain? I'm not sure."

"Something *I* must forfeit?" she asked.

"Possibly."

"I suppose I'll know soon."

Her eyes wandered the trees as her mind searched through everything she had learned from the Wells of Power and the words of the prophecy. She went over the visions again like a mantra: someone named Tarrick begging his father to repent and undo things, his father refusing and cursing the *gods*, a woman giving the previous Keyholder a choice, the Keyholder refusing to walk through the darkness at the penalty of starting it in motion, and now the words from Zara's lips that she knew as deep as her soul . . .

> burning, burning, all burning, all consuming
> it must be paid in full

What must be paid in full? Those were the lines that frightened Octavia the most. Was this why the previous Keyholder refused to walk into the darkness? What did he know that she did not? What awaited her at the Well in Hritza?

She gritted her teeth, summoning her courage. The only line of the prophecy that gripped her soul was the first: *a millennium and not a vessel willing*. One way or another, she would be willing. She had to be. She would end this. The reality of everyone dying was too grave a consequence to ignore, and she refused to let it happen.

"I am willing," she whispered to the *gods*.

"What?" Azariah asked.

"Nothing." She kicked her horse forward, pulling closer to Azariah. "How are we going to get across the outlet with our horses? I remember you said there's a bridge, but it's guarded? How well guarded? Can we get across it?"

Octavia didn't like the idea of once again having no food and no things. If they couldn't use the bridge, they would have to swim again, and she didn't want to give up the horses so quickly—but she also didn't want to get captured.

"We will go to the bridge first," Azariah said. "I'd like to keep our things, if possible. But if we can find no way across it unnoticed, we'll swim like we did before."

She was relieved that he was thinking the same thing. "How far are we from the bridge?"

"Two hours, possibly less if we hurry. The cover of night will work in our favor."

"As it always does," she added with a smile. "Let's ride." Octavia urged her horse into a gallop, and Azariah took off after her.

As the night dwindled slowly onward, they approached the outlet. Still hidden in the trees, Azariah had them stop, dismount, and tie their horses up to the low-hanging branches of a pine.

"We'll scope out the bridge on foot. It will be easier to stay hidden that way. Here." He handed Octavia a sheathed dagger, and she tucked it into the waistband of her pants.

They crept through the trees, stopping just shy of the edge of the forest to keep themselves hidden. The start of the bridge was a mere dozen feet away, and it was massive, easily spanning the width of twenty horses if the creatures rode side by side. Immediately, Octavia could tell that crossing the bridge undetected was not going to be an option. It was crawling with Zoharthian guards. There were forty men, and that was only what she could see from this end of the bridge. Who knew how many more were stationed on the other side?

Her hopes fell.

"Azariah," she whispered. "We can't. We'll have to swim. Let's ride back to the spot we swam across before."

He rubbed his forehead, clearly disappointed, but he nodded in agreement. "Looks like we're leaving our horses."

They were just about to retreat through the trees when a piercing shriek split the night. Azariah tensed, and he drew his sword. Octavia's heartbeat spiked. Fumbling with the dagger in her waistband, she drew the blade out and held it aloft. They both froze, hidden behind the pine trunks.

The cry had alerted those at the end of the bridge nearest them, and all of the men turned. Swords were drawn, and those who were lazing about stood. For a few seconds, there was only silence, and then more cries sounded. The Zoharthian soldiers pointed at something Octavia couldn't see, and then they charged across the bridge, away from the place where Octavia and Azariah had hidden themselves.

"What's happening?" she hissed, standing close behind the bounty hunter.

"I don't know."

Azariah's eyes did not leave the bridge, and he did not lower his sword. Then the source of the noise emerged, and the shouts of dying men grew thick in their ears. The Zoharthian soldiers were fighting other soldiers, and blood splattered the bridge as the Zoharthian soldiers were cut down.

Octavia gripped her dagger so hard that her nails pierced her skin. She recognized the newcomers from their dark red garb and metal armor. They were from Xadia. Immediately, Azariah backed up a few paces and grabbed Octavia's free hand, squeezing it tight.

The bloodbath continued, and Zoharth's men screamed in agony as they fell by Xadia's hand. The skirmish was over quickly, and soon, the end of the bridge swarmed with a hundred Xadian soldiers. And from their midst, Pierre Zarqel strode forward. His bald head and uniform were spattered with blood, and a triumphant gleam lit his barbaric face.

Octavia could feel all of the blood drain from her cheeks. He was alive. Pierre Zarqel was alive . . .

Stomach acid climbed up her throat. How were they going to

escape this? Any second now, Octavia was sure she'd see flashes of blue and hear shouts of triumph. She could already feel the phantom touch of Pierre's hands around her throat and his hot breath against her face. She wanted to run, but her body wouldn't move. All she could do was grip Azariah's arm as he pulled her deeper into the shadows behind one of the thicker pines.

A sharp whistle sounded, and then Pierre called out to his men. "To the Well of Power, boys! Everyone take a parcel! She can't have gotten far. The Keyholder must return to the darkness sooner or later, and when she does, we'll be waiting."

They didn't have a single parcel with them? Disbelief nearly choked her. The *gods* were surely working in her favor to have allowed all of Xadia's parcels to be lost to the darkness in the chaos of that night . . .

Xadia's soldiers marched forward toward the tree line, and Octavia buried her face into Azariah's chest. He wrapped his arms around her, and they crouched low, getting as small as possible as they huddled together. The night, along with the thick branches of the trees, helped shield them, but the soldiers were passing so close to them that Octavia could feel the dirt below her feet tremble. She quieted her breathing, even though her brain was screaming for more air than she was permitting into her lungs.

The footsteps kept going. On and on. It felt like forever, although it was probably only mere minutes.

Once the men had passed the spot where they hid, the two of them still didn't move. Azariah kept his arms around her, his strong hands steadying her, and it helped to suppress some of the fear beating within her chest.

When the noise faded, they both peered toward the bridge again.

Octavia almost yelped, but she clamped a hand over her mouth to stop herself. Pierre Zarqel was standing at the end of the bridge closest to them, peering back across it toward the side that led to the desert. Dead bodies lay everywhere in the moonlight, but he didn't look at them. He was as still as a statue, waiting for something.

From across the way, a boy emerged, walking over the bridge. He stared down at the bodies, wide-eyed, and did his best to avoid stepping on them. Once the boy finished his trek, he stopped at Pierre's side, and it was only then that Octavia recognized him.

It was Absalom, the bondservant who had helped her escape when the darkness swept Xadia's encampment.

Pierre stared at the boy with a nurturing expression—one that didn't fit his cruel features. "Do you know why I asked you to come along with our little hunting party instead of having you stay back at camp, boy?"

Absalom shook his head. "No, Commander." His sickly face grew more sweaty as his attention fell back onto the dead Zoharthian soldiers.

"Take a good look at them." Pierre pointed around at the bloodied men that lay at his feet. "What do you see?"

Absalom clasped his bony hands together. "I see dead men, Commander."

"Take a closer look." Pierre grabbed Absalom's upper arm and pulled him toward one of the men sprawled onto his back with his open eyes toward the sky. His limbs were at odd angles, and blood oozed from his mouth. "What do you see?"

"I . . . I don't understand the question, Commander," Absalom replied, his voice coming out with a squeak.

"Then let me explain." Pierre drew himself up to his full height, keeping a firm grip on Absalom's arm. "I see a man who was too weak to protect himself. All of them. Too weak to protect their kingdom.

And that's why they were cut down tonight. They did not have the strength to stand against their enemies, and when one does not have the strength it takes to make a stand, they have already lost."

Pierre's savage stare went from the dead man to Absalom.

"Do you know why I am searching for the Keyholder, boy?"

"Because you want her to walk through the darkness in the name of Xadia."

Pierre's upper lip twitched, and he clenched his teeth. The scar that went from his cheek up to his bald head made him look like a brutish animal. "Try again."

Absalom winced in Pierre's grasp as his fingers clamped harder over the boy's arm. "I don't know, Commander. Please, you're hurting me!"

Pierre released Absalom, and he stumbled back, looking up at his commander with fearful eyes. Absalom's mouth trembled, and his arms shook.

"Xadia is not weak. Xadia is *not* vulnerable. But if another kingdom claims the Well of Eternal Healing before us, we may become like these men—too weak. If we are to be the greatest of the kingdoms, it cannot come to pass without the Keyholder." Pierre's gaze burned into Absalom. "How is it that when I returned to my war tent on the night of the darkness, the Keyholder was gone? I had her chained hand and foot. Can you explain how she was able to get free?"

The silence that stretched on as Pierre stood there filled Octavia's veins with ice.

"I . . . I do not know, Commander," Absalom replied shakily. "I ran from the darkness along with the rest of the soldiers. I did not see what happened."

Pierre stroked his thick gray mustache and turned away from Absalom, staring up at the moon. He seemed to bask in it, drawing in a huge breath that let his chest expand all the way.

"Do you want to know how *I* think she escaped?"

Absalom took a step back from the commander. When the boy did not reply, Pierre faced him, a murderous look entrenched in his cold features.

"I think *you* unchained her."

Absalom shook his head. "No! I would not defy you like that, Commander Zarqel. I didn't touch her. It must have been another . . . or else . . . she must have slipped out of her chains."

A creeping calm quieted the fierce look on Pierre's face, but he didn't break eye contact with the boy. He tutted, pursing his mouth. "You know," he mused. "It's a shame. I was hoping to hear the truth from your lips . . ."

Pierre moved so fast that Absalom didn't even have time to gasp. There was a flash of silver, and Pierre buried his knife into the boy's chest, thrusting it upward and holding it there. Octavia had to fight with herself not to scream. Absalom's eyes grew so wide that they seemed to pop from his sickly face.

Pierre snarled in Absalom's ear. "My second in command saw you go into my war tent, and when you emerged, so did *she*! *You* freed the Keyholder! And now you will *die* for it! May you rot in the darkness."

He wrenched the blade free, and Absalom collapsed onto the dirt at the foot of the bridge. Without even so much as a backward glance, Pierre stalked forward toward the tree line and followed in the direction his men had marched.

31

Go and Save Us

Octavia crouched in Azariah's arms, stunned. Tears immediately wet her face. She could hear Absalom's labored gasps in the quiet of the night as he fought to draw in breath. They waited a minute longer to make sure Pierre was gone, and then Octavia glanced up at Azariah. The moment he gave her a nod, she stood, running from the trees and falling to her knees by Absalom's side. The bounty hunter quickly followed her.

The boy's spasms of pain were like daggers to Octavia's heart. His chest was covered in blood, and it dripped from the corner of his mouth too. He looked so small and vulnerable lying in the dirt.

"Absalom! It's okay!" Octavia whimpered, pressing her hand to the knife wound. "You're going to be okay! Just lie still!" Blood sprang up over her jittering fingertips, and the boy's eyes lit with surprise at her presence.

"Y-you?" he gasped.

"I'm going to help you," she assured him. "You'll be alright. You'll see! I'm going to open the Well of Eternal Healing, and you will be okay. And your family will be so happy to see you again!" Octavia looked up at Azariah with desperation. "Please, help him! There must be something we can do!"

He didn't respond.

Octavia shook her head, her voice turning thick with anguish. She couldn't give up on Absalom. She wouldn't. "No! He saved me! He saved both of us. We have to help him!"

"Octavia . . ."

"NO!" she cried, pressing down harder in her attempts to staunch the blood.

Absalom whimpered, and his body began to shake. He clung to Octavia's wrist, and with what little strength he had left, he smiled at her as tears coursed down his face onto the dirt. The way he smiled reminded her of Bowan . . .

More blood dribbled from his mouth, and in a hoarse whisper, he said, "It w-was my honor to s-serve you, Keyholder. May t-the *gods* bless y-you."

Then he grew very still. His hand fell from her wrist, and his eyes lost the light that had been there moments before.

"Absalom!" she whimpered. "Absalom, don't go!"

Octavia bowed her head over his and let out a soft cry, her heart breaking. She was supposed to heal him. She had promised him. He was supposed to live. Of all the people she had encountered since gaining the key, this boy had been the most pure of heart. The *most* worthy of bearing the blessings of the *gods*.

Hatred for Pierre coiled up in her throat and built like a scream.

Gently, Octavia closed Absalom's eyes.

"Octavia, we have to go," Azariah urged. "Time is running out. It's not safe for you here. By killing the Zoharthian soldiers, Pierre has incited an act of war. Zoharth will retaliate against Xadia for this. We must get you to the darkness before anyone else can capture you, or I fear things will get far worse."

She looked up at him with tear-stained cheeks, and grief for the dead boy ripped her heart in two, but Azariah was right. If Pierre had ordered a hundred of his men to get a parcel of *waters* each from the Well of Prophecy, then there was little she could do to avoid them if she wasn't safely within the bounds of the darkness. It was only a matter of time before they would find her again.

She rose from the ground, her hands covered in Absalom's blood. Azariah's face carried compassion, and she sank into his chest. He wrapped his arms around her, and she stood there for a few seconds, gathering her strength. Her mouth trembled as she took one last look at the boy who had saved her life.

"May the *gods* carry your soul into the afterlife with honor, Absalom," she whispered. "I owe you everything."

She pushed herself out of Azariah's embrace, wiping her face with the back of her wrist. Then her expression hardened, and anger spurred her onward. Octavia would not let Pierre Zarqel capture her again. She would be in the depths of the darkness long before he ever got the chance.

"Let's go."

The two of them slunk back into the trees on high alert to retrieve their horses, and then they rode quickly across the bridge filled with the dead. They traveled as fast as the thick forest and the dark would let them, putting as much distance between themselves and the bridge as possible. All the while, Octavia's mind was fixed on the darkness. Absalom's dead eyes were burned into her mind, and it strengthened her desire to end this. She cursed Pierre's rotten soul to the *gods*.

May he pay for every ounce of suffering he has caused, she thought.

For an hour, the two of them did not let up. They rode in silence, pushing their animals to keep pace with one another. Soon, the trees began to thin, and then the edge of the forest appeared. The terrain was starting to look similar to that of Xadia's encampment where Pierre had held them captive.

Octavia slowed her horse, bringing it to a halt at the edge of the sparse forest, and so did Azariah. Exhaustion swept her body. She hadn't slept properly in days. But they could not stop to fall asleep—as much as she wanted to.

"Where do we go from here?" she asked. "How far now?"

"From here, it's nothing but desert until we reach the darkness. The land is open, so there will be nothing to hide us if we come upon anyone."

A shiver flew down her spine, and she gazed out across the desolate desert in the bright moonlight. "I'm done hiding."

"We will come upon the darkness any time now." Azariah pulled his horse forward a few steps, getting closer to her. "Once we see it, I cannot continue with you. If I get too close—"

"I know," she said.

She remembered the prongs of black mist that had shot across Xadia's camp like snakes. Azariah needed to stay far away to avoid its snares. She grimaced, her stomach seizing uncomfortably. Her hands turned clammy and sweat beaded along her hairline. She could feel a brewing storm in her soul, and the key that had burrowed into her flesh tingled in response.

She took a shaky breath, straightening her posture and pulling her shoulders back, but this did little to calm her nerves.

"Hey." Azariah's soft tone brought her eyes to his. He appeared so intense and calm at the same time. He was looking at her like he was trying to memorize every feature of her face. "You can do this, Octavia. I believe in you. Remember, you are the Keyholder, savior of all the lands, blessed by the *gods*, and you stand for all of us—by your own words."

She tried to smile, but it fell flat.

"Thank you," she whispered.

"Are you ready to continue?"

She wasn't even though she knew she had to. "Yes."

With a "yip," Octavia kicked her horse forward before her mind could find another reason to stall her. They rode, the open terrain around them making Octavia feel exposed and vulnerable, though not another person was in sight as far as her eye could see.

The moonlight above them lit the night well, and the stars joined in. It was a vast and beautiful sky, spread out like a scroll before them. It was the kind of sky that reminded Octavia of home and happiness, and so, she turned her thoughts to her family. To Mama, who she wished with all her heart might actually be healed as a result of this. To Bowan, who she longed to hug and hold in her arms again. And to Papa, who she prayed would remain safe wherever Rustwick's army was.

Abruptly, a stark burning sensation seared Octavia's palm, and she gasped, gazing down at the key. Its sparkling surface dazzled in the moonlight. Nothing about it looked different, but a churning sensation cascaded through her stomach, and dread filled her heart. They were close. She could feel it. Though she couldn't see the wall of darkness yet, they were nearly upon it.

The responsibility of the key weighed heavy in her palm and on her heart. She was the Keyholder for all. The gravity of that sentiment sank into her like an avalanche, but it also bolstered her resolve and sealed her determination.

Half an hour later, a rumbling shook the ground beneath their horses. It was soft at first, but then it grew in intensity, and there, brewing in the distance, she finally saw it. The immense wall of darkness frothed like a beast, small from their vantage point, but still terrifying—and it was made of a blacker substance than the night, standing out starkly against the stars.

It looked like it would be another hour's ride toward it, and Octavia pulled on the reins of her horse to stop the animal in its tracks.

She locked eyes with Azariah. "You can stop here. You don't have to go any farther."

"I will go with you only a little longer," he said. "I will let you know when I cannot continue."

The comfort she felt from this gave her another burst of courage. Truthfully, they were still far enough away for Azariah to be safe, but if he had wanted to stop here, she wouldn't have blamed him.

"Yip!" she cried, jamming her heels into the belly of her horse.

The hooves of the animals pounded against the sand, and the closer Octavia got to the darkness, the more the key seemed to pull on her soul, drawing it toward the wall of black tar that festered over the horizon like a cancer.

Every minute, the breadth of the darkness grew, and it took all of her self-control not to turn around and flee. Every piece of her survival instincts was telling her to run away, but the time for running was over.

When Azariah pulled his horse to a stop, Octavia stopped too. They were still a good distance from the wall, but she knew it was time to say goodbye to the bounty hunter.

"This is where I must leave you," he said.

The look on Azariah's face was a mix of sadness and respect. He was staring at her in reverence, and deep in his eyes, he wore no fear—whether he felt it inside or not, he was showing her the best of himself.

She brought her horse up next to his. So many emotions were crowding her mind. She didn't want to tell him goodbye, and she was grateful to him beyond what she could express. If not for him, she would've been dead several times over. He had saved her again and again, and now it was time for her to save everyone else.

Her eyes burned with tears, and one slipped down her face.

"Azariah Ronan," she said, smiling at him. "I am in your debt. You have indeed helped save all the lands, just as Zara said, and the *gods* are smiling down on you. Thank you for everything you have done for me."

She wanted to embrace him. She wanted to kiss him again. But in her heart she knew that if she did, she might not ever leave him. So instead, she held out her right hand, palm open to the sky, and Azariah took it. She felt the warmth of his skin against her own. His rugged hand was strong. Tender. She squeezed it tight, and the two of them stared at each other.

"Go and save us," he said with a nod. He gave her the kindest smile he could offer, one that was filled with somber encouragement. "I will still be here when the darkness falls."

With that, their hands fell apart, and Octavia looked up at the darkness as it rumbled slowly across the ground. She urged her horse into a gallop, leaving the bounty hunter behind, and with him, a piece of her heart . . .

Only ten minutes later, Octavia halted her horse, deciding it was best to continue on foot, lest the poor creature die within the clutches of the darkness. She was close enough now to see the edge of the ashy substance clearly, and as her eyes scoured the scene, she noted that no tendrils of black slithered out from the wall as they had before. It was simply a billowing smoke slowly creeping toward her.

She dismounted, feeling the trembling of the earth beneath her feet. She turned the animal around and gave it a slap on the rump, sending it back the way it had come.

As she stared out into the distance, she couldn't see Azariah anymore, so she faced the brewing blackness, taking in its massive, all-encompassing prowess. It was hard to keep breathing properly in its presence. It seemed to pull all the strength from her limbs, sucking her dry and leaving her resolve desolate.

It was paralyzing . . . finally standing in its presence. Her heart was ramming itself into her ribcage relentlessly, and for a moment, Octavia thought she might die simply from her body giving out on her.

No one survived the darkness. *No one.* Not in a thousand years. The very idea of intentionally reaching out to touch it was so terrifying that Octavia couldn't bring herself to move. For a long time, she simply stood there, gazing up at the wall that crept forth to blot out the stars. It was like standing at death's doorstep. To step forward would be to invite death to claim her. And she didn't want to die . . .

The key would protect her. It had to.

That was all Octavia could repeat in her mind. It was the promise passed down by legend, surviving the sheer span of time like a steadfast beacon of hope.

She clenched her shaking hands, bringing her eyes down to the sand at her feet to momentarily give herself respite from gazing at the soul-crushing sight.

"Only the Keyholder can walk through the darkness," she murmured hoarsely.

She still needed to walk a fair distance to reach the edge—at least a hundred yards—but she lifted her head to the sky, peering up at the stars that were splashed across the night like paint on a canvas.

Octavia pressed her fingernails into her palms and whispered to the *gods*, "I am willing, and I am ready. Show me what you must."

32

Not a Vessel Willing

The key prickled in her palm like a guiding force, and an all-consuming sense of purpose crashed into her. Whether it was the *gods* prodding her forward or her own determination, Octavia took her first purposeful step toward the darkness with the mindset of intentionally walking into it . . .

Flash.

A blinding light radiated from all around Octavia. It was so violent and so bright that she threw her hands up to shield herself from the intensity. For a moment, her sense of sight was completely overwhelmed. Everything was white. Brilliant. Dazzling. It was like she stood inside the sun itself. The luminescence around her seared her eyes, and she clamped them shut to find relief, but none came.

She stumbled, sinking to her knees, and her hands reached forward to catch herself, but instead of feeling sand beneath her fingertips, there was something hard and smooth.

Octavia blinked, now able to open her eyes.

She wasn't kneeling in front of the darkness. In fact, the darkness was gone altogether. All that shone around her as far as she could see was brilliant white nothingness set upon a floor of shimmering glass that spread out forever in all directions, like an endless perfect sea.

"Octavia Fletcher," a soft, ethereal voice spoke.

Octavia spun around, leaping to her feet, her heart ramming against her chest. There, floating five feet from her, was a golden woman with robes of pure white. Her hair was made of silk that shone like the stars, her skin was brilliant and flawless, and her face was cloaked in a dazzling glory that shielded her eyes so that Octavia could not see her features.

Immediately, reverence for this woman took hold of Octavia's heart, and she dropped to her knees, laying herself flat on her stomach and casting her gaze down to the glass, for she knew she was in the presence of a *goddess*. As if a spell had been cast over her mind, Octavia suddenly became aware of the fact that this was the same woman from the memory she had seen in the Well of Prophecy at Zoharth.

Octavia couldn't find the words to speak. She was in awe. She felt so unworthy and exposed, as if this woman knew every thought, decision, and experience Octavia had ever had.

"Raise your head, child, and stand to your feet," the woman said.

Octavia obeyed, and it was only then that she realized she wasn't wearing her clothing from before. She was dressed in white robes just like the woman, although Octavia's robes didn't shine.

Standing in the presence of the *goddess* was so paralyzing that Octavia was unable to use her voice. Nothing felt worthy enough to leave her lips, so she simply stared in astonishment.

"It is time for you to learn what every Keyholder before you has learned," the woman said, spreading her shimmering hands open wide. "And then you must make a choice."

The *goddess* moved toward Octavia so that she was less than a foot away. She looked down into Octavia's face, but even this close, the glory around her eyes made her features impossible to discern. Tears formed in Octavia's eyes from the devotion stirring in her soul.

"Are you ready to see, Octavia Fletcher?"

Octavia's mouth struggled to move, but she found her words at last, speaking them with courage. "I am."

The woman offered her hand to Octavia, but Octavia dared not touch the *goddess*. It felt wrong. She was too unworthy to even stand in her presence, let alone feel the light of her spirit.

"Take my hand, child," the woman encouraged. "It is alright."

So, Octavia did . . .

Brilliance captured her every faculty, and a tug pulled her forward.

Octavia found herself in a grand throne room made of rose marble. She didn't have a physical body anymore—she was spirit only. She existed, but not in a corporeal way.

Octavia drifted from the throne room onto a balcony that overlooked the lands, and the view was astonishing. Set atop a high hill, this grand palace opened up to the forest beyond, and in the distance there were two different specks of water—lakes—with the Restless Sea to the right of the landscape and the Kraven River to the left.

In her heart, Octavia knew that she was in the throne room in the Kingdom of Hritza.

"Look at it, Tarrick," a deep man's voice chimed. "Look at how the lands shine in the light of the sun."

Octavia turned to see two men standing on the balcony.

One was clearly the king. He was dressed in rich robes of blood red, and his crown was spiked and made of gold. Curly black hair came down to his shoulders, and his full beard was groomed to perfection. Next to him, a young man not much older than Octavia herself stood staring out at the view. He also was dressed in red fabrics, and he carried a sword on his hip. He looked like the king—his spitting image—with curly black hair and piercing green eyes, although the young man's hair was trimmed short.

"Our kingdom is beautiful, Father."

The king turned to face his son. "I have a dream in my heart, Tarrick. One that I wish to share with you."

"What is it?"

"One day, you will be king, and I want to leave you with a legacy unparalleled since the dawn of humanity. It is a legacy I hope we can build together."

Tarrick placed his hands on the railing of the stone balcony. "Tell me, what does your dream entail?"

"I want Hritza to be the greatest kingdom on earth."

The young man raised an eyebrow at the king.

"But Father, Hritza is already the greatest of the kingdoms. The *gods of old* have blessed us with the Well of Eternal Healing. No other Well of Power is as coveted or as useful. The kingdoms all come to us for their needs. You are King Elak Jethro, the most revered royal in all the lands. People worship you."

Tarrick scrunched his nose at the word "worship," as if it made him uncomfortable.

"Honestly, Father, we want for nothing in trade agreements or riches. What could you possibly mean by saying you want Hritza to be the greatest kingdom on earth?"

King Elak took in a slow and strong breath. "I want to share our greatness with all. But to do that, we must take action. The other Wells of Power . . . they do not belong to us."

"Belong?" Tarrick repeated. He shuffled his stance, tilting his head to the side. "We can use the *waters* from any Well of Power. Our trade agreements allow it."

"I'm not talking about our trade agreements," the king countered, a hungry gleam in his green eyes. "I'm talking about control. If Hritza controlled all the Wells of Power, then we would truly be the greatest kingdom on earth."

Tarrick swallowed, his Adam's apple visibly bobbing in his throat. "Control all the Wells of Power?" He paled considerably. "Father, don't you think that will make the *gods* angry?"

"The *gods* are the ones who gave us our positions of power!" the king snapped. "It is our duty to use them to create a better world. Imagine with me, for a moment, a future in which there is no war over the Wells of Power because the option simply does not exist. If all the Wells of Power belonged to Hritza, peace would last forever."

"What are you talking about? We have peace!" Tarrick's voice was unwavering, and he shook his head. "There are no wars, Father."

At this, the king got angry, and his tone grew harsh. "Are you so foolish to think that no other kingdom might try to war with *us* to gain the Well of Eternal Healing? We have peace now, Tarrick, but it is simply an illusion. The truth of the matter is, the Well of Eternal Healing may belong to another kingdom in the future simply because of our lack of vision in protecting it in the present. But if Hritza owns all the Wells of Power, then no war could ever come about."

King Elak's broad hands slid over the stone railing of the balcony as he gazed out at the landscape again. The breeze tossed locks of his black curly hair behind his shoulder.

"We will provide lasting peace while forever solidifying our status among the lands. Hritza is the greatest, but she will be *greater* still."

Tarrick appeared uneasy at the look of desire that shrouded his father's face, but before Octavia could observe anymore, her ethereal form was whisked away . . .

She appeared in a stone war room. In its center, there was a large stone table with maps and scrolls. Cubes of metal acted as props, purposefully placed across the maps. King Elak Jethro stood at the head of the stone table with Prince Tarrick by his side, and a dozen other men were present too, all studying the maps.

"Sire, Hritza's army is ready to march."

The person who spoke was standing on the opposite side of the stone table from the king. He was tall and commanding, with skin of rich brown and long hair as black as night. His dark brown eyes were unfeeling and calculated. He looked like the commander of Hritza's army.

"It will be easy to secure the Well of Prophecy in Zoharth. It shouldn't take many soldiers. Zoharth's army is lacking, and its people are nomadic. I'm not worried about them—or Vrelia's Well of Beauty either. Vrelia is small and doesn't have an army at all. Those kingdoms are not our priority, and they will not pose a threat. The real crux of this is going to come down to Xadia and Urtha. Xadia is well-endowed with weapons due to the Well of Costly Metals, and Urtha is the largest of the kingdoms by far. But if we move swiftly and attack those two kingdoms simultaneously, then neither one can help the other. It is the element of surprise that will work in our favor."

"Do we have enough men to coordinate a simultaneous attack?" King Elak asked, his hand to his chin.

"Indeed," the commander replied. "Every able-bodied man. As you requested."

"Good. What about Omari and Rustwick?"

"Once our forces secure Urtha's Well of Euphoria, we can deal with Omari. The Well of Fertility will not be hard to take. Rustwick, however, may be a thorn in our side. Its kingdom and people are strong, but I have confidence that if we possess Xadia and Urtha, then Rustwick may yield without a fight. And if they don't, sire, I can assure you, we will take the Well of Bountiful Harvest by force."

The king looked pleased, a wide smile splitting his mouth. He pointed to one of the metal pieces on the nearest map, but before he could speak, Prince Tarrick beat him to it.

"Father, this is not right! We have peace! We should not do this! The other kingdoms have never given us a reason to think they might attack us to gain the Well of Eternal Healing. We are doing this unprovoked. It is *wrong*!" Tarrick searched the faces of the men present, pleading with them. "Surely you can see that this is wrong?"

No one spoke. They all simply stared at him.

"We are starting a war! And for what?" Tarrick demanded, slamming a hand down on the stone table.

"Silence!" King Elak warned, glaring daggers at his son. "That is enough."

"I will not be silent!"

"YOU ARE NOT THE KING!" he roared.

"I do not have to be the king to *speak* in this war room!"

Elak drew his hand back and struck Tarrick full across the face with a blow that echoed off the stone. It was hard enough to knock the young man to the floor, and Tarrick lay there, stunned.

The king's gaze hardened, and his green eyes flashed with rage. "You would do well, Prince Tarrick, to check where your loyalties lie. We are doing this for eternal peace! The Kingdom of Hritza will last forever, and it will control all of the Wells of Power gifted to humanity by the *gods of old*. I vow it!"

Taking a moment to compose himself, King Elak tugged on the front of his blood-red robes. He cleared his throat and turned back to address the commander.

"Do all of our soldiers have two parcels each?"

"Yes, sire," the commander replied with a nod. "Every soldier will be able to heal himself twice over if needed. Our forces will remain strong. The dead will not be from Hritza, I can guarantee it."

"Excellent."

Tarrick let out a frustrated growl, now rising from the floor to challenge his father anew. "The *gods* are condemning us at this very moment. They see and hear all of us. They know our hearts! We will bring destruction upon ourselves if we proceed. Do you not hear the words you are speaking?" He pointed at the commander. "You speak of dead men—men that do not have to die at all! Father, I beg of you, do not do this! We are blessed by the *gods*, but they will curse us if we take what is not meant to be ours."

King Elak turned his murderous gaze toward his son. It looked as though he might hit him again. "Guards, please escort Prince Tarrick to his room. Lock him within and do not leave the door unattended."

The guards standing at the entrance of the war room promptly obeyed their king, walking up to Tarrick swiftly and arresting his arms. Tarrick did not fight them, but his eyes burned with tears, and he spoke harshly as the guards pulled him from the room.

"You will bring wrath upon us all!"

Octavia was transported from the war room, and her spirit was placed in the center of a battlefield on an open plain. In the distance, the smooth white marble domes of Urtha rose up from the ground, reflecting the light of the sun as it scorched down upon a bloodbath.

Men with swords were cutting each other down without mercy. Screams tore through the air, and horses whinnied in panic. An Urthan soldier cried out in agony as a blade dug into his arm, nearly severing it in two. As he fell to the dirt, blood spurted from the wound, but before he could scream again, a sword buried itself into his chest, and the light vanished from his eyes. The man who had killed him panted heavily, bleeding profusely. He groaned in pain, but then he pulled a parcel of *waters* from his armor, unstoppering the vial with his teeth and drinking the *waters* straight.

Shimmering gold flickered from his injuries, lighting up his wounds in a dazzling display of magic. Within seconds, his skin cleared up and his eyes grew sharp. He stood tall, no longer labored with pain, and a deep gash that had been torn through his calf muscle healed itself, leaving nothing behind—not even a scar.

The man moved on, joining a knot of soldiers a dozen yards away and charging back into the fight. Octavia watched as the battle grew more fierce, and the blood of the dying soaked the earth . . .

There was a rumble that shook everything around her, and in the twinkling of an eye, Octavia found herself at the Well of Euphoria in Urtha. Hritzan soldiers swarmed the temple, killing the Wellminders and their assistants without restraint. The white marble was stained crimson as the sparkling black rock and blue *waters* were surrounded and secured.

The cries of Urtha rang in Octavia's ears, and suddenly, she wasn't in the temple any longer. She was floating in the sky over the top of the great kingdom, and her soul felt the pain of every dead and dying man, woman, and child who stood in Hritza's way. It was a deluge of terror and grief that tore through her soul like fire.

In a collage of catastrophe, Octavia's spirit was flung from the Kingdom of Urtha to the Kingdom of Xadia, and all over again, she watched the bloodshed. The Well of Costly Metals fell to the invading forces, and the rustic and mountainous kingdom was painted red, its dirt streets, metalsmitheries, and taverns overrun.

Bang.

The scene changed with a violent shudder, and a new setting formed. Octavia was back in the Hritzan palace, and Prince Tarrick stood on the balcony of a vast and spacious bedroom, staring out at the brewing storm clouds that hung in the sky like an omen of death from the *gods*.

The door to his bedroom opened, and King Elak entered along with four guards. Prince Tarrick turned at the sound, his whole body tensing at the sight of his father.

"You have started this, haven't you?" Tarrick whispered, the anger in his shaking voice palpable.

"We've taken the Well of Costly Metals at Xadia and the Well of Euphoria at Urtha," he responded, his tone even. He eyed his son with a sense of caution, holding his hands up like Tarrick was a wild dog that might bite him if provoked. "This will be over soon, Tarrick. The only true stronghold left is Rustwick. Zoharth, Vrelia, and Omari will not fight us. I am sure of it."

Prince Tarrick's green eyes burned with grief. "The blood of the innocent cries out against you, Father. I can hear it on the wind! We will not escape judgment for this."

"I have done this for *you*! For your future! For *everyone's* future!" the king snapped.

"No, Father, you have done this for *yourself*. I have no part in this!"

"You are my son! By the very nature of your blood, you have taken part in this." The king strode over to Tarrick, grabbing his upper arm and dragging him to the bitter edge of the balcony. He motioned outward across the stormy landscape. "All of this will be ours. Every piece of it. *All* the Wells of Power. How can you not see that what I have done is for the salvation of all future generations?"

Tarrick ripped his arm from his father's grasp. His chest heaved as his voice grew more harsh. "You are blinded by your greed!" He pointed toward the guards blocking his bedroom door. "You have imprisoned me for speaking out against you!"

"I have been more than *kind* considering your insubordination in front of my advisors," he snarled. "I could have locked you under the palace and thrown away the key if I had wished it. You are simply under house arrest. You do not have to be a prisoner, Tarrick. I have only done this so you can see reason, and once you do, you will be as free as you were before."

Tarrick gritted his teeth. "The day I see *murder* as *reason* is the day I die, Father."

Elak's face hardened. The cold hatred in his expression became piercing, and he stayed silent for several beats. "I see you need more time to think about where your loyalties lie."

The king turned on his heels and left the bedroom, the guards following in his wake. The door slammed shut, and the lock clicked back into place.

Octavia rose from the balcony of Tarrick's bedroom high into the sky until she was just below the dark storm clouds. She could see the entire palace that sat atop the hill that housed the magnificent Kingdom of Hritza. The towering spires of stone and the intricately carved craftsmanship were spectacular to behold.

Boom.

A clap of thunder shook the air, and rain poured across the earth. Time seemed to blur, and so did the force of the storm.

Then Octavia's spirit dove straight down, falling through the palace walls until she was inside a vast and vaulted room that shone like diamonds. The walls, floor, and ceiling were made of glass, and at the far end of the space, paneled by three floor-to-ceiling mirrors, was the Well of Eternal Healing, its sparkling black rock dazzling like the universe beyond the night sky.

King Elak stood with his hands on the rim of the Well, gazing into its glowing blue *waters*. At the entrance of the glass room, doors of silver metal flew open, and a group of four guards escorted a disheveled

Prince Tarrick in. He looked like he hadn't slept in days. His curly black hair was unkempt, and his green eyes were haggard with dark circles beneath them.

"Leave us," Elak instructed the guards.

They retreated from the room, leaving Tarrick alone with the king. Elak turned from the Well to stare at his son. For a few seconds, only silence hung between them. Then the king beckoned Tarrick over.

Tarrick hesitated, but then walked to his father's side, and the two of them both beheld the Well of Power with admiration, peering into its depths.

Still, neither of them said a word.

It was only when Tarrick broke his gaze away from the *waters* to look his father in the face that King Elak spoke. It was a whisper, but the echoey nature of the glass room picked up his voice and amplified it.

"It is finished. All the Wells of Power now belong to Hritza."

Tarrick's eyes immediately glistened with tears, and he buried his head in his hands. His breath came out strained, his whole body shook, and he sank to his knees in front of the black sparkling rock, placing a hand out to touch the Well of Power.

King Elak gazed down at his son. There was no hint of compassion behind his eyes. "Drink from the Well of Eternal Healing, Tarrick, and put away your resistance. It is over. You are unwell. The guards have told me that you have stopped eating, and you are even refusing to drink. You cannot fight me anymore."

"No, I will not drink from the Well."

"Do you want to die!?" The king's retort was jarring. "Your body wastes away before my eyes—and all for nothing. Your fast will not undo what has been done."

Tarrick glared at his father, still sitting in front of the Well of Power.

His gaunt face and tired eyes made it seem like he was on the verge of passing out.

"I have had visions. Nightmares. From the moment you sent out our army to shed innocent blood. I have dreamed of a darkness that will cover this kingdom. A destruction so severe that no one will escape it. It has consumed my every waking moment."

"If you would only drink from the Well and eat, you may feel better."

"Food tastes like ash in my mouth, Father!" Tarrick cried. "Aren't you listening to me? Hritza has been marked for destruction!"

"Nonsense."

King Elak turned back to the blue *waters*, and the glow lit up his face. He closed his eyes and breathed in deeply. Then he pulled a vial from his robes and put his hand down to draw a parcel from the Well.

"I have been drinking from the Well every day since the start of this, and I have found that my body and mind are the strongest they've ever been." He shot a disgusted look at the young man on the floor at his feet. "I may live forever if I continue, and it seems that I must since you have refused your rightful place at my side—and your birthright of becoming king after me."

Elak took the vial of *waters* and downed it in one gulp. The rejuvenation that lit his face made his skin gleam for a few seconds. He held his hands up to the ceiling, basking in the glory of the Well of Eternal Healing as it revitalized his body and brightened his eyes. He seemed to be less old now, only by the smallest noticeable amount.

"I am like the *gods*, Tarrick, and I will rule over the lands to provide an eternal peace that all—both great and small—will cherish. Now, I will offer this grace to you only once more: drink from the Well with me and join the everlasting dynasty of Hritza or perish at my feet."

Without hesitation, the king drew his sword and pointed the tip of it down toward Tarrick's face. The young man lifted his chin in defiance, narrowing his sunken eyes and clenching his teeth.

"You are a wicked man, Father. May the *gods of old* bring down the destruction they have shown me."

With a growl, Elak cut his sword through the air, hurling it toward Tarrick's neck, but the moment the blade made contact with his flesh, it shattered like glass, and a bright white light flashed over the Well of Power, flinging the two men back from it.

Both the king and the prince skidded across the glass floor. Then a commanding chorus of voices all spoke as one, and it came from a ball of radiant light that now hovered over the opening of the Well.

The power of the *gods'* voices echoing in unison shook the foundations of the room.

"King Elak Jethro of Hritza, the blood of the innocent cries out to us from the ground, and we have heard them. Because of your greed and corruption, no one will drink from the Well of Eternal Healing again. Not until you have righted this wrong."

A violent flash of blue was followed by a cracking noise, like the earth beneath the palace was splitting open. The Well of Power shuddered, and then the sparkle of the black rock rim died. It looked like the outside of the Well was now made of ash instead of stone. The blue *waters* vanished, and in its place, black, tar-like liquid filled the inside until it came up to the lip—but it did not spill over.

Then, from the ball of shining light, a woman appeared. She was crowned with glory, her features so bright they were indiscernible. The two men gawked in alarm at her presence.

She walked over to the king, who was still prostrate on the glass floor, and in a jerk of movement, the woman's hand commanded him to stand.

The king was compelled to his feet, bound by invisible strings, unable to move a muscle. His green eyes bulged as the *goddess* took her hand and reached toward his chest. His royal robes melted away as if they were made of ice, and then the *goddess's* shimmering hand plunged into King Elak's chest right where his heart was. He cried out in agony as light burrowed into his flesh. His screams went on and on as the light grew, and when the *goddess* drew her hand back, there was a small silver key that sparkled like diamonds melded into his flesh above his heart.

King Elak tumbled to the floor, released by the invisible strings. He grasped his chest, gaping at the key that had burrowed into his skin. The *goddess* towered above him, her voice like a raging storm.

"You wanted to be like the *gods*, King Elak Jethro? It is now as you have wished! In your flesh you carry a power no other mortal does. You possess the key that will unlock the Well of Eternal Healing. We offer you this chance of salvation: withdraw your forces from the other kingdoms, give back the Wells of Power you have stolen, and then return to this place to undo what you have done." The *goddess's* eyes flashed with lightning. "Climb into the Well of Eternal Healing and drown yourself in its *waters*. Only by this sacrifice may your sins be paid in full. Only *then* will the Well be as it once was!"

King Elak's eyes widened in horror, and he shook his head, backing away from the golden woman. He looked down at his chest again, and his fingers clawed at the key, but it did not come loose. It was a part of him.

"No! You cannot make me do this!" he shouted at the *goddess*. "I will not bend to your whims! I am King Elak Jethro, the greatest of all kings! You have no right to take the Well of Eternal Healing from me! From *us*! Humanity will curse you for this!"

The woman's eyes burned. It was so blazing that Tarrick and Elak had to shield their faces from the luminosity of her wrath.

"By your own actions, Keyholder!" the *goddess* cried.

She cast her shimmering hands toward the Well, and then her form flew back into the ball of golden light that still hovered there. With a flash, the ball of light vanished, and the entire room went dark, no longer lit by the glory of the *gods* or the blue *waters*.

Several seconds of silence followed this.

Then a frothing gurgling noise issued from the Well, and the black tar-like substance began to spill forth over the rim.

Both the king and the prince gasped, scrambling up from the floor and backing away from darkness. The two of them looked at each other, fear etched into both of their faces. Without hesitation, they fled the glass room just as a burst of darkness slammed through the doors, streaking out into the hallway beyond.

The guards standing there cried out in shock as the tendrils of black wrapped around their bodies. In the blink of an eye, they dissolved into ash like they had never existed in the first place. Elak and Tarrick screamed, pelting down the hall away from the growing destruction.

A violent wind tore over the Kingdom of Hritza, and Octavia was sucked from the palace back into the sky. She watched from above as the cataclysmic force of the *gods'* wrath was poured out from the cup of their fury . . .

As the darkness engulfed the palace, a column of fire fell from the heavens, scorching the kingdom below. It tore through the streets, demolishing everything in its path, and the curse from the Well of Eternal Healing swirled over the living in tandem, taking life as soon as it touched it.

Octavia experienced the terror of every person who died from the expanding punishment—whether by fire or by darkness. The darkness spilled over the land like a wave, claiming the innocent and reducing them all to dust. To blood and bones. To puddles of slime. To nothingness.

Octavia felt like she was watching time move on fast forward. The darkness consumed the entire Kingdom of Hritza. It seeped like ink spilled from a bottle, unceasing and unrelenting. And then suddenly, it stopped, the blackened mist pooling up against an invisible barrier at the edges of the endless trees beyond.

The column of smoke that rose into the sky over the fallen kingdom spit ash into the air a thousand feet high and spread it on the winds like chaff.

Flash.

Octavia was now standing outside of the darkness, staring up at it alongside King Elak and Prince Tarrick. The two men were panting and bleeding, both injured from their flight. The king had sustained several large gashes to his chest, which still bore the sparkling key, and Prince Tarrick's right forearm was thick with blood from a gouge mark the size of an apple, as if a beam had fallen and clipped him.

The forest sheltered them within its branches at the perimeter of the *gods'* fury, but the ash in the air was still so thick that they could barely breathe.

Tarrick's eyes were filled with tears. He fell to his knees, crying out in anguish over the loss of the kingdom. His hands tore through his hair, and the scream that left his mouth was hair-raising.

King Elak, however, looked relieved to be alive, and his face hardened with a look of hatred that festered deep in his soul. He cursed aloud, yelling at the *gods* with all of his might. "YOU ARE DEATH ITSELF!"

The forest lit up, and the *goddess* stood before the king once more, her presence burning like the stars of the heavens. Her wrath turned upon the king, and with a voice that sounded like the winds of the earth, she said, "There is but one more chance for you, King Elak Jethro. Because you carry the key, the darkness cannot harm you. Walk into it, return to the palace, and drown yourself in the Well. If you do, we will extend mercy upon the lands and resurrect all that have perished by this plague. We will roll back the darkness. It is only *your* death we require. For your sins, the darkness will ravage your soul, but the lands will be cleansed, and all will be as it once was. That is the price. Only the Keyholder can undo this!"

The king stood in front of the *goddess*, defiance in his tone. "I will not! *You* have caused this. Not me!"

"It is your choice, Keyholder."

The radiance from the *goddess* shattered through the trees, and it slammed into the king and the prince, flattening them to the ground. They both lay there at the edge of the darkness, stunned, and when they looked up, the *goddess* was gone.

Tarrick glared at the king, anger curling his tone. "The *gods* are giving you a chance to undo this, and you mocked them to their face!" The prince leapt to his feet, advancing on his father, and this caused the king to jump to his feet as well. Tarrick slammed his hands against his father's chest. He pointed to the diamond key. "You do not deserve your life after what you have done! Fix this! Save all of us! Resurrect the life you have taken!"

Elak countered by shoving his son's hands away. "The *gods* branded me with this! This isn't my doing!"

Prince Tarrick's tone swelled with outrage. "You have ruined us all! Look at what you have done! Look at Hritza—how she burns in the darkness!"

The ruins of the fallen kingdom sweltered behind the prince, fueling his words.

"The *gods* cannot compel me to do this, Tarrick. They will not force my hand," the king countered, his bare chest heaving. The key shone bright against his pale and bleeding skin.

"Father, repent! There is nothing left for us. You have gone too far, and the *gods* themselves have punished the entire kingdom for it. You were wrong. And *still*, they have given you the chance to undo this. Please, I beg of you. Listen to them."

The look of rage that flushed Elak's face was palpable. "I will not! I have done nothing but strive to make Hritza great. From the onset, I have proven that Hritza is deserving of power. I was going to create the greatest kingdom on earth! But the *gods* . . . they are hateful. Controlling. Undeserving of our worship and adoration."

Tarrick gaped at his father. "You would blaspheme them so openly? So brazenly?"

"*Yes*! Humanity has outgrown them. I was about to be a god among men—and Hritza the jewel of the earth—and they saw my greatness as a challenge."

"The blood of our brothers and sisters cries out from the ground to testify against you, Father. You have done a wicked thing!"

"The gods are the wicked ones. *They* have brought this destruction. Not me! And I will *not* bend my knee to the tyrants in the sky, Tarrick."

The prince stood there, aghast, with his mouth open and his eyes streaming. The disbelief and anger coursing through him was carved into his soul. It was as if, from the moment of his imprisonment, Tarrick had built in himself a wrath all his own. His hands trembled, and then his sorrow turned into an untamed fit of rage.

Tarrick launched himself at his father, pushing him back and screaming, though no intelligible words came out. It was only a guttural, anguished cry of loss. The king grappled with his son, caught off guard by the sudden assault, but this did not deter Tarrick. Tarrick shoved him again, beating his hands against Elak's chest with brutal force.

Abruptly, the king's foot caught on a thick root that jutted up from the ground, and he tumbled backward. With a sickening thud, Elak Jethro's skull cracked into a jagged rock by the base of a pine, and his body went eerily still . . .

Tarrick stood there, his chest shuddering as sweat licked his forehead. Then his mouth parted, like he couldn't believe what he had just done. Immediately, regret stole over his face, and he clasped his hands together. Blood dripped from his forearm onto the dirt, and Tarrick's eyes were inexplicably drawn from his father's dead body to the gaping wound on his own arm.

The only sounds present were that of the raging fire that burned beyond the darkness and Tarrick's uncontrolled breathing . . .

A cannon-like noise split the forest air, and Tarrick shrieked, throwing his hands up.

He cringed away from . . . nothing. He peered around. Not another soul was in sight. The cannon noise boomed again, and this time, Tarrick fell to his knees, wildly searching the trees for the source of the sound. But still, nothing revealed itself. For a third time, the cannon noise tore through the forest, and Tarrick's entire body shook like a leaf in a strong wind.

Then a dazzling light lit up King Elak's chest, right where the key was, and a ball of brilliance rose from his skin. It hovered in the air for a few moments before chasing after Prince Tarrick. Then a violent flash lit up the entire forest as the young man scrambled away from the light, but before he could escape it, it had burrowed deep within his forearm, melding to his flesh.

Tarrick screamed, clawing at the key, but it was too late. It was already a part of him. He stared at the thing in horror, and when he looked up at the towering wall of darkness, the *goddess* had returned.

Her burning glory was now directed at Tarrick, and he retreated from her, trembling.

"We offer you the same chance, Keyholder," the *goddess* said. Her eyes flashed. "Walk into the darkness, drown yourself in the Well, and pay for the sins of Hritza. Only then will this curse be lifted."

"But . . . what?" Tarrick shook his head as understanding shattered across his desperate face. "This was not my doing! I was against my father's plan from the beginning. Please! I didn't mean to do this. I didn't mean to kill him. I'm sorry. I—" Tarrick's bulging eyes went to his father's lifeless form. "It was an accident! Please! There must be another way. Bring him back. I'm begging you! Give him the key again. I will convince him to—"

"There is no other way. You have taken the life of the one who was meant to bear the punishment for the sins of Hritza, so now the key belongs to you. Since you are his blood, we extend the offer of resurrecting all those who have perished to you, Prince Tarrick Jethro. However, should there be another Keyholder beyond you who is willing, only the fall of the darkness and the restoration of the Well will be granted. The choice is yours."

And in that moment, Octavia knew that despite his noble heart, Prince Tarrick Jethro was too afraid to do as the *goddess* had asked . . .

Octavia Fletcher began to live hundreds of lives.

Keyholder after Keyholder.

The dazzling inch-long key melded to an old man's face, then it latched onto a young woman's hip, then it buried itself into a king's foot. Over and over again, the key changed hands, and the cannons sounded. Blood spilled in an endless cycle—the greed of every person's heart palpable and present. They all sought glory for themselves. And each time, when the truth of what it meant to bear the key came to pass, the *goddess* would appear, and the Keyholder would cry out in anguish at the cost of what their decision to kill for the key meant . . .

A thousand years passed, and Octavia felt all the years in her soul. It was endless. It was like living forever, but at the same time, only minutes transpired.

Finally, she was standing at the edge of the darkness once more, and she was beside a young man. Recognition lit her spirit. This was the last Keyholder before her. The *goddess* was back, floating in front of him, having just shown him the true cost of the key, but this time, there was a new condition, and Octavia understood in her heart that the *gods of old* were tired of humanity's greed, and they felt sorrow for allowing the Wells of Power to exist at all.

"A millennium and not a vessel willing," the *goddess's* voice boomed. "Unless the wrong is righted, all will perish. You have seen, and now you know. You must make your choice."

The young man sank to his knees, trembling. "No . . . NO! I don't want to do this! There must be another way. Surely, you cannot think I would do this! I want out. Please!"

"There is no way out."

"I will not walk into the darkness. Give me another way! I'm begging you! There must be something else I can do. Give me something else to do, and whatever it is, I will do it!"

The *goddess's* ethereal form illuminated the trees beyond the edge of the darkness, and her anger burned. "Is your decision final?"

"P-please . . . you . . . you cannot do this . . ." the young man sobbed.

"You understand what your refusal means, don't you? What it will cost?"

"Please. P-please! I—I can't—I w-won't—"

"I will ask you one more time. Will you walk into the darkness?"

The young man tore at his hair, backing away from the *goddess*, and crying aloud. "Oh *gods*! Oh . . . I . . . it's not fair! It's . . . This isn't what I wanted! This isn't the glory promised! How could you do this to me!? To everyone before me!? You . . . you are sick! Perverted! I cannot . . . I . . . No! NO! I WILL NOT!"

"Then by your own words, you have cursed all that draw breath. From this moment forward, the darkness now moves, and it will swallow the land. The blood of every innocent man, woman, and child is now on your hands, Keyholder."

With a roar, the swirling darkness began to edge forward, slow and creeping, but deadly in its path, and the young man screamed, scrambling back from it.

With a jarring flash, the *goddess* vanished, and Octavia's spirit was pulled to Zoharth, where a woman with curls of deep red hair and eyes of amber stood gazing over the Well of Prophecy in shock. Her whole body quaked, and she fell to the dirt next to the sparkling black rock, and from her lips, the words of the prophecy flowed like a river.

And when she was finished, Zara rose from the ground and set her sights on the Zoharthian palace, determining in her mind to tell King Bastian Jasper the words she had learned . . .

Everything all around Octavia shone brighter than the sun. It overwhelmed her senses, casting her spirit from history back into the realm of the *gods* until she was in front of the *goddess* standing on the same glass floor that spread out in all directions endlessly.

The golden woman looked down at Octavia, her eyes shrouded in glory. Her voice sounded like a trumpet call. "You have seen, and now you know. You must make your choice, Keyholder."

33

Double Insurance

Octavia's eyes were rimmed with tears. A hollow pit had formed in her stomach, and her body felt like a shell, useless and fragile. She beheld the *goddess*, and her voice came out as a hushed whisper.

"I must die?"

Saying the words aloud caused her chest to seize and her mind to go numb. This couldn't be the cost . . .

The woman floated in front of Octavia, her glory shining. "That is the price. Only then may the darkness fall, for its wrath must be satisfied. Your soul in exchange for humanity. You as the vessel for the curse or the end of all things."

Octavia sank to her knees, unable to draw breath. The sheer terror that consumed her body was too much to bear. It turned her blood to ice in her veins. It wrapped around her throat and tore through her resolve like paper.

The words of the prophecy came back to her:

greed will be the undoing, and forfeit the gain

Her life. That's what she must forfeit. And the gain will be the Well of Eternal Healing and fall of the darkness—the salvation of all.

She couldn't speak even though she wanted to scream. All Octavia could do was lift her gaze to the *goddess* in anguish. Whether the *goddess* felt any pity for her, she didn't know.

A shiver crawled across Octavia's skin, and something in her mind snapped into place. It was from living the lives of all the Keyholders. In every instance, after the memories of Hritza, the *goddess* would address the Keyholder in front of the darkness, for it was only by choosing to take a step toward it with the intention of entering into it that the truth was revealed. But Octavia was not in front of the darkness now. She was still on the endless glass sea dressed in white robes—she was still in the realm of the *gods.*

A sinking feeling burrowed through her, and the *goddess* seemed to read her thoughts.

"You have not yet walked into the darkness, Octavia Fletcher," the *goddess* said. "You are not yet beyond the reach of wicked men. We have shielded you so that you may know the truth. But it is time for you to return to your mortal form."

"You've shielded me? What does that mean?" Octavia asked, desperate.

"An army has seen you. An army awaits. They are held back by our light, but once you return to your body, we cannot shield you from them."

Octavia got to her feet, her heart thundering in her chest. How close was this army to her physical form? How long had she been standing in front of the darkness learning the truth from the *gods*? Long enough for a whole army to come upon her?

Her thoughts spiraled. Could she run toward the darkness and make it into its depths in time to escape them? Octavia hadn't even had time to process what she must do. To end this all at the cost of her life and soul? Maybe she could truly make her choice inside the darkness, safe from the clutches of those who sought her.

She would have to run . . .

"The decision, as always, remains with you, Keyholder," the *goddess* said, sweeping her hands open wide. Her palms shone bright.

"Wait!" Octavia cried. "Please, give me more ti—"

The brilliance of the realm of the *gods* shattered around her, and Octavia was cast into a light that burned her eyes.

Returning to her physical form felt like slamming into the earth from the stars. Octavia fell, and she fell hard, her soul sucked back into her body with the force of a whip. She was supernaturally frozen in place a hundred yards from the edge of the darkness, and she could see the veil of light that protected her, cloaking the place where she stood. It was like a bubble of gold that radiated out from her skin.

But then another light caught her attention. Flashes of blue surrounded her on all sides, and it took Octavia's mind a moment to recognize it, but when she did, her stomach sank. Parcels of *waters*—dozens of them—all clutched in the hands of soldiers that crowded around the place where the light shielded her.

With a burst of energy, feeling rushed back into Octavia's limbs, and she gasped, drawing in breath like she had been underwater. In that very same moment, the ethereal shield faded into nonexistence, and at the fall of the light, the soldiers charged toward her.

Octavia didn't even have a chance to run to the darkness before hands grabbed her. She twisted her body, yanking her arms in a desperate attempt for freedom, but there was no escaping them. The soldiers dragged her away from the edge of the darkness kicking and screaming, and her mind went so wild with panic that she couldn't see straight.

She felt like she was suffocating. She couldn't get enough air into her lungs. This couldn't be happening. Not again—not when she was so close. She fought and fought, pulling against the men who clutched onto her and begging them to let her go.

And then . . . Octavia's strength failed her entirely.

All of the fight drained from her body, and she went limp. A black fabric bag was forced over her head, rope bound her wrists together in front of her, and she could do nothing to resist it.

More hands grabbed her, lifting her from the ground. Then her feet scraped against something hard—it felt like wood—and someone forced her to sit. Two soldiers held her there, their nails digging into the skin of her upper arms.

Voices called out, yelling at one another to get away from the darkness. There was a violent tug, and whatever Octavia was sitting on moved at the pace of a galloping team of horses.

The sheer terror she was feeling was like an out of body experience. In her mind, she knew what was happening, but her body had simply given out on her. She was unable to command her own muscles. They felt like puddles against her bones. All she could do was sit there, utterly numb. She couldn't see, and she felt like her brain was shutting down. Only her heartbeat told her she was still alive.

Which army had captured her?

The thought of Pierre drove itself like a spike through her chest, and it made her want to scream, but even that failed. Her voice was gone, evaporated like her strength.

For twenty minutes, the only thing Octavia could do was breathe as the cart she sat in moved along toward *gods*-knew where. And when it finally stopped, an icy dread filled her veins.

The soldiers holding her yanked her up to her feet, and her knees buckled.

"Walk!" one of them snarled.

She couldn't . . .

So they dragged her instead.

They hooked their arms under hers, hauling her across the dirt, and the black fabric bag over her head blocked everything from view. She could only hear the sounds of more voices and the crunch of feet against sand.

The soldiers holding her pushed her down into a sitting position again, and she felt her back lean up against something flat. It felt like a wooden post. The ropes at her wrists were loosened, and then her arms were pulled behind her and rebound so that she was tied to the post. The fibrous cords dug into her wrists to the point of hurting, and Octavia's panic turned to tears.

She whimpered underneath the cloth covering her face. Her cheeks and knees were tingling, and the sensation crept through her joints, draining her strength even further.

"Move out of the way!" a harsh voice commanded.

The soldiers stepped back from Octavia. Boots fell against the ground—too many to know the number that surrounded her. Someone crouched in front of her, and then the black fabric sack was pulled off of her head.

Octavia squinted in the harsh light of day. There was no denying it. She must have been standing in front of the darkness for hours as the *gods* showed her the true cost of the key, because it had been night when she had chosen to walk into its depths.

She took in her surroundings quickly. She was in the middle of an open expanse of desert, and in the distance, the darkness brewed with wrath above the horizon. Soldiers crowded together, peering at her intently, and the man who knelt before her bore an excited yearning on his face. Octavia had never seen him before.

He had pale skin, light blue eyes, vibrant red hair, and a full red beard and mustache. He also wore a crisp copper-brown uniform. Whoever he was, this man looked like a commander, and Octavia felt the smallest shred of relief that it wasn't Pierre Zarqel.

"Well, well, look at what the *gods* have so favorably bestowed upon us today," the man mused, searching Octavia's face. "King Asa will be pleased."

Octavia's eyes widened, and she swallowed against a dry throat. This was Rustwick's army. Immediately, she searched the faces around her, but none of them were Papa. So Octavia sent a desperate prayer up to the heavens that he was far from this place, because if Rustwick's army discovered their tie, she had no doubt they would use Papa against her . . .

"I'm Commander Elthron Kaz," the red-headed man said. "We have been searching for you for quite some time. What luck to have finally found you at the doorstep of the darkness itself." He cocked his head, narrowing his eyes. "Let's be straight with each other, shall we, Keyholder? You will walk into the darkness to claim the Well of Eternal Healing in the name of Rustwick, by decree of King Asa Draydon, and after—"

"I will not."

She stared at the commander in defiance, and though her body had no strength at all, her voice gained it like a storm.

The overwhelming revelation the *gods* had bestowed upon her gave her a spite she did not have before, and the foolishness of this man's greed angered her. He didn't understand anything. None of them did.

In this moment, Octavia felt closer to the *gods* than she ever had before. It was her choice, they said. Hers, and hers alone.

If she walked into the darkness at all, it would be for *everyone*. And no man could make her claim the Well of Eternal Healing for their kingdom. For their greed. For the thing that started this in the first place.

"You may have stolen me away from the edge of the darkness, but you have no hold over me! You are only delaying what I must do at the cost of more lives. Release me."

Commander Kaz eyed her in a calculated manner. "You think I have no hold over you?"

"You cannot make me claim the Well for Rustwick!" she spat. "If I do this, I do it for *all* the lands—not for you. Not for any king either. Release me!"

The commander stood from his crouched position, backing away from her. Then he looked around at his men, an amused smile hooking his mouth. "Did you hear that, gentlemen? We've come all this way for nothing! We might as well pack up and go home."

Laughter flitted through the soldiers, and Commander Kaz's face hardened, his smile now gone. He stared at Octavia. "I don't know who you are or where you're from, Keyholder, but I think I have something you want. Let's see if this changes your mind."

Elthron Kaz snapped his fingers, motioning to people beyond Octavia's view, and into their midst, the soldiers dragged a man who was bound hand and foot with a black fabric sack over his head. Octavia's heart sank all the way to her toes. Even with his face covered, she recognized him, and tears sprang to her eyes as the soldiers dropped the man to his knees in front of her. The black fabric sack was ripped from his face.

It was Azariah . . .

He gritted his teeth against the leather gag in his mouth, staring at Octavia with streaming eyes. He looked far more injured than he had when they had parted ways. The whites of his eyes were streaked with red, his long black hair was caked with blood, and there was new bruising along his jawline.

Octavia felt like she couldn't breathe. She wanted to scream. Her heart was going to tear itself from her chest.

Commander Kaz walked behind Azariah, his eyes fixed on Octavia. "He's a traveling companion of yours, is he not?"

When Octavia didn't respond, Kaz withdrew a dagger, grabbed a fistful of Azariah's hair, and yanked him back, placing the blade to his neck. Azariah groaned in pain.

"Stop! Oh *gods*, stop!" she yelped. "Don't hurt him!"

Kaz smiled at Octavia's reaction. "I thought so." He pulled the blade away from Azariah's neck and released the hold on his hair. "My men caught him as we approached the darkness, and I thought, who would be out so far, *this* close to the darkness, all alone, unless their reason was *you.*"

Octavia couldn't lie her way out of this one, and she couldn't pretend she didn't care. Azariah had her whole heart, and she would do anything to protect him.

"I'll do it. I will walk through the darkness and claim the Well in the name of Rustwick. Just don't hurt him! I'm begging you."

Elthron Kaz's triumphant smirk lit his features. He approached Octavia, crouching down again. "See? That wasn't so hard, was it?" His eyes flicked up to a soldier standing behind her. "Unbind her. Put her companion against the post instead."

Rough hands attacked the knots at Octavia's wrists, and then she was free. Her limbs still felt like puddles, and she had to be hauled to her feet by the soldiers. Two men held her up, while more soldiers dragged Azariah to the wooden post. They sat him against it, wrapping rope around his torso to secure him there.

Octavia's anxiety was like a beehive buzzing underneath her skin. All she could do was stare at Azariah as he stared back at her. How was she back here again? Bargaining for his life to cruel and wicked men.

"Commander, the scouts are back!" someone shouted.

Beyond the group of soldiers, the sounds of horses drew near, and Commander Kaz looked up at the new arrivals. Three men on horseback rode up, parting the crowd, and there was an urgency to their demeanors.

"Speak quickly. What news do you have?" Kaz demanded.

"Commander, Xadia's forces are drawing near. They are less than half a day's journey from us," the first man said breathlessly.

"And Zoharth's army marches across the outlet as we speak," the second man added. "We are running out of time. The Keyholder must go to the darkness now, or we will have a whole different fight on our hands."

The third man pulled his horse forward, a stark look of shock on his face. He was so pale he looked like death itself, and as Octavia's eyes lifted to his, her heart nearly gave out.

No . . .

"Octavia?" Papa murmured in disbelief.

Commander Kaz's attention snapped to Papa, and then it went back to Octavia. A horrible feeling slithered through her entire body.

"What is this!?" Papa demanded, prodding his horse all the way up to the commander. "Why do you have my daughter? What's going on!?"

"This is your daughter?" Kaz's eyebrows raised.

Papa leapt from the horse, walking up to the two soldiers holding Octavia. She stared up at him, too overwhelmed to speak. Tears traced her cheeks.

"Release her at once!" Papa demanded. "What is the meaning of this?"

Commander Kaz took Papa by the shoulder and pulled him back from her. "This is the Keyholder." His light blue eyes went from Papa to Octavia as brutish amusement split his mouth. "And it looks like our little Keyholder hails from Rustwick. How poetic."

Papa looked like he had been slapped in the face. He gaped at Octavia. "She can't be the Keyholder. This must be a mistake."

"See for yourself," Kaz said, sweeping a hand toward Octavia.

The soldier holding Octavia's left arm grabbed her hand and held it forward. The key sparkled, causing those around her to stare at it in awe. Papa's eyes went from the key to his daughter's face, and anguish fell over him. His soft brown eyes glistened with disbelief. "It can't be . . ."

Kaz gave a quick nod to his men. "Bind him. We don't need any interference."

The soldiers moved quickly, obeying their commander, and Theodin Fletcher was pulled away from Octavia and restrained with rope.

"No!" Octavia cried, pleading with Kaz. "Leave him alone! He has nothing to do with this! I have already promised to walk through the darkness in the name of Rustwick. Please! Let him go!"

"Let's call it double insurance, Keyholder. Now you have *two* reasons to claim the Well of Eternal Healing for Rustwick," Kaz threatened. He breathed in the dry desert air like he was savoring the moment, delight written into his countenance. He called out in a loud voice. "The *gods* are truly smiling down on us today!"

He walked up to Octavia so that his face was inches from hers, and his stale breath trailed into her nose.

"To the darkness, my dear."

"Let me speak with my father and my companion."

"No."

"I only want a minute with them!" she countered. "Your salvation can spare me a minute! They are both my whole life. *Please.*"

Octavia's voice was the only strong thing about her. She could barely keep herself upright. Her legs were weak, her limbs shook, and she hung in the soldiers' grip nearly limp. Her fate in the darkness was a permanent decision. Only she knew what was about to happen. With desperation, she prayed in her heart to the *gods* that Commander Kaz would allow her this final grace. She had to say goodbye.

"Only a minute," Kaz relented.

He gave the soldiers holding Octavia a stiff nod, and they dragged her over to Papa, who was now gripped between two soldiers himself. He had tears in his eyes and seeing him cry made Octavia's face wet with more grief. She forced herself to put more weight onto her feet, and she shrugged away from the soldiers, but they did not let go of her.

"Let me stand!" she said resolutely.

At a look from Kaz, the soldiers released her, and Octavia wobbled, but she was able to keep her balance. Without hesitation, she wrapped her arms around Papa and buried her face in his chest. She had to quell the sob that had lodged itself in her throat.

"I'm so sorry, Papa," she whispered. "I'm so sorry for how much trouble I've gotten myself into." She looked up at him through glassy eyes. "When this is over, Mama can be healed. Bowan can have his father back, and you three will live long and happy lives. I vow it."

"Octavia, how did this happen to you? What is going on?"

She let out a whimper. She wanted to explain everything to him—all that she had endured over the past few weeks—but there wasn't time for that. So she said what was important, for it was the only thing she had the strength to do. "I love you so much, Papa. It's going to be okay. The darkness is going to fall. Just . . . promise me you will take a parcel to Mama. And hug Bowan for me. Tell him I love him, okay? And tell Mama too."

She gripped him in the hug more fiercely now, tears spilling down her face. She didn't want to let him go, but she forced her hands to release Papa's clothing. Then she turned toward the bounty hunter, and her unsteady legs carried her to the wooden post. The soldiers parted, allowing her through, and she dropped to her knees in front of him.

Azariah's breathing was labored—shallow—and his injuries were horrible. Whatever beating he had received upon capture had been severe. He sounded like he was suffering greatly, and it scared her, because even after their escape from Pierre, he hadn't been this hurt. Octavia's hands reached up to his face, and gently, her fingertips worked the knots of the leather gag.

"You will leave him as he is!" Kaz growled.

"He can't breathe!" Octavia shot back with venom. "He's hurt! Have you no mercy? He can't escape you."

Kaz did not say anything more.

She loosened the gag, pulling it from his mouth, and Azariah coughed, a trail of blood dribbling down his chin. She peered at him with tears in her eyes, and then she brought her forehead to his as her hands held either side of his face.

"I'm—s-sorry—Octavia," he sputtered, wincing in pain. "I'm s-so sorry."

"This isn't your fault," she whispered.

Her lungs constricted as affection for him overwhelmed her. Azariah had done so much for her. He had protected her relentlessly, and now she would protect him.

"The *gods* have shown me what to do." She swallowed hard, more tears spilling down her face. "Everything's going to be alright. I will open the Well, and then Commander Kaz can heal you. I will make him promise me. He can heal you, and then you can leave this place. You can be free to find the happiness you deserve. Promise me you will find happiness, Azariah."

He stared at her, his pained face burdened. "W-why are you s-speaking like this? What must happen t-to open the Well?"

Octavia's heart felt like it was shattering in her chest. The reality of her own death stormed through her body, weakening it even further. She had to die. She was going to die. As she held her forehead against Azariah's, Octavia's heart broke for everything she would never get to do. For every moment she would never get to have with him. How could she tell him the cost of the key? She couldn't . . .

With all the tenderness she owned, she pressed her lips to his, kissing him for the last time, and tears fell down her face onto his chest. He kissed her back, and she let out a quiet sob.

The kiss lasted far too short a time, and when she pulled back, she simply stared at him, memorizing his features. His kind face. His lips. His brown eyes. The stubble of his beard. There was still so much she wished she could say to him, but the only thing she had left to say was the only thing she had yet to fully experience.

Mama's soft words came back to her: "People might say a few weeks isn't enough time to know, but for me, it is."

For Octavia, it was too.

She spoke it for the life she could have had with Azariah.

She said it for herself—and she said it for him too.

"I love you, Azariah Ronan. May you truly know happiness again."

She rose to her feet, knowing that if she did not leave him now, she may never find the will to do so. A strength that must have been granted by the *gods* flowed through her legs, and Octavia walked up to the commander, staring at him with a ferocity fueled by the key embedded in her palm.

"Promise me you will heal him," she stated. "When the Well is open, swear to me you will give him the *waters*."

Commander Kaz's upper lip pulled tight to expose his teeth. "As long as the darkness falls and the Well belongs to Rustwick, you have my word."

"I will do my part," she said with authority. "Whatever is to become of me, as the *gods* are our witness, if you do not follow through with this, may the wrath of the heavens fall upon you to consume your soul, Commander Elthron Kaz. You *will* heal him."

The conviction of Octavia's tone caused the commander to falter a bit, and he shrank back at her presence. An unnatural calm descended upon her. It was a peace she could not describe. Perhaps it was the knowledge that this would be over soon.

"Take me to the darkness," she said.

As the soldiers led Octavia away, she looked back at Azariah one last time, and she thanked the *gods* for the short time she had been granted with the man she had come to love.

34

It Must Be Paid In Full

Octavia stood at the edge of the darkness as it swirled above her. Its vastness was paralyzing. The soldiers who had escorted her back to its edge stood in the distance, well away from its clutches, and now all that was left to do was walk forward.

This was it. She was finally going to step into it, and she knew that once she did, she would never come back out. It was an unreal experience, knowing that she would die, but that was the cost. At the penalty of all perishing, she would do this. For her family. For the man she loved. For everyone who was innocent.

She only hoped that after the fall of the darkness, humanity would be wise enough to realize that they should never repeat history, lest the *gods of old* change their minds.

Octavia put one foot in front of the other, bringing herself up to the bitter edge of the frothing substance as it leaked across the earth toward her. She looked back over her shoulder, gazing out at the expanse of desert, then she wiped her face of the last of her tears.

She put her left palm forward, the smallest part of her still fearful that she would die upon touching the barrier, but as she took another step, her hand went into the ashen substance, and she felt no pain.

Octavia took a deep breath and crossed the threshold.

Immediately, all sounds ceased to exist, and she was cast into thick darkness. She walked forward blind, with her hands outstretched, and fear tore through her chest. How was she supposed to find the Well if she couldn't see anything at all?

However, with only a few more steps, Octavia emerged from the pitch-black section onto a stretch of desert. But everything looked different now.

The sun didn't shine above her, the air was gray like ash, and the land was cracked and desolate. It was dim. Not dark enough for her to be fully blind—but almost. And rot weaved through the earth as decay filled her nose.

There was no sound. Nothing at all. It was so quiet that Octavia's own breath was like an avalanche. The blood pulsing through her veins magnified in volume, and for several minutes, all she could do was stand there unmoving.

"Walk," she whispered to herself.

Her own voice roared through the quiet. It was the most terrifying silence of her life—with no earthly experience to compare it to. It was simply the absence of every sound, sucked into a void of nothingness, and it drove her mind crazy with desperation to hear something other than herself. But the silence was relentless. Unbreakable.

Octavia scanned over the landscape, her breathing shallow and uneven. Far in the distance, she could see a massive hill with a crumbling structure atop it. The ruins of the Kingdom of Hritza rose like an omen of death from the blackened ground. It would take her forever to walk to the base of it and climb up, but Octavia had nothing left to do but move forward.

With her heart beating like a drum magnified like cannons, she started her trek. The key was the only comfort she carried, for it shone like a beacon, helping to light the path across the cracked earth.

As she left the bubbling edge of the darkness behind, the scent of death filled Octavia's nose, making her gag. It was putrid. She pulled up the front of her tunic, trying to breathe through the fabric to give herself some relief. Slipping, she fell to her hands and knees, and her palms squished into the decay beneath her.

Octavia gagged again, sick coming up her throat.

This wasn't natural. It had been a thousand years, and yet it smelled as if the carnage had happened mere weeks ago . . .

The key burned in her palm, and she sucked in a gurgling breath, pushing herself to stand and run a few paces in the hopes of getting away from the scent. Her lungs felt like they were being squeezed, and she found that the air here was thinner than anything she was used to. She gasped, slowing her pace. Running wasn't going to be an option. There simply wasn't enough substance to breathe in.

Octavia curled forward, vomiting, and her stomach emptied itself of what little contents it contained. The atrophy of the ground was overpowering, and her eyes watered.

She just had to keep moving.

Octavia tore a strip from her tunic and tied it around her mouth and nose, hoping that the fabric would help her manage the rancid smells. It only tempered them slightly, but it was all she could do.

For an hour, Octavia pushed herself forward, locking away all of her emotions deep into the recesses of her mind simply to force her body to cooperate. The rot was not gone, and she was not used to its smell, but it had lessened slightly as the palace of Hritza drew near.

Time didn't seem real here. The suffocating silence worked against her, siphoning her resolve and pushing her thoughts to fall prey into backing out of this. She could still run. She could still leave this place. She hadn't drowned herself in the Well yet.

"No," she whispered. "I am willing."

She had left her tears beyond the darkness, and she had resolved in her mind to pay the price. Octavia would not turn away like every Keyholder before her. The words of the prophecy came back to her again:

greed will be the undoing, and forfeit the gain

She would go through with it, for the sake of all.

The base of the massive hill towered in front of her, and she peered up at the dilapidated and charred ruins overhead. How many people lost their lives that day? How many burned for King Elak's sins? And how many innocents were swallowed by the curse that came out of the Well?

From Hritza's memories, Octavia knew where to go, and it was only by filling her mind with thoughts of her family that she was able to keep walking. She replayed the years of going to the harvest festival—the pig races, bobbing for apples, eating pie, drinking beer. She went over the nights she and Bowan had lain out in the wheat fields looking up at the stars, talking about nothing and everything. She relived Mama's good days, when she was happy and lucid. She thought of Papa and how hard he had always worked for his family. And then her mind moved to the feel of Azariah's lips against her own, the feel of his hands on her waist, his strong arms, the way he had made her feel . . . She clung to the happiness. Only the happiness. For her heart wanted to go back to him. She didn't want to die, but there was no alternative.

She would save him.

She would save all of them.

The sharp incline of the hill had her gasping for breath in the ashen and dim atmosphere. She dug her hands into the festering dirt, pulling herself up. One handhold after another. One foot in front of the other. Higher and higher, she climbed.

Sweat slicked down her back and covered her forehead. The ripped cloth over her mouth was suffocating, so, despite the corrosive smells, she tore it from her face, discarding it on the hill.

Upward. Onward. To the Well.

Her mind grew more desperate as her body weakened from the strain of the climb, but at last, she reached the outer wall of the palace and collapsed to the ground, lying there for a few minutes to collect her strength.

As she stared up, all she could see was the brewing storm of the darkness. It blotted out anything beyond its clutches. No stars were visible, and no life was visible either. It was all destruction. And the stone of the palace itself was blackened, cracked, and crumbling. Ruin—that was all that was around her.

She pushed herself up, standing unsteadily, and with her eyes cast upward, she entered the decomposing courtyard. The moment she stepped foot onto the grounds of the ancient Hritzan palace, the key scorched her palm. She gasped, looking down at it. Its light brightened, and a deep unearthly pull tugged at her whole body. The Well was close. She could feel it. It was calling to her soul, whispering to her to come step into its *waters*.

Here, the smell of death strengthened. The walls of the courtyard looked wet, like the blood from those who had perished all those years ago had not yet dried.

Silence.

Oppressive, fear-inducing, bone-chilling silence.

It made her want to scream.

Octavia's breath shuddered as she crossed through the courtyard and climbed the steps leading up to the entrance. The doors were withered away. All that remained was a gaping opening that looked like a cave.

She crept forward, walking into the belly of the palace. The disintegrating structure looked like it might collapse over the top of her, and it was so dark that she could barely see anything at all. Only the key provided enough light to see where to place her feet.

She peered through the dark.

In the corner of the entryway, a spiral staircase extended upward, and when Octavia held her left palm forward to light the way, her heart dropped into her stomach. Even in the near-dark, she could tell that the spiral staircase wrapped itself around the base of the Well of Power.

She gaped at the sight. How deep did the Well of Eternal Healing go? If Octavia was being honest, she didn't know the depth of any of the Wells of Power, but for this Well's opening to be at the top of the Hritzan palace, its depth had to be staggering.

She approached the staircase, which was slick with a crimson liquid that covered the black weeds riddled over its surface. Tentatively, she placed a foot on the first step, and when it did not give way beneath her weight, she climbed up.

The spiral took her to the pinnacle of the palace. The Well pulled on her soul again, instilling her with a primal fear, and the key responded in tandem, prickling at her flesh. Octavia stepped from the staircase into a hallway she recognized from the memories. This was the place Elak and Tarrick fled the start of the darkness . . .

Her breath came out strained and broken. Her heartbeat thundered through her, like it was a bird desperately trying to flee for its life. Octavia ground her teeth together and balled her right hand up, digging her nails into her skin.

She kept her left hand aloft so the key could light her path, and with forced steps, she moved to the doorway of the room that housed the Well of Power.

The once grand glass room was cracked and atrophied, like the walls themselves had been a living organism that had died and decayed. At the far end, the black rock rim of the Well was just as it had been in the memories: ashen, like a fire had scorched it.

For minutes on end, all Octavia could do was stand there in the deathly silence at the entrance to the room, staring at the Well of Eternal Healing. Once more, she fought with her desire to run. To hide. To get as far away from the Well as possible and not give her life and soul in exchange for humanity.

What was it going to be like to die? Would it hurt? But far worse than that was the question regarding her soul. What did it truly mean to give her soul to the darkness? Would she cease to exist? Would it destroy her soul completely or would she be bound to it for eternity? Octavia had always believed in the afterlife—one blessed by the presence of living with the *gods*—but was that even an option for her anymore? Would the *gods* see her act of sacrifice and pull her soul from the pit? Or would she stay there forever paying for the sins of King Elak Jethro?

"Please," she whispered to the room. "Let there be another way." She stared up at the broken ceiling, which was cracked open to the darkness above it, and her heart desperately pleaded with the *gods*. "Please."

But there was no answer.

The silence continued on . . .

The key and Well once again worked together to call her forward, and Octavia reluctantly walked all the way to the rim. She peered into it. The *waters* were black and still. Her entire body was sapped of all strength as she stared within.

One last time, she prayed to the *gods* to take this from her—to give her something else to do. Again, there was nothing but the certainty of death that clawed its way through her, and no word from the *gods* to stop her.

She swallowed hard, her skin sticky with sweat, and her limbs numb with fear. How could she drown herself if her mind and body would fight back against it? She was certain her panic would pull her from the *waters*, and her lungs would refuse to give up their breath.

Octavia scoured her surroundings using the light of the key. Thick vines weaved together along the crevices of the room, so she approached one, pulling a strand free from the wall. It was about five feet in length, and sturdy enough to not break. Then she continued her search. At the base of the Well, a piece of the rock had broken completely off.

That would have to work . . .

Her eyes watered as she tied the vine around her waist. She knotted it twice, and then she took the other end of the vine and wrapped it around the fragment of rock, binding it and tugging on it to make sure it wasn't going to come loose. Then she hoisted the rock into her hands. It was heavy, and she could barely manage to carry it.

Then Octavia peered into the black *waters*, and only anguish filled her spirit.

She sat on the rim of the decaying Well, putting her feet in. It was freezing, and her lungs spasmed at the frigid temperature. Even though Commander Kaz had Azariah and Papa, and even though Octavia had said she would claim the Well for Rustwick, she knew in her heart that she wasn't going to. She was doing this for everyone, and no threat from the despicable men below could stop her. The only thing that tore her apart was the fact that she would never know if Azariah and Papa would be okay. All she could do was pray for their safety.

She gazed at the key and drew what little strength she could from its shimmering surface, imagining herself walking amongst the *gods* in eternal peace, free from pain and free from the clutches of wicked men.

She had to do it now, or she wouldn't have the courage to do it at all . . .

Octavia looked up one last time, and whispered to the *gods*, "For every person who does not deserve the darkness, I do this for them."

She pushed the rock into the Well, and it yanked her into its bitter cold depths. She plunged, down and down. She kept going long after she felt like she should have reached the bottom, and the pressure of the *waters* built around her, crushing her chest and ears.

When the rock stopped, Octavia barely had any strength left to hold her breath. She panicked, her body fighting her like she knew it would. But she was far too deep to surface in time, even if she had not tied herself down.

Darkness was the only thing around her, her brain cried out for air, and then pain attacked her body like knives.

Everything hurt.

Water filled her mouth and lungs.

She tried to pull the vine loose from her waist.

But then her mind stopped fighting, her limbs grew still, and her heartbeat slowed . . . until eventually, it stopped . . . and in the silence, in the darkness, in the Well of Eternal Healing . . . Octavia Fletcher died.

35

Moments of Faith

Octavia was on a smooth glass surface, and she was naked, but that word felt incorrect, for she didn't have a body anymore. She was spirit only. All around her, there was light. She didn't know how she could see it, because she didn't have eyes, but this place was familiar. The glass sea extended endlessly in all directions.

She tried to speak, but she had no mouth and no tongue. Octavia didn't know what her form was, so she looked down, hoping to get a glimpse of it, but she saw nothing. The only thing she knew for sure was that she existed . . .

What happened? She searched her thoughts, but each time something concrete was on the cusp of her understanding, it slipped away. She didn't know why she was here or what was going on . . .

"Octavia Fletcher," an ethereal voice chimed.

She turned, suddenly in the presence of the *goddess*, and the glory of her appearance sparked the memories of Octavia's whole life, flashing them before her like lightning. She had drowned herself in the Well of Eternal Healing.

Octavia tried to speak again, but it was impossible.

"You will speak only when it is time," the *goddess* said. "We are in deliberation over you, Keyholder." She extended her hand, ushering Octavia to her side with a flick of her finger. "Come."

Octavia's spirit was caught up with the radiance of the *goddess*, and in a flash of brilliance, she found herself in the center of a circular diamond room. There were a dozen great golden thrones that rose up like pillars all around her, and seated on the thrones were six *gods* and five *goddesses*, with one throne empty for the sixth *goddess* who still stood with Octavia. Each of their faces was cloaked in majesty, hidden from her view.

The overwhelming awe she felt being in the presence of the *gods* was enough to make Octavia wish she had never existed at all. If she could have lain prostrate on the floor before them, she would have, but she did not have the ability to do so.

It was strange, existing without a form—feeling without a mind or a heart.

The *goddess* who had whisked Octavia's spirit to this place took her seat on the open throne, and when she did, the entire room dazzled brighter than anything in all of the heavens.

"We are here to weigh your heart, Octavia Fletcher. For this very day, the course of humanity's fate will change."

A booming voice deeper than thunder spoke. "I do not understand why we have come together to discuss this. The Keyholder has willingly offered to pay the price. The darkness must have a vessel to satisfy its wrath. That was always the end of this."

"I believe things have changed," the *goddess* said. "And so must we."

A *god* whose voice sounded like a soft rain chimed in. "Speak plainly. Why is the Keyholder in our midst when her soul should be burning in the darkness?"

All of the divine beings looked to the *goddess*, and she held out her hands. "This girl did not take the key out of greed. She is the first in a thousand years to not murder for it—to not seek its glory."

"It does not matter," the booming thunderous *god* countered. "The darkness must claim her soul for the Well of Eternal Healing to open. The sins of Hritza must be paid in full."

"What was our purpose in creating the darkness in the first place?" the *goddess* challenged. "Speak, for we all know."

A new *god* answered, and his voice was like that of a powerful wind upon the sea. "To punish the wicked hearts of the men for their greed, for they thought they could hoard the gift of the Wells of Power for themselves instead of sharing the *waters* in peace as we intended."

The *goddess's* face flashed. "Precisely, and after a thousand years, humanity has not changed. When we gave the words of the prophecy to Zara the Wise, murder resulted. Instead of humanity coming together to face the darkness, they fought over the Keyholder to gain the Well. Even now, their armies march to wage war over gaining its power. They have learned nothing."

"Then they do not deserve any of the Wells of Power!" another *goddess* lilted, her voice as musical as every note under the heavens. "The darkness should consume them all."

"The darkness," the thunderous *god* boomed, "should consume who it was *meant* to consume. The Keyholder's destiny was tied to the darkness the moment the key melded to her flesh. Her soul is no longer ours."

Fear ripped through Octavia at the thunderous *god's* statement. She wanted to say something, but she had no means to say it. She simply existed in the center of the diamond room, captive to the *gods* without a way to express anything at all.

"The purpose of creating the key was to make a wicked man pay for the wickedness in his heart, and with each change of the key, we saw only wickedness abound. But not in her," the *goddess* said. "Let us weigh her heart, for I believe we must take it into account."

"To what end?" the musical *goddess* asked. "What will change as a result of examining her? The darkness must have a vessel in order to fall. The Keyholder was always meant to redeem humanity in our eyes at the price of their soul. We can't break the darkness if we have no place to send it. It was born from humanity's greed and must be satisfied with a price."

The thrones lit up, reflecting the glory of the *gods* as their words grew more heated.

"Perhaps the cost of being the Keyholder can be more than what we originally intended it to be," the *goddess* offered. "As we have seen, humanity has not learned from this. They have not changed as we hoped they would."

"Speak plainly now," the thunderous *god* said sharply. "What are you suggesting?"

"I propose we charge the Keyholder with the task of bringing peace to the lands, for I fear that the evil hearts of men will force our hand again. A new darkness may yet come, and the destruction of all things will follow. We had already decided to eliminate humanity with the Keyholder before Octavia Fletcher, for when he refused to walk into the darkness, we set it in motion. We did not expect to find anyone willing to bear the curse. But from the moment this girl gained the key, I have watched her. She is not like the others. She has sacrificed herself for a world that is still wicked, and I believe we should give humanity another chance because of her actions."

"If we are weighing her heart, then let us truly weigh it," the *god* who sounded like a soft rain said. "Let us see her moments of faith—if indeed she has been true."

The *goddess* stood from her throne, walked to the center of the room where Octavia was, and threw her shimmering hands up. The diamond room brightened like the stars, and Octavia's prayers were displayed for the *gods* to see. Every single one of them since gaining the key flashed across the thrones: praying during her flight through the trees that she would get away from Voramir, imploring the *gods* for their protection as Azariah led her away from Rustwick, asking the *gods* if they would allow her to make it to Zoharth without anyone else capturing her, pondering in her heart the nightmare about the darkness growing across the ground like a weed . . .

The moments came sharper now, each one more focused than the last.

What am I supposed to do? Her own thoughts echoed all around her. *What were you trying to show me?* She was leaning up against a pine tree, sifting through what she had seen in the Well at Urtha.

The next moment, Octavia was on horseback having just escaped the people who had drugged her. She was desperately searching for Azariah, praying to the *gods* that she would spot the blanket she had slept with. She searched and searched, and right as she was about to turn away and give up, the *goddess* herself stood by Octavia's side, right next to the horse. There was a flick of her golden hand, and Octavia's attention turned toward the trees, finding the blanket and then the bounty hunter . . .

She was chained in Pierre's war tent, and she sneered at him as he wrapped his hand around her throat. "You're avoiding the question, and my patience is wearing thin!" he growled. "I'm going to ask you one last time, Keyholder. How do I get the key?"

Octavia's prayer to the *gods* to help her trick Pierre burned like a fire in her chest as she spoke. "You can't. I already told you. I'm the last Keyholder. *I* am the one who must walk through the darkness, or there will be no one to walk through it at all. That's why it's moving—it started when *I* got the key."

Pierre's grip on her neck vanished, and he backed away from her. "*You* caused the darkness to start moving?"

"Yes! The *gods of old* are tired of humanity's greed, and they've decided to take back all the Wells of Power with the darkness. If something happens to me, or if I choose *not* to walk through the darkness—which I *can* do—then everyone will die. The *gods of old* are ending this with me."

The diamond room of the *gods* glowed brighter, moving to the next scene.

In one moment, Octavia was thanking the *gods* for Absalom and his kindness, and in the next, her voice was desperate. It echoed off the golden thrones as the *gods* watched her strain against her chains.

"Help me! Please help me! I don't know what to do!"

The *goddess* stood in the war tent, peering at Octavia with eyes shrouded in glory. And with her luminous hands stretched out wide, the *goddess* granted Octavia's prayer for help, calling the darkness across the land toward the place where Xadia camped.

The perspective shifted, and the scene unfolded from the vantage point of the heavens.

Seeing the events from above was chilling. A piece of the darkness pulled ahead of the rest, sweeping toward Xadia's camp silently at the will of the *goddess*, and when it came upon the edge of the tents, the *goddess* unleashed it, and it roared like a monster, killing all in its path.

The focus of the vision zoomed into Pierre's war tent.

"Unchain me!" Octavia cried. "ABSALOM! You have to unchain me! Please!"

The boy ran to grab the key to her restraints, but then he clutched it to his chest. "If I unchain you, you have to walk through the darkness in the name of Xadia! I need you!"

Octavia's devotion to all stirred in the throne room of the *gods*. "I will walk through the darkness in the name of *everyone*! You will drink the *waters* and be healed! You and so many others!"

Absalom started to cry. "You are going to run!"

"I am. But, Absalom, you need to trust me, and you have to free me! Please! I cannot save anyone if I am chained and the darkness sweeps over this tent!"

The focus of the memory sharpened with a roar. Octavia was free, and she put both of her hands on either side of Absalom's face. "I swear to the *gods*, I will walk through the darkness and unlock the Well of Eternal Healing. You will be healed, Absalom. You will! May the *gods* protect you! Your bravery today will not be overlooked."

The scene shifted again, and Octavia threw herself in front of Azariah with a scream as a tendril of darkness flew toward his chest. The key shone like the stars, and then the darkness claimed another victim instead . . .

A new prayer surfaced.

Octavia and Azariah were at the edge of one of the tents in Zoharth, waiting to steal a moment for Octavia to look into the Well of Prophecy. Her heart cried out for the favor of the *gods* in seeing what she was meant to see. She was earnest and open, ready to receive their instruction.

And then she was sitting at the mahogany table with King Bastian Jasper in the Zoharthian throne room, praying for the *gods* to tip the scales of Bastian's heart so that she could learn the words of the prophecy . . .

Flash.

"I am willing," she whispered as she rode on horseback away from the Kingdom of Zoharth toward the outlet.

"I am willing," she whispered as she stood at the edge of the darkness before learning the true cost of the key.

"I am willing," she whispered as she walked toward the base of the hill where the ruins of the Hritzan palace stood.

One final prayer appeared on the golden thrones, and she asked the *gods* to take this from her—to give her something else to do—but they didn't.

Her last words echoed all around the realm of the *gods*. "For every person who does not deserve the darkness, I do this for them."

Octavia cast the rock into the Well and plummeted into its depths . . .

The entire diamond room seared with heat and light, overwhelming Octavia's spirit, and the show of prayers ended. Once more, Octavia tried to speak, but she had no vocal cords to use. She was silent before the thrones.

The *goddess* addressed the room with the sound of a trumpet call. "This Keyholder is not like the others. She is of pure heart and intention. No one can deny this. We have all searched the hearts of every Keyholder before her, and that is why we decided to start the darkness in motion in the first place, because none were righteous. None were willing. And we were sorry in our hearts for making the Wells of Power and gifting them to humanity in the first place. But this girl . . . I can find no fault in her for the things she has done. Her reverence for us is undeniable, and her heart for what is right is true. Let us return her to the mortal realm to try and bring about peace, for we all know that the wickedness below will cause destruction again. The cycle will start over, and we will blot out humanity for their sins. If a new darkness comes, there is no more grace left in the realm of the *gods*." The *goddess* opened her arms wide. "But what if we could offer grace *now*? *Before* a new darkness can come? This girl could be humanity's final chance."

The thunderous voice was back. "The truth of matter remains: the sins of Hritza must have a vessel, or the darkness cannot fall from the land at all. Its wrath must be satisfied. Are you suggesting the Keyholder should not pay the price because she is pious?"

The golden thrones blazed. All of the *gods* and *goddesses* began to speak over each other. The noise of their voices was so frightening that Octavia was surprised she did not perish on the spot. She also couldn't understand what they were saying anymore. They chorused into a violent symphony that sounded like a deluge of natural disasters.

But once they stopped booming together as one, their words came clearly again.

"I have a solution that may satisfy the wrath of the darkness," the *goddess* said.

"She *must* be the vessel!" the thunderous *god* stated resolutely.

"She will be, but let us not cast the darkness into her soul," the *goddess* countered.

The musical *goddess* chimed up. "Then where do we cast it?"

"Let us cast it into the key, for it was made with the intention of protecting the Keyholder from the darkness until they could drown themselves in the Well."

"But . . ." the musical *goddess* hesitated. "Can the key hold the darkness indefinitely?"

"The key *can* contain the wrath, but it will be measured by humanity. If peace can be found among men, the darkness can be sealed up. But if peace cannot come about, the key won't be able to hold the darkness back forever."

There was a great murmuring around the thrones. The *goddess* spoke again.

"Let us give humanity this one last grace. We can return the Keyholder to her mortal form. The Well of Eternal Healing can open again, and perhaps, with the Keyholder residing *with* humanity instead of burning in the darkness, there can be a chance for peace."

The glory that shone around the twelve thrones was sealed in silence as the *gods* pondered the proposal. The silence seemed to last forever, but it also only lasted mere moments.

The *god* whose voice was like that of a great wind over the sea said, "Let us ask the Keyholder. Open her mouth."

Suddenly, it felt like Octavia had lungs again. She hadn't even been aware that she wasn't breathing until air was pulled back into her.

"Octavia Fletcher," the *goddess* said, peering down at her. "We want to offer you a chance to redeem humanity. We want to send you back to your mortal form. The darkness will reside in the key, contained only for a short time, and you will be tasked with bringing peace to all the lands for the sake of those who are innocent. War over the Well of Eternal Healing is brewing, and it *will* pull the darkness forth again if nothing changes. And if that happens, there will be no salvation. Not even you will be able to escape." Her aura lit up brighter than the sun. "Do you accept this task? Will you walk among men again and fight to bring about a world where all the Wells of Power are shared as we intended them to be?"

Octavia felt overwhelmed. How was she supposed to achieve peace in a world rife with wickedness and greed? She was only one person, and she didn't have political power or an army at her disposal, let alone the influence to acquire any of that.

But despite the seemingly impossible nature of the monumental task, she would do it. She wanted to live again. She would accept the cost if it meant that her soul had a chance to be spared from burning in the darkness. Humanity could do better. It could *be* better, and she would figure out a way to help them.

Her voice was small and insignificant in the presence of the *gods*. So many questions flew through her spirit, but the only thing she could get herself to say was:

"I accept."

The *gods'* chorus of agreement thundered around the throne room at her response, and the *goddess* floated closer to Octavia.

"Are you ready, Octavia Fletcher?"

"I am."

The *goddess's* hands moved over Octavia's form, and light streamed around her. In the twinkling of an eye, she was cast down to earth, falling from the stars until her soul hovered over the ruins of Hritza, which was still covered by the darkness.

She fell, passing through the stone like it was made of mist, and then her spirit stopped over the Well of Eternal Healing. The black *waters* stirred, and from its depths, Octavia's body was pulled upward and deposited onto the shattered glass floor next to the Well.

Her lips were blue, her face was gray, and her skin looked pale and water-logged. Her hair was plastered to her cheeks, and no life was in her eyes. It was horrifying to see—the corpse of her flesh laid out like a shell before her . . .

An intense pull hooked around her, and her soul was slammed back into her corporeal form. Her lungs expanded, her eyes popped open, and her body shuddered. She sat up, coughing out water and then gasping for air like she couldn't get enough of it. Blood pumped through her veins again, and her heart pulsed alive within her chest. Color returned to the flesh of her arms—she could feel it in her face too—and life surged through her with abandon. Abruptly, Octavia was pulled to her feet by a supernatural force that infused a renewed energy into her bones.

A rumble shook the ground beneath her.

The Well began to froth, the black *waters* spilling from its edges. The key blistered in her left palm, and without warning, the *waters* shot upward, arcing above her and then spiraling down toward her hand where the key lay buried in her flesh.

Octavia was anchored in place—but it was not of her own doing.

The force of the *gods* commanded her body, and they pulled her left hand up to the heavens so that it was raised high above her head. In a torrent of devastation, the darkness slammed into the key. The force of the boiling black tar against her palm was excruciating. Devastating. She felt like her entire arm was on fire. It leached down to her bones, and she screamed into the whirlwind of black as it tore around her.

Gale force winds whipped her face and chest. The darkness roared, shaking the whole earth. The stream of it was endless. It poured into the key without mercy, its fury rich with wrath. Like a never-ending flood, the blackness tucked itself into the key with the violence and ferocity of a thousand years of retribution.

All Octavia could do was stand there and bear it with a cry that tore her lungs to shreds and felt like razors in her throat. She squeezed her eyes shut, her arm still stretched to the sky, and when the last inkling of black had tucked itself into the key, the *gods* released her, and she collapsed to the floor of the room.

Her breath shook in her chest, her body covered in a sheen of sweat.

When she opened her eyes, the light of day was pouring over the top of her, filtering through the broken ceiling of the Hritzan palace and reflecting off of a glass floor that now had no cracks.

The deafening sound of silence that had plagued the darkness was no longer present. Instead, nature, with its soft breeze and quiet melodies, hummed in her ears. And the rotting decay of the curse was gone, although the ancient palace still appeared broken and crumbling.

Octavia got to her feet unsteadily, and she stared at her left palm. The key, which had always dazzled like diamonds, was now as black as tar, and veins of the black slithered under her skin around the edges of the object.

A pull as deep as her soul caused her to look up. The sensation was coming from the Well. Its outer rim was sparkling once again, its black rock perimeter shimmering like the other Wells of Power. She approached it in awe, her heart filled with veneration, and when she peered into its depths, the *waters* shone blue, glowing with the power of the *gods.*

Octavia's parched lips parted. It was an incredible sight to behold. The Well of Eternal Healing was open for the first time in a millennium, and she was the first to gaze at its *waters*.

A golden glow illuminated the side of the Well, and three glass vials appeared out of thin air, perched on the edge of the rim. Octavia looked up into the heavens, and in her mind, she knew the *gods* were giving her permission to draw from the sacred Well—to be the first.

With trembling hands, Octavia dipped the vials into the *waters*, collecting the three parcels and capping them off. She tucked the parcels into her pocket. Then a fourth vial appeared, and with it, the *goddess* whispered in her ear, "Drink from the Well, Octavia Fletcher, and find your strength, for you will need it. The armies of men draw near."

Although Octavia could not see the *goddess*, she felt her presence in full measure, and she obeyed, dipping the fourth vial into the *waters* and bringing it to her lips.

She emptied it in one gulp.

The sensation that flew through her limbs was incredible. Invigorating. It was a lifeforce unparalleled by anything that existed in the mortal realm. All of Octavia's wounds were healed with bursts of sparkling gold that flickered from her skin, and her body gained strength like she could run for miles on end and never tire.

With one last glance at the Well of Eternal Healing, Octavia strode from the room, walking into the hall beyond, and as she looked down over the landscape from the towering heights of the Hritzan palace, she could see the armies of Rustwick, Xadia, and Zoharth approaching in the distance, like ants spilling from a hill.

Her heart beat resolutely in her chest, sending blood through her veins to remind her that she was *alive*, and with strength in her voice and wrath in her heart for the wicked men below, she whispered, "Azariah Ronan, I am coming for you."

Octavia Fletcher's story continues in:

Wrathwielder (The Wells of Power Book 2)

Want to explore the world of Keyholder even further?
I've written a **bonus chapter from Azariah's POV**,
which can be found on my website for FREE.
It's a rewrite of chapters 19-23 (the Pierre section of the book).
Check it out at djharringtonbooks.com

Acknowledgements

I'VE PUBLISHED MY fifth book already? This story was incredible! It took hold of my mind and heart in such a profound way that I simply couldn't stop writing it. I craved this adventure like air, and I had so much fun telling Octavia's story and building this world.

I have never drafted and edited something so fast. I started writing Keyholder on December 24th, 2023. I drafted the whole thing in 63 days and did developmental edits the following 23 days. Then the manuscript was whisked off to the beta round. Final edits started on April 15th, 2024 & concluded on May 15th, 2024. I thank God for the wonderful gift of storytelling he has instilled in me and the vast support network he has given me to see my dreams become a reality.

None of this would have been possible without the amazing team of people who helped me craft this world and pushed me to meet my daily word count goals. Some HUGE thank you's are in order.

First, to my wonderful husband, Steven. I remember the day you told me you didn't want to know anything about Keyholder. "I want to experience a Danielle Harrington book." That's what you said to me. So I begrudgingly agreed, and I didn't tell you a single plot point ahead of time. I simply let you *experience* the book. I will admit, it was fun shocking you a few times throughout this story, HOWEVER, I distinctly remember saying to you: "Don't ever make me do that again!" Plotting this book all by myself was HARD! Like . . . I'm proud of myself, but DANG that was difficult! I missed my partner in crime, but I am exceedingly grateful for your support when it came to brainstorming the world-building of Keyholder. The enticing danger of Urtha and the rich uniqueness of Vrelia were your brain children, and boy did I take those concepts and run with them! I love you so much, Steven. Thank you for always being so supportive and for helping me create incredible stories. And SUPER thank you for being my copy editor.

Now, to my wonderful critique partner and developmental editor, Josh. We've worked on 3 books together, and you never cease to amaze me with your notes. Your sense of pacing is INCREDIBLE! I know I've told you this before, but your eye for storytelling is phenomenal, and some of the scenes that made it into the final edit of Keyholder were entirely from your pacing notes. The depth of despair and the richness of human connection I was able to explore in Keyholder was enhanced by your critical eye. Thank you, friend, for all of the time and care you put into this book. You are so amazing!

Next, there are two ladies in particular I need to thank for how fast I was able to draft Keyholder. Kayla and Stephanie. My writing besties! My sprinting ladies! I love you two so much. Writing can be such an isolating venture, but you two gave me an experience I've never had before. Who gets to say they've written their ENTIRE book WITH their friends from start to finish? Our nightly writing sprints started early January 2024, and we did not stop until ALL 3 of us finished our drafts. We wrote/edited together every single night for nearly 3 months. Every. Single. Night. Also! It was so special for Kayla and I to finish our books on the same night within minutes of each other. Truly an incredible and encouraging experience. And I've met so many new writer friends as a result. The writing community is incredible. <3

To my alpha reader and beta readers!<3 You ladies were amazing. Danna, I appreciate you for reading Keyholder early through all the messy beginning drafts. And thank you for re-reading scenes over and over again as I worked to get them just right. You were tough on Octavia, admittedly to my dismay at times, but you pushed me to make her even stronger. Michelle, Gabby, Skyler, Molly, Sarah, Sophia, Monica, and Kayla …

WOW! I had a lot of notes to sift through, but they REALLY enhanced the story. In particular, chapter 29, The Pain In The Payment. That chapter grew into something breath-taking from a combination of feedback. It was hard to get right, but I'm so happy with it, and I couldn't have done it without your help.

A special shoutout to Molly and Sarah for all the DMs during Keyholder's line edits. That was a whirlwind of a month, but I absolutely loved our daily chats and how you two made me feel so excited about my book every single day even when I was feeling exhausted and burnt out. <3

Tony, thank you for proofreading Keyholder. You've been with me from the start of my author career, and your work has been amazing. I bow to you, sir! How you find the things that have slipped through the cracks of the editing process, I will never know.

I also want to thank Efa (my internal illustrator) for the beautiful work she has done. <3 It was truly a pleasure to work with you. Thank you for bringing Keyholder to life and producing STUNNING scene art. This honestly is the prettiest book I've ever written.

To my family: Mom and Dad, thank you for your continued support for my storytelling. I love you two so much! Michelle and Gabby, I'm so happy I got to include you in the process of creating this book. Your excitement and support is amazing. Luke and Katherine, it's always fun to hear your thoughts post-publication. Thank you for consistently buying and reading my books. It really does mean a lot to me.

To my readers: thank you for trusting me to take you on another adventure. You are the reason I write. I hope my stories continue to give you heart-pounding emotion and much to think about. Thank you for supporting me, for buying my books, and for all of the kind messages along the way. If you enjoyed Keyholder, consider leaving a review. Reviews help me reach more readers.

I promise to give you more harrowing adventures with high stakes and dastardly villains. I hope to continue to break your hearts, ensnare your senses, and have you feverishly turning the pages to find out what happens next. There is more to come for Octavia Fletcher. And I can't wait!

Finally, my Kickstarter posse! WOW! Thank you for a wonderful Kickstarter experience. Your excitement for my book made all the hard work SO worth it. In particular, I want to thank Kayla for her time and effort in teaching me how to create and run a successful campaign.

Without further ado, here are the names of everyone who pledged to my campaign:

- A hamlyn
- Abby Johansen
- Adelle Williams
- Adrianna Ferrannini
- Adrienne Hiatt
- ALB
- Alexandra Corrsin
- Alexis
- Alisha
- Allie Hawver
- Ally
- Alyssa Heck
- Alyssa Pressley
- Amanda Balter
- Amanda Ciuriuc
- Amy Standage
- Angela Morse
- Angela Powers
- Ann
- Anna Gergerich
- Antoinette Sturniolo
- Ashley Bultena
- Ashley Haynes
- Ashlie Donaldson
- Astridd
- Beka Laing
- Brooke Engles
- Bryce Harriet/ John Edson
- C. Stilianessis
- Carissa Anne
- Carl Spitzer
- Carly Carlson
- Carolee S
- Catherine Kopf
- Caylie M
- Christina Palma
- Courtney Marie
- Cristy Bowlin
- D. E. Carlson
- Dan Kenner
- Danae T
- David Holzborn
- Deanna Magee
- Dennis K. Crosby
- E. Kim
- E.H. Demeter
- EJ McFadden
- Elizabeth Crawford
- Elizabeth W.
- Elle A.
- Emily Nolden
- Emma Hill
- Emma Shirley
- Erica L. Coe
- Felicia
- Fleur DeVillainy
- Gabby Lizotte
- Gavin Oxley
- Georgianna J Myers
- Haley Schutzenberger
- Heather Lizotte
- Holly Davis
- Holly Morgan
- Holly Penney
- Isabel K.
- J Bruckner
- J. Gabriel Gates
- J. Glaude
- Jamie Taylor
- Janine B
- Jasmine K
- Jenna
- Jenni
- Jennifer P.
- Jenny Darlington
- Jessica Beatty
- Jessie McSpadden
- Jillian Yetter
- Jo Holloway
- Jordan Clifton
- Jordan P. Barnes
- Joshua Del Toro
- Jules Dyrud
- Julia Rose
- Justin Beaver
- Katherine Carney
- Katherine Malloy
- Kathryn Weese
- Kati Kirsten

- Katie Marie
- Kayla Ann
- Kayleigh M
- Kelsey
- Kerrie Koopman
- Keverlie Jones
- Kiersten Pavoncello
- Kim Ashworth
- Kimberlee Cloutier
- Kimberly Cash
- Kinsey Eason
- Kristina R
- Kyliegh
- Laura Abbeflower
- Leanna V.
- Lindsay Mason
- Lindsey Redd
- Liza Clarke
- Luke and Katherine
- Lynae Ford
- Maria Milanova
- Mariah L. Rosewood
- Marissa Brightly
- Marlene Renteria
- Mary Andrews
- Matthew Romeo
- McKenzie French
- Meggy Klepto
- Megyn "Sapphi" MacDougall
- Michael H.
- Michelle Fearon Scales
- Michelle Fierro
- Michelle McKuhen
- Mike McCue
- Molly Douglas
- Monica
- Morgan G.
- Mustela
- Myranda Nowak
- Natalie
- Natalie Colburn
- Natasha Rueschhoff
- Nathan Keys
- Nellie Slowiak
- Nevin Skye
- Nichole Heydenburg
- Nicole
- Nicole Clayton
- Nicole Geiger
- Nicole Oke
- Nicole Triptow
- Nika Schrauf
- Nikki T
- Nikole C.
- Olivia Morgan
- Page Vanover
- Phoenix
- Priscil87
- PunkARTchick "Ruthenia"
- Qavee
- Rachel Lowe
- Rachel Stadeli
- Rachel Walker
- Rebecca White
- Rebekah
- René
- Renske
- Reyna Michelle
- Rhianne R
- Rike
- Ruby Sutton
- Ruth Alstot
- S Simmons
- Sam Christopher
- Samantha Mendell
- Samantha Miland
- Samantha Newberry
- Sara Francis
- Sarah
- Sarah Bryant
- Sarah Limardo
- Sarah Lynn Abigail
- Scott & Judy Lizeffers
- Shannon Tusler
- Shayla Morgansen
- Sherri
- Skylar Nezat
- Skyler Wry
- SLM
- Solène
- Sophia
- Stacey Trombley
- Starr Z Davies
- Stephanie Bos
- Stephanie Crachiolo
- Stephanie Meredith
- Stephanie Price
- Stephanie Whitfield
- Stephen Prendergast
- Sydney Moses
- T Laine
- Tanya Young
- Taylor Hare
- Taylor Kimble
- Tea
- The Araujo Family
- The Bronleys
- Tiffany Goldman
- Tyrean Martinson
- V. M. Lyton
- Valhalla Erikson
- Vanessa Luu
- Vannessa Goodwin
- Veronica Rodriguez
- Victoria Townsend
- Vivian Rolfe
- Wendy Martinez
- Xyvah
- Yvette Garcia

About the Author

DANIELLE HARRINGTON is a stay-at-home mom, award-winning author, and hardcore science nerd. She earned her undergraduate degree in chemistry from Biola University and taught high school chemistry for five years before becoming a full-time writer and editor. Her inner fangirl perks up at the mention of Quidditch, BookTok, Middle Earth, and the perfect hand-crafted chai tea latte. Danielle lives in Idaho with her husband, daughter, and three cats. She's published a four-book young adult dystopian series called The Hollis Timewire Series, and what she loves more than anything is to give readers twists they don't see coming and imaginings that keep them thinking long after the story ends.

FIND THE AUTHOR—
Instagram: @djharringtonwriter
TikTok: @djharringtonwriter
Online: djharringtonbooks.com

www.ingramcontent.com/pod-product-compliance
Lightning Source LLC
Chambersburg PA
CBHW020556310726
48979CB00008B/1236/J

* 9 7 9 8 9 9 0 6 5 0 2 1 3 *